Advance Praise for *The Mapmaker*

"Tom Young's terrific new thriller, *The Mapmaker*, offers penetrating insights about the secret war in Nazi-occupied France during World War II—beginning with how Allied sabotage and bombing campaigns depended on hand-sketched maps drawn by French resisters who lacked photo equipment and supplies. The tension mounts unbearably as the 'mapmaker' and her colleagues struggle against the Gestapo's murderous tentacles."

—**David O. Stewart**, author of *The Lincoln Deception*

The Mapmaker

A NOVEL OF WORLD WAR II

TOM YOUNG

A KNOX PRESS BOOK
An Imprint of Permuted Press
ISBN: 979-8-89565-124-7
ISBN (eBook): 979-8-89565-125-4

The Mapmaker:
A Novel of World War II
© 2025 by Tom Young
All Rights Reserved

Cover art by Jim Villaflores

This book, as well as any other Knox Press publications, may be purchased in bulk quantities at a special discounted rate. Contact orders@posthillpress.com for more information.

This book is a work of fiction. People, places, events, and situations are the product of the author's imagination. Any resemblance to actual persons, living or dead, or historical events, is purely coincidental.

No part of this book may be reproduced, stored in a retrieval system, or transmitted by any means without the written permission of the author and publisher.

Permuted Press
New York • Nashville
permutedpress.com

Published in the United States of America
1 2 3 4 5 6 7 8 9 10

In memory of Lieutenant Colonel Joe Myers

CHAPTER 1

Philippe Gerard

SUMMER, 1943

For Lieutenant Philippe Gerard, a permanent darkness cloaked France. He saw his Nazi-occupied homeland only at night, when he flew his Westland Lysander into clandestine airstrips on missions for the British Royal Air Force.

The last flush of daylight faded from the ramp at RAF Tangmere in West Sussex as Philippe ran up his engine for another sortie. He checked his propeller RPM and oil pressure. Wondered whether tonight would be the night he didn't make it back.

He hoped so. Death in combat could clear his name.

Tonight's passenger sat behind him in the Lysander's tandem cockpit. Philippe did not know the man's name. He knew only that the man was an agent in the French Resistance. In the event of capture and torture, the less Philippe knew, the better.

"Are you ready to depart?" Philippe asked over the interphone.

"*Oui,*" the agent answered. "*Vive la France.*"

Philippe slid his canopy closed and locked the side windows. Under a rising, rose-colored moon, he taxied to the departure end of the runway. Observing radio silence, the tower flashed a green light signal for takeoff. Philippe eased the throttle up to full power. Vibration from the big Bristol Mercury engine rattled the instrument panel and set the needles dancing. The Lysander began to roll. A few seconds later, the airspeed indicator came alive and the tailwheel rose. In less than a hundred yards, the gull-winged aircraft lifted into the night.

The English countryside, bathed in moonlight, scrolled beneath Philippe's windscreen. He kept his cockpit lighting dim to preserve his night vision. Only landmarks and an aeronautical chart would guide him to his destination: a reasonably flat pasture owned by a patriotic farmer in Centre-Val de Loire.

Philippe eased the control stick to the right and rolled the Lysander into a bank. The compass mounted between his knees at the base of the instrument panel spun to a southerly heading. No lights glittered from the ground. Under blackout orders to protect from German bombers, villagers kept their windows shut tight. Towns appeared as ghosts of themselves, dark suggestions of gabled roofs, church spires, and streets. Philippe climbed to two thousand feet and leveled off.

With the aircraft trimmed for level flight, Philippe had little to do but steer. The Lysander was a much simpler airplane than the twin-engine Bloch MB.174 he'd piloted in the French *Armée de l'Air*. Philippe and his crew had flown reconnaissance missions three years ago, during the Battle of France in 1940. He felt he'd contributed little to the war effort; the aerial photographs simply chronicled a rout. France collapsed under blitzkrieg in six weeks.

Many of Philippe's squadron mates fell to *Luftwaffe* fighters, left smoking holes in fields and woods. His unit's most famous member, the author Antoine de Saint-Exupéry, described their sacrifices as glassfuls of water dashed onto a forest fire. Saint-Ex was in America now. Though his age could have excused him from combat flying, he'd risked his life for France. Yet there were malign whispers of disloyalty because of Saint-Ex's differences with General de Gaulle, the self-appointed leader of the Free French.

Similar whispers plagued Philippe, for different reasons. Sometimes he wanted to shout into the wind, "Then *you* get out of your armchairs and fly with us. *You* tangle with the Messerschmitts. *You* visit your best friend in the hospital with his face burned off. *You* make life-and-death decisions and then live with them." Those who did not go to war roared like lions.

Under the faint glow of a cockpit map light, Philippe adjusted the chart clipped to his kneeboard. Placed his finger on the town of Chichester. From Chichester, he would set out across the English Channel to an occupied France.

France was defeated, but not entirely prostrate. Brave men and women like the one sitting silently behind him carried on the fight.

Going in, passengers said little. No doubt the inbound *résistants* were pondering their mission and its risks. Philippe had heard horror stories about interrogations at 84 Avenue Foch, the Gestapo headquarters in Paris. Fingernails ripped off. Eyes gouged out. When one agent reached his pain limit, he leaped from a window to protect his secrets.

Others were less successful, if one could call it that. Some gave up critical tidbits of information under torture. A few, perhaps to protect family members, became turncoats and collaborated with the Germans on a continuing basis. A trusted friend might deliver you into the ropes and chains, knives and needles of Avenue Foch.

Chichester passed under the Lysander's wings as a jumble of shadows. Beyond the town, the English Channel's waves crested in moonlight like liquid copper. Philippe scanned beneath him, but no lights appeared. Ships ran dark, hunted by invisible U-boats.

After several minutes over the water, Philippe checked his compass heading and refolded his chart to reveal the Normandy coast. Glanced at his wristwatch, noted his airspeed.

"An hour and a half," he announced.

"Roger," the passenger replied in English.

He's done this before, Philippe thought. Learned flyboy lingo from the Brits. Perhaps a high-ranking officer if he's transiting back and forth. Probably coordinating with the Special Operations Executive about tactics and strategy.

No matter. The procedures remained the same, whether Philippe was flying a low-level courier or Resistance chief Jean Moulin himself. Agents on the ground would wait for the sound of the Lysander's engine, then flash a Morse code signal. If the signal was correct, the pilot would flash a response with his landing light. Then the ground personnel would switch on three flashlights arranged to indicate wind direction. The pilot would land into the wind for the slowest possible groundspeed on touchdown. Roll to a stop in less than 150 yards. Offload cargo or passenger and take off again within three minutes.

Ahead, the night horizon revealed irregular angles, the coves and outcroppings of the French shoreline. Philippe eased back the throttle and descended below one thousand feet. He didn't know if German radar operators would care about something as small as a Lysander; they probably worried more about formations of heavy bombers. Still, he didn't want to make it easy for them. He crossed the beach low enough to watch the surf crash into rocks and slide, foaming, back into the ocean.

Here, too, blackout orders prevailed. The towns lay dark. That actually made navigating easier for Philippe. He depended not on city lights for reference, but a river. In darkness, he could more readily spot moonlight on the water. On this southerly heading, he would find the Loire, a ribbon through central France.

Philippe and his passenger flew without speaking for a while. Then a series of flashes lit the horizon, perhaps a hundred miles away.

"*Merde*," the agent said. "They are bombing."

"My RAF colleagues," Philippe said.

Now that France suffered under Nazi occupation—or Nazi *infestation*, as Philippe considered it—the Germans had converted her industry to their war aims. French factories became targets for the Allies. The Lancasters and Stirlings might be pulverizing a Renault plant, the workers mere sacrificial lambs. The RAF struck by night, the USAAF by day. To the strategists, occupied France was an enemy, and they bombed it like an enemy.

The flashes receded as Philippe angled south, and his passenger fell once again into silence. Philippe began to sweat, so he unlatched the canopy to let in a rush of air. He felt hot because he wore two layers of clothing: Underneath his uniform he wore a peasant's shirt and trousers. If he were forced down, he would burn the plane, lose the uniform, and take shelter with the Resistance. Wait for instructions and a ride back to base.

The agent in the back seat had also taken precautions about clothing and personal effects. His bag contained nothing to connect him with Britain: no tag from Savile Row, no tin of English biscuits. A woman from the Special Operations Executive had searched his luggage to make sure.

Philippe ran his eyes over his compass and fuel and oil pressure gauges. The Lysander was running well tonight, and he had more than enough petrol to get back to Tangmere. He turned his attention to the ground, scanned the fields and woods. Finally, up ahead, he found his guiding landmark.

The Loire reflected the moon as a dappled orb. Trees lined the riverbanks. Philippe nudged the control stick and rolled into a turn. Followed the river through the Loire Valley.

He had landed several times in this region, but not at tonight's field. He checked his chart, noted a particular bend of the river. When Philippe reached that bend, he turned onto a heading of 150 degrees.

"Ten minutes," he said.

"Roger."

The aircraft crossed a series of fields and hedgerows. Then Philippe found a pasture oriented roughly north to south, perhaps half a mile long and 500 yards wide. More than enough: A pilot could land a Liberator here, let alone a Lysander. He descended low, waggled his wings. Turned for another pass.

The ground remained dark. No signal light. Without the proper signal, Philippe would not land. It had happened before; sometimes a rendezvous would cancel at the last minute because German forces were too close, or worse, an agent had been arrested.

Philippe overflew the field again and worked quick mental math. He had enough fuel to loiter for half an hour and still make it back to England. He would not wait that long, though. That much buzzing around could alert the wrong people. He decided to give it fifteen more minutes.

"I'll give them a few more passes," Philippe said. "Then back to Tangmere."

"*Oui.*"

The man sounded downcast. Philippe understood why. When you had a dangerous mission, you wanted to get on with it. Nothing was worse than the waiting. Philippe remembered the feeling well from his days flying recon missions in the MB.174: *If the Germans must send me down in flames, then damn the weather and let them do it now.*

On his third pass, Philippe spotted the signal light. The light emitted a series of short and long blinks. He didn't catch the pattern at first, so he turned to make a fourth pass and take a closer look. Then he recognized one short blink followed by three long ones: *dot, dash, dash, dash.* Morse Code for the letter *J.* The correct letter of the day.

Philippe rolled into a 180-degree turn to overfly the field again, and he placed his finger on the switch for the landing light. With his landing light, he signaled the coded response: *dash, dash, dot, dot.* The letter *Z.*

Though he understood the reasons for such careful authentication before landing, part of him resented the need for tradecraft at all. The only way he could go home to France was to sneak in like a thief in the night—and he could plan to stay only three minutes.

He pulled up and banked again, waited for the next set of lights. He was expecting three lamps for wind direction.

The field went dark. Philippe circled and waited. He glanced at his watch. Ten minutes had passed since he'd signaled with his landing light. All they needed to do was plant three sharpened poles into the ground with flashlights taped to the ends.

Philippe eyed the field. Nothing looked suspicious, no clues on the ground. That meant little, however. He recalled from his recon days how even a full-on land battle, especially a small-unit engagement, sometimes offered little evidence to an aerial observer. A wisp of smoke, perhaps. A rare glimpse of tracer fire.

Defeat, on the other hand, was obvious. Abandoned villages burning to keep the enemy from taking shelter in the houses. Streams of overloaded cars and trucks clogging the roadways as civilians fled the German advance. Philippe's unit, Reconnaissance Group 2/33, hopscotching from one temporary base to another as France yielded territory. Headquarters became a farmhouse here, a schoolhouse there. All the while, Philippe and his squadron mates launched on pointless sorties—"awkward missions," as Saint-Ex called them: *The Panzers are ten miles closer than yesterday. What did our general staff expect?*

Philippe had flown over this very region, the aircraft's camera whirring to document capitulation. And now here he was again, as if he couldn't get enough. Saint-Ex would find this droll.

Finally, lights winked on in the field below. But not in the pattern Philippe expected. Instead of a skinny triangle, three lights appeared in a straight line. That made no sense; the wind could be coming from either direction along that line.

"*Stupide*," Philippe muttered.

"What is wrong?" the agent asked.

Philippe explained the foul-up.

"Most of our agents know little of flying," the man said. "Perhaps they are new at this."

Philippe considered the situation for a moment, then asked, "Do you feel comfortable going in?"

"Their letter of the day was correct, no?"

"*Oui.*"

"Then we land."

Philippe throttled back to descend for landing. Unlike the MB.174, the Lysander had fixed landing gear. No gear handle to remember.

He lined up on the three lights with no idea if he was landing into a headwind or a tailwind. In this case, it didn't matter much. The long pasture gave him plenty of runway, even with wind on his tail.

At a hundred feet off the ground, Philippe eased the power up to ten inches of manifold pressure. Carrying just a little power made for a softer touchdown. He pulled back the stick to raise the nose into the landing attitude. The wheel came to within inches of the grass.

In the corner of his eye, Philippe saw what appeared as faint sparks. Muzzle flashes.

Bullets slammed into the Lysander's fuselage. Something struck Philippe's left boot as if smashed with a sledgehammer.

"*On nous a trahis,*" the agent said. We are betrayed.

Philippe jammed the throttle all the way to the stop. Pulled the nose higher to go around. The Mercury engine screamed as the Lysander clawed for altitude.

Another burst raked the aircraft. Philippe heard rounds punching through the canopy behind him. He pitched for the steepest climb the plane could give him, the faster to get out of gun range.

Several miles from the airfield, he leveled off and took long breaths. Tried to calm himself, take stock of his situation. Checked all his gauges. The engine was running normally, and fuel did not appear to be leaking, thank God.

He reached down and felt his left boot. It was wet. In the light of the instruments, he looked at his hand. Bloody. Philippe had been shot in the foot. No pain yet; he felt only numbness.

"Are you all right back there?" he asked.

No answer.

"Do you read me on interphone?" Philippe asked.

No response.

He turned a rheostat to bring up the cockpit flood light. Twisted in his seat to look behind him.

The agent lay slumped to one side. A bullet had torn off the side of his head. Blood and brains spattered the canopy. *Why could they not have gotten me, too?* Philippe thought.

He turned forward and set a course for Tangmere. He did not look aft again.

CHAPTER 2

Charlotte Denneau

Staccato slams of automatic gunfire woke Charlotte Denneau from a sound sleep. She rose in utter confusion, momentarily unsure where she was. Charlotte and her fellow Resistance fighters moved so often, slept in so many different safehouses, that it became hard to keep track. Then she remembered: She was at a farmhouse outside Cahors, in the department of Lot, in southern France. At a place the Resistance deemed secure. What had gone wrong?

She threw the sheets off the bed. Charlotte always slept in her clothes in case she needed to move fast. She reached for the STEN gun, which hung by its sling from a wicker chair. Checked the magazine and ran to the stop of the stairwell.

"Charlotte, get your bags," a voice shouted from downstairs.

It was Jacques, the team leader. She did not grab her bags. She picked up an ammunition case and stumbled down the steps as quickly as she could.

At the base of the stairs, she found Jacques kneeling by a first-floor window. He fired a burst from his STEN out into the gray light of dawn. At the other windows, teammates Georges, Edmund, and François also manned weapons. From somewhere in the field outside, gunfire chattered. Rounds smacked into the front of the house. A bullet punched through the clapboard. The slug missed Charlotte's arm by inches and flung splinters against her cheek. She slid to the floor. Took a position beside Jacques.

"Gestapo?" Charlotte asked.

"I think they're Milice," Jacques said.

The Milice were the Vichy regime's hated paramilitary force. Fascist thugs, to Charlotte's mind. Worse than the Gestapo, because the Milice were Frenchmen who betrayed their own nation's ideal of *Liberté, Égalité, Fraternité*. They worked closely with the Gestapo to track down Resistance fighters. Charlotte knew horror stories of agents tortured to death in Milice dungeons. That was part of the reason she worked under the code name of "Tigresse." Only the agents she trusted most knew her real name.

Charlotte thrust her barrel through the window's broken glass. Shadowy figures advanced across a wheat field toward the house. She clicked off her safety and fired a burst. The figures went down, but she couldn't tell if she'd hit anything or if the enemy was just taking cover. Her nine-millimeter brass casings clattered on the hardwood floor. Burned gunpowder stung her nostrils.

"Surrender," a voice called from the field. "You cannot escape."

Jacques and the other men answered with stitches of fire. Georges yanked an empty magazine from the left side of his STEN and inserted another. Fired again. At least they had plenty of ammunition. They'd been resupplied a few nights ago with an airdrop by a British Halifax bomber.

The Milice returned fire. Three slugs punched through the door and slammed into the wall. Plaster showered the floor. To Charlotte's right, François moaned and slumped behind a window sill. Blood spattered the chaise behind him. Charlotte put down her weapon and scrabbled on her knees to his side.

Blood pulsed through a wound in his neck. He stared up at the ceiling, scraped at the floorboards with his heels. Tried to speak, but managed only a gurgle.

Heedless of bullets, Charlotte rose to her feet and ran to the kitchen. Found a first-aid kit, also supplied by the Halifax. She unzipped the pack and fumbled for gauze pads. Sprinted back to François's side, kneeled and placed one pad over the entrance wound. She reached under his neck and tried to cover the exit wound, as well. Blood soaked through both pads and seeped between her fingers.

François appeared to sigh, to let out a long breath. His chest did not rise again, and he made no more sounds. His blood spread across the floor and began to soak into a rug beside the chaise.

"He's done for," Georges said. "Take your things and leave."

"No," Charlotte said. She picked up her weapon and resumed her place beside Jacques. Fired through the window again. The blood on her fingers felt sticky against the gunmetal.

"Charlotte, they cannot get your drawings," Jacques said. "Leave us now, before it's too late."

Jacques was right, she realized. Her heart broke to admit it. She'd always known a moment like this might come. Because of her skills and what she knew, she might have to leave her friends. Quickly, without a goodbye.

She had begun by sketching diagrams, a skill she had first honed as an art student at the Sorbonne. When it came to reconnaissance, the Resistance seldom enjoyed the luxury of photographs. Very difficult to find the chemicals and create a darkroom for developing pictures. Charlotte helped fill the need by drawing. If the fighters wanted to blow a trestle, for example, she would sketch the scene, including possible egress routes. Operatives armed with this knowledge stood a better chance of succeeding at their missions and surviving to fight again. She made her diagrams especially useful by marking them in English as well as in French. Charlotte had grown up speaking both languages at home; her father was an American diplomat, and her mother was French. She felt she had two hometowns: Washington and Paris.

Charlotte drew maps, as well. When the Resistance learned of a German troop position or a V1 rocket emplacement, Charlotte would note the location. *Les Forces Françaises Libres*, the Free French Forces, considered her information reliable enough to pass it up the chain of command. On two occasions, RAF Lysanders had made night landings at clandestine airfields to pick up Charlotte's maps. She had no idea what became of them after that. But a week after one of the pickups, the United States Eighth Air Force sent heavy bombers to obliterate a V1 launch site she had identified.

Outside, three of the Milice rose from the wheat field and ran toward the house. Charlotte fired another burst. This time, one of them spun as he went down, obviously hit. The others dived for the ground. Charlotte fired again at where they'd disappeared into the wheat. The weapon went silent when her magazine emptied.

"Go!" Jacques shouted.

More Milice sprang from the field and sprinted forward. The men fired from the waist as they ran. A round ricocheted off the ancient candelabra that hung from the ceiling. Fragments of candle wax joined the plaster, broken glass, and empty cartridge casings on the floor. Jacques grunted and fell back from the window. Charlotte reached to help him, but he pushed her away. Blood began spreading down his shirt.

"Leave now!" he said.

Charlotte fought her emotions. She ran up the stairs as more slugs punched through the walls and into the living room. In her bedroom, she snatched up a map case and a knapsack. The map case contained her notes and drawings, along with pens, pencils, and colored markers. The knapsack was her go-bag. It contained toiletries, a change of clothes, and an American .45 pistol. It also contained her latest work-in-progress. This was to be her masterpiece, her greatest contribution to the war effort: a map of French railways, with as much detail as possible on marshalling yards, locomotive repair facilities, and rail tunnels. The Resistance's Plan *Vert*, or Plan Green, called for destruction of railways to hinder German troop movement when the Allies invaded France. There were other plans in progress, as well. Plan Blue targeted power plants. Plan Violet targeted communications. But none were more important than Plan Green, aided by Charlotte's pens.

Charlotte slung the knapsack and case over her shoulder. She fairly leaped down the stairs, skipped two and three steps at a time.

At the landing, she saw Jacques had pulled himself back to the window. He was firing one-handed. Edmund flung away an expended magazine and slammed in another. Georges lay still in a pool of blood.

"*Je t'aime*, Jacques," Charlotte shouted.

Without another look, she fled through the kitchen and out the back door. Just off the back steps, a bucket and chain hung over an open well. Beside the well, a decade-old motorcycle rested on its stand.

Charlotte mounted the Peugeot P104. Kicked the starter. The engine sputtered to life, belched blue smoke. She shifted the bike into gear and twisted the throttle. The rear wheel spun, fishtailed, and threw dirt against the side of the well.

A dirt path led away from the farmhouse, between two fields. Beyond the fields lay a forest of oak and poplar. Charlotte sped down the path. She hunched low over the handlebars to present a smaller target. The 350cc engine screamed. Charlotte did not look back at the Milice, who by now must have spotted her and started firing. If she could reach the woods, she could weave through the trees. Whatever vehicle the Milice had used could not follow her there.

The Peugeot struck a dry mudhole. The front wheel lifted into the air. When the wheel contacted the ground again, the bike skidded sideways. Charlotte shifted her weight to correct. Something stung her left calf, but she ignored the pain. At the edge of the forest, the bike fishtailed once more. Leaves flew from underneath the rear wheel.

The tire found purchase again, and Charlotte vanished into the trees.

MEMORANDUM
REGARDING: Operation Donar
Gestapo Counterintelligence Corps,
Federal Intelligence Service, Lyon
Lyon, France 23 June 1943
TO: Reich Security Main Office, Berlin
FROM: Klaus Barbie, Hauptstürmfuhrer

Targeted infiltration of terrorist cells in France has met with initial success. Interrogation of captured subversives, carried out here at the field office in Lyon or at Gestapo headquarters in Paris, has yielded valuable intelligence. Our Operation Donar seems to have rendered ineffective a primary terrorist network, codenamed PROSPER by the enemy. As detailed in previous memoranda, some high-ranking terrorist leaders are now in the custody of the Reich. In many cases, French citizens loyal to the Aryan cause have helped penetrate these cells. In some cases, effective interrogation methods have extracted information from prisoners not otherwise willing to cooperate. Radio direction-finding technology has proven especially valuable in suppressing terrorist communications with London. Our operatives have captured alive at least two enemy radio operators. They have continued their transmissions under our supervision. This has yielded information regarding enemy airdrops and landing grounds in support of terrorist cells. Recommend continued use of radio DF vans.

Heil Hitler,
Klaus Barbie, Hauptstürmfuhrer

CHAPTER 3

Philippe Gerard

A pall darker than the cigarette smoke hung over the briefing room at Tangmere Cottage. The cottage, loaned by a private owner, served as the operations center for Philippe's unit, the No. 161 Special Duties Squadron of the RAF. In better times, the place would have made a charming rural home for a West Sussex family. Now it headquartered some of the most secret and dangerous missions of the Second World War.

Philippe and a half dozen of his fellow pilots awaited a briefing from a "high-ranking visitor." That almost certainly meant an officer from the British Special Operations Executive. The SOE's mandate covered espionage, sabotage, and reconnaissance against Nazi Germany, including No. 161's efforts to aid the French Resistance. Winston Churchill had commissioned the SOE in more colorful terms: "Set Europe ablaze." Unofficially, SOE was called "The Ministry of Ungentlemanly Warfare."

Dry British humor on such a topic didn't sit well with Philippe. With his homeland under the jackboot, he had little use for witticisms. Especially today, when signs pointed toward things taking a turn for the worse. First, there had been his own disastrous flight, when he'd descended into gunfire and come back with a dead man behind him. Philippe's foot still throbbed from the bullet that had punched through near the rudder pedals, grazed his foot, and filled his boot with blood. After eight stitches and a course of antibiotics, a flight doctor had pronounced Philippe fit to fly again.

Another bad omen had come last evening while Philippe listened to the BBC's nightly broadcast into occupied France. The program, *Les Français parlent aux Français*, opened with the first four notes of Beethoven's Fifth Symphony—which sounded like Morse code for the letter V.

V for Victory.

But what followed didn't sound victorious. After the usual news and information to counter German propaganda, there came cryptic messages, disguised as personal notices, for specific Resistance networks. One of them said, "Caroline is feeling ill."

That was a message to someone or some group to go to ground. Cease operations. Hide.

Philippe wasn't supposed to know that, but he did. He knew it because his sister, Lisette, was a member of the PHYSICIAN network, one of the largest Resistance circuits. He wasn't supposed to know *that*, but you learned things when you worked for the SOE. He was proud of Lisette but worried about her constantly. And one of the war's myriad cruelties was that the nature of their work meant neither could contact the other. No letters, and certainly no telephone calls. He had not heard from her since he'd left France. During that time, their parents had passed away. Their mother had died from a stomach infection that could have been treated with antibiotics. But wartime shortages left none available. Then their father drank himself to death. Lisette was the only family Philippe had left. On some days, the thought of rejoining her in a liberated France kept him going. On other days, he realized how unlikely that was, and he hoped only for a quick death in combat to clear his name.

A one-word command, soft-spoken yet authoritative, interrupted his dark thoughts: "ATTEN-SHUN!"

The order came from 161's young commander, Squadron Leader Hugh Venable. Philippe did not know him well. In fact, Philippe knew none of his squadron mates well and tried to keep it that way. But Venable had earned Philippe's respect, if not his friendship. The commander had already received the Distinguished Flying Cross for leading a unit tasked with cloak-and-dagger operations. At twenty-five, the man had nothing left to prove. A former fighter pilot, Venable displayed none of the machismo common to that breed. He adorned the nose of his Lysander not with snarling teeth or blazing pistols, but with the cartoon character Jiminy Cricket. Modest, for a man of Venable's accomplishments.

The pilots rose to their feet.

"Our guest today is Mr. Milton," Venable said. "One of the Baker Street Irregulars."

Philippe knew that was another nickname for the SOE. These British with their drollness. He also knew the man's real name was anything but Milton.

"As you were," Milton, or whoever he was, said. The men took their seats.

The man standing beside Venable looked more like an Oxford don than a spy. He wore a gray tweed jacket and vest, with a red pocket handkerchief folded perfectly into three points. His red tie matched the handkerchief. Thinning hair, more gray than black.

"Chaps," he said, "first I must congratulate you on your smashing work. Your deeds are noticed all the way up to Downing Street."

Some of the men nodded. Venable stood with his hands behind his back and showed no expression.

"However," Milton continued, "this has been a rather bad summer for our friends across the Channel. I am sorry to report that Resistance leader Jean Moulin was arrested by the Gestapo on 21 June."

Philippe's squadron mates looked at one another, eyes widened. Some of them, including Philippe, had met Moulin, who was president of the National Council for the Resistance. Philippe and Venable had flown him in their Lysanders.

Venable looked as shocked as the rest of the men. "Sir," he asked, "how did this happen?"

"You mean who betrayed him?" Milton said. "Unknown. All we know is that he attended a meeting near Lyon. The Gestapo were not invited, but they also attended. The Germans themselves have confirmed it for us. They've been trumpeting the arrest on RRG."

That was Reichs-Rundfunk-Gesellschaft, Nazi propaganda radio. Philippe had heard RRG broadcasts before he left France. Though he didn't speak German well, he understood enough to wonder how anyone could believe the anti-Semitic filth that spewed from RRG transmitters.

Philippe realized he shouldn't feel so surprised at Moulin's capture. Betrayal presented an ever-present risk. The Resistance comprised factions of all political stripes: Gaullists, ultra-nationalists, Communists, Socialists, and Christian Democrats, just to name a few. Who knew where the rivalries could lead? And there might have been no deliberate betrayal at all. Any Resistance member might break under torture and reveal information. Any Resistance member could make a sloppy mistake—one moment of poor tradecraft. To survive, French patriots had to get it right every time. The Gestapo had to get lucky only once.

"I'm afraid that's not the only bad news," Milton added. "We've lost one of our own. The Jerries have captured Francis Suttill. You knew him by his code name, PROSPER."

Venable drew in a sharp breath, stared at the ceiling. Then he scanned the room, as if trying to gauge the reaction of his men.

Philippe could hardly imagine a worse development. Suttill was Lisette's commander, and he had managed the largest network of Resistance agents. Technically, that network, or circuit, was code-named PHYSICIAN. But so critical was Suttill to its operations that the circuit had become known by the moniker of its leader. More than once, Philippe and his squadron mates had plucked Suttill from a moonlit French field and brought him to England for consultations.

If the enemy could get to him, they could get to anyone. The Gestapo or the Abwehr, German military intelligence, must have infiltrated his circuit like termites destroying a house from within. What did this mean for Lisette?

Perhaps the entire Resistance effort had been doomed from the start, Philippe thought. Though SOE officers like Suttill were professionals, they led networks often composed of dedicated amateurs—students, farmers, and shopkeepers who refused to accept Nazi domination. These amateurs found themselves hunted by a ruthless police state with the world's most highly trained investigators and interrogators. Perhaps the war was already over. For France, maybe it had been over since 1940.

"I know this is a lot to take in," Milton said. "I wish I had better news. Do any of you have questions?"

"Sir," Venable said. Then he paused as if struggling for words. "What—what do we do now?"

"For now, we cut our losses," Milton answered. "Mitigate the damage. Over the next few moon periods, you will extract from harm's way whomever we can save."

Fitting to mark time that way, Philippe thought. The pilots of 161 lived not from day to day or week to week, but from the waxing of the moon toward full bright, through its waning, until it no longer illuminated landmarks.

"See to your ships," Venable ordered. "Get with your mechanics. Anything that needs repair, do it now. We are about to get very busy."

That afternoon, Philippe inspected his Lysander. The RAF's maintenance personnel continued to impress him. Fabric specialists and sheet-metal men had already patched the bullet holes in the fuselage and the landing gear struts. Both tires had been changed. This contrasted with Philippe's experience with the French air force during its final days. The mechanics, through no fault of their own, barely had time to work on the aircraft. The squadrons were always either flying missions or falling back to another makeshift base. The airplanes flew with whatever problems they had until the engines wouldn't start—or until the *Luftwaffe* sent them spinning and burning into the ground.

Philippe climbed the ladder to the rear cockpit. Maintenance had yet to replace the rear canopy; three white bullet holes marred the acrylic. He slid the canopy to its aft position.

After the dead man had been removed for burial with military honors, the ground crew had done their best to clean the aircraft. They had replaced the seat cushion and scrubbed the interior. But they could not wash away every trace. Rust-colored stains still splotched the shoulder harness. The final signature of a hero who had given all for France.

When he inspected the front cockpit, Philippe opened the maintenance log and noted the open write-up for the canopy glass. Checked the date of the latest oil change. Closed the log cover, where some poetic mechanic had pasted the image of the aircraft's namesake: the Spartan admiral Lysander, whose fleet destroyed the Athenian navy in the Battle of Aegospotami in 405 BC.

The small, unarmed airplane, made partly of cloth, had a lot to live up to.

Two days later, as the moon gleamed past its first quarter, Philippe received orders for his next mission. He sat next to his commander in a leather armchair at Tangmere Cottage. Books lined shelves on either side of the cold fireplace. A summer breeze ruffled the curtains of an open window. But for their uniforms, the two men might have appeared a pair of gentlemen whiling away an evening at their club.

"Your passenger will be a woman," Venable said. "Her name, for our purposes, is 'Tigresse.' According to the latest intelligence, she narrowly escaped a Milice raid a few days ago."

A female passenger? That was unusual.

"Who is she?" Philippe asked.

"She is an officer with F Section," Venable said. "A French-American, actually."

Even more unusual. Venable explained how the SOE's French Section had recruited "Tigresse," daughter of a French mother and an American father who'd been stationed as a diplomat in Paris by Theodore Roosevelt. She was a little older than many Resistance fighters, in her thirties now.

"After France fell, she made her way to Lisbon," Venable continued. "SOE was sniffing about in Portugal, looking for people with the right talents and motivation. When they saw her university transcript, they trained her up in cartography. And a few other, less pleasant things."

"Have our contacts confirmed the pickup location and time?" Philippe asked. He knew communication with Resistance networks was never easy. Radio operators worked from haylofts, church steeples, and attics—anywhere they could string an antenna and hide from the Nazis. They never stayed in the same place for long, and they never transmitted lengthy messages. The Germans had developed direction-finding technology, and they prowled France with their DF vans, searching for furtive signals.

"They have not," Venable said. "When SOE last contacted the wireless operator, he responded with a duress code."

That meant the radio man had been arrested. But the Germans had not killed him. At least not yet. To exploit this capture, they had forced him to continue his work as a radio operator, hoping to glean intelligence. But at the end of his last transmission, he had keyed a secret Morse signal that meant, essentially: *There is a Gestapo officer at my elbow.*

"Where is this 'Tigresse' woman now?" Philippe asked.

"Unknown."

CHAPTER 4

Charlotte Denneau

Charlotte spent a week on the run, trusting no one. She ate what she could steal from gardens and orchards—an apple here, a tomato there. She slept on beds of forest ferns, always taking care to hide her motorbike in the underbrush. The graze wound on her leg pained her. She made no attempt to contact the Resistance. With the network in tatters, she had no idea who might have been compromised. The only person she spoke with was a gas station attendant, who must have wondered why she looked so dirty and disheveled. The bandage on her calf must have made her look even more suspicious. She used the last of her francs to fill the fuel tank on her Peugeot.

She felt she'd taken a long chance even with that brief encounter. Like a feral cat, Charlotte wanted to stay as far away from people as possible. The Gestapo and the Milice were everywhere, it seemed. How could they have found that safehouse? The infiltration must have been worse than anything in her most paranoid imaginings.

With little plan other than to keep moving, she continued on her way. She felt like one of the downed fliers assisted by the Underground, constantly running to avoid capture. She had met one of those poor souls once—a British pilot horribly burned when he'd bailed out of his

Lancaster. Charlotte had aided him along his escape route to Spain. She did not know whether he'd made it or not.

One afternoon, as she motored down a narrow country road, the grass tall along its shoulders, she witnessed a strange sight. In the sky, far above the scattered cumulus floating with the breeze, dozens of white lines began etching across the blue. At the leading tip of each line, Charlotte noted a dark dot. These were the condensation trails of American heavy bombers, she realized, on their way to strike a target.

Her own maps and drawings had been used to help select targets, but she had never seen the Liberators and Flying Fortresses in action. She had *heard* them before: faint thumps as the bombs struck miles away. But this scene, both majestic and terrible, was her first visual contact. She stopped her motorbike to watch.

More lines joined the aerial sketch. But the new lines were not straight; they curved with the maneuvers of aircraft. Charlotte puzzled for a moment, then guessed the curving trails marked the paths of attacking German fighters.

Then one of the lines changed color—from white to black. This also puzzled Charlotte, until she supposed the black was smoke from a bomber that had been hit. This proved correct when the black line arced toward the ground. Flames puffed from the tip of the black line. The smoke thickened as the aircraft spiraled downward and disappeared beyond the tree line. The crash site was miles distant. She saw the billow of flame before she heard the faint crump of the explosion.

"*Mon Dieu*," she whispered.

Attacks by enemy fighters continued, and a second aircraft fell. Then another. But the bulk of the formation pressed on, condensation trails extending, seemingly as inexorable as time.

The formation's passage fixed in Charlotte's mind the importance of her role. Grand strategy might depend on small details—like the details she drew on her maps and charts. A dot on a piece of paper could launch a thousand bombers. Nothing was unimportant. She could not hide from the war and her duties.

Charlotte watched the condensation trails spread and dissipate until she came up with a plan. Probably not a good plan. Certainly not a safe one. But purpose returned for her when she decided where she was going. She was no longer aimlessly fleeing. There were *résistants* in this territory, she knew. But not the kind with expensive British training. The trick was to find them.

She rode farther into the country. She eyed a farmhouse here, a barn there. Nothing she found looked worth taking a chance. Charlotte rode until she ran out of fuel again. Then, for the last mile, she pushed her motorbike. Outside a small farming village, she came upon a stable: a two-story structure with horse stalls on the first floor and a hayloft up top. White paint peeled from the clapboards. Two open-bed trucks and a car sat parked outside. One would not normally see that many vehicles at a farmer's stable, which gave Charlotte hope she had come to the right place. She did not know this region well; she was taking a guess. And a risk.

With the toe of her boot, she lowered the motorbike's kickstand and left it on the path. Dropped her knapsack beside the Peugeot, her pistol still inside. She held her hands at her sides, so that any occupants of the stable could see she wasn't holding a weapon. She approached the stable slowly, watching for any movement.

"*Arrêtez*," a voice called from inside. *Stop right there.*

Charlotte froze. The stable door slid open.

Out stepped three men. The first carried a double-barrel shotgun, sawed off so that it was almost more sidearm than shoulder weapon. A bandoleer filled with ammunition stretched across his chest.

The second man held a STEN. Suspenders across a dirty collarless shirt supported his canvas britches. The third man wielded an automatic pistol like Charlotte's. An American-style Bowie knife hung from his belt. He wore a black beret in the style of the Basques. All three sported mustaches and several days' growth of beard.

These had to be the *Maquis*: rural fighters named for the tough scrub brush that clung to Mediterranean islands. More guerrillas than spies or saboteurs, they were perhaps the most unpredictable element of the Resistance. The hardest for de Gaulle to coordinate and control. They cared little for secret signals from the BBC, or from anyone in London, French or British, telling them what to do.

Thus, they were probably the hardest cells to infiltrate. Even the Gestapo feared them. If Charlotte could trust anyone now, maybe it was this band of cutthroats.

The *Maquisard* with the shotgun leveled the weapon in Charlotte's general direction. He kept his finger off the twin triggers, but his thumb rested on the safety. He took a drag from his cigarette. Exhaled the smoke. Flicked away the butt.

"Who are you?" he asked. "What do you want?"

"My name is Tigresse," she said. She decided to keep things simple. She would tell them as little as possible. But what she did tell them would be true. "I am—I was—with PROSPER. I do not know if it is still operational."

The man with the STEN glared. "No good can come of this, Pierre," he said. "Just shoot her."

"Quiet," Pierre hissed. "Look, she is wounded." Blood had begun seeping through the bandage on her leg.

Pierre, evidently in charge, regarded Charlotte for a moment. She stood still. Tried not to show fear. Considered what little she knew of these men: They spoke with the accent of the Pyrenees, mountains on the border with Spain. Not very far from here. Unschooled but not unintelligent, given that they had survived this long. Resourceful.

"I am sorry to disturb you," Charlotte said. "I know this is awkward. The Milice raided my cell's safe house. I believe I am the only survivor." Her eyes welled as she thought of Jacques and the others. During her days on the road, she had tried hard not to think of them.

"There are none lower than the Milice stooges," Pierre said.

This jibed with what Charlotte had heard about the *Maquis*. Like all patriots in France, they despised anyone and anything associated with the occupation. But they especially hated the Milice, recruited from Frenchmen willing to cooperate with the Gestapo. The *Maquis* were known to lie in ambush for them.

"I do not know your countersigns," Charlotte said. "I cannot offer authentication. But I doubt very much a spy would come to you this way, wounded and half starved, pushing a motorbike without fuel."

Pierre did not respond, but he seemed to consider her words. Finally, he said, "How did you find us?"

"Purely a guess."

Charlotte explained that during PROSPER's better days, she had known a courier from this region. The woman worried about her son, who was to be drafted into the *Service du travail obligatoire*, a forced labor program. The young man said he'd rather risk death than work for the Nazis. Like many of his friends, he disappeared into the hills and joined the *Maquis*.

"What was the woman's name?" Pierre asked.

"I do not remember."

"She's lying," STEN man said. "Shoot her."

"Shut up, Christophe," Pierre said. "If she were lying, she would have a name, supplied by the Gestapo."

The man with the pistol and the Bowie knife finally spoke. "If she were lying," he said, "she would have a better story than this."

"Indeed," Pierre said. He lowered his shotgun. "Come inside, my dear. Perhaps we can find you something to eat. And tend to that wound." Pierre picked up her knapsack and carried it inside for her.

Charlotte let out a long breath, felt relief wash over her. Blinked as she entered the stable. Shafts of daylight provided the only illumination. The windows, if one could call them that, contained no glass. They were simple openings in the walls, with small doors on rusting hinges, to provide fresh air for the animals. Two rows of stalls, separated by a central corridor, lined the building. The stalls sat empty except for one, where a horse munched hay.

The *Maquisards* appeared to have camped in the stable for at least a few days. Their bedrolls lay on the corridor's plank floor. On a workbench, Charlotte noticed weapons in various states of disassembly: the barrel of a Browning automatic rifle, parts of STEN and BREN guns, a large-caliber revolver. Dirty dishes littered a rough-hewn table. From underneath the table, Pierre lifted a basket covered with a cloth napkin.

"Take whatever you like," he said. "Our host has been generous."

"*Merci*," Charlotte said. She took the basket and sat on a wooden milkstool. In the basket she found baguettes, a round of cheese, and a jar of olives. She had not eaten since early yesterday, and that had been only a stolen tomato. For Charlotte, the world offered nothing finer than the aromas from that basket. She broke the round of cheese in half and bit into it as if it were an apple.

For ten minutes, she could not stop herself from eating. She ignored the dirt under her fingernails, ate the olives from the jar with her bare hands. Dipped the bread into the olive oil and tore off large chunks with her teeth. Pierre handed her a canteen, and she took a long pull of water.

"I am sorry," she said finally. "I have forgotten my manners."

"Manners are a luxury these days," Pierre said.

At the workbench, Christophe lifted the Browning barrel and wiped it with a rag. Stared at Charlotte for a moment.

"I guess I was wrong," he said. "Anyone working for the Boche would not be so hungry."

"Christophe is our armorer," Pierre said. Then he pointed to the man with the Bowie knife. "And this is Aloïs. His uncle owns this farm."

Aloïs nodded. "You are a wisp of a girl," he said. "What are you doing fighting Nazis?"

Charlotte considered his question for a moment.

"I have a pistol like yours," she said, "and I know how to use it." She lifted her knapsack from where Pierre had dropped it on the stable floor. Opened the flap to reveal rows of pens and colored markers in sleeves along the pack's front side. "But these are my real weapons."

She explained her specialty, described how she drew maps and diagrams. She emphasized how her work could provide details not always visible from the air. Specifics not found on the usual roadmaps. Helpful for sappers, saboteurs, and target planners.

"Ah," Pierre said. "A mapmaker. I can see how your skill is useful."

"I have some things here I need to get out," Charlotte said. "Charts and diagrams. Do you have a radio? Or do you know anyone who does?"

She didn't bother with the details, but she had standing orders to contact her handlers in London in the event of an emergency. Her current situation certainly qualified. But with her network's radio operators dead, captured, or compromised, PROSPER was effectively silenced.

The *Maquisards* exchanged glances. Charlotte presumed they were deciding how much to tell her.

"We do not do much chatting on the radio," Pierre said. "The Germans have ways of finding radios."

"I have heard of this," Charlotte said.

"Even if we could take you to a radio man," Aloïs said, "could he reach your people? Correct frequencies and all that?"

"I do not know," Charlotte said. "Our communications are always difficult. And dangerous."

Pierre stood, and he motioned for his men to join him at the stable entrance. The *Maquisards* whispered together for a few moments. Then Pierre said, "We can take you to a radio man, provided he has not moved. And he moves often. It will be a long drive."

"*Merci*," Charlotte said. "I am in your debt."

The next morning, Charlotte and the three *Maquisards* set out in a battered Renault truck. Pierre and Christophe rode in the cab, while Charlotte and Aloïs leaned against the wooden slats lining the truck's bed. Charlotte kept her .45 hidden in her pack. Aloïs hid his under a burlap sack, and he'd left his Bowie knife behind. Pierre had told everyone to look as harmless as possible, to appear as a group of farmers on the way to their field. They had loaded a pitchfork, two hoes and a milk bucket into the back of the truck, purely for appearances. A pair of outsized trousers covered Charlotte's wound, which was improving now with sulfa powder and fresh gauze.

Charlotte hoped the Milice wouldn't patrol this far out in the country—but her safe house had been pretty remote, and the Milice found it. So she took no chances. She and Aloïs kept their handguns loaded, as were the shotgun and the STEN up front.

28

With Pierre at the wheel, the *Maquisards* kept mainly to dirt roads. The Renault swayed and groaned across mudholes, wheezed and belched blue smoke. In the back, Charlotte and Aloïs rode in silence for an hour. Finally, Charlotte asked him, "Do you still have family in this area?"

The tip of his cigarette glowed red as he took a drag. Held the smoke in his lungs a long time before he exhaled to answer her.

"No longer," he said. "My parents lived in a village in Tarn-et-Garonne. When the *Wehrmacht* tried to requisition their home for officer billeting, they resisted. They were both shot dead. My brother also joined the *Maquis*, but he is as good as dead. He was captured, and is now in the Amiens prison."

Charlotte knew of the prison, named for the town where it was located in northern France. The Nazis kept Resistance fighters and political prisoners in Amiens. As far as Charlotte knew, no one ever left that place alive.

The truck turned off the dirt road and onto a farm path. Pierre slowed to walking speed to negotiate the ruts. The path led alongside a vineyard, the vines heavy with purple grapes. Charlotte supposed any wine made from these grapes would end up on a Nazi officer's table. The Germans plundered the best of France's produce. Charlotte knew of Frenchmen who had lost hair to malnutrition. City dwellers caught pigeons for a rare taste of meat.

Pierre stopped by a grove of pines. At first, Charlotte saw nothing to suggest a reason for stopping. No building, no place for a radio operator to set up shop. But then she noticed a crumbling structure obscured by weeds and branches. The remains of an old stone barn, she imagined, perhaps last used in the days of Napoleon. Intrigued now, she scanned more closely. From behind the ruins, an antenna extended up the trunk of a pine.

"Maurice," Pierre called.

No answer.

"Maurice," Pierre repeated. He opened the driver's door and stepped to the ground. Charlotte got out of the truck and stood beside him.

"*Ici*," a voice called.

An arm emerged from the barn's entrance. Swept away a curtain of vines and pine straw. A man ducked to clear the low passageway. Stepped out into the sunshine.

Unlike most *Maquisards*, he was old. Gray beard, hair down to his shoulders. No taller than five feet. His peasant shirt lay open to the waist, revealing a paunch covered with black and gray hair. Black beret, like Aloïs's, only more ragged. A hand-rolled cigarette burned between the fingers of his right hand.

"So they haven't killed you yet, you old *poilu*," Pierre said.

Charlotte recognized the nickname. Translated literally, it meant "hairy one." The French used it as a term for low-ranking riflemen of the Great War, much the way Americans referred to "GIs" or "dogfaces" nowadays. Presumably, Maurice had fought the Germans before.

"Not for lack of trying, the bastards," Maurice said. "Say, who is this pretty girl you brought to me?"

"She is Tigresse. Or that is one of her names, anyway. She has joined our struggle."

"*Très bien*. Can she shoot?"

"She claims so, but that is not her specialty." Pierre described how Charlotte drew maps. He told Maurice she needed a call to London.

Maurice's eyes narrowed. He took a long drag from the stub of his cigarette, then dropped the butt and crushed it with his boot.

"Do you trust her that much?" Maurice asked.

"She came to us starving, and she showed us her drawings. Railroads, location of a Panzer division, that sort of thing."

Maurice turned toward Charlotte. "You want them to fly you out, my dear?"

"I want them to come and get my latest maps. I do not know if they will tell me to leave with them."

Charlotte decided not to add any explanation. She wondered if she'd already said too much. But she'd said enough to satisfy Maurice. He bade them to come inside.

The interior was lit by a single oil lamp. A bedroll lay on the dirt floor. A rifle stood propped in a corner; it was an RSC M1917, a semi-automatic weapon from the previous war. A bit like the newer M1 Garand issued by the United States. But what impressed Charlotte most was the radio on Maurice's table: a Type 3, Mark II set designed by the SOE.

A red leather suitcase contained the radio's transmitter, receiver, and power supply unit. Wires ran from the radio to a generator, and from the generator to a bicycle mounted on a stand, with its rear wheel removed. Another wire connected the radio to a tiny Morse key. Charlotte was not a trained radio operator, but she knew enough to know this model was state of the art.

She discussed frequencies with Maurice. Charlotte did not know the specific channel PROSPER's radio operators had used to communicate with her handlers. Maurice could offer only an all-purpose frequency, one of several monitored by young women on duty at receiving stations in Britain and Cairo, poised with their headsets and typewriters. Charlotte would request a pickup, then wait for a response. The message would have to go through several hands. Hardly the ideal process for such life-and-death matters, but everything about this business was a calculated risk. To complicate matters, Maurice could not spend more than five minutes on the air at one time. Not only were the SOE women listening—so was the *Funkabwehr*, German counterintelligence with their damnable radio vans.

Maurice pedaled his bicycle, charged up his battery. Switched on the radio. The set glowed and hummed as it warmed up.

He began to transmit. Tapped the key so quickly that Charlotte, who knew Morse code, could barely keep up. He finished in less than two minutes, then waited. A terse response came back: *message received.*

Now Charlotte and Maurice could only wait. She had suggested a pickup, two nights hence, at the farm owned by Aloïs's uncle. Maurice would listen for confirmation from SOE and send for Charlotte when it came.

Charlotte and her new friends climbed aboard the truck for the ride back to their camp. They passed the vineyard, then rattled alongside an overgrown pasture, occupied by a sole Holstein milk cow. The cow raised her head to watch the Renault roll by. The rest of her herd, Charlotte imagined, had been slaughtered for beef long ago.

Farther along, smoke rose from a farmhouse. Beside the house, an elderly woman stooped in a kitchen garden. Though Charlotte normally would have expected to see animals in a farmyard, she noted their absence. Not a chicken nor a goose. No goats or guineas. Not even a dog.

The truck came to a curve where the dirt track disappeared into a forest. Ahead, four men stepped out of the woods. All carried long guns. They took up positions blocking the road. Raised their weapons.

"Gestapo," Aloïs said.

MEMORANDUM
REGARDING: Operation Donar
Gestapo Counterintelligence Corps,
Federal Intelligence Service, Lyon
Lyon, France 2 July 1943
TO: Reich Security Main Office, Berlin
FROM: Klaus Barbie, Hauptstürmfuhrer

Rigorous interrogation of terrorist elements reveals increased coordination between those elements and Allied command center. Thus far, we have been unable to ascertain a timetable for major enemy operations. However, a clear pattern emerges: Terrorist groups appear to be shifting away from individual attacks on targets of opportunity. Rather, they seem to be preparing to impede and harass Reich forces en masse, *upon commencement of Allied movement into France.*

This office has made numerous recent arrests, with more expected soon. Recommend further interrogation of captured terrorists incarcerated at Fresnes, Fort Montluc, and Amiens. Prisoners whose interrogations are completed within this jurisdiction will be eliminated.

Request additional personnel for counterintelligence operations in southern France.

Heil Hitler,
Klaus Barbie, Hauptstürmfuhrer

CHAPTER 5

Philippe Gerard

Over the Channel, Philippe rolled his Lysander into a thirty-degree bank. The turn raised his left wing and framed the moon in the struts. The reddening orb lit the scattered clouds with a pale fire and cast a rose-colored sheen across the water. Visibility was good—at least ten miles.

Other than a clear night, Philippe had little else going for him on this mission. For one thing, navigation was a problem. He adjusted a utility light to shine on the chart clipped to his kneeboard. The chart was folded to a region of France farther south than most of his landing zones—one he'd never visited before. This time he would not have the River Loire or any other obvious landmark to guide him. He'd have to rely on dead reckoning—just chart, compass, and watch—to get him reasonably close, then scan for a light signal from the ground.

Worse, there had been no acknowledgment from "Tigresse" after SOE confirmed her pickup request. The listening post in Cairo had received her initial call, which had come from a wireless operator she had never used before. The authentication signal had been correct, with no distress code. But after that, nothing. Radio silence.

Normally, a mission under such circumstances would not have been approved. But London had decided "Tigresse" was important enough to take a chance.

"You don't have to fly this one," Venable had told him. "I'll go."

"No, sir," Philippe had answered.

The more dangerous the mission, the better. Perhaps tonight he might die for France and clear his name. And if he didn't die, perhaps he'd get this brave woman out of harm's way, and get whatever she was carrying to Allied commanders, who seemed to want it badly.

When the Lysander crossed the French coast, Philippe glanced at his RAF-issued wristwatch. Noted the sweep of the second hand across the cream-colored dial. Leveled his wings and adjusted the throttle to fly at exactly 150 knots. Held course for five minutes, then turned forty degrees and checked his watch again. He stayed on that heading for ten minutes. Noted a slight wind drift from the north. Dimmed his cockpit lighting and surveyed the ground.

Hilly terrain, foothills of the Pyrenees, undulated below him. West of Toulouse, the country became sparsely populated. Philippe hoped "Tigresse" had found a proper landing ground. The Lysander could roll to a stop in less than a thousand feet, but those thousand feet needed to be reasonably flat. Ideally, with no tall trees at either end.

The moon revealed wooded slopes, fields bordered by hedgerows, winding narrow roads. No lights of any kind, not even the headlamps of a car. Anyone driving at this hour would use blackout shades for minimal lighting. As Philippe scanned the terrain, for a moment he felt like the reconnaissance pilot he used to be.

Back then, most of his flights were farther north, as the Germans rolled into France. In the MB.174, he didn't fly alone; his crew included an observer, who was an officer like the pilot, and an enlisted gunner. Philippe had liked his crew. The observer, Jean-Luc, was a privileged man from a privileged family. Yet he was a brave man. His father's connections could have gotten him a safe job on the ground, but Jean-Luc flew. The gunner, Marcel, was the son of a Jewish butcher.

At the time, Philippe thought he was helping save France. Gathering intelligence to form what his squadron mate Saint-Ex called a "blueprint of the war."

But now he felt he'd only been wasting fuel. And headquarters had been wasting crews. If the recon units managed to gather useful intelligence, that intel seldom made it to the Command Staff. The French collapse happened so rapidly that the Staff was always moving—and there was no way to communicate with them. Roads choked. Telephone lines fell. Radio frequencies jammed.

And there was that one mission—one pointless mission—that had changed nothing in the war but everything for Philippe.

Thirty thousand feet over Metz, he had called for an oxygen check. A routine procedure done frequently at high altitude to make sure the crew was conscious and alert. If an oxygen mask failed or if the supply depleted from a leak, hypoxia could kill. A crewman might fall asleep at his station and never wake up. The pilot could not see all the crew; the only way to make sure everyone was okay was to call on interphone.

"Oh-two check," Philippe had called.

"Observer good," Jean-Luc responded. Mid-mission, his camera was whirring, snapping photos of enemy positions below.

Then silence. No call from the gunner.

"Gunner?" Philippe called. "Gunner, check in."

No response other than hiss on the interphone.

Apparently, Marcel had passed out from lack of oxygen. Normally, a pilot would dive in this situation, to get the stricken crew member back down to breathable air. But there were enemy positions below. Philippe had a judgment call to make: Risk German gunfire or stay high and let Marcel die of hypoxia? He thought for about a second. Then made his decision.

He pulled his throttles to idle. Pitched down to accelerate. Eyed the airspeed indicator to stay just below 530 kilometers per hour—the Vne, or "never exceed" speed for the MB.174.

The rush of air across the canopy increased to a roar. The altimeter began unwinding: 29,000, then 28,000, then further. The vertical speed

36

indicator dropped until it pointed to Philippe's boots; the needle pegged and could go no lower.

The cockpit grew hot as the aircraft dived into thicker, warmer air. Sweat oozed along Philippe's arms and chest. He wore a heavy flying suit designed for the frigid temperatures of high altitude. As the altimeter spun through 15,000 feet, black bursts of smoke erupted all around the MB.174. The explosions of German *Fliegerabwehrkanone*, or "flak," sent claws of shrapnel slashing the aircraft.

"Taking fire," Jean-Luc called from the observer's station. No emotion. No shouting. Just a simple statement of fact.

At 10,000 feet, needles of tracer fire joined the flak bursts. Philippe leveled the aircraft and banked hard to the right.

No use. The tracers followed him through the turn. Four loud thumps sounded as large-caliber rounds slammed into the fuselage.

Normally, a reconnaissance plane like the MB.174 sought high altitude as a safe haven. Now Philippe could do only the opposite—dive as low as possible to increase his angular velocity over the Boche guns. He pitched down. Forests and fields loomed in his windscreen.

At the treetops, Philippe leveled. The tracers still chased him, so he pitched downward again. Blasted across a cornfield so low he heard stalks slapping the fuselage. A tree line loomed ahead. He climbed to clear it.

That's when he noticed oil pressure at zero on the starboard engine. Ground fire must have punctured the oil reservoir. The airframe shuddered as the engine seized. Black smoke trailed from the engine. Fire wreathed the cowling.

Philippe punched the extinguisher button. Feathered the prop.

The flames disappeared. But now he had to limp home on one engine.

"Gunner, check in," Philippe called.

No answer.

"Observer?"

Nothing.

Though sweat soaked his flight suit, Philippe now felt a chill. And a twist in his gut. Were both his friends dead?

Philippe took in a deep breath. Forced himself to concentrate. He still had an airplane to land. Clear of the enemy now, he climbed to a thousand feet. Checked his chart. Turned onto a heading to take him to his unit's latest temporary base—a schoolhouse outside Le Mans. The third temporary base in ten days. An adjacent pasture had become a grass landing ground.

On the radio, Philippe called operations and reported his emergency. "Very well, sir," came the answer. Perhaps there would be an ambulance. He knew there would be no crash truck standing by—the squadron was on a shoestring. If upon landing he rolled the aircraft into a flaming ball, there would be no help.

He banked his wounded aircraft over the schoolhouse. Extended his landing gear, lowered a notch of flaps. Leveled in the turn to final approach to bleed off airspeed. His unit was now down to six planes, and he saw only two parked in the playing field that served as a make-shift ramp. The rest were either out on sorties or lost. His own might also be lost for further missions, depending on the damage.

On final now, Philippe dropped another notch of flaps and pulled the throttle for his good engine to idle. Let the MB.174 glide to earth.

The grass strip was not as flat as a proper airfield. The ground undulated, and Philippe's main wheels touched down as the terrain rose to meet him. The aircraft bounced, settled back to earth. Philippe's molars cracked together with the hard landing. The nose yawed left—Philippe corrected with his rudder pedals.

In a spray of dust and grass, he pivoted the MB.174 to turn into its parking spot. More than anything, he wanted to get out of his harness and check on his friends. But he knew the best thing he could do was to stop the airplane and shut it down so medics could approach. He pulled the port engine's fuel mixture to idle cutoff. The propeller spun down. Now the aircraft made no sound save for the popping of an engine cowl as it cooled, and the static hiss of the radio. Nothing but silence from the other crew positions—no words, no movement. Philippe flipped the battery switch to OFF, and the plane went completely dead, perhaps never to fly again.

A mechanic came running with a fire extinguisher. When he saw no flames, he put down the extinguisher and peered into the observer's compartment. The mechanic then looked up at Philippe with an expression of utter sadness.

Philippe unplugged his headset cord and oxygen mask. Unbuckled his harness and turned to look behind him. Two bullet holes pocked the aft canopy, and gore spattered the glass. A round had torn through Marcel's neck. Oil dripped from the starboard engine cowling. Blood dripped from the fuselage. Two medics arrived with an ambulance, but there was nothing for them to do.

A brief investigation found a kink in the gunner's oxygen hose. Perhaps, mercifully, Marcel had been unconscious when the German bullet hit him. Not so for Jean-Luc, who had bled to death after shrapnel sliced through the aircraft's skin and his femoral artery. Philippe suffered not a scratch, though he suffered and would suffer more. Jean-Luc's father, his thoughts twisted by grief, accused Philippe of diving to alert the Germans they were under surveillance.

Philippe's commanders dismissed the accusation as preposterous. But they questioned his judgment. The mission was more important than one crew member. In trying to save Marcel, he had put one man above the mission, and he'd gotten another man killed.

All that had happened three years ago, but Philippe's psychological wounds remained raw and untreated. He knew untimely deaths were part of the human condition, and routine in wartime. After all, his country had lost nearly one-and-a-half million soldiers during the Great War. Then came the Spanish flu, and now another damnable war. To Philippe, it seemed the Reaper and his blade had a special preference for the French. So, sometimes the rational part of his mind asked why two particular deaths pained him so. But he always came back to the same answer: Those were the only two for which he felt responsible.

With his fingertips, he eased the control stick to the left, turned the Lysander under the moonlight. Scanned the darkened ground beneath him.

Nothing.

No signal, no light of any kind. Not even a stray sliver from behind a blackout curtain at a farmhouse.

Philippe wondered if he'd made a navigational error. He twisted a rheostat to bring up his map light. Checked the chart clipped to his kneeboard.

As a cross reference, he tuned his ADF receiver to Radio Paris, the hated Nazi propaganda outlet. Philippe listened to the garbage crackling in his headset—"England, like Carthage, shall be destroyed"—only long enough to identify the station. Then he turned down the volume and watched the needle on his radio compass. Based on his bearing from Paris, he was in the right place.

He could not loiter for long—the fuel gauge crept ever lower, and soon it would force a return to England. And if "Tigresse" had been captured or turned, there might be men with guns down there, waiting for the sound of a Lysander. The possible reasons for a failed contact were endless. Perhaps there had been a simple miscommunication.

During all Philippe's flights with the RAF Special Duties Squadron, night had been his element. Darkness meant a haven, a protection—however thin—from discovery and German bullets. A few hours in which he could enter his homeland, and perhaps, just perhaps, make a difference.

But tonight, the darkness felt hostile. Philippe let his mind wander to bleak words from Lord Byron that he'd read back at Tangmere Cottage:

> *I had a dream, which was not all a dream.*
> *The bright sun was extinguish'd, and the stars*
> *Did wander darkling in the eternal space,*
> *Rayless and pathless....*

Sometimes the war felt like a bad dream. What had happened to his dear Lisette? Had France really fallen? Did jackboots really echo through Parisian streets?

But it was not all a dream; it was all real. Philippe's dark thoughts over dark terrain brought him low. He considered pushing the stick forward for a terminal dive. Ending his pain in a splash of flame. The fire would probably flicker for a few moments, then burn out. The darkness would again become complete.

He would become merely the latest casualty, hardly worth a mention in intelligence reports. Few questions would be asked. The war and the world would go on without him.

But that would waste military resources: this expensive aircraft and his expensive training. His mind and his hands and his eyes belonged not to him but to the cause. Philippe loved France even if France did not love him.

One last time, he scanned the ground beneath him. Nothing but gloom. Checked his fuel gauge. Pushed up the throttle for climb power, and set a course back to Tangmere.

CHAPTER 6

Charlotte Denneau

In a farmhouse cellar, Charlotte and Aloïs tended Pierre's wounds. Or at least they tried. Shot twice through the shoulder, Pierre had lost a lot of blood. Worse, by now his wounds seemed to be infected. Sweat beaded his forehead. Charlotte and Aloïs had no thermometer, but they could tell simply from touching Pierre's forehead that he was running a high fever. Their hosts—a brave couple with a Christian-Democratic faction known as Combat—had sent for a doctor. But there was no word on when the doctor might arrive.

Christophe was dead. He had been killed outright in the firefight at the Gestapo roadblock. Maurice, the old *Maquis* radio operator, also was dead. Evidently located by one of the enemy's radio vans, he had gone down fighting rather than submit to arrest. Charlotte did not know if her coded message to London had been intercepted, but she had to assume the worst. That's why she had missed her planned pickup last night.

For the moment, she focused on tending to Pierre. With a pair of scissors, she cut through his bandages, filthy with dried blood. Until the doctor arrived, she could do little for him but change his dressings and offer aspirin for pain. He had begun going in and out of delirium. His eyelids fluttered, and he looked up at Charlotte.

"The fish are not biting," he said.

"What's that?" Charlotte said.

"No fish," Pierre whispered.

"He's out of his head again," Aloïs said.

Not necessarily a bad thing, Charlotte thought. Perhaps in his delirium, Pierre was out of the war for a moment. Maybe in his mind, he was a boy sitting by a stream with a fishing pole. Perhaps the young Pierre's biggest problem was catching another grasshopper for bait. If his altered consciousness had found a peaceful place, Charlotte considered, then let him stay there for a while.

In her own mind, she replayed the horrors of the roadblock shootout with the Gestapo. As soon as the four Germans positioned themselves across the road, she and Aloïs crouched low in the back of the truck. At the wheel, Pierre slowed and stopped. Up front in the cab, he and Christophe spoke not a word. They just started firing.

Pierre's sawed-off shotgun must have come as an awful surprise to the first goon to die. With a single swift motion, Pierre lifted it from the truck seat, pointed the double barrels. Pressed the trigger. The load of buckshot, delivered at point-blank range, practically took off the German's head. At the same time, Christophe opened up with his STEN. He cut down one of the enemy on his side of the truck.

The other two Germans raked the cab with their *maschinenkarabiners*. They fired wildly. The spray of bullets caught Pierre so quickly that he never fired his second barrel. Rounds stitched Christophe from his head to his gut.

Unseen by the Germans until it was too late, Charlotte and Aloïs raised their pistols from the back of the truck. Charlotte leveled her .45 at the goon who had just shot Pierre. With both hands, she aimed at her target's center mass and began firing. So close it was impossible to miss, she hit him four times. Aloïs put down the German on the other side of the vehicle.

It was over in five seconds.

After the roar of gunfire, there came a beat of silence. Burned gunpowder salted the air. Cattle lowed in the distance.

"I'm hit," Pierre called.

The truck began to roll forward—Pierre's foot must have slipped off the brake. Charlotte jumped down from the vehicle, opened the front door. Reached in and set the parking brake.

The scene in the cab turned her stomach. Blood streamed from Pierre's two wounds, spattered the seats and windshield. On the passenger side, Christophe had bled so profusely that blood pooled on the floor. Intestines bulged from his shirt. Brain matter flecked the dash. Christophe's eyes stared sightless. His right hand still clutched the STEN. Aloïs opened the passenger door, took the weapon, and dragged the body from the cab.

Charlotte helped Aloïs lift Christophe into the truck bed. Bile rose in her throat when his guts dragged in the dust. At least he'd died quickly and not suffered.

They left the Germans on the ground. Aloïs took the wheel, and Charlotte climbed in on the passenger side. Christophe's blood soaked her trousers and stained her shoes. Pierre sat between them. He leaned on Charlotte's shoulder, his face contorted with pain.

They drove fast on backroads. Prayed not to encounter another ambush or checkpoint. With a dead body in the back and a wounded man up front, their identity as Resistance fighters was obvious. And under no circumstances could they lose Charlotte's maps.

"Where can we go?" Charlotte asked.

"Anywhere but home," Aloïs said. Charlotte assumed that by "home" he meant his uncle's farm.

The other options were thin. This part of France had been called the *Zone Libre*, the Free Zone, until last year. That was an exaggeration at best. The *Zone Libre* was run by the collaborationist Vichy government. And when the Allies invaded North Africa, the Germans took over all of France.

Aloïs headed toward the town of Valence, on the River Rhône. He explained that he knew people there who might help.

"They worked with Renouvin," Aloïs said. "They've lain low since he got arrested, but I think they're still with the cause."

Charlotte knew that name from her intelligence briefings, but she kept that information to herself. Jacques Renouvin had fought during the Battle of France. He was wounded and captured, then managed to escape from a hospital. Renouvin went on to organize Combat cells, which naturally put a target on his back. The Gestapo had finally caught up with him last January at a train station in Brive-la-Gaillarde.

Outside Valence, Aloïs stopped at the farmhouse. The couple there—Lyam and Marie Blanchet—were not happy to see him. They became even more disturbed when they learned they needed to dispose of a corpse and treat a wounded man. But they did not turn away fellow patriots. While they buried Christophe in the orchard, Lyam leaned on his shovel, wiped his face with his sleeve and said, "It is very dangerous here."

Aloïs laughed out loud—without any trace of mirth. "You think we don't know that?" he asked.

"I think it's worse than you know." Lyam rammed his shovel into the mound of soil over Christophe's body. Looked over at Aloïs. "Do you know the name Klaus Barbie?"

Aloïs shrugged. "Just another Boche. So what?"

Charlotte didn't know the name, either. She had been briefed on the identities of high-ranking Nazis, but she'd never heard of a Klaus Barbie.

"He is the local Gestapo chief," Lyam said. "He keeps his headquarters up in Lyon, at the Hotel Terminus. I have heard stories about his interrogations that would turn your stomach."

"All the Gestapo are bastards," Aloïs said.

"Yes, but this one is especially so, and especially effective."

"Is this why everything has been falling apart for us?" Charlotte asked.

"It's part of it," Lyam said. "If you fall into Barbie's hands, you will tell everything you know, and then you will die."

"Then we don't fall into his hands," Charlotte said. "Simple as that."

"That's what the L-pills are for," Aloïs said.

No one spoke for several minutes. Yes, that was what the L-pills were for. Charlotte had her own. More than one, in case some got lost. L stood for "lethal." Potassium cyanide, to bring quick death to avoid torture.

Charlotte, a lapsed Catholic, had thought long and hard about whether she would use an L-pill. If you committed suicide, did that mean eternal damnation? She decided the question was irrelevant. If you bit down on cyanide while facing capture, you didn't do it because you *wanted* to die. You wanted to live on, to continue the fight. Better yet, to see peace and enjoy life again. But you sacrificed yourself to protect your brothers and sisters in arms. It was really no different than a soldier falling on a grenade to shield his friends, or a pilot remaining at the controls of a burning aircraft so his crewmates could bail out.

It wasn't suicide at all. It was just tactics.

The doctor arrived too late. He had come from Valence, only a few miles away. But for the sake of security, he had not come by a direct route. He had taken two days to get to the Blanchet farm, and no one blamed him. But by then, Pierre was beyond saving. His wounds had become septic. He had lapsed into continual delirium. The doctor said antibiotics would do no good now. Better to give Pierre morphine to ease his final hours. Only by courage and wits did the doctor have antibiotics and morphine at all. The Germans had taken most medicines for themselves.

Charlotte caressed Pierre's head as the needle went into his arm. The doctor depressed the plunger, and the lines around Pierre's eyes shallowed almost immediately. Though he was semiconscious at most, he seemed to feel the pain lift away from him. His jaw muscles relaxed, and he opened his eyes. Looked straight at Charlotte.

"Complete your mission," Pierre whispered.

Those were his last coherent words. He lapsed back into delirium, and he died around sunset. The Blanchets sent for a priest they knew to say a few words for Pierre and Christophe. That was the nearest they could come to a proper funeral. With informants all around, public ceremonies for two men who had died of gunshot wounds were too risky.

Charlotte took Pierre's final request to heart. Though the Resistance seemed shattered, and the Gestapo and informers were everywhere, she still had a job to do: Plan Green. Map the rail system. Find targets. Sooner or later, she still believed, the Allied armies and waves of their aircraft would come across the Channel. She could give them something to shoot at.

Her rail maps were fairly good for central and northern France. But here in the south, they remained a little thin. After the priest left, Charlotte plotted her next move. She met at the kitchen table with Aloïs, along with Lyam and Marie Blanchet.

"My job is the railroads," she explained. "Especially places where aircraft might bomb, or sappers could place explosives."

"Such as?" Lyam asked.

"Tunnels and trestles," Charlotte said. "Roundhouses and marshalling yards."

"Are you mad?" Marie said. "You want to scout such obvious targets now? All of France is crawling with Gestapo and Milice. Barbie and his henchmen seem to know what we're doing before we do. We should wait this out. Bide our time."

Marie folded her arms. Stared out the window as if expecting armed men at any moment. She startled when her cat, a gray tabby, leaped onto the windowsill and flicked its tail.

"Bide our time for how long?" Aloïs asked.

"Until it's safer," Marie said.

"It will never be safer," Aloïs said. "Not until we make it safer." He told the Blanchets about the death of his parents, and about his brother in Amiens prison.

A tense silence hung over the kitchen. Finally, Lyam said, "So we press on. We don't fight Fascists because we are guaranteed to win. We fight Fascists because they are Fascists."

"Very good," Charlotte said. "What do you know about the trains in this area?"

"Not much," Lyam said. "Only that there is a rail line that connects Lyon to Marseille."

"Marseille is a port," Aloïs said. "That railroad would be important to the Germans."

"*Absolument*," Lyam said.

"Where is a weak point, or a choke point, on that line?" Charlotte asked.

Lyam fished a pack of Gitanes from his shirt pocket. Tapped out a cigarette, placed it in his mouth, and lit it. Charlotte guessed he needed a minute to think; perhaps he was unused to this type of target mapping. Or perhaps he needed a minute to consider how much risk to undertake. Lyam and Marie exchanged glances. Lyam took a puff from the cigarette, exhaled through his nostrils.

"There is a trestle that crosses the Rhône," Lyam said finally. "It is south of here, near Avignon."

"Does it get much traffic?" Charlotte asked.

Lyam shrugged.

"How shall we get there?" Aloïs asked.

A fair question, to Charlotte's mind. Normally, she did this sort of work alone, traveling on her motorbike. But she had been forced to leave it behind, and there was no going back for it now. And driving anywhere near a town required some thought. Drivers needed special permits. Farmers usually had those permits, but any task with a farm truck had to look like farming, or something related.

"We could drive you close to Avignon," Marie said. "Walk the last few miles. If you're going to the river, take fishing poles."

The suggestion relieved Charlotte. So Marie was on board with this. Back in the fight. And the fishing poles were an excellent idea. Cover story.

"When?" Lyam asked.

"First thing tomorrow," Charlotte said.

Morning fog ghosted across the still surface of the Rhône. Charlotte and Aloïs stepped with care through the stones that lined the riverbank. Dew clung to the weeds and dampened their trousers. Charlotte found a rock large enough to sit on, then swung her pack off her shoulder. She took out a pad and pens, and began to sketch the iron structure of the railway bridge, along with surrounding landmarks. The bridge reminded her of the Long Bridge that spanned the Potomac, but she kept the thought to herself. She never spoke of her French-American heritage, of how she volunteered for the Resistance right after the fall of France, well before the United States entered the war. No telling how the enemy might use that information.

For appearances, Aloïs carried two cane poles and a tackle box. The poles were already rigged with line, corks, and hooks. Aloïs pulled a hook from where it was embedded at the base of one of the poles. Twisted the pole to unwind the line from around it. Swept his boot through the weeds until he found a grasshopper. Caught the insect, and impaled it on the hook.

"A fine morning for fishing," Aloïs said.

"Funny," Charlotte said. "I think Pierre was imagining a scene like this during his fever."

Aloïs considered that for a moment. "I hope so," he said finally. "Better than so many other things he might have had in his head."

A rumbling grew in the distance. The bridge began to vibrate with the train's approach. On the far shore, a locomotive appeared. The bridge groaned when it took the weight. Dirt and rust fell from the girders, sprinkled the water. As the train passed, Charlotte counted eight boxcars and two flatbeds. Each flatbed carried two Panzer IV tanks. Charlotte noted the time and scribbled the data on the upper right corner of her sketch.

After the train passed, Aloïs swung a line into the river. The cork plopped onto the surface and settled atop the water. To Charlotte's right, movement caught her eye—about fifty yards downstream. A man and a woman were walking toward Charlotte and Aloïs, along a riverside path. They were older, in their sixties. Maybe a retired couple out for a morning stroll.

A cry from Aloïs diverted Charlotte's attention. "Hey, I got one," he said. Charlotte turned to see the cane pole bent, its line taught. Aloïs pulled against a fish of some size; whatever it was, he could not lift it out of the water.

When Charlotte looked up again the man and woman were closer. Within ten yards.

"*Bonjour*," Charlotte said. She received no reply.

The man raised a Leica. Pointed it directly at Charlotte and Aloïs. Snapped a photo.

CHAPTER 7

Philippe Gerard

The hospital corridor smelled of antiseptics. The tile floor glared with light from the mercury-vapor lamps overhead. As Philippe walked with Squadron Leader Venable, their heels clacked and echoed along the hallway.

Venable had brought Philippe here in London to meet someone who might help unlock the mystery of what was happening with "Tigresse." She had sent a signal requesting a pickup, then not shown up. Was she dead or in distress? Or had she been turned? Had she tried to set up a trap? No one had heard from her since Philippe's wasted trip over southern France.

"You need to prepare yourself for what you're about to see," Venable said. "Try not to look shocked when you meet him."

Flight Lieutenant William Chadwick had commanded a Lancaster bomber sent to strike an arms factory at Rouen several months ago. Shrapnel from antiaircraft rounds punctured the fuel tanks and set the aircraft afire. Chadwick ordered his crew to bail out of what had become a flying torch. Two of the gunners never escaped the aircraft. Chadwick remained at the controls until he thought everyone was out. By the time he unbuckled his harness, flames had enveloped the flight deck. He plunged through the fire to reach an escape hatch.

At a private room in a wing reserved for war wounded, Venable knocked on the door. No answer. Venable knocked again.

"Enter," a voice called, barely audible.

Inside the room, Philippe needed a moment for his eyes to adjust to the darkness. Curtains shut out the noonday sun. On the other side of the hospital bed, a man sat in a wheelchair with his back to the door.

At a glance, Philippe could see the man had been there for a long time. In some ways, the room looked more like a permanent flat than a hospital chamber. Framed photos stood on a nightstand. Bookshelves held dozens of volumes. Magazines were strewn across the bed. The Union Jack hung from a wall.

"Flight Lieutenant Chadwick?" Venable said.

The man turned his wheelchair. Even in the shadows, the flames' devastation became obvious. Chadwick's nose and lips had burned away. Scarred skin sagged from his cheeks like melted wax. Blue veins streaked the scar tissue. A single tuft of hair remained on top of his head. Only by sheer force of will did Philippe stifle a shudder. He had seen something like this once before. This time it was worse.

Chadwick gripped his armrests, began to stand.

"As you were, Flight Lieutenant," Venable said. "If anything, I should be saluting you."

The lieutenant let himself drop back into his wheelchair. "Very well, sir," he said. Gravel in his voice. "What can I do for you?"

"We'll get to that," Venable said, "but how are you doing?"

A long silence passed. Perhaps Chadwick thought that was a foolish question. But finally, like a good British officer in the presence of a superior, he formed an answer.

"With a series of surgeries, they hope to reconstruct enough of my face to make me look nearly human," Chadwick said. "I do not believe it is worth the pain." He described how each operation involved scraping away scar tissue. For reasons he did not completely understand, the doctors could not fully anesthetize him.

Chadwick's burns appeared worse than those suffered by Philippe's old squadron mate Sagon. Philippe recalled going with Saint-Ex to visit

Sagon in the hospital back in 1940. Philippe saw then that Sagon was giving more than his life to his country. The agony, the long recovery, the disfigurement of such a cruel injury surely were worse than quick death in a crash. Every mirror would reflect the terror, replay the worst moment of one's existence.

"I can only imagine your journey to avoid capture with those burns," Venable said. "Not even the Victoria Cross is enough to honor your endurance and courage."

"Thank you, sir. I just didn't want to fall into the hands of the Nazis. Simple as that."

"Actually, your journey is the reason we came to see you," Venable said. "A woman called 'Tigresse' aided you, yes?"

"Indeed, she did."

"Then the rest of this conversation must remain secret."

Venable explained that 'Tigresse" remained in the field, with critical information for the Allied cause. The No. 161 Special Duties Squadron was tasked with getting her out. But now they could not find her.

"And you want to know if you can still trust her," Chadwick said.

"Exactly," Venable answered. "She has done good work. But everyone has weaknesses. Everyone has limits."

"Believe me, I know," Chadwick said. "And I have followed the news from France. Apparently, the Gestapo has ways of finding those weaknesses."

"They do."

"I can tell you only what I saw. And that was months ago. But I believe if 'Tigresse' was ever going to quit, she would have quit while smuggling me into Spain."

Chadwick described his good fortune in parachuting into an open field. Temporarily blinded, he could not steer his chute away from trees. The field was owned by a French farmer who had lost his only son in the war. Grief had made the man fearless; the Nazis could no longer take away anything he cared about. The farmer took in the downed flier, sent for a doctor. The doctor thought Chadwick would die. For a week they kept him as comfortable as possible in the farmer's cellar, mainly with alcohol. But when it seemed he might survive, they had to start moving him.

"I told them not to take the risk," Chadwick said. "I told them to shoot me and bury me. It would not be murder; it would be mercy. But they wouldn't hear of it."

That's where 'Tigresse" came in. She knew the routes and safe houses. Transporting Chadwick was especially difficult because at times he had to be carried. She arranged for men to move him on a stretcher. Sometimes she carried one end of the stretcher herself.

"I thought the travel was arduous until we reached the Pyrenees," Chadwick said. "Then it became worse. I'll never understand why they didn't leave me in the snow, but they didn't."

At the border, the Spanish section of the network took over, and 'Tigresse" remained in France. Chadwick eventually made his way to Lisbon. But even in neutral Portugal, he had to remain out of sight. His burns made it obvious he was a downed aviator. And in Lisbon, the Nazis had eyes everywhere. Eventually, the SOE spirited him out on a diplomatic flight.

Philippe considered what the rest of Chadwick's life might look like. In his condition, would he ever know the love of a woman? Would he ever start a family? Could he find work? Perhaps the government would provide him a disability pension. But even in the best of cases, the war would never end for this man.

Meeting Chadwick made Philippe feel a little ashamed. He had wanted to die over his regrets, over his loss of esteem. Esteem among fellow pilots was no small thing. But suddenly his own problems seemed a mere inconvenience compared to those of the man before him.

Philippe tried to think of something appropriate to say, but words failed him. In the end, he kept it simple: "It has been an honor to meet you, Flight Lieutenant," he said.

"I am not sure how I have helped you."

"In the intelligence business," Venable said, "every little bit helps."

"Very well, sir."

After Philippe and Venable left the hotel, Venable hailed a cab.

"Back to Tangmere, sir?" Philippe asked.

"Not yet. We're staying in London tonight. There's someone else here you'll want to see."

"Who's that, sir?"

"Oh, you'll know him when you see him."

The commander wore a wry smile—a rare thing for someone with such heavy responsibilities. Philippe asked no more questions. Better to play the game and wait for the surprise.

The taxi drove past blocks of homes destroyed during the Blitz. Mounds of rubble littered once-beautiful neighborhoods. The Luftwaffe bombing campaign seemed to have ended, at least for now. But Philippe wondered if this was merely a lull, if the Germans had some new aircraft or weapon under development. It wasn't like them simply to quit. During the Battle of Britain, the RAF had beaten them back. However, Philippe suspected those brave British pilots in their Spitfires and Hurricanes had, at best, only bought their nation more time.

The cab rolled by the Houses of Parliament. Philippe imagined Churchill himself inside, intoning words of inspiration. The vehicle stopped at St. Ermin's, a luxury hotel that dated to the previous century.

"We're staying here, sir?" Philippe asked.

"Oh, not on the RAF's shilling," Venable said. "A friend of yours extends his generosity."

A suspicion formed in Philippe's mind. But he kept his thoughts to himself, let Venable's plan play itself out.

Inside, they found the bar crowded with late-afternoon drinkers. Cigarette smoke drifted among the chandeliers. Officers in uniforms of all the Allied nations chatted with one another and with attractive young women. Philippe noted an RAF pilot here, a Canadian infantryman there, and several American majors and lieutenant colonels. A gramophone spun out "There'll Be Bluebirds Over the White Cliffs of Dover" by Vera Lynn. Philippe would have preferred Josephine Baker, but he was happy to hear music of any kind. Men in civilian clothing joined the mix. Diplomats, presumably, or agents who worked in the shadows. St. Ermin's carried a reputation as a hub of anti-Nazi intrigue.

Even in this elite gathering, Philippe's old squadron mate stood out. At better than six feet, he towered over most of the men in the room. Antoine de Saint-Exupéry was not in uniform; he wore a pin-striped suit with a checkered tie knotted tight at his collar. He kept his right hand stuffed into his coat pocket. In his left hand he held a whiskey tumbler and a cigarette. Philippe would have recognized the balding pate and the slight upturn in the nose anywhere. Saint-Ex responded with an easy smile to something said by one of the women surrounding him. Then he recognized Philippe.

"*Mon ami*," Saint-Ex called. Waved with his drink and cigarette.

Philippe pushed through the crowd. Embraced his friend. Felt part of Saint-Ex's drink slosh down his back.

"Ah, Philippe," the author said in French. "I see the Boche haven't shot you down."

"Not yet, anyway," Philippe said.

Saint-Ex took a step back. Eyed Philippe's uniform. "And you are with the Brits now," he said.

"I fly for France," Philippe said, "however I may."

Philippe introduced Venable. He would have liked to explain all Venable had done in support of the Resistance. For the sake of security, he said only, "This is my commander. He is one of France's best friends."

The author took a drag from his smoke, regarded Venable. Even while addressing a British officer, he continued speaking French.

"Yes, I know of him," Saint-Ex said. "I thank you for your work, sir."

Venable nodded.

"How did you know to send for me?" Philippe asked. "This is a pleasant surprise."

Saint-Ex explained how their old reconnaissance unit, the 2/33 Squadron, was reconstituting in North Africa. The Americans were outfitting 2/33 with a photorecon variant of the P-38 Lightning, one of the hottest fighters in the skies. The campaign against Nazi Germany had begun in North Africa to provide a foothold for attacks in Europe. Now the Allies could launch from bases in Algeria, Libya, Morocco, and Egypt.

"You should come back with us," Saint-Ex said. "It will take some paperwork, but I am sure the clerks know how to transfer you from the RAF back to the *Armée de l'Air.*"

"Perhaps," Philippe said. "Perhaps."

He had not expected an offer like this. He would have liked nothing better than to rejoin 2/33. But...there was unfinished business. He exchanged a glance with Venable. The commander's face remained expressionless. Philippe decided to make no commitment, at least not on the spur of the moment. Instead, he asked, "What brings you to Britain?"

"A meeting with my British publisher. It seems de Gaulle is displeased with *Pilote de Guerre.*"

Saint-Ex referred to his memoir of flying during France's brief struggle before falling to the Nazis. He used the French title for a book published in English as *Flight to Arras.*

"And?"

"And who cares what de Gaulle thinks? He thinks the book is defeatist. But it merely says what happened. Does he think France won?" Saint-Ex's tone made it clear he wanted to talk about something else.

"So, how do you like the P-38?" Philippe asked.

"She is a flying torpedo," Saint-Ex said. "Very fast. Very advanced."

"Ah," Venable chimed in. "You must love it."

"*Je ne sais pas,*" the author said. "So many switches and dials. The pilot becomes more of a chief accountant."

To Philippe, that sounded so much like Saint-Ex: a man who praised modernity in his writing, yet hated to learn new technology. During a brief and undistinguished stint as a test pilot, Saint-Ex had nearly drowned himself and his crew in a seaplane. He'd failed to pull the nose of a Latécoère 293 high enough on landing. The floats dug into the water, and the aircraft flipped. Saint-Ex, along with a naval officer and a mechanic, bobbed up, spitting seawater.

Saint-Ex stubbed out the nub of his cigarette in an ashtray on the bar. Took a pack of Camels from his pocket. Evidently, he had stocked up on good American cigarettes during his time in the United States. He lit a fresh smoke, exhaled through his nose. A shadow seemed to cross his face, and Philippe felt sorry his question had led to a mention of de Gaulle, who was always a sore subject for Saint-Ex. The author had always felt General Henri Giraud would make a better leader of France. Giraud was now leading what forces he could muster in North Africa.

"Are you writing now?" Philippe asked.

"*Toujours*," Saint-Ex said. *Always*. "A work I call *Citadelle*."

"What is it about?"

Saint-Ex took the Camel from his lips, stared up at the ceiling. For a moment Philippe feared he had offended his friend with a question that did not merit an answer. But finally, Saint-Ex said, "It is about what is a civilization. Why are we here? What are we doing here?"

"Fine questions for the times we are in," Venable offered.

"Especially for France," the author said. "These times will define us."

CHAPTER 8

Charlotte Denneau

N ight insects trilled in the forest. Breeze murmured in the pines. The constellation Scorpius glittered overhead, unobscured by clouds, undimmed by any moonlight.

The sinister image of a scorpion seemed fitting to Charlotte. She and Aloïs were on the run. They had to assume the couple with the camera were informants. They had to assume their cover was blown. There was no question of going back to the Blanchets' farm; that might only lead the Gestapo there. Aloïs was making the decisions now, and he didn't seem entirely sure of himself.

"Tell me again where we're going," Charlotte said as Aloïs held a tree branch for her to follow him.

"Périgord province," Aloïs answered, "if he is still there."

"Who?"

"*El Espectro.*"

That made even less sense. The code name, or nickname, or whatever it was, was Spanish, not French. The specter. The ghost. Some figure in the *Maquis*, Charlotte gathered. Aloïs had told her little else.

They had nothing in the way of provisions. Charlotte had brought only her knapsack to the river, so she still had her maps and drawings, thank God. She also still had her .45, as did Aloïs. Already she felt tired, hungry, and filthy. To reach Périgord on foot would take days.

They came to the edge of the woods, which opened onto a field. Darkness made it hard to tell, but the field appeared to have been left fallow. There was no crop that Charlotte could discern; just weeds and grass. Perhaps a farmer was letting the field rest for the season. Or maybe the farmer was dead.

A deep rumble came from the sky. Not thunder, but a low, sustained tone from the north. Charlotte looked up but saw no aircraft. A formation of British bombers, she guessed, flying toward some target with lights off. From what she understood, the British bombed by night and the Americans bombed by day to hit the enemy around the clock.

Dim lights on the ground brought her to more immediate problems. Across the field, a couple hundred yards away, she spotted a column of trucks. They drove slowly under blackout headlamps. A German unit, no doubt, repositioning itself.

Charlotte and Aloïs waited for the column to pass. When they felt it was safe, they waded through the weed field and crossed the road. They entered a narrow stand of trees, bordered by a stone fence. Beyond the fence lay another field, also fallow, and beyond the field, a farmhouse. Lamplight glowed from a window. A small outbuilding, perhaps a toolshed, and a barn stood near the home.

"Let's just watch it for a time," Aloïs said.

"*D'accord*," Charlotte answered.

She imagined what Aloïs was thinking: This could be a source of help, maybe someone who could offer food, perhaps a change of clothing. But it could just as well be someone who would turn them in, or shoot them outright. Not a time to make snap decisions.

The first blush of dawn pinked the eastern sky. Roseate streamers lit the horizon, and somewhere near the farmhouse, a rooster crowed.

A side door slammed, and a woman appeared. She appeared young; brown hair extended past her shoulders. She wore a peasant dress with a white apron. A farm wife, presumably, coming out to gather eggs or feed livestock.

But she carried no basket for eggs. No feed bag for animals. There was nothing in her hands but a small knife. Charlotte supposed she might be about to cut vegetables from a kitchen garden.

But she never stooped to gather a tomato or a gourd. Instead, she leaned against a fencepost and watched the sun rise. She pulled a cloth from her apron and dabbed at her eyes; the woman was weeping.

Then she put the knife to her wrist.

Aloïs sprang from his hiding place. Charlotte followed close behind. They sprinted across the field, jumped a wooden fence. By the time they reached the woman, blood dripped from her fingers. She had made one cut and was starting another. Aloïs tackled her.

The woman screamed. "Leave me alone," she shouted. On the ground now, she dropped the knife. Twisted away from Aloïs. "Go away!" she cried.

Charlotte grabbed the knife from the dirt. Flung it away. The woman rose to her feet. Dirt and grass flecked her hair. She tried to run for the knife. Charlotte caught up with her. Clutched her around the waist.

By now, blood spurted from the cut on her wrist. Splattered her dress and apron.

"This is not the way," Charlotte said. "We know things are bad. They are bad for everyone."

The woman stopped resisting. Breathed hard. Placed her bloody hand to her forehead. Sobbed.

"What do you know?" she said. "You know nothing."

"I know you need to let me put a bandage on that wrist."

The woman stared into the distance. She let her arms fall to her sides. Blood dripped from the fingers of her left hand and spattered into the weeds.

"Let's get you inside," Charlotte said. She placed her hand on the woman's arm. Led her toward the house.

At the door, a black cat skittered from the steps. Aloïs opened the door, and Charlotte led the woman into a kitchen. The woman sat at a rough-hewn table. She paid no mind to the blood dripping onto her table and floor.

Aloïs found a dish cloth and wet it in a washtub half filled with cold water. Twisted the cloth to squeeze out the water. The woman held out her injured wrist, but she did not look at him. He began wiping away the blood. The wound kept bleeding. The cut gaped open and kept filling with blood.

"That needs stitches," Charlotte said.

"Leave me and let me bleed to death," the woman said.

"Fortunately, I don't think you got the artery," Charlotte said. "Where are your sewing things?"

The woman shrugged.

"I'll see what I can find," Aloïs said.

He disappeared into the home's interior. Charlotte wrapped the wet cloth around the cut and applied pressure to stop the bleeding. She heard Aloïs opening closets and drawers. After several minutes, he came back with a spool of red thread, a pair of scissors, and a sewing needle.

Charlotte tried to recall her training in field medicine. "Aloïs, do you have a match?" she asked.

"*Oui.*"

"Put a flame to that needle, to sterilize it."

Aloïs struck a match and followed her instructions. Then he blew out the match and held the needle to let it cool.

"This will hurt some," Charlotte said. "I am sorry, but we need to close that wound."

The woman stared at the table and made no reply.

"Can you find me a dry cloth?" Charlotte asked.

Aloïs searched the kitchen and found a napkin that looked fairly clean. Handed it to Charlotte. Charlotte patted the wound to clear away as much of the blood and she could. Threaded the needle. Took a deep breath and pierced the woman's arm.

The woman winced, but gave no other sign that she felt any pain. She held her arm perfectly still. She seemed hardly to feel pain, and she seemed not to care whether her wound got treated or not.

Charlotte made four stitches. Tied each one and trimmed the knots with the scissors.

"You'll need to cut these out in a few days," she said. "When you do it, be careful and take your time."

The woman offered no reaction. She seemed not to hear the words at all.

Aloïs disappeared again. Came back with a gauze bandage.

"Ah," Charlotte said. "So you do have first-aid supplies."

The woman did not reply.

Charlotte wrapped the bandage over the cut. Tried to tie it securely but not too tightly.

"Is that all right?" she asked.

Again, no answer.

Charlotte considered what else to say, if anything. Finally, she asked, "Why did you want to do this?"

For long seconds the woman said nothing. Charlotte thought she was not going to get an answer. She and Aloïs were taking chances by being here at all. Just as she thought to get up and leave, the woman spoke.

"My husband is a prisoner of war," she said. "I have not seen him for three years. I do not know if he is alive. A German major is billeted here. He makes me cook for him and his friends. He beats me. He uses me for his pleasure. He says I am his whore because French men are cowards and cannot fight. He is half right, anyway."

"We will wait for him," Aloïs said. "We will show him about fighting."

"Shh," Charlotte said. She knew German officers requisitioned French homes. She had not heard of this particular brand of abuse, but she wasn't surprised.

"What is your name?" Charlotte asked.

"Valerie."

"You are not a whore, Valerie. You are a victim of a war crime."

"Not after today," Aloïs said. "We will kill him."

"We can't do that," Charlotte said. "If we do, you know what they will do to her."

"She can come with us." Aloïs pulled up a chair and sat beside Valerie. "You can come with us if you want."

Valerie looked at him. "Who are you?" she asked.

62

Charlotte considered what, if anything, to tell her. But before she could decide, Aloïs said, "We are *Maquis*."

Valerie's eyes widened. She appeared more fascinated than afraid. She sat in silence, regarded Charlotte and Aloïs. The appearance of *résistants* had clearly surprised her. And perhaps altered her calculations.

"I, I would love to escape this hell," she said. "But I am no soldier. I would just be in your way. And if my husband ever makes it back, I need to be here for him. I need to endure this for him."

Her eyes glistened at the mention of her spouse. She wiped away a tear with her good hand. Then she shuddered—perhaps at the thought of what she had to endure.

Charlotte considered the woman's situation for a few minutes. Then she said, "There is another way you could help, and maybe help yourself, too. You have an enemy officer under your roof. You can gather information."

Valerie's eyes met Charlotte's. Again, she seemed interested, but skeptical. "I am no more a spy than a soldier," she said.

"You don't need to be," Charlotte said. "All you need to do is listen."

"Listen? And how would I tell you what I hear?"

"Let us worry about that. We may not be able to get back here to learn what you know. But we might. Or someone might. Just listen and wait."

"This is very good," Aloïs said.

"I will do this," Valerie said.

"Good," Charlotte said. "Remember, don't ask any questions. Don't show any curiosity. Don't write anything down. Just listen."

"I can do that."

"Excellent."

Valerie thought for a moment and added, "I have no vehicle. He travels sometimes in a black Citroën and sometimes in an army truck. If you see any vehicle here at all, that means he is here."

"Very good."

"May I know your names?" Valerie asked.

"No," Charlotte said. "It is better if you do not."

"I see."

Valerie sat up straight. She took the wet cloth from the table and began wiping blood stains from her fingers. Her manner changed so much that Charlotte felt they had given her hope. Then she decided hope was too strong a word. But maybe they had given her…purpose.

"We should go now," Charlotte said. "If we go, will you be all right?"

Valerie shook her head, shrugged. "I don't know. Yes. Well, I have something I can do now, anyway."

"Yes, you do," Aloïs said.

"Can I offer you anything? Do you need food?"

"Yes," Aloïs said. "And water. Anything will help."

"A change of clothing, too," Charlotte said, "if you can spare anything."

"Oh, yes," Valerie said. "I have trousers that might fit you. I'll get some of my husband's old clothes, too."

Valerie left the kitchen for a while. She came back with a muslin sack filled with clothing. She found another sack and went outside to the garden. Returned with tomatoes and onions. Passed the sacks to Aloïs. Filled an old-fashioned wineskin with water and gave that to him, as well.

She embraced Charlotte. Shook hands with Aloïs. Then Charlotte and Aloïs left through the kitchen door and slipped back into the forest.

They continued toward Périgord. They moved slowly and with care, mainly in the dark. They subsisted on the vegetables from Valerie, along with what Charlotte called "salad," simply grass and leaves. Above all, Charlotte made sure to keep her knapsack dry to protect the maps and drawings inside. They bathed in streams, and the fresh clothes felt like a luxury. They avoided roads and came into contact with no one else. After three days, they came to a stream that flowed past a set of stone cliffs. Trees studded the cliffs; their roots took hold through cracks in the stone. More trees lined the base of the cliffs.

"This is the place," Aloïs whispered, "if he is still here."

They lay flat to the ground, hidden in vines and scrub. For a time, they saw nothing. But eventually Charlotte spotted men moving through the trees. All carried weapons. Their clothing varied; none wore uniforms. These were clearly *résistants* of some description. One man led a horse, another a pack mule.

"Where are they coming from?" Charlotte asked. "I don't see any tents."

"There is a cave," Aloïs said.

"A cave?"

"I will go see if they will have us. I do not think they will shoot me. But if they do, just run away."

Aloïs smiled when he said that, but Charlotte knew he wasn't joking. He rose from the ground and crept through the pines and hackberries. He stayed gone for so long Charlotte wondered what was wrong. But at least she never heard a shot.

Finally, Aloïs appeared at the edge of the woods and waved. Motioned for Charlotte to come. She looked around, decided it was safe. Shuffled downhill, picked her way across the stream on wet rocks. Joined Aloïs, who was accompanied by three men.

Those three were the roughest *Maquisards* Charlotte had ever seen. Aloïs looked well-groomed by comparison. Beard stubble, torn clothing. Muddy boots. Rope for belts. One carried a Mosin-Nagant rifle, a Russian-made bolt-action from the previous century. The other two had Winchester lever-actions—and where in heaven's name had they found those? They looked in their forties, but in their condition it was hard to guess their ages.

"*Bonjour*," Charlotte said.

The men laughed. Without speaking, they led Charlotte and Aloïs to the entrance of a limestone cave. Firelight flickered from inside. One of the men bade Charlotte to enter, and she ducked through the opening. Aloïs and the men followed.

Charlotte's eyes needed a moment to adjust to the dim light. A cooking fire gave off woodsmoke aroma. Meat sizzled on a grate. Not beef or chicken, Charlotte guessed, but wild game shot by these renegades. Two women tended the fire. Four men sat on the cave floor, wiping rags over disassembled weapons. Another man, clearly the one in charge, sat in a folding campaign chair. He studied a map by the light of an oil lamp on a table beside him. An Astra 400, an automatic pistol of Spanish make, also lay on the table.

Ancient drawings graced the walls: images of deer and bison left by prehistoric artists. The paintings, the shadows, and the flames put Charlotte in mind of a nether world, a Hades. A more primitive war in a primitive time. Who the hell were these people?

The man looked up from his map. He wore a black beret and a checkered flannel shirt. Stroked his long mustache. A long scar marked the back of his hand. The man puffed a cigar; its end glowed red. He blew out the smoke. Regarded Charlotte.

"I am *El Espectro*," he said. "What can I do for you?"

MEMORANDUM
REGARDING: Operation Donar
Gestapo Counterintelligence Corps,
Federal Intelligence Service, Lyon
Lyon, France 10 July 1943
TO: Reich Security Main Office, Berlin
FROM: Klaus Barbie, Hauptstürmfuhrer

Radio intercepts, along with prisoner interrogations, are beginning to reveal identities of key terrorist figures. At this point, it is unclear whether these figures are homegrown French troublemakers, or whether they are agents of the British SOE or the American OSS.

Some of these operatives may be females. This office has ascertained a code name: "Tigresse." She is believed to be working within this jurisdiction.

This office is aware of the Führer's Commando Order of last October, stating that Allied commandos and parachutists shall be summarily executed without trial. We shall follow the Führer's order without fail, after extracting whatever intelligence any captured terrorist or commando can provide.

Heil Hitler,
Klaus Barbie, Hauptstürmfuhrer

CHAPTER 9

Philippe Gerard

The dark of the moon brought a lull to Philippe's flying and a darkness to his mood. His unit always stood down between moon cycles, since the pilots depended on moonlight to navigate. He hated the down time. It gave him too much time to think.

At Tangmere, he tried to keep himself busy by studying aeronautical charts. However, he already knew the landmarks of southern France nearly well enough to navigate from memory. He reviewed the pilot's manual for the Lysander, but he'd already memorized the aircraft's procedures and limitations.

The radio didn't help. He listened to *Les Français parlent aux Français*, and the program brought little but bad news. The RAF's Bomber Command had tried to hit the Peugeot works at Sochaux. The Germans had converted the automobile factory to weapons production, and the Allies wanted it out of commission. But most of the bombs had missed. Instead of flattening the target, they had struck French homes.

When Philippe wasn't flying, he worried. He worried about Lisette. He worried about his country. He worried about his reputation. Tonight, he thought mainly about Lisette. He longed for a letter or a phone call, but of course, that was impossible given her work for the Resistance.

He didn't even know if she was still alive, and the uncertainty burned inside him.

He'd last seen her three years ago, right after the fall of Paris. His unit, Group 2/33, had fallen back to the Bordeaux-Mérignac airfield. French aircraft of all types lined the ramp. Philippe preflighted a Bloch MB.174 reconnaissance bird. Pilots from other units salvaged Caudron fighter planes and Breguet bombers. The *Armée de l'Air* was retreating to Algiers to continue the fight from North Africa. Saint-Ex had found a Farman 220, a four-engine bomber big enough to carry several passengers and a load of spare parts. He wasn't checked out on the Farman, but he was flying it anyway.

Lisette had volunteered as a nurse trainee for the French military. That made her eligible for a military evacuation flight, and Philippe assumed she'd fly on Saint-Ex's Farman to Algiers. But as other passengers lined up on the tarmac, she changed her mind. Philippe took the news like a punch to the gut.

"Why in God's name would you stay?" he asked. He was pulling on his flight gloves, about to board his MB.174.

"I can fight the Nazis better from here," she said. "I know people who are organizing already."

"They will kill you. What do you know of guerrilla fighting? You are a nurse."

Across the ramp, the Farman's number one engine sputtered and smoked. The prop began to turn as Saint-Ex started the motor.

"Get over there, Lisette," Philippe shouted. "He's getting ready to take off. Get in that damned airplane, and I'll see you in Algiers."

Lisette shook her head. "I'm staying, brother," she said.

Some of Philippe's other squadron mates were beginning to start their engines. He didn't have long to debate.

"Are you doing this because…of me?" he asked.

"What do you mean?"

"Because they reprimanded me for getting my crew killed. Are you trying to prove something on behalf of the family?"

Lisette's mouth fell open. She dropped the knapsack she was carrying. Spread her arms in exasperation.

"No!" she shouted. "That's absurd. I can't believe..." Lisette looked about as if trying to think of words to express her frustration. She never finished her sentence. Engine noise drowned her out. She grabbed her knapsack, turned and walked back into the terminal.

Philippe climbed aboard the MB.174. Steadied himself on the canopy rails and let himself drop into the pilot's seat. Strapped in and tried to concentrate. Where was the damned battery switch?

Only through rote procedure and muscle memory did he get through his startup checklist. But the engines fired, the oil pressures came up, and all the magnetos checked good. The Bloch seemed to want to keep fighting, whether its pilot could focus or not.

Philippe released his parking brake, took his place on the taxiway behind a line of other aircraft being ferried to Algiers. Exhaust and dust from prop blast filled the air. When his turn came, he lined up on the runway and pushed his throttles forward. Checked his manifold pressures and let the aircraft accelerate. He felt strange taking off alone, but there was no need for a gunner or observer on this ferry flight. Alone with his thoughts, which didn't help. He blamed himself for Lisette's decision. Of course it was because of him; why else would she do something so foolhardy?

He lifted off into a ragged sky, clouds torn by windshear. Adding insult to injury, turbulence rocked his airplane as soon as he brought up the landing gear. The rough air never subsided. Philippe checked in on the radio with the flight leader, then joined up in a formation of three other MB.174s. *Stupide*, he thought, to try to fly formation in turbulence through marginal weather. But he held position as best he could. Kept eyes on his airspeed, vertical speed, and altitude. The instrument panel rattled and the needles danced with every bump.

Below him, when he could see through the undercast, the Mediterranean looked angry. Whitecaps spilled across black waves. At one point, perhaps halfway across the Med, he noticed a strange sight: A column of smoke rising through the broken cloud layer. Heavy smoke, too, not just a gray wisp.

"Ares Flight, Ares Lead," a voice crackled on the radio. "You see that?"

Philippe liked the call sign. The Greek god of battle. "In sight," he answered.

"Fucking U-boats," another pilot called.

As the formation drew nearer, Philippe spotted the source of the smoke. A tanker listed on the surface and burned like fury. A French tanker, perhaps, torpedoed on its way to North Africa. *Perfect*, Philippe thought. *We'll get to Algiers and have no fuel.* Lifeboats bobbed on the swells. He offered a quick silent prayer for the sailors.

Philippe hoped his unit could resume its recon flights as soon as tomorrow. That would keep his mind off Lisette and everything else. But Group 2/33 couldn't turn a prop without fuel. Maybe some tankers had gotten through, or perhaps some aviation gasoline remained on hand at the African airfields.

Finally, the formation went "feet dry," crossed over the coastline. Breaks in the clouds revealed brown patches of ground, the arid terrain of North Africa. Philippe followed the flight leader in a descending turn to Maison Blanche airfield at Algiers. Chatter filled the radio: A harried tower controller tried to bring order to the chaos of a dozen aircraft, some low on gas, all wanting landing clearance.

When Philippe's turn came, he pulled his throttles to idle, lowered his landing gear. As he began to flare for landing, a fuel truck blundered across the runway. He muttered curses, shoved up the throttles, and went around. Well, at least there was fuel. He climbed back to pattern altitude. Noted the ragtag assortment of airplanes on the ramp. Turned from his base leg to final approach, and touched down uneventfully this time.

He taxied onto the ramp and parked next to an Amiot 354, a twin-engine light bomber. Oil pooled under its right engine; perhaps the thing had blown a seal. That raised another question: Would the *Armée de l'Air* have the parts and mechanics to keep flying?

The Bloch's propellers spun down when Philippe pulled the fuel mixture levers to idle cutoff. He swung himself out of the cockpit, retrieved his duffel bag from the observer's compartment. The bag contained the entirety of his worldly possessions: a few toiletries, two extra flight suits, underclothes and socks, and a couple sets of civilian clothing. He'd also brought a passbook with the number for his savings account in a Paris bank, perhaps worthless now, and a signed copy of *Vol de Nuit*, or *Night Flight*, by his friend Saint-Ex.

Three airplanes away, Saint-Ex was helping civilians climb down from the Farman. Some were military and Red Cross nurses, and Philippe cursed that Lisette wasn't among them. He joined Saint-Ex in a hangar lined with cots. The higher-ups hadn't yet figured out officer billeting. For tonight, at least, home would be a blanket on a cot among the mechanics, gunners, nurses, and refugees.

"I didn't see your sister," Saint-Ex said. "Isn't she here?"

Philippe explained Lisette's decision. "I think she did it because of me," he added.

"*Arrête tes bêtises,*" Saint-Ex said. *Stop talking nonsense.* "We make life-and-death decisions every day, with little time to think. You have risked your life for France many times. That we are here together at all means we are like cats, with nine lives."

"I pray Lisette has nine lives, too."

"She's a brave woman," the author said, "and my respect for her just went through the clouds. But know this: Her courage is separate from yours. She might be trying to prove herself, but she has nothing to prove about you. Neither do you, for that matter."

Saint-Ex's words soothed Philippe a bit; he considered the author a very wise man. But Saint-Ex was also very kind. Philippe wondered if he was speaking from wisdom or kindness, cold analysis or sympathy?

There was no way to know—and there were more immediate problems to deal with. Like getting organized for the next missions. How soon could 2/33 start flying again? A clue came with an announcement written on a chalkboard in the main hangar: MANDATORY BRIEFING, ALL FRENCH MILITARY PERSONNEL, TOMORROW 1400.

When the time came, there were no rows of folding chairs set up for a proper briefing. No charts on the wall, no sealed envelopes with flight plans. The men stood around in knots, speculating, curious about their next moves. Philippe noticed most of them were *Armée de l'Air*, some were French army, and some were navy. A few wore civilian clothes; perhaps they were from the diplomatic or intelligence corps.

Finally, an air brigade general strode in. He carried no notes. No aide accompanied him. He wasn't wearing service dress; he wore a rumpled flight suit like the rest of the crews. And he looked grim. He didn't need to call the men to attention; they all fell silent. The general stepped up onto an ammunition box.

"Gentlemen," he said. "I regret to inform you that an armistice has been signed with Germany."

Groans rose from the assembled airmen and soldiers.

"The document was signed last evening," the general continued, "near Compiègne, in the same rail carriage where Marshal Foch accepted the German surrender in 1918." He spat the words, clearly disgusted by the location chosen by the Nazis and the insult it implied.

Philippe and Saint-Ex looked at one another. Saint-Ex's eyes welled.

"I am sorry to say," the general added, "that you are all demobilized."

The hangar erupted with shouts and curses. Philippe opened his mouth to speak, but he could think of no words. How could this be? How could France have collapsed so quickly? Philippe gestured toward the ramp.

"We have aircraft," he cried. By now there were scores of them parked in rows. "We still have the means to fight." And the means to prove himself, he thought. Would he never get that chance?

Later that day, the radio brought more bad news. Adolf Hitler had taken a victory tour of Paris. The bastard visited Napoleon's tomb, had his photo taken in front of the Eiffel Tower. He called it the greatest and finest moment of his life.

Philippe, Saint-Ex, and the other officers checked into the Hôtel Aletti in Algiers. In better days, the Aletti, with its grand views of the harbor, had hosted the likes of Charlie Chaplin and Josephine Baker. Now it became a barracks for the defeated, a shelter for refugees.

While the officers waited there, they received more news from France. None of it was good. The armistice divided their country into two zones: one under German occupation, the other at least formally under a French government. A collaborationist government, to Philippe's mind. He and Saint-Ex vowed they would not serve the Vichy regime.

British spooks sniffed about, looking for Frenchmen who might be useful. Saint-Ex took a ship to Marseilles, eventually to make his way to America. Philippe hopped a C-47 to England.

Three years later, he was still in England. Things didn't look much better for France. Revisiting bad memories of his flight to Algiers only put him in a worse mood. So, Philippe was happy for something to do when Hugh Venable called him into the briefing room at Tangmere.

"We have a mission for you on the full moon," Venable said.

"Tigresse?" Philippe asked.

"No, her location is still unknown. But I think this flight will interest you. We're bringing out your sister."

Philippe's eyes widened. He opened his mouth to speak, but he needed a moment to form the words.

"Lisette? So she's alive! That's wonderful," Philippe said. "How do we know this?"

"Her network still has one secure radio operator. But the Gestapo seems to be closing in. That's why she's scheduled for transport."

Philippe forced himself to control his emotions, to maintain his military bearing. "Why?" he asked. "What happened?"

"I don't know the details," Venable said, "but she is wounded. The Gestapo and the Milice have been known to pull people out of hospital wards. That's why we're getting her out."

"Wounded? How?"

"A bullet wound. That is all I know. By the way, if this mission is too close to you, we can get someone else to fly it. I'll fly it myself."

"No, sir. No, no. I'll do it. Thank you for letting me." Philippe took in a deep breath, tried to calm himself. "When do we go?" he asked.

"The next full moon."

"Very good, sir. I assume she is stable enough for travel."

Venable didn't answer at first. He put a cigarette in his mouth, flicked his lighter. Seemed to consider how to answer.

"No, Philippe. She is not. But we're getting her out anyway."

CHAPTER 10

Charlotte Denneau

Charlotte became aware of milky light spilling into the cave entrance. Halfway between sleep and wakefulness, she could not remember where she was. Then she realized she'd slept in a proper sleeping bag, actually quite comfortable. For a change, her stomach felt satisfied, too. She and Aloïs had feasted on roast rabbit and slices of venison, washed down with bitter wine, courtesy of *El Espectro* and his band of guerrillas.

His real name was Pablo, and he'd told her to call him that. His fighters called him that, too. As the camp came to life, there was no saluting, no barking of orders. Pablo seemed to run things in a collegial manner. He laughed with two women preparing dough for breakfast bread. He offered cigars and pipe tobacco to the men. But he was in charge without question.

A coffeepot steamed on the fire grate. When Pablo offered Charlotte a mug, she asked him how he'd managed to get coffee.

He laughed and said, "We make it ourselves, my dear, with acorns and herbs. Coffee without coffee."

Charlotte took a sip. It tasted awful, but it was hot.

"I thank you," she said. "This is very good."

Aloïs joined them and accepted a mug from Pablo. They chatted about old times, referred to people and places Charlotte did not know. But from their conversation last night, she'd learned Pablo was a veteran of the Spanish Civil War. He'd worked as a pipefitter, and he'd led a trade union. When the union formed a militia, he led the militia. When the militia was asked to fold itself into the larger Republican Army, Pablo resisted. He remained in the hills and he hit Fascists as he pleased. He racked up a body count, and Franco's army never found him. His team could ambush and disappear like ghosts. The enemy feared him so much they dubbed him *El Espectro*.

During that time, Charlotte had considered joining the fight in Spain. The International Brigades recruited volunteers from all over, and many Americans served in the Abraham Lincoln Battalion. But the International Brigades' Communist ties put her off, and she decided not to go.

Part of her had always regretted that, especially after she read *Homage to Catalonia* and *For Whom the Bell Tolls*. But this morning she felt as if she'd stepped into the pages of Orwell and Hemingway. Perhaps this was how things were meant to be: If she'd joined the fight in Spain, she might not be here now to fight for France. And France was where her heart was, even if she did hold an American passport.

"Pablo," she said, "if you don't mind my asking, what brings you to fight for France?"

"I hate Fascists wherever they are," Pablo answered. "And Franco wants me dead so badly that it's probably safer for me here, if you can believe that."

Charlotte explained her own mission, and how she needed to get her maps out. She was pretty sure she knew the answer to her next question, but she had to ask: "Do you have a radio?"

Pablo shook his head.

"I have no use for a radio," he said. "All I can offer is food and shelter. Maybe a weapon if you want one. You can stay with me for as long as you don't get in my way."

Charlotte considered her situation. She certainly couldn't wait out the war here indefinitely. But to complete her mission she needed to remain alive and free. For now *El Espectro* at least offered her that much.

"I thank you," she said. "Aloïs and I will try to stay out of the way, and help if we can. But we'll take our leave when we have to."

"I understand," Pablo said.

When Pablo asked about news of the war, Charlotte told him the Allies had taken Sicily. Apart from that, she had little good news. Things in France were going to hell. She did have one bit of tactical information: She described how she and Aloïs had met Valerie, and how a German officer was billeted in the woman's home. Charlotte told Pablo the rest, too.

"Sons of bitches," Pablo said. He looked out through the cave entrance, off into the distance. Stroked his beard. "This woman said she would help?"

"She did. But we can't just shoot him there. Aloïs and I already talked about this."

"Yes, yes. I know."

Pablo shared breakfast with Charlotte and Aloïs. The guerrilla leader sat cross-legged with his back against a tree. He sipped his coffee substitute, ate his fried cornmeal, smoked another cigar, and got up to confer with his lieutenants. When he came back, he'd made a decision.

"Let us go see your friend Valerie," he said.

From his group of twenty fighters, Pablo chose just six. Charlotte took one look and considered them hopelessly outgunned. Each carried an ancient Spanish Mauser. But after exchanging a few words in Spanish with Pablo, two of them went away and came back with additional weapons. Charlotte recognized their Lee-Enfield rifles. But the Lee-Enfields had been modified. Both muzzles sported British No. 68 rifle grenades.

"Where in heaven's name did you get those?" Charlotte asked.

"We have our sources," Pablo said. He flashed a rare grin. Rested his right hand on the pistol holster attached to his web belt. Took a self-satisfied puff of his cigar.

Charlotte asked no more questions. She seriously doubted SOE had ever dropped supplies to these wild men. She doubted SOE even knew they existed. But Pablo probably had friends and friends of friends, and they likely did a lot of bartering. Perhaps that boded well for eventually getting to a radio.

As the men finished gearing up, Charlotte could see how they gained their reputation for stealth. They filled their canteens to the brim. "When you drink, you finish it all," Pablo said as he offered canteens to Charlotte and Aloïs. "No sloshing."

They made sure their magazines were full of ammunition, and each ammo pouch on their web belts contained only one mag. Nothing to clink or scrape. They snapped shut every pocket of their field jackets. With parachute cord—*and where did these guys get parachute cord?*—they tied the ends of their pistol holsters to their thighs. Nothing to flap against their legs. No necklaces or dog tags. No change in their pockets.

Their efforts toward silence reminded Charlotte of stories she'd heard from her British friends about man-eating tigers in India: They stalked and killed so quickly and quietly that their victims did not get a chance to scream. These deadly cats often earned nicknames like Ghost or Spirit. Or *El Espectro*.

She'd thought she knew something about unconventional warfare. In fact, that was the subject of all her training. But this was a thing apart. Pablo and his fighters had somehow remained alive while being hunted by Fascists since 1936. You didn't do that without learning a thing or two.

Charlotte and Aloïs followed Pablo's instructions. They sound-proofed their own gear, tied their holsters to their legs. Charlotte kept her knapsack with her maps and drawings, naturally, but she got rid of some metal pens that might clink. Taped the remaining pens in place. She took off her wristwatch. Placed it in a pouch within the knapsack. No need to let the watch's crystal reflect a glint of sunlight. Filled an extra magazine with rounds for her .45. She placed the magazine in her pants pocket and made sure the pocket contained nothing else.

Pablo led the team away from the camp. In addition to his ever-present Astra 400 pistol, he brought with him a Hotchkiss M1922 machine gun. The weapon sported a folding bipod and a box magazine filled with 7 mm Mauser rounds. Pablo carried the big gun as if it weighed no more than a broom. He stepped with no sound, like a cat on the hunt. When Charlotte's boot cracked a twig, she earned a glare from the man with the rifle grenade. She watched her footing more closely after that.

During the three-day hike back to Valerie's home, Pablo and his comrades appeared completely in their element. For Charlotte, the woods presented a survival challenge. She could get by, but barely, and with discomfort and little sleep. For the *El Espectro* band, wilderness was a haven. They seemed never to tire. They moved soundlessly as deer. They lived off the land—even thrived. They snared squirrels and roasted them on spits. They picked morels. They fashioned fishing poles from branches and somehow found fish in streams so narrow one could step across them in one stride.

On the second night, they treated Charlotte and Aloïs to trout sauteed over an open fire. The filets sizzled in a mess kit, along with sliced morels and shallots.

"*Mon Dieu*, Pablo," Charlotte said as she took a bite. "If you are married, your wife is a lucky woman for a husband who cooks like this. I only imagine what you can do in a proper kitchen."

Pablo stared into the fire. He stared for so long Charlotte feared she'd said something wrong. Then he confirmed it.

"I was married," he said. "My wife and child are dead."

He explained how his young family had lived in the town of Málaga, in Andalusia. A beautiful port on the Costa del Sol. Pablo thought his wife Maria and son Juan would be safe there while he was at the front. Republicans held most of Andalusia; the region seemed safe as any other in Spain. But the Fascists assembled a force that greatly outnumbered the Republicans. They rolled in with fifteen thousand soldiers, including Italians and Germans, backed by Nazi tanks and planes. Málaga fell on the eighth of February, 1937.

Thousands of civilians—mainly women, children, and the elderly—fled. They trudged along the N-340 coastal road to Almeria, about 120 miles away. Aircraft from the German Condor Legion bombed and strafed them. Artillery and naval guns shelled them. A massacre with no military purpose killed as many as five thousand people; Pablo didn't know the exact number.

"I never got to bury Maria and Juan," he said. "There wasn't enough left of them to identify."

"I'm so sorry," Charlotte said.

Pablo shrugged. "It's a common story," he said. "You can hear a thousand variations in Spain. I am not unique, except maybe that I still seek vengeance."

"You're effective," Charlotte said. "I will give you that much. But you could be more so if you came in with SOE."

Pablo tossed a stone into the fire. Embers swirled from the impact. He shook his head.

"I hear that a lot," Pablo said. "But I care nothing for flags and factions."

He described how the Republican side in Spain comprised different groups—the POUM, the PCE, the PSUC. Squabbling between them hastened their defeat. Leftist groups even came to open street fighting in Barcelona.

"Our side wasn't perfect, either," he said. "One of my men raped a nun and beat her to death with a crucifix."

"What did you do?" Aloïs asked.

"I shot him in the head."

They reached Valerie's at midmorning. Fog still hung over the fields and forests. Nothing interrupted the silence but the call of a lark. The group watched the house for a quarter of an hour. No vehicles were in sight. Evidently, the major had already left. Nothing moved, until finally, Valerie opened the kitchen door and let out the cat.

"Aloïs and I will make contact," Charlotte told Pablo. "I will motion for you if she wants to see you."

Pablo nodded.

Charlotte and Aloïs approached the house. When Charlotte knocked on the door, the cat curled around her ankles. Valerie opened the door. She did not seem at all surprised to see them.

"I was hoping you would come back," Valerie said. "But I did not expect you so soon."

Valerie's appearance put Charlotte at a loss for words. Her cheek bore a deep blue bruise. She had a black eye. Her lower lip had been split; the cut oozed pale red. Her hair looked thinner, as if a fistful had been torn out.

Charlotte sighed. "We brought some friends," she said. "They would like to solve your problem permanently."

"Where are they?" Valerie asked.

Aloïs gestured toward the woods. "Out there," he said. "Seven men. Would you like to meet them?"

"Very much."

Aloïs opened the door, beckoned to Pablo and his men. They emerged from the trees, carried their weapons across their chests.

"They are rough Spaniards," Charlotte said. "But I think you will like them."

"Spaniards?" Valerie said.

"Long story."

When Pablo entered the kitchen, he started to offer a greeting. But then his mouth hung open when he saw Valerie's wounds.

"Oh, my dear," he said in accented French. "Please let us help you."

"*Tout à fait*," Valerie said. "And I thank you."

They sat at the kitchen table. Charlotte let Pablo ask most of the questions. Valerie explained how the major usually traveled in a black Citroën. She retrieved a Michelin road map from a bureau in the living room. Handed it to Charlotte.

"Lately," she said, "some kind of open truck goes ahead of the car. It has a big machine gun in the back. Be careful."

"Sounds like a Kübelwagen," Aloïs said.

Pablo nodded.

Charlotte opened the road map. Notes had been handwritten on it in German. Valerie pointed.

"We are here," she said. She briefed them on the country lanes surrounding her farm. At no point did she sound emotional. She shed not

82

a single tear. To Charlotte, Valerie sounded almost…professional. Such was her determination to get revenge. Or at least to end her torment.

"He varies his times," Valerie said. "He varies his routes. But at some point, he must always take the Old Chapel Road."

"That is all we need to know," Pablo said.

TOM YOUNG

MEMORANDUM
REGARDING: Operation Donar
Gestapo Counterintelligence Corps,
Federal Intelligence Service, Lyon
Lyon, France 03 August 1943
TO: Reich Security Main Office, Berlin
FROM: Klaus Barbie, Hauptstürmfuhrer

This office's pursuit of terrorist elements continues unabated. A female criminal, believed to be operating under the code name "Tigresse," remains at large. Others have been captured and interrogated. Still others have been identified and will be brought in shortly. Further memoranda will outline any intelligence extracted by resulting interrogations.

The pace of operations against these terrorists and saboteurs has increased. Pursuant to that, hospitals and clinics across France have been instructed to report anyone treated for suspicious injuries such as gunshot wounds. Even injuries sustained in vehicle accidents are to be reported, as automobile permits are restricted, and traffic accidents could be the result of fleeing terrorist elements.

Heil Hitler,
Klaus Barbie, Hauptstürmfuhrer

CHAPTER 11

Philippe Gerard

The clear twilight beckoned Philippe. A full moon floated above the tree line and promised fair skies. But the weather officer told a different story. A front pushing down from the North Sea into France would bring low clouds and gusty winds spitting rain. The forecasters recommended scrubbing the mission. Nonetheless, SOE said fly.

Philippe was fine with that. To get his wounded sister out of harm's way he would have flown through a hurricane. At least he wasn't alone. Squadron Leader Venable would lead a two-ship formation—a rarity for 161 Squadron. They would bring out Lisette and two other injured Resistance fighters.

From the cockpit of his Lysander, Philippe watched the mechanics prepare the two aircraft. Both planes had sat idle since the last new moon, so the nine-cylinder Mercury engines needed to be pre-oiled. Otherwise, those big pistons would grind themselves to scrap on startup.

A man in oil-smeared coveralls removed a screen from the crankcase of Philippe's aircraft. Connected an oil line from a heated tank. Pumped warm oil into the aircraft's crankshaft, supercharger, and reduction gears.

Next to Philippe's plane, another mechanic completed the same process on Venable's aircraft. Philippe admired the nose art on the commander's ship: the cartoon character Jiminy Cricket, with a V for victory added for each mission into France. Philippe's plane now had its own nose art. The mechanics had honored him by painting the Cross of Lorraine, adopted as a symbol of the French Resistance.

When the mechanics finished, they disconnected the external oil lines, buttoned up the access panels, and pulled the props through. Moved their toolboxes away and signaled for engine start. Philippe cycled his priming knob several times to pump fuel into the carburetor. Then, with his thumb and forefinger, he pressed the boost-coil and start buttons.

The engine coughed, trembled, barked, and fired. The Mercury settled into a smooth low idle. A whiff of exhaust wafted into the cockpit. The propeller turned in lazy circles, slowed by the reduction gearing so that one could almost count the blades. Philippe turned on his radios. When they warmed up, he heard a greeting from Venable.

"Good show, old boy," the commander said. "Are you ready to fight some weather?"

"*Certainement*," Philippe said.

"*Très bien.*"

Ten minutes later, the two Lysanders climbed above West Sussex. Philippe had not flown formation for quite some time, but the skill came back easily. He locked onto the RAF roundel on Venable's fuselage and held position. Ahead, skies were already darkening—both from the sunset and looming clouds. Over the Channel, the two pilots dropped low to the water and skimmed the waves.

Philippe forced himself to concentrate, to try to think of this flight as just another mission. That was impossible, of course. Muscle memory and habit filled in where his mind left gaps. For SOE to order evacuation of an injured agent not stable for transport, in marginal weather at that, suggested the Gestapo was closing in hard. What kind of animals would drag patients out of hospital wards? And why did they want his sister so badly?

He knew only the barest details. Back in June, the Resistance had somehow destroyed hundreds of tons of tires at the Michelin factory in Clermont-Ferrand. Lisette had reportedly taken part in that, though

86

Philippe didn't know how. And that was months ago; she must have been on the run ever since. He smiled at the thought of the black smoke towering into the French sky like an obscene gesture to the occupiers.

Two clicks sounded in Philippe's headset. That was Venable double-tapping his push-to-talk switch: a signal to break formation. Apart from taps and clicks, they would try to maintain strict radio silence. Philippe nudged his stick just slightly to the right to begin veering away from the commander's aircraft. Cloudy weather ahead would make it dangerous to fly close formation. Beginning at the French coastline, they would navigate independently.

Philippe checked his chart, noted the time. Navigation helped settle his thoughts somewhat. Yet he longed to know more about Lisette's condition. The mysterious SOE intelligence officer, Mr. Milton, had briefed him yesterday about the mission. But the briefing raised more questions than answers.

"How badly is she hurt?" Philippe had asked.

"Unknown," Milton had answered.

"But she has gunshot wounds?"

"She does."

"Where?"

"Unknown."

"Is she in a hospital now or has she been moved out?"

"Unknown," Milton had said. "But if she is not out yet, she certainly will be tomorrow."

Milton didn't have much information on Venable's passenger, either, except that the man was a colleague of Lisette's, and he'd also sustained gunshot wounds while fleeing the Gestapo.

You don't know much, do you? Philippe wanted to ask. *What kind of intelligence briefing is this?* But he'd held his tongue. In this business, you never had all the information you'd like.

Rain began to fleck Philippe's windscreen. The weather officer had estimated the cloud ceiling over the Channel at two thousand feet. A low-flying pilot could work with that easily enough. However, the forecast called for lower ceilings over the continent. Venable's plane remained in sight, but now it was a dim speck a half mile ahead, moving just above the water.

Turbulence rocked the Lysander. Philippe found it difficult to hold a steady heading. The compass mounted between his knees bounced and trembled, as did the needles in all the other instruments. Whitecaps flecked the water below. Foam curled over the wavetops and slid down the crests. Philippe watched the orientation of the foam and realized he faced a direct headwind.

He'd expected a headwind—just not such a strong one right on his nose. The strong wind meant a slower groundspeed and greater fuel consumption. Philippe was cruising at an airspeed of 180 miles per hour, but he felt like a salmon swimming upstream. He'd hacked his chronometer as he crossed the English coast. When he crossed the French shoreline, he would stop the second hand. The time spent to travel that distance would tell him his speed across the ground.

Philippe flipped a switch to his left. That illuminated the tubular fuel gauge mounted on top of the tank behind the rear cockpit. He loosened his shoulder straps, twisted in his seat. Turbulence sloshed the fuel in the gauge, but the reading already looked lower than usual for this point in a Channel crossing. The Lysander carried about 100 gallons of high-octane aviation fuel. Tonight, would that be enough? Refueling in France was not an option.

Eternal minutes later, the dark line of the Normandy coast loomed ahead. As the beach passed under his landing gear, Philippe stopped his chronometer. Noted the elapsed time. With a gloved thumb, he spun a wheel on his flight computer and calculated a groundspeed of 135.

Not good. No doubt Venable had the same problem. And they couldn't count on a tailwind during the return trip to make up the difference. For tactical reasons, they planned to take a different route back to England—one that might not bring a direct tailwind. Philippe wanted to call Venable and ask his thoughts, but he couldn't do that under radio silence. Nothing to do but press on to the destination.

Mist shrouded Philippe's windscreen. He'd entered the clouds. The ceiling, as forecast, was dropping.

Merde, he thought. *Tonight, the weather is on the side of the Boche.*

The Lysander was not equipped for instrument navigation, so Philippe needed to see the ground to find his way. He pushed forward on the stick. Dropped to one thousand feet.

The aircraft might as well have been a submarine sinking into the depths. Philippe still could see nothing. The cloud cover obscured all moonlight. Under blackout, French villages below had disappeared. No streetlights, no headlights, no anything. *Rien.*

Philippe focused on what instruments he did have, though they were basic. He glanced at his vertical speed indicator. Eased back on the stick until the needle showed a descent rate of zero. Cross-referenced the altimeter to make sure it showed a steady altitude. Then he noted his compass heading. The compass card was turning; he was in a bank. Nudged the stick to level his wings.

That felt wrong. Now he seemed to be tumbling to the left. But the needles told him otherwise.

Trust the gauges, he told himself.

During Philippe's training, he'd learned the human body was not designed for flight. The inner ear could misinterpret movement or lack thereof, especially when eyes offered no help. In the dark or in the clouds, a flier could become convinced he was turning when he wasn't. Or vice versa. Pilots had been known to become disoriented when they could not see. They'd roll into a bank and the nose would drop. They'd see the descent on the altimeter but not feel the turn. So they'd pull back on the stick. That tightened the turn and increased the descent.

Instructors called it the death spiral.

Philippe's sense that he was falling to the left increased. His mammal instincts screamed for him to correct, to yank the stick to the right. But his training told him to watch the needles. He relaxed his grip on the stick, held it with his fingers.

Panic began to burn somewhere inside his gut. A strange sensation. He'd felt a range of emotions during his combat flying, but never panic. There had been times when he would have welcomed a crash. But not tonight. Tonight he had a purpose. Tonight he must live, if only so Lisette might live.

This is vertigo, he realized.

For a moment, the aircraft felt motionless. Then Philippe perceived a diving turn to the right. The urge to correct came with such force that he almost started to yank the stick and stomp the rudder pedals. Yet the altimeter held steady, registered no descent. He stopped himself.

You've got the leans, he realized. The leans could kill a pilot.

Bile rose in his throat from vertigo-induced nausea. He swallowed hard, took deep breaths.

No, no, no, he thought. *I will not get airsick. That is for beginners.*

A light passed under his left wing—perhaps the headlamp from some Nazi granted the privilege of driving at night. And perhaps the Nazi had foregone blackout lenses, thinking no bombers would fly on a night like this.

In any case, it was enough to fix the ground for Philippe's vestibular cortex. The nausea faded. The leans went away. The instruments made sense, for a change. The darkness became more haven than hazard.

"*Mon Dieu*," Philippe said aloud. "I thought I was better than this."

Disorientation could have made him fly a perfectly good airplane into the ground. He would not have been the first. And he still had a mission to fly.

Now that he'd managed not to create a smoking hole in the ground, Philippe needed to sort out navigation. Tonight's landing ground was in the Auvergne region, deeper into central France than most of 161's missions.

The flight plan called for him to locate a dormant volcano, the Puy de Dôme. The Puy de Dôme was one of several ancient lava domes and extinct volcanoes in the Massif Central region. The hilly territory wasn't ideal for nighttime visual landings, but the Resistance had identified a plateau that offered more than enough flat distance to put down a Lysander.

From the map case on the left side of the cockpit, Philippe pulled a reconnaissance photo taken of the landing ground. A specially outfitted

Spitfire from the Photographic Reconnaissance Unit at RAF Benson had taken the image from high altitude on a clear day. Philippe swiveled a utility lamp to study the photo.

The field looked like any other in rural France: one patch in a patchwork quilt of fields, pastures, fences, and hedgerows. The photo was beautiful, with the field so easily identifiable from twenty thousand feet. Down here it was another story, crawling through the mist at night.

Philippe cross-referenced his aeronautical chart. Noted the time. Twisted aft to check his fuel quantity again. When he turned back, a radio tower loomed in his windscreen. But for a shaft of moonlight through a cloud break, he never would have seen it.

"Damn it!" Philippe shouted.

As he cursed, he shoved the throttle forward. Pitched up. Banked hard to the right.

The Mercury engine howled. The aircraft clawed for altitude.

Philippe watched the needle on his vertical speed indicator point to the sky. Felt his cheeks sag with the g-forces that were doubling his weight.

The landing gear barely cleared the guy-wires that supported the antenna tower.

Philippe climbed away from the tower, then leveled off. That put him in the clouds, in the blind. He eased back the throttle to descend enough to see the ground. His heart thumped as if it would jump out of his chest. He glanced at his chart again.

"Son of a bitch," he said aloud in English. "The Germans don't have to shoot me down. I keep trying to do their job for them."

Where his thumb rested, the tower was clearly marked on the chart. His eyes had seen it, but his mind hadn't registered it. He'd had so much to consider that his brain just couldn't—or didn't—factor in one more bit of critical information.

Concentrate, he told himself. *Get your thoughts together or die.*

He took several deep breaths. Dropped below one thousand feet above ground level.

Down low, visibility improved a bit. Not full moonlight, but better than scudding along the bottom of a cloud layer. Turbulence still bounced the Lysander. Philippe's shoulders strained against his harness.

A dark shape rose in front of him. Yes, there. The Puy de Dôme.

He banked left, began a turn around the remains of the dead volcano. With the Puy de Dôme positively identified, he took up a new heading and again hacked his chronometer. He was looking for a field at Thalamy, just west of Clermont-Ferrand. Venable had warned him Thalamy was perhaps the worst of the landing grounds set up by the Resistance. It was hard to find, with no closer landmarks than Puy de Dôme. Pilots of 161 Squadron hated the hills that rose around it. Plus, heather liked to grow in its boggy soil. You could find yourself landing on soft ground with your propeller chewing into underbrush.

The chronometer's second hand swept past the 4 for the third time. That meant the field should be close. Philippe scanned outside. He saw nothing. No light, no anything.

He rolled into a turn. Pushed forward on the stick to stay underneath the lowering cloud deck. He was looking for the flarepath, three flashlights tied to poles, their beams arranged to form an L.

Still nothing.

Where were they? Frustration tinged with a hint of panic began to curdle in Philippe's gut. Didn't they know this was his sister? Of all nights, of all missions, this was not the time for a foolish mistake.

Philippe checked his fuel again, worked quick calculations. He could loiter for half an hour before his fuel status would force him to head for England.

Part of him wanted to burn through all his fuel if that meant he could finally see Lisette. But he would do no good to pick her up only to run out of gas and go down within sight of a German patrol.

He kept the Lysander in a bank, orbited the field. When no lights appeared for ten minutes, he widened his search. Shifted his holding pattern to the south. Perhaps wind had caused a navigation error.

The hills below remained dark. The terrain undulated like a patch of wrinkled black velvet.

Fifteen more minutes passed. Philippe began to suspect the mission might end with an abort.

Finally, just as he reached for the chart with the segments back to base, the flarepath appeared beneath him. Philippe leveled his wings, swept low over the field. As he did so, another flashlight signaled *dash, dash, dot.* The letter G. Tonight's code for all clear.

Philippe turned for another pass. Flicked his light switch with the answering signal. Set up on a base leg, turned onto final. Throttled back and felt the slats and flaps deploy automatically—a peculiarity of the Lysander.

He eased the power up to carry just a bit of manifold pressure into the landing, hoping to touch down gently.

Despite his best efforts, the Lysander crunched hard into the heather. Bounced, then settled back into the scrub. Shreds of vegetation filled the air. The left main landing gear dug into the wet soil. The Lysander ground-looped, spun itself around. Philippe felt himself yanked sideways against his harness straps. The tail tipped upward. That nearly forced the nose into the ground, which would have destroyed the prop. But the plane dropped back into a normal landing attitude. Came finally to rest.

The Resistance welcoming party approached—three men. At the edge of the landing light's beam, Philippe saw another Lysander, one with Jiminy Cricket on the side. Venable had made it in.

Philippe drew his flashlight from a flight suit pocket. Slid open his canopy. Shined the light down onto his landing gear.

The wheels were mired to the axles. And there was no sign of Lisette.

CHAPTER 12

Charlotte Denneau

Charlotte and Aloïs watched Pablo study the terrain. The way he chewed his cigar, still unlit, put Charlotte in mind of a scholar studying a manuscript. The way he slung the Hotchkiss gun across his shoulder put her in mind of a farmer carrying a hoe. He had chosen a spot where the Old Chapel Road intersected a paved two-lane highway. The highway ran atop a knoll. Beyond the intersection, the Old Chapel Road sloped downhill. That road must have been used for centuries, Charlotte guessed. Horse hooves, wagon wheels, and then truck tires had worn it deeper and deeper until it sank several feet below the surrounding fields.

"So we have a sunken road," Pablo whispered to his six men. "If we set up a parallel ambush, we can direct our fire downward enough not to hit each other."

"*Sí*," a fighter answered.

A barley field bordered one side of the road. Corn grew on the other side. Charlotte had no infantry training, but she could see clear advantages and disadvantages. The vegetation would provide concealment for the ambush team. But it would also limit their view along the road.

Pablo must have been thinking the same thing. "I will position myself up there," he said. He pointed to a spot in the barley, about thirty yards up the hill. "When I see them coming, I will start firing. If you hear a vehicle and I do not fire, let it pass."

The men nodded. They seemed to have done this before, perhaps many times. But one expressed a concern.

"This is very close quarters, *jefe*," the man said.

"Yes, it is," Pablo answered. "A knife fight. But at this range, we cannot miss."

The man smiled and nodded.

Charlotte had her own concerns. The ambush point was far enough from Valerie's home that she wouldn't be the obvious suspect in the major's death. But that didn't mean the Germans wouldn't kill her anyway. She had already gone into hiding, under protection of Pablo's *El Espectro* guerrillas. Valerie had been reluctant to leave her home. She'd clung to hope that her POW husband might return any day. But Charlotte finally convinced her the war wasn't near its end. And it would do no good for the husband to get home and find his wife had been executed.

Still, there would be repercussions if the ambush succeeded. The Nazis liked to avenge deaths of their officers tenfold. One of the worst examples had taken place a little more than a year ago. Charlotte had been briefed on Operation Anthropoid, the assassination of Reich Security Chief Reinhard Heydrich by Czech Resistance fighters in Prague.

The Czech team intercepted Heydrich's Mercedes at a sharp turn on the route to his office. One of the fighters dropped a coat that had concealed his STEN gun. He tried to fire, but the weapon jammed. Another fighter hurled a grenade. The blast mortally wounded Heydrich.

Nazi vengeance came quickly. They executed thousands. Wiped two Czech villages off the map. During the manhunt, the fighters took refuge in a cathedral. They held out against *Waffen-SS* troops for as long as they could. Then they took their own lives rather than face capture and interrogation.

Charlotte doubted the assassination of the major would bring reprisals on that scale. A rapist mid-level officer wasn't nearly as big a fish as Heydrich. Yet she knew the Germans would want some sort of revenge.

But German vengeance did not matter. If the Resistance stopped fighting because of enemy reprisals, the enemy would win.

Pablo's men took their places. Three hunkered down in the barley. Three kneeled across the road in the corn. The middle man on each side had a rifle grenade. The others carried their Spanish Mausers. Pablo himself settled into the barley uphill from the rest of the assault team. Charlotte watched him unfold the bipod and set up the Hotchkiss gun. When he took a prone position behind the weapon, he all but vanished from view.

Charlotte and Aloïs retreated to the safety of the forest at the far end of the barley field. If the ambush went badly, their plan was to slip away with Charlotte's maps and drawings. Aloïs had wanted to add his pistol fire to the ambush, but Charlotte reminded him about the priority of her mission. From their vantage point, they could see the intersection and the sunken road that would become Pablo's kill zone. But they could not see Pablo or any of his men. The crops hid them completely.

They waited. And then they waited some more.

"What do you think?" Aloïs whispered.

Charlotte shrugged. "Valerie said he didn't always come back at the same time."

A pair of ravens wheeled over the cornfield. Their caws echoed across the farmland. Apart from the birds, silence reigned. In the quiet, one could imagine the war over. France free and at peace.

Maybe someday.

A reminder of reality came in the form of the *Luftwaffe*. A low hum joined the ravens' calls. The noise grew, and Charlotte looked up to see a Junkers Ju 52, a twin-engine transport aircraft, accompanied by two Messerschmitts riding shotgun. The aircraft were flying low, beneath a solid overcast.

"What's that?" Aloïs asked.

"Who knows?" Charlotte said. "Perhaps some Boche general on his way somewhere."

"Too bad we can't shoot him down."

Charlotte nodded. "One target at a time," she said.

The afternoon wore on toward sunset. A battered farm truck turned down Old Chapel Road, and Pablo's men let it pass. An hour later, a horse pulling a cart came the same way. The man at the reins never glanced to his left or right. He remained oblivious to the firepower hiding on either side of the road.

The sun began to sink below the tree line. The cloud layer dulled the sunset, which manifested only as a vague orange glow. The overcast hung ever lower, and a soft, mizzling rain set in.

"Do you suppose Valerie gave us bad information?" Aloïs asked.

"I doubt it," Charlotte said. "She said he varies his times. I'm sure they all learned from what happened to Heydrich."

"Probably so."

At dusk, the rain grew cooler. Droplets beaded on Charlotte's field jacket. She drew the jacket tighter around her and held her position. She supposed Pablo and his men would lie in wait all night if necessary. Pablo showed himself only once. He raised to survey the terrain one more time before full dark. Stretched himself. Then disappeared into the vegetation again.

Nightfall brought the deepest gloom Charlotte had ever witnessed. Overcast blocked the moon and stars. Blackout orders obscured or extinguished whatever lamps might have burned in distant homes. Nothing seemed to exist but the cool rain and the hard ground beneath her. Aloïs remained next to her, but he could have been a thousand miles away. She wondered how Pablo and his men would see to aim. Then she realized that in such close quarters, they wouldn't need to do much aiming.

Finally, the rumble of vehicles broke the silence. On the ground, not in the air. The sound came from beyond the hilltop. In the darkness, Charlotte detected motion along the road. No clear outlines, just an ephemeral hint of something traversing the night.

A faint glow flickered through the corn stalks: headlights dimmed by blackout lenses. The engine noise dropped an octave as the vehicles downshifted and slowed.

"Here they come," Aloïs whispered.

Headlights swept the barley field as the first vehicle turned onto Old Chapel Road. The light played across the spot where Charlotte had last seen Pablo, but the barley hid him. She recognized the vehicle as a Kübelwagen. Just as Valerie had said, the Kübelwagen mounted an automatic weapon in the back. A soldier manned the gun. His knees swayed as the vehicle dipped through a rut.

Behind the gun truck, another vehicle followed. Charlotte couldn't tell its make, but by its shape, it could have been the Citroën described by Valerie. The vehicle turned onto the Chapel Road.

For a moment, it seemed that Pablo had decided to let the vehicles pass. The Kübelwagen upshifted. Began to accelerate.

The barley erupted with fire.

Staccato slams from the Hotchkiss gun convulsed the countryside. Muzzle flashes lit the scene like a jerky old movie. The German soldier in the back of the Kübelwagen never fired a shot. He appeared to dance for half a second, a macabre marionette. Then he dropped from view.

A streak of light speared from the cornfield. An instant later, an explosion illuminated the Citroën. The rifle grenade struck the car square in the middle. The Citroën veered into a ditch. Thudded to a halt.

From the barley, just downhill from Pablo, another rifle grenade fired. The round hit the car's engine compartment. The detonation came so loud that it seemed to pierce Charlotte's eardrums. Two seconds of silence followed. Then a *whoosh* went up as gasoline ignited.

Screams sounded from within the car. When the fuel tank lit off, the explosion drowned out the cries.

Two shots registered from the Kübelwagen. Perhaps its driver remained alive and was firing a pistol. Pablo answered with his Hotchkiss. Raked the truck with fire.

The Citroën burned like a torch. Flames towered over the corn and threw shadows flickering across the fields. The gunfire stopped. So did the screams. The only sound came from crackling flames and from metal groaning as it heated and warped.

The odor of burning steel and flesh stung Charlotte's nostrils. She and Aloïs held their positions. Waited to see what Pablo and his men would do next.

The ambush team began to emerge from their hiding places. Their shadows loomed, then shrank as flames flared and fell. In the firelight, Charlotte could easily imagine Pablo and his men as specters, avenging wraiths who could strike and vanish like smoke.

Moans emanated from one of the vehicles. Pablo stepped across the ditch, Hotchkiss gun across his shoulder. He placed the Hotchkiss on the ground. Peered into the wreckage of the Citroën. Drew his sidearm. Fired two quick shots from the Astra 400. Holstered the weapon.

"I think it's over," Charlotte said.

"So fast," Aloïs answered.

Pablo's men gathered around him. They carried their rifles with the muzzles down. That confirmed for Charlotte that all the enemy were dead. Pablo placed his cigar between his teeth. Produced a lighter, and lit the cigar. For a moment, the lighter illuminated his face. To Charlotte, he looked more sad than triumphant. He turned toward the spot where Charlotte and Aloïs were hiding. Beckoned for them to approach.

They waded through the barley. As they neared the kill zone, the stench of scorched flesh joined with the odor of burning metal and gasoline.

"The major will trouble Valerie no more," Pablo said.

"He will not trouble anyone anymore," Aloïs said.

"You showed him mercy, *jefe*," one of Pablo's men said. "You should have let him burn."

"I know."

Pablo lifted the Hotchkiss gun. Took a long puff from his cigar. Then he flung the cigar into the fire and led his team into the night.

CHAPTER 13

Philippe Gerard

Trapped in an ink-black, muddy pasture, Philippe did something he'd never intended to do during a mission into occupied France: He shut down his engine. Normally the Lysanders spent only three minutes on the ground. They needed to get in and out quickly, because even the most competent Resistance fighters could have been followed. At any moment, any landing field could become *brûlé*, or burned. Discovered by the Gestapo.

But there was no safe way to dig the plane out of the mud with a propeller spinning. Philippe placed a gloved hand on his fuel mixture lever. Hesitated just a moment. Pulled the lever idle cutoff.

The Mercury engine sighed, and the prop spun to a halt. The only noise the aircraft made now came from the whine of the gyroscopes spinning down. Philippe flipped the magneto and battery switches, and the instrument panel went dark. He unbuckled his harness. Slid open the canopy. Climbed out of the cockpit and lowered himself to the ground.

His boots squished into the mud. The splattering sound drained his hope: Would they ever get this airplane moving again?

Philippe looked over at Venable's plane. It sat with its engine running, the commander still in his seat. A pair of Resistance agents were helping two wounded men climb into the rear cockpit. The patients would ride in the two aft-facing seats in the back. One of the patients wore a sling around his arm. Beyond that, Philippe couldn't tell much about their wounds. But both men moved slowly, with evident pain.

Two other men ran to Philippe's aircraft. They played their flashlights across the wheels. One of the men carried a shovel.

"We will dig you out," one of them said in French.

"*Merci*," Philippe said. "Where is Lisette?"

"She is coming. She is coming."

"She's not here yet? What happened?"

"We came in three cars by three different routes."

Proper tradecraft, Philippe thought. But had the car bringing Lisette been stopped by the Germans or the Milice?

The man with the shovel bent to his work. He scooped muck from in front of the right wheel well, tossed the mud over his shoulder. The other man kneeled and began digging with his bare hands.

"I'll be right back to help you," Philippe said.

Philippe slogged over to Venable's plane. Mud spattered onto his flight suit. But he felt the ground become firmer as he neared the commander's Lysander. Apparently Philippe had suffered the bad luck of rolling into the wettest part of the field.

He climbed the ladder to Venable's cockpit. Shouted over the engine noise: "I'm stuck, sir."

"I see that. I'll wait for you."

That wasn't how the mission was briefed. If one Lysander was disabled, the other one left anyway. No sense letting the enemy capture two pilots.

"You can't do that, sir."

"They'll get you out in a minute or two."

"I doubt it, sir. It's a mess over there. And Lisette's not even here yet."

In the dim glow from Venable's instrument panel, Philippe saw the tension in the commander's face. He didn't want to leave a man behind. But orders were orders. And the mission procedure had been decided far above Venable's pay grade.

"I'll be okay, sir. I'll see you at breakfast at Tangmere. But if I can't get out I'll burn the plane and blend in with these renegades."

Venable shook his head. "Bloody hell," he said. "I don't like it, but all right."

The commander extended his hand. Philippe shook it with a firm grip.

"Godspeed, Lieutenant," Venable said. "Bloody hell." He slid his canopy forward. Latched it shut.

Philippe stepped back from the aircraft. The engine noise rose from an idle to a growl, and the plane rolled forward into the darkness. Venable lined up on the longest section of the pasture. His Lysander swayed and bounced as it accelerated. By the time it lifted off, Philippe had lost it in the gloom. Its engine faded into silence. Now Philippe could hear nothing but the shovel slapping into the mud around his own airplane.

He helped with the digging. Got down on his knees beside the tailwheel and took off his gloves. Scraped mud with his bare hands. He scooped out what looked like a clear path for the tailwheel. He hoped the men digging at the main wheels could free them in a similar fashion. Then perhaps with three or four men pushing on the wing struts, they could move the aircraft out of this mudhole and onto firmer ground.

Philippe stood. Wiped his hands on the front of his flight suit. Mud now covered his clothing. Only his gloves remained clean. At least he wouldn't dirty his instruments and switches if he ever managed to fly out. But still there was no sign of Lisette.

"Where is she?" he asked.

"Soon," one of the agents answered. "Soon."

Was that a real answer or just wishful thinking? No way to know.

"I believe we can move the airplane now," another man said.

"Then let's push," Philippe said. He placed his hands on the left strut. Another man joined him. Two others positioned themselves at the right strut. "Heave," Philippe called.

For a moment, the aircraft did not budge. "Heave," Philippe ordered.

The Lysander rocked, rolled forward. Slid back into the ruts.

"Again," Philippe called

With all his strength, he pushed against the strut. The men groaned with the effort. The plane rolled farther this time.

"Keep it moving," Philippe said.

The man beside him slipped and fell. Picked himself up from the mud and pushed.

"Swing it around," Philippe said. The men turned the plane. Pushed it onto a patch of ground that seemed to have more grass than muck.

"I think I can taxi from here," Philippe said. *If the damned engine will start*, he thought to himself. That big Mercury radial could be cantankerous. Sometimes it didn't like to start up again when it was still hot.

Now, there was little to do but wait for Lisette. Philippe checked his watch. The luminous dial told him it was barely past two in the morning. He decided to wait until just before daybreak, if need be. Then he would take off. He hated the thought of leaving without his sister. But he would only endanger her more if he let the Lysander sit here in broad daylight.

Finally, two faint pools of light appeared in the distance: a car, navigating the rural road by blackout lenses. The vehicle stopped at the edge of the pasture. The Resistance men went to greet the occupants. Philippe ran to catch up with them.

He found Lisette sitting in the back seat, next to a balding man in a shirt and tie. When Philippe pulled open the door, she did not seem to recognize him. She looked at him through half-opened eyes.

"Lisette," he said. "It's me, Philippe. I'm getting you out of here."

She smiled. Leaned her head against the seat back.

"What's wrong with her?" Philippe asked.

"Morphine," the bald man said. "I am Dr. Thibodeau. I have been treating her. She has two bullet wounds to her shoulder, with a lot of pain."

"I thank you," Philippe said. "But what took you so long?"

The driver answered: "*Abwehr* officers were at the hospital, asking many questions. We decided to get the doctor out, too. We took a longer route in case we were followed."

Philippe pointed to Thibodeau. "You mean he's flying with us?"

"Yes," the driver said. "We hate to lose him, but we would rather lose him this way than have him arrested."

"Very well."

Though Philippe kept his thoughts to himself, this was good news to him. Clearly, Lisette was in no shape to fly. But who better to accompany her than a physician? And the doctor looked like he weighed no more than 150 pounds. Not heavy enough to cost much fuel.

The men helped Lisette from the car. She leaned on the doctor. Took Philippe's hand. They walked her to the aircraft. At the ladder to the aft cockpit, Philippe said, "Lisette, you're going to have to climb up. Can you do this?"

She placed her left hand on the first rung. Looked up. Shook her head. "I, I...cannot," she said.

"We will get her in there one way or another," Thibodeau said.

The doctor climbed into the aircraft. Turned and reached for his patient. Pulled her by her left arm. Philippe and one of the Resistance men lifted her by her legs.

Lisette screamed.

The sound pierced Philippe's heart. How badly were they hurting her if the pain punched through the morphine?

Thibodeau placed her in one of the aft-facing seats. Sat beside her in the other seat. Philippe showed him how to buckle the harnesses and put on the headsets. Then Philippe pulled on his flight gloves and climbed into the front cockpit. Donned his leather helmet.

In quick succession, he flipped the battery and generator switches. Set the propeller pitch for coarse. Opened the cowl flaps. Pulled the fuel primer handle and cracked the throttle open. Pressed the starter button.

The starter clutch engaged, and the big prop began to turn.

"*Allez, allez, allez,*" Philippe whispered. *Go, go, go.*

He let one prop blade rotate across the nose. Released the starter. Pressed the button again. Watched another blade come around. Repeated the process a third time. Venable had taught him this trick to persuade the Mercury to crank. Finally, Philippe pressed the starter button and held it.

"Start, you son of a bitch," he hissed in English.

The engine fired, belched smoke. Settled into a low idle. Philippe watched his oil pressure rise, and he set the prop pitch. Switched on the radios and interphone. The whine in his helmet told him the circuits were alive.

"Can you hear me back there?" Philippe asked.

"*Oui*," Thibodeau said.

"How is Lisette?"

"In some pain, but all right."

A faint female voice came over the interphone: "I am here. Thank you so much, Philippe."

She sounded more lucid now. Maybe the morphine was wearing off. Philippe didn't know whether that was good or bad. Mentally, he pushed his emotions down into some small place. Time to concentrate on his job.

"Are you ready?" he asked.

"*Absolument*," Lisette answered.

Philippe held the hand brake. Pushed the throttle up to 1800 RPM. Checked his voltage, temperatures, and pressures. Eased off the brake. To his relief, the aircraft began to roll. He taxied forward, lined up, and advanced the throttle to takeoff power.

The Lysander accelerated. Philippe felt the tailwheel rise, and the aircraft lifted into the night. He set a course back to Tangmere, rolled the aircraft onto the initial heading. The few lights visible on the ground vanished when he climbed into the overcast. Philippe concentrated on his instruments. Held the wings level and the rate of climb constant until he broke through the cloud layer.

Above the weather, stars glittered. Moonlight cast a bronze glow across the horizon. Philippe leveled off. Set the trim tabs so he could keep the plane on heading and altitude with just his fingertips.

"Everyone still okay back there?" he asked.

"*Oui*," the doctor said. "Beautiful night."

"It is now," Philippe said. He thought for a moment, then decided to ask: "How did she get hurt?"

Lisette answered for herself. "A Milice raid," she said. "I barely got away. Some did not."

Her voice sounded stronger now. That encouraged Philippe. He decided to see if she could satisfy his curiosity.

"What were you doing?"

Long silence. Perhaps she was considering how much she should tell him. Finally, she said, "When I talk to you, we are not transmitting, no?"

Someone had trained her well.

"No," Philippe said. "When you speak on the interphone, only the doctor and I can hear you."

"Very well. It was Plan *Tortue*. Turtle. Sabotage the roads. Slow German traffic when the Allies come."

Very interesting. Philippe wanted to know more, but he decided not to ask. In this business, no good came of knowing more than necessary to do your job. Still, he found it encouraging that there were plans forming. He and his squadron mates had taken crazy chances bringing agents in and out of France. Above his pay grade, wheels were turning. Clearly, there was more to the Resistance than taking random potshots at German soldiers. He thought of 'Tigresse," this woman he was supposed to find and bring out of France. She seemed to have disappeared. Maybe she was dead. But if not, what was she doing? Perhaps something more important than he could imagine.

A flash of light interrupted his thoughts. Spears of flame off his right wing.

Twenty-millimeter cannon fire. From a night fighter.

Philippe shoved his stick to the left and stomped the rudder pedal. The Lysander rolled hard.

Just in time. More cannon fire passed behind his tail.

He had long feared this moment. Philippe knew the Germans had outfitted some of their Messerschmitts and Heinkels with that damnable Lichtenstein radar. With the airborne radar, an enemy pilot could spot you on a cathode ray tube even if he couldn't find you visually. Then he could close in for the kill.

Philippe turned hard again. From the back, he heard Lisette yelp in pain. Perhaps his abrupt roll had slammed her against her harness. Her comfort no longer mattered.

More fire slashed by on his left. The bastard was maneuvering.

The Lysander could never outrun a high-performance fighter. Early in the war, the RAF had used Lysanders as light bombers, and the *Luftwaffe* slaughtered them. That's why they were relegated to the liaison role.

In the corner of his eye, Philippe caught a glimpse of his nemesis. Its black shape loomed like a shark from the depths of murky waters. The Messerschmitt Bf 110 nearly collided with him, roared across the top of his canopy. In the moonlight, the twin-engine *Nachtjäger* turned for another pass. Death itself, coming around again.

Dear God, let him be low on fuel, Philippe thought. His only hope was to keep turning inside the *Nachtjäger*. The larger, faster plane needed a wider radius to turn.

Philippe jammed the stick down and to the right. A hard descending turn.

Cannon fire sliced to his left. A round struck his left wing.

The Lysander rocked with the impact. Philippe fought to keep control.

The aircraft rolled back to level flight. But it handled differently. Less responsive now. Surviving this lethal ballet would have been hard enough to begin with. Now Philippe had a wounded ship. He knew he couldn't keep this up for long.

He twisted in his harness. Saw the fighter come around again.

Just before the *Nachtjäger* reached his six o'clock, Philippe shoved his throttle to the stop. Yanked back on the stick for a sharp climbing turn.

He felt his wings shuddering on the edge of a stall. Thrust the stick forward. Let the Lysander's nose drop through the horizon.

Philippe dived for the clouds. Pierced the overcast. He leveled two hundred feet off the ground. Prayed there were no powerlines at that height.

Down low beneath the cloud layer, Philippe hoped the German pilot had lost visual contact. And perhaps the bastard's radar wouldn't spot him in the ground clutter.

Just in case, he turned again. Flew a complete circle.

The fighter was gone.

MEMORANDUM
REGARDING: Operation Donar
Gestapo Counterintelligence Corps,
Federal Intelligence Service, Lyon
Lyon, France 03 September 1943
TO: Reich Security Main Office, Berlin
FROM: Klaus Barbie, Hauptstürmfuhrer

It is with great regret that I inform you of the terrorist murder of Major Helmut Fischer, along with his driver and three other enlisted personnel. This heinous act took place in the southern section of this jurisdiction, in the Périgord region.

Thus far we have little information about suspects. The woman who lived in the house requisitioned by Major Fischer has disappeared. Aggressive questioning of other local residents has yielded little information.

This office shall be ruthless in its pursuit of the criminals.

Heil Hitler,
Klaus Barbie, Hauptstürmfuhrer

CHAPTER 14

Charlotte Denneau

For weeks, Charlotte and Aloïs stayed with the *El Espectro* guerrillas. Pablo's scouting parties found heavy enemy response to the strike against the Nazi major. German patrols crisscrossed the countryside. No doubt they searched Valerie's home, probably more than once. But they never found her because she remained under the protection of *El Espectro*. Pablo paused operations during the enemy patrols, which Charlotte considered wise. But she made it clear she needed to move on as soon as it was safe, to find some way to communicate with London.

While Valerie sheltered with the guerrillas, she became one of them. Pablo and his men taught her to shoot, to disassemble and clean weapons, to find cover and remain quiet in the woods. Revenge and resistance had given her purpose. She would no longer wait passively for her husband's return.

Summer yielded to fall. The forest turned red and gold, and then the leaves fell. Mornings brought frost. The fighters huddled closer around their cooking fires. Charlotte began to fear her rail maps would never reach Allied planners in time to do any good. But one evening, Pablo called her, Aloïs, and Valerie to a meeting. He sat in his folding chair, placed his cigar in an ashtray. Called for four clean glasses. He poured Calvados and raised a toast.

"To my new *amigos*," Pablo said. "I have enjoyed our association. But it is time for new missions. My men and I are heading for the French Alps. You and I must move on."

"The Alps?" Charlotte said.

"Yes, to join a larger force," Pablo said. "Beyond that, I cannot say more. And for you, I have made inquiries."

Charlotte clinked her glass with the others, took a sip. She hadn't tasted liquor in months. The apple brandy burned all the way down. And she could hardly wait for Pablo to explain what he had in mind for her.

"I have contacted friends in Limoges," Pablo said. "Their methods are more conventional than mine. They have bosses and radios. They may be able to help you communicate."

"That is good news," Charlotte said. "Who are these friends?"

Pablo explained that he knew people with *Francs-Tireurs et Partisans*, or FTP. A Communist-led Resistance faction. The French Communist Party had not taken a side at the start of the war. But when Hitler turned on Stalin and invaded the Soviet Union in 1941, the FTP formed to fight the Nazis. Charlotte had little sympathy for Communists, but she needed help and would take it where she found it.

"I believe they trust me," Pablo said. "But they took their time deciding whether to trust you."

"Understandable," Charlotte said.

"To travel, you will need false identity papers," Pablo said. "They are sending a man to provide those."

A week later, Pablo brought Charlotte and Aloïs to a safe house outside Limoges. A sign above the door read *Boucherie*. Perhaps the place had once been a butcher's shop, but it showed no sign of recent business. A metal bucket rested on the front stoop. Pablo explained how that was a sign that it was safe to enter. He knocked at the door.

After a long pause, a tall woman with silver hair answered. Despite her age, she remained trim and attractive. Something heavy weighed a pocket of her peasant dress. Charlotte assumed it was a handgun. The woman lowered her spectacles and said, "You must be the famous *El Espectro*."

"I do not know about famous, madame," Pablo said, "but I am he."

"Come in," the woman said. "Comrade Yannick is here for you."

In the dim front room, a coal fire glowed in a fireplace. An empty wooden counter was all that remained of the butcher shop. A young man sat at a folding table. On the table, Charlotte noticed a small camera, bottles of chemicals, a typewriter, and stacks of paper and cardboard.

The man stood. He wore glasses, a gray pullover sweater, and an oversized set of trousers held by a rope belt. Charlotte guessed he was no more than nineteen. His youth explained why he wasn't a POW or a *Maquisard* hiding out in the woods; he would have been too young to fight when the Germans invaded France in 1940.

"Yannick is my nephew," the woman said. "I am Genevieve."

"We thank you for your help," Charlotte said.

"I lost my husband in the Great War," Genevieve said. "I lost my son in this one. There is nothing left for me but the struggle."

The words hung in the air for a moment. Charlotte tried to think of something appropriate to say. She could come up with nothing better than, "I am sorry for your loss." Genevieve nodded. Clearly, she'd heard it before.

"You are taking chances to help my friends," Pablo said. "I appreciate your effort. What can we do to make this easier for you?"

Genevieve raised her spectacles to her forehead. Placed her hands on her hips. Looked like someone used to being in charge.

"You can disappear," she said. "I understand you are skilled at it, and I mean that in a good way."

"I like to think you are right," Pablo said. He waved to Charlotte and Aloïs. "My friends, I wish you well." Without another word, he left.

"I need to take your photographs," Yannick said. He pointed into the next room. "You will find some plain shirts in there. Find one that fits you, and put it on over your clothing."

Charlotte chose a brown flannel blouse. She took off her jacket and donned the blouse over her own shirt. Buttoned it to the throat. Aloïs found a black cotton shirt. Yannick directed Charlotte to sit on a wooden stool positioned against a wall of white plaster. He opened a Lumière folding camera and snapped three photos. Repeated the process to take pictures of Aloïs. Then he gathered chemical bottles and retreated into a back room.

While they waited for Yannick to develop the film, Charlotte said to Genevieve, "I salute you for the work you do, and your son for his sacrifice."

Long silence. Finally, Genevieve said, "My son died at Dunkirk. He almost made it out. In fact, he *had* made it out."

Genevieve explained how her son, *Capitaine* Laurent Garnier, fought hard when the Germans invaded in 1940. By the time France fell, he was among the British, Belgian, and French forces cornered in northern France. The British launched Operation Dynamo to evacuate as many troops as possible from the port of Dunkirk.

"On the 29th of May, he boarded the HMS *Crested Eagle*," Genevieve said. "It was an old paddle steamer that left the port with about 600 men."

The *Crested Eagle* didn't get far, Genevieve explained. Shortly after her crew cast off, a flight of Stukas dive-bombed her. With the ship on fire from stern to bow, the skipper ran her aground to give survivors a chance to swim for shore.

"I am told Laurent was in the water, pulling a wounded man by his lifejacket," Genevieve said. "The Stukas came back and strafed them. His body was never recovered."

"No wonder you continue the fight," Charlotte said.

"I am told you can still see the wreck of *Crested Eagle* at low tide. A ghost ship, remaining with the ghosts of her dead."

When the photos developed, Yannick set to work at his typewriter. "Your new name is Simone," Yannick told Charlotte. "Simone Lejeune. Aloïs is now your brother, and his new name is Lucien."

Yannick opened an inkpad. Lifted a wooden-handled rubber stamp. Dipped the stamp onto the ink and stamped an official-looking seal onto a piece of card stock. Used scissors to size the photographs and glued them onto the card stock. When he finished, he handed Charlotte a *carte d'identité* that looked as authentic as any she'd ever seen.

"Crease it a little," Yannick said. "Make it look like you've carried it around for a while." Charlotte bent the ID. Placed it on the floor and scuffed it with her shoe. "That's the idea," Yannick said.

Charlotte picked up the document from the floor and examined it more closely. The palm-sized folio folded into halves. The round stamp on the top half read: *République Française*. The line below it read: *Préfecture de Police*. Yannick had filled in the blanks with her false name and a date from six months ago.

Yannick gave Aloïs a similar fake ID.

"Good work," Aloïs said. "Have the Boche ever arrested anyone caught with one of these?"

"Not with mine," Yannick said. "Every detail must be correct. They know the common mistakes to look for."

Aloïs nodded.

"The two of you need something else to pass unnoticed," Genevieve said.

"What's that?" Aloïs asked.

"A shower."

"I do not doubt it," Charlotte said.

The FTP provided Charlotte and Aloïs with showers, fresh clothing, a hot meal, and a decent night's sleep in real beds. The next day, the forged IDs got their first test. Genevieve led Charlotte and Aloïs to the Limoges train station. They bought tickets for Rouen, in northern France.

"Why Rouen?" Charlotte asked.

"We are not in contact with your SOE," Genevieve explained. "But our contacts in Rouen know some of your people."

Charlotte was curious. But she didn't ask questions for the usual security reasons. She did know that members of the BRICKLAYER circuit were still operating in that part of France. Maybe someone there had a wireless.

At the train station, Charlotte tried her best to look nonchalant. She stuffed her fists into the pockets of her new wool overcoat, which she needed now in the November chill. She could watch her breath join with the morning fog. She carried her map case buried in a canvas bag with a shoulder strap, much like a large purse. That way, she hoped she looked more like a day traveler. A knapsack or a suitcase was more likely to get searched. Aloïs wore a heavy sweater. His false papers identified him as a factory machinist, an essential worker not subject to forced relocation for labor in Germany.

The train hissed and screeched into the station. When Charlotte and Aloïs lined up, a conductor and two *Feldengarmen*, German military police, checked their documents. Charlotte's palms sweated, and she prayed the officers would not look in her bag. The police nodded to her, motioned for them to board.

For long minutes, the train sat at the station. Charlotte feared the police had changed their minds, that they would search everyone. To appear unconcerned, she pretended to sleep. Real sleep, of course, was impossible. Charlotte almost worried that people around her could hear her heart pounding.

Finally, the train lurched into motion. Rumbled through highway crossings guarded by German soldiers. Chugged by bombed-out villages. Passed a field littered with the burned remains of a downed aircraft. Charlotte could not tell if it was an enemy or an Allied plane; the wreckage was unrecognizable. But it looked to have been something big, which suggested an American Liberator or a British Lancaster.

At various stops, people boarded and disembarked. At one point, two Gestapo officers in their black trench coats escorted a handcuffed man. The man kept his eyes downcast, looked at no one. The whites of his eyes were no longer white; they were shot through with blood. Charlotte forced herself not to stare. Had this man talked, had he given up names? Or was he going to his death a hero? She shuddered at the thought of whatever prison or concentration camp awaited him. And she knew she could expect the same fate if she got careless. Or even if she just got unlucky.

When the train pulled into Rouen, Charlotte and Aloïs got away from the station as quickly as possible without drawing attention to themselves. Train stations were never good places to linger, with all the soldiers, police, and informants milling about. As instructed, they strolled along the Seine, overlooked by the centuries-old Rouen cathedral. They stayed within sight of its spires, looking for an old man in a blue felt hat.

When Charlotte spotted the blue hat, she asked the man, "Is this where they burned Joan of Arc?"

"Dumped her ashes in the Seine," the man replied.

That was the correct countersign. The man led them to a home at the edge of the city. The stone house was so old and dilapidated that wooden shoring propped up its walls. Smoke curled from a chimney with missing bricks. When the man opened the door and bade Charlotte and Aloïs to enter, an elderly woman greeted them. The man's wife, Charlotte presumed. Wordlessly, the woman served them a supper of potato soup.

Charlotte hadn't eaten all day, and the warm soup felt good going down. While she ate, she said, "We were told you might have a radio."

No one spoke for several seconds. Charlotte wondered if she'd said the wrong thing. But then the woman said, "The men have an S-phone. They will bring it tonight."

Charlotte had heard of that device, but she'd never used one. Unlike the typical W/T set that transmitted Morse code, the S-phone was used for voice communication, primarily with aircraft.

Around midnight, two men appeared at the home. The elderly couple greeted them like old friends. One wore a long woolen overcoat and a flat, cabbie-style hat. He spoke with a Polish accent and introduced himself as Jacek. The other stranger was French and was called Remy. Charlotte assumed both were code names.

The old man climbed a ladder into his attic and called for his guests to follow. Flipped a light switch to reveal steamer trunks covered with dust—artifacts of travel in better times. The light also illuminated a hatch in the ceiling. The man climbed through and motioned for his guests to follow. Atop the flat roof, he sat with his back against the chimney. He lit a cigarette as if he'd seen all this before.

THE MAPMAKER

Night air cooled Charlotte's lungs. Starlight spun through scattered clouds.

Jacek removed his overcoat. Beneath the coat he wore a canvas harness loaded down with battery packs, a transceiver, a headset, a microphone, and a collapsible antenna. With practiced motions, he set up his gear and switched on the set. Tubes glowed inside.

"Do you worry about the Germans homing in on you?" Charlotte asked.

Jacek shook his head. "Beam goes mainly up," he said, pointing to the sky. "For airplanes. Enemy would have to be close to hear on ground."

"But we still take precautions," Remy added. "We move around."

When the S-phone warmed up, Remy kneeled next to Jacek. Donned the headset and lifted the microphone. Pressed the talk switch.

"Any station, any station," Remy called. "This is Roland."

Charlotte recognized the call sign: Roland was a French war hero of legend, dating back to the 700s.

"Any station, this is Roland," Remy repeated. "Do you read?"

No answer. In fact, no answer came that night at all.

"We try again tomorrow," Jacek said, "somewhere else."

The next evening's call, from atop another home, brought no better results. On the third night, at the crest of a wooded hill, they tried again. This time they waited until they heard aircraft engines. They hoped to catch the RAF on a night mission. The weather was good for flying; stars sparkled overhead like diamonds ground to dust. Light breeze rustled the bare limbs of trees.

"Any station," Remy transmitted, "this is Roland. Do you read?"

No response.

Remy repeated the call several times. Charlotte began to think this was all a waste of time. But when the aircraft engines grew louder, Remy tried again. He had his headset volume turned high enough that Charlotte could hear the answer:

"Roland, this is F for Frankie. Have you loud and clear."

CHAPTER 15

Lisette Gerard

At St. Peter's Hospital in the Whitechapel district of London, Lisette opened her eyes. She had undergone two operations for her bullet wounds, and the doctors said she was improving. A tube for an intravenous drip snaked from a bottle hanging above her head.

As she woke up, she recognized Philippe sitting in a steel chair across from the bed. He folded his copy of *The Times* and smiled at her.

"*Bon après-midi,*" he said.

"Is it afternoon already?" Lisette said. "I lose track."

"You do not need to keep track. All you need to do is rest and heal."

Lisette nodded. Then winced.

"Are you in pain?" Philippe asked.

"Some. It comes and goes."

"I'll get the nurse." Philippe placed his newspaper on the floor and started to get up.

"No, there's no need. They will come around with morphine later."

Philippe sat back down. "What can you tell me about how you got wounded?" he asked.

"I got shot running a roadblock."

Lisette added that it happened after an operation related to Plan *Tortue*, the effort to impede German military movements. But she didn't tell her brother the whole story. Her team broke into a Michelin factory at Clermont-Ferrand. Resistance snipers waited for the night watchmen to present an easy target. When the watchmen met at the front gate for a cigarette break, the snipers fired. Then the team crashed the gate with a truck.

After that, they found no opposition. The Germans worried about aerial bombing of factories, but here, at least, they hadn't anticipated sabotage. The team took their time pouring kerosene on stacks of new tires. Rows and rows of them. Lisette lit the first match, watched the flames spread through the warehouse. The *résistants* escaped just before sunrise. Dawn revealed a tower of black smoke above Clermont-Ferrand. The flames destroyed 300 tons of tires.

But every success by the Resistance came with a cost. The Gestapo ran a dragnet. They sealed off train stations. They set up highway checkpoints. At a rural crossroads, Lisette and two companions had to make a quick decision. Three German soldiers guarded the checkpoint. One of them lowered a cross-hatched wooden barrier and motioned for the driver to stop. Lisette sat in the back seat.

"May I see your vehicle permit?" the soldier asked.

"You may," the driver said.

"Here it is," Lisette said.

From underneath a blanket she raised a Winchester Model 12 trench gun. Fired a blast of American-made buckshot through the window. The soldier died instantly. Lisette racked the slide, chambered another round. Killed the second guard as her driver, Baptiste, stomped the gas pedal.

The acceleration pressed her back in her seat. Smoke from her shotgun tinged the air. For a moment she felt the thrill of escape.

But behind her, the third guard opened up with his machine pistol. The rear glass shattered. Something hit her shoulder like a sledgehammer.

The impact pitched Lisette forward. For a moment, she didn't realize the blood on the back of the seat in front of her was her own. Then she felt the bullets' burning path through her left shoulder.

"I'm hit," she shouted.

No one answered her. Baptiste concentrated on the road. He whipped through a turn, skidded, corrected. Sped along a straight stretch. Slammed on the brakes for a hard right turn.

Claude, in the front passenger seat, was dead. Blood and brain matter flecked the dashboard and windshield.

Lisette knew she could not go to an emergency room. Baptiste took her straight to the home of Dr. Thibodeau. Using only chloroform for anesthesia, he performed surgery on her two bullet wounds in his wine cellar. Sneaked her into a hospital ward in the wee hours, aided by a patriotic nurse. Treated the off-the-books patient with antibiotics as best he could. He never quite got her stabilized; she'd lost a lot of blood. But he arranged her evacuation when the Gestapo began searching hospitals and clinics. He had treated wounded *résistants* before. Pushed his luck farther each time. SOE decided to evacuate him, too, before his luck ran out.

"So you finally got an airplane ride with me," Philippe said. "I am sorry about the circumstances."

When he first began his flight training, Lisette always asked in her letters for a ride. A teenager then, she did not understand why her brother could not just give her a hop in a military aircraft. Now she was 22. But she suspected he still saw her as a little sister—to shield and protect.

"It was quite a ride," Lisette said. "Dr. Thibodeau said we nearly got shot down."

"Yes, it was close. Is Dr. Thibodeau here at St. Peter's? Is he still taking care of you now?"

"He is. He is not on the staff here, of course. At least not yet. But he is advising them on my condition."

Lisette did not to tell Philippe that Dr. Thibodeau was more than a physician. He held high rank with F Section. Right now he was back in London, debriefing with SOE leaders. F Section had already begun debriefing Lisette, as well. They had updated her with the latest intelligence from the continent. And the news was not good. She steered away from the subject of Dr. Thibodeau.

"Have you been working?" Lisette asked.

Philippe nodded. "I have," he said. "Things are going…better," he added. "In fact, we spoke recently with a colleague of yours."

"Someone I know?"

"Probably not. But a colleague nonetheless. The RAF dropped a W/T set to her, so she's talking with us again. We've been trying to get her out for a long time. I hope to pick her up on my next flight."

"Very good. I hope that flight is less eventful than ours."

Philippe chuckled. "So do I," he said. "And I hope the rest of the war is less eventful for you."

There he went—trying to protect her again. She recalled when they'd parted with angry words after the fall of France. He'd tried to get her to take a flight out of Bordeaux-Mérignac airfield. But by then, she'd decided to stay in France and fight rather than evacuate to North Africa. What would he say if she could tell him the latest?

During Dr. Thibodeau's latest visit, he had brought with him two other gentlemen: one from SOE, and one from MI6, or military intelligence. They did not offer their names. Guards sealed off part of the ward. For an hour, not even doctors could enter Lisette's room. She sat up in her bed.

"Are you sure you feel up to this?" Thibodeau asked her.

"I am," she said. Despite her discomfort, she was very curious about what they had to tell her. Yes, there was a war on. But what could be urgent enough for a hospital room briefing?

"We remind you this briefing comes under the Official Secrets Act of 1939," the MI6 man said.

"I understand," she said.

"An unfortunate development has taken place in our area of operations," Thibodeau said. "The 2nd SS Panzer Division has transferred from the Eastern Front to France."

Lisette sat up higher in her bed. She knew the Waffen SS was bad news. But she didn't know details about this particular unit.

"What can you tell me about them?" she asked.

The SOE man opened a manila folder marked MOST SECRET. Lifted the top page of its contents. Passed the page to Lisette.

"This is a summary of their sordid history in the Soviet Union," the man said. "The men of the 2nd are so fanatical their division is called *Das Reich*."

Lisette skimmed the summary page. In Russia and the Ukraine, the 2nd SS Panzer Division had worked with the *Einsatzgruppen*. The *Einsatzgruppen* had no military purpose. Their job was simply to slaughter civilians—Jews and other targeted populations. They recruited local thugs to work with them as a force multiplier. *Das Reich* had coordinated the murder of nearly one thousand Jews in Minsk. In Kharkiv, at a ravine called Drobytsky Yar, the Germans killed 15,000 Jews in one day.

But *Das Reich* also had combat experience. They had fought in the Battle of Kursk, a ferocious tank battle, only half a year ago. At the Battle of Yelna they had destroyed the town and burned most of the houses.

"So, as bad guys go," Lisette said, "these are some of the worst."

"Quite true," the MI6 man said.

"Our sources tell us Hitler himself chose Montauban as the new base for *Das Reich*," Thibodeau said.

Montauban was in southern France, a short drive north of Toulouse. Now, Lisette understood why these men were telling her all this, and how it related to her work. From Montauban, a battle-hardened Panzer division could race to the coast, wherever the Allied invasion landed. Unless impeded by the Resistance and Plan *Tortue*.

The enemy's war ministers could launch aircraft, deploy navies, command armies. And a handful of determined Resistance fighters could trip them up.

"How can I help?" Lisette asked. Perhaps SOE wanted her in London for consultations. She would enjoy some time in London.

"We want to strengthen Plan *Tortue* preparations against *Das Reich*," the SOE man said.

"You have already done more than your share," Thibodeau said. "But after you heal, and when you're ready, these men would like you to go back in."

122

Lisette stared at Thibodeau, then at the men from SOE and MI6.

"We will not order you," the SOE man said. "This is purely voluntary. If you decline, you may remain in our employ here in Britain. F-section will award you all the honors you have earned."

Lisette shifted her torso, tried to find a more comfortable position against the pillows behind her. The pain was coming back worse now; it was time for another shot of morphine. She sighed, locked eyes with Dr. Thibodeau.

"I'll do it," she said.

CHAPTER 16

Charlotte Denneau

At a landing site in northern France, codenamed ARTEMIS, Charlotte pulled her overcoat tight around her. Clutched the canvas bag that contained her map case and .45. Chill permeated the midnight air. At long last, she waited for the RAF plane to land and pick her up. With help from fellow Resistance fighters, she had made contact by S-phone. SOE had worked out details through a W/T set sent by airdrop. Then the weather turned sour, and two pickup dates got canceled at the last minute.

Now it was early December. And tonight, the weather didn't look a lot better. A full moon shone through breaks in the clouds. But those breaks came seldom. And when the clouds scudded over, they mizzled cold rain.

Aloïs waited with Charlotte, along with the two ruffians who had provided the S-phone communication, Jacek and Remy. The SOE had decided Aloïs would leave with Charlotte, so he could brief London on *Maquis* activities. Perhaps later, they'd send him back in.

"I have never ridden in an airplane before," Aloïs said.

Charlotte chuckled. "You chose a heck of a way to start," she said.

"I did not choose this."

"I know."

THE MAPMAKER

"Is flying frightening?"

"Not under normal circumstances."

Charlotte didn't bother to add that this was anything but normal circumstances. Aloïs had agreed to fly to Britain reluctantly, and despite Charlotte's assurances, he looked scared—which surprised her since he was fearless in a gun battle. He had never traveled outside of France, he spoke no English, and he wasn't sure he could help SOE. But London insisted; the *Maquisards* were the most difficult of the Resistance fighters to coordinate, and they wanted whatever insight he could provide.

Jacek checked his watch. "The plane is late," he said. He and Remy had set up the flarepath an hour ago. The lights, lined up in an L shape, glowed in the mist. The two men had worked efficiently; Charlotte gathered they'd done this often.

A faint buzz rose in the distance. At first Charlotte dismissed the noise as another German military truck speeding along a highway. But as the buzz grew louder, she allowed herself to hope the aircraft was finally on its way. At last, she—and more importantly, her maps—might get to London.

The buzz rose to a growl, and eventually Charlotte heard an aircraft whoosh overhead. Between the clouds, backdropped by the moon, she caught a glimpse of the aircraft. Only its silhouette; the plane flew without navigation lights. The aircraft circled the field for several minutes. Charlotte guessed the pilot was trying to spot the flarepath through breaks in the clouds.

After several minutes, the plane turned and descended. The aircraft vanished in the mist and then reappeared, now lined up with the flarepath. Remy raised an Aldis lamp and flashed a signal. The pilot flashed a response with his landing light. The aircraft banked, came around for another pass, and began its final approach.

"Thank you for your help," Charlotte said to Remy and Jacek. Beyond that brief remark, there was no time for sentiment or speeches. She knew the drill: The pilot wanted no more than three minutes on the ground. Climb up, strap in, fly out.

The engine noise grew louder. Charlotte knew little of flying, but she guessed the pilot was adjusting his power for some reason. The descent seemed fast, though Charlotte hadn't seen enough of these landings to know what was normal. The cylinders growled still louder.

As the aircraft neared the ground, Charlotte recognized it as a single-engine Lysander. The Lysander pitched its nose a few degrees higher. Thudded to earth on its main wheels.

A strange sight happened when the aircraft touched down. Ice shattered from the wings. In the dim light of the flarepath, shards glittered like diamonds cast to wind. The Lysander bounced back into the air. When it touched down again, more ice broke off. A sheet slid from the tail and splintered like a glass pane.

Charlotte knew *that* wasn't normal. She wasn't sure how ice could affect a plane's flying, but it certainly couldn't help.

"Did you see that?" Remy asked.

"Yes," Charlotte answered. "What happened?"

"He picked up a load of ice coming down through the clouds. He's lucky he got here at all."

The Lysander taxied to the side of the flarepath. The canopy opened, and the pilot unbuckled his harness and stood up. Played a flashlight across the wings. Apparently satisfied, he beckoned for his passengers to board.

From her training, Charlotte knew the drill. She approached the aircraft from behind to stay away from its spinning propeller. She led Aloïs to the aft cockpit, motioned for him to climb the ladder. She followed him, carrying her map bag and the case containing her W/T set. Sat beside him in one of the two aft-facing seats. Showed him how to fasten his harness and don his headset.

When she put on her own headset, she heard a greeting from the pilot.

"Good evening, friends," the flier said in French. "I am Philippe. I cannot tell you how good it is finally to meet you. But we talk later. Now we go."

He offered nothing else about his identity. No surname or rank.

Charlotte closed the aft canopy. Waved to Remy and Jacek. Offered a short silent prayer that the two of them would survive the war. Offered another that she, Aloïs, and the pilot would survive the next ten minutes.

Philippe pushed up the throttle. The Lysander lumbered through the pasture, lined up with the flarepath. The engine howled, and the aircraft began to roll.

The airplane vibrated as if it would come apart. The vibrations increased as the plane accelerated. Finally, it lifted off, and the vibrations eased.

The Lysander levitated into the night sky. The darkened hills fell away. For a moment, moonlight played across the wings. Then the aircraft entered a cloud. The world disappeared, the Lysander shrouded in mist.

"Here we go again," Philippe said on interphone. Unsure what he meant, Charlotte guessed the pilot was talking to himself. The engine surged. Charlotte felt the nose pitch up. "I want to try to climb through this stuff as quickly as I can," the pilot added.

Above Charlotte's head, translucent haze formed across the canopy. Ice, she realized.

The Lysander continued to climb, or at least Charlotte felt like it was climbing. Yet it never broke out of the clouds. Charlotte turned in her seat to watch. She could see little but the back of the pilot's head and the blur of the propeller. She glanced up at the canopy. The ice was thickening. Was that on the wings, too?

Charlotte wondered how much danger they were in. Could this cause the aircraft to crash? She clutched the bag with her maps. Those maps carried details available nowhere else. She thought more of her work than her life: What if after all this, these maps burned up in a crash?

A wing dipped. The Lysander rolled to the right. The engine surged again. The aircraft began to vibrate. Not like the vibrations during the takeoff roll, but something worse. Charlotte turned around again. Some sort of spray seemed to flash from the propeller. For a moment, the vibrations eased. Charlotte guessed she'd just seen the propeller sling off a load of ice. But at this rate, more would surely form.

A wing dipped again, this time on the left side. Aloïs sat silent and wide-eyed. Charlotte gripped his hand. She looked up. Now the canopy was opaque with ice. Could the pilot see at all?

For what felt like an eternity, though it was only minutes, Philippe fought with the elements. Fought with his airplane.

"Hold on," he shouted over the interphone. "I am sorry. I have to put this thing down before I lose control altogether."

The engine's tone softened. Charlotte felt herself descending. Aloïs squeezed her hand tighter, crossed himself.

She could not tell when the Lysander descended out of the clouds. By that point she could see nothing through the glass. She doubted the pilot could see anything either. Perhaps he just hoped to hold the airplane steady and pray it was over an open field. The wings dipped left, then right. The engine roared, hushed, roared again. The aircraft staggered through its descent. Charlotte braced herself. Waited…waited.

The Lysander slammed to earth. The crunch came with the sound of ice shattering. Sheets of it broke from the canopy, shattered off the wings. The pain of impact stabbed through Charlotte's hips and shot up her backbone. Aloïs cried out.

The airplane bounced, went airborne again. Touched down once more, and ice shattered again. The Lysander spun in a loop. Pitched forward. The propeller struck the ground. The engine instantly went silent.

For a moment, no one spoke. The only sounds came from the hum of the interphone and the creaking of bent metal. Then the pilot said, "Get out as fast as you can."

Charlotte and Aloïs unbuckled their harnesses. Charlotte reached for the canopy latch and tried to slide open the canopy. It would not budge.

"I think it's jammed," she said. Evidently the fuselage was bent, making it difficult for the canopy to slide along its track. She shoved again. The only result was a jolt of pain through her bruised hips. *Thank God there's been no explosion*, Charlotte thought. She guessed that danger was why the pilot ordered them to get out quickly.

Aloïs helped her push. This time the canopy slid halfway open. Charlotte grabbed the bag with her maps and let it fall to the ground.

Lifted the case with her W/T set. Squeezed through the partially open canopy, climbed down the ladder, and dropped to the ground. That brought another jolt of pain. She hurt all up and down her legs and hips, but judged nothing was broken. Aloïs followed her out of the aircraft. The pilot racked open the forward canopy and climbed out.

"Step away from the plane," he said.

All three moved a hundred yards from the Lysander. Charlotte felt cold mist on her face. She began to shiver. In the dark, under cloud cover, she could see almost nothing. Just the vague silhouette of the broken aircraft against a distant line of trees. The propeller blades were bent; it was clear to Charlotte the plane was going nowhere soon.

"What went wrong?" Aloïs asked. His voice shook like he was frightened. Or angry or confused. Maybe all three, Charlotte supposed.

Philippe took a moment to answer. He folded his arms around himself and appeared to look down at the ground. Perhaps he closed his eyes; Charlotte could not be sure in the darkness. He seemed to have trouble accepting what had just happened.

"The airplane became so coated in ice that it could not fly," he said finally. His voice shook as he spoke. Maybe he was cold, or maybe he was trying to control his emotions. "I am so sorry," he added. "Are you hurt?"

"I do not think so," Aloïs said.

"Neither am I," Charlotte said. "Just a bit sore. I know you did your best."

Again, the pilot hesitated before answering. Standing near the wreckage of his aircraft, he seemed a vision of misery. Charlotte tried to imagine what he felt. He'd planned on getting back to England tonight, completing his mission. But forces beyond his control had swatted him to the ground.

"We should have chosen another night," Philippe said. "But if we waited for perfect conditions we would never fly."

"I have faced gunfights," Aloïs said, "but I have never been so scared." And to Charlotte, he looked like he was *still* scared.

Philippe stared at Aloïs. Opened his mouth to speak, but changed his mind. Charlotte wondered what he would have said. Obviously, he was struggling with guilt and regret—whether he deserved it or not.

"We are still alive," Charlotte said. "That is something. And we are not in the hands of the Gestapo."

"We must keep it that way," Aloïs said.

"Philippe, where are we now?" Charlotte asked.

The pilot kneeled. Dug into a pocket of his flying suit. Withdrew a map and a small flashlight. He unfolded the map, shielded the flashlight lens with his hand. Studied the map for a moment. Folded the map, pocketed the flashlight, and stood.

"Near Amiens," he said. "We did not get far."

"Amiens?" Aloïs said. "My brother is in the prison there."

"What do we do now?" Charlotte asked.

"Something I never wanted to do," Philippe said. He began walking back toward the Lysander. Charlotte and Aloïs followed him. When they came within twenty yards, he said, "Do not come any closer. You have all of your maps and gear out of the plane, yes?"

Charlotte nodded.

Philippe stooped, then crawled underneath the aircraft. He turned some sort of valve or petcock. Fluid began to drain from the Lysander.

"What is that?" Charlotte asked.

"Fuel," Philippe said.

A pool of gasoline formed beneath the plane. Fumes stung Charlotte's nostrils. Philippe reached into a pocket and found a pack of cigarettes. Placed one between his lips. For a long time, he did not light it.

He motioned for Charlotte and Aloïs to move farther away. Fumbled for a lighter. Lit the cigarette and took a long drag.

"I need to wait until I have a large puddle of fuel," Philippe said. "Stand back."

The pilot smoked the cigarette down to half. Stared at his airplane in silence. Then he stepped forward. Flicked the cigarette toward the fuel. The orange tip arced into the gasoline pool.

THE MAPMAKER

The fuel made a whooshing sound as it ignited. Flames enveloped the Lysander. Fire swirled over the fuselage, blackened the Cross of Lorraine on the nose. The wings, covered in fabric rather than sheet metal, burned to skeletons. Sparks and smoke rose into the night sky and mixed with the ice-laden clouds.

CHAPTER 17

Charlotte Denneau

In a cold, muddy forest, four miles from the crash site, Charlotte switched on her W/T set. Above her, in the branches of a leafless maple, Aloïs strung the antenna. She waited for the Type 3 Mark II set to warm up, prayed it had enough power. She hadn't charged the battery since Remy and Jacek had used it to set up the Lysander pickup. She hadn't expected to use the radio again.

She also prayed she could remember proper procedures and make contact. Charlotte had received rudimentary training on clandestine radios, but she wasn't a specialist. The Resistance had people—like Remy and Jacek—whose entire job was communications.

The pilot, Philippe, held his flashlight for her. He shivered beside her in French peasant clothing. The freezing mist settled on his plain tunic and trousers. As his aircraft burned, he had unzipped his flight suit, balled it up, and tossed it into the flames. He'd worn the plain clothing underneath. Now, he no longer looked like an RAF pilot. But he'd retained his gun belt, which carried a Webley revolver.

Aloïs climbed down from the tree, joined Charlotte and Philippe by the radio.

"Is it working?" he asked.

THE MAPMAKER

"Well, it's on," Charlotte said. She donned a headset from the radio's leather case. Plugged in the transmitting key. Took a deep breath. Reviewed in her head the Morse code for her first transmission. Then she tapped out "QRV." The code for *Are you ready to copy?*

The tones sounded in her headset. That was good—at least the radio was transmitting. But how far? The signal needed to reach London or Cairo. And she could try only so many times. The Germans and their damnable direction-finding vans were listening, too.

No answer. Charlotte tapped again: QRV.

After a few seconds, tones sounded in her headset. "Thank God," she whispered in English. She concentrated. Translated the Morse:

London here.

She thought hard, tried to recall the encryption codes. She had to assume the enemy was listening, too. She could say nothing in plain English or French. She began tapping again:

Broken wing. The Road Not Taken.

Then she tapped numbers for her authentication code and a reference to her approximate location. An answer came quickly, in English. But not much of an answer:

Stand by.

Presumably the person on the other end was consulting with an operations officer: *A Lysander has been forced down. Pilot and passengers need nearest help.*

After long minutes, another transmission from London:

Amazing grace. Peter and Paul.

Charlotte had to think about that one. She mentally reviewed the codes she could never write down. Then she pieced it together: In her vicinity there was a clergyman who could be trusted. If she found him, he would authenticate himself by saying, "Amazing grace." She would authenticate herself with the code words "Peter and Paul."

Vague, but better than nothing. Charlotte tapped her key again:

Out.

She switched off the set. Nodded to Aloïs to pull down the antenna wire. Explained what she'd heard to Aloïs and Philippe.

"They could not be more specific than that?" Aloïs asked. "A clergyman. No name? No church?"

"They cannot be more specific about a lot of things," Philippe said. "The Gestapo is listening, too."

"I see."

"We can only wait for first light," Charlotte said. "Then we look for a church with a rectory."

"This area is pretty rural," Philippe said. "At least we don't have to search every church in Paris."

The three huddled beneath a canopy of dripping trees. They shivered and spoke little as the hours passed. Aloïs looked glum. Philippe appeared to try to hide his emotions, but at one point he excused himself, walked behind a tree, and retched. Charlotte simply felt tired and hungry.

At daybreak, they began hiking. They kept to the woods and fields, avoided roads as best they could. Aloïs carried the W/T set. Charlotte carried her map case. Sleep deprivation and cold numbed her limbs and thoughts. Only by sheer force of will did she put one foot in front of the other. Finally, they found a small chapel by a crossroads. Philippe and Aloïs remained hidden while Charlotte knocked at the church door. No answer. She knocked at the door of the house nearby.

"Who are you?" a woman's voice called from inside.

"My car has broken down," Charlotte said. "I need help."

"We cannot help you. Go away!"

Charlotte did not argue. Under occupation, everyone was afraid. Afraid of spies. Afraid of the Gestapo and the Milice. Afraid of betrayal. She could not blame the woman.

They kept searching. Before noon, they approached a small Catholic church on the outskirts of Amiens. Its steeple overlooked a stone courtyard. Next to the courtyard stood a parish house made of the same stones as the church. Smoke wafted from its chimney. A pair of white hens wandered the yard.

Charlotte walked to the front door and knocked. No answer. She knocked again.

The sounds of whispered conversation came from inside, but still no answer. Finally, a peephole in the door slid open and an eye appeared.

"Who are you?" a male voice asked. "What do you want?"

"My car has broken down," Charlotte said.

The peephole slammed shut. More whispers from within.

Finally, the door opened. The priest looked to be in his fifties: a tall man with gray hair and a gray beard. He wore a black shirt with a white tab collar. Charlotte felt warm air roll through the doorway. Along with it came the scent of baking.

"I am not much of a mechanic," the priest said. "But God's amazing grace has brought you here." As he spoke, he did not make eye contact.

"I believe we have met before," Charlotte said, "At the feast of Saints Peter and Paul."

The priest looked up at her. "Come in," he said. But he did not smile. In fact, he did not look happy at all to see her. Behind him, a woman toiled at a wood-fired stove. The priest's cook, presumably. "I am Father Fontaine," the priest said.

"Thank you," Charlotte said. "I have two comrades with me—"

The priest did not let her finish her sentence.

"You are already causing me trouble," the priest said. "But we must carry the burdens the Lord gives us. Now get inside. Hurry."

Charlotte motioned for Aloïs and Philippe to approach. All three entered. The priest closed the door behind them. Philippe began to introduce himself.

"I am Philippe—"

Father Fontaine held up his hand.

"I do not need to know your names," the priest said. "You may take shelter in my cellar. I will fetch someone to help you. You must not go outside for any reason until they come. Those are my conditions. Either accept them or be on your way this instant."

"We accept them, sir," Charlotte said.

She wondered why Fontaine was so short with them. With wartime hardships, everyone was under stress. That went double for anyone helping the Resistance. But this man seemed especially agitated by visitors who had been properly authenticated.

The priest ushered Charlotte, Philippe, and Aloïs into a cellar lit by a single naked light bulb. The light revealed two barrels of potatoes. An earthy odor filled Charlotte's nostrils. Dried herbs hung from the ceiling by strings. But there was no sign of meat—no sausages or smoked hams. Three dusty wine bottles occupied an otherwise bare shelf.

"If you need a toilet, we will bring you a chamber pot," Father Fontaine said. "Do not go outside."

"We understand," Charlotte said.

"Are you hungry?"

At first no one spoke. Then Aloïs said, "A bit, sir."

"Very well. My cook will prepare you something. She will also try to find you dry clothes. Now you will excuse me. You have given me much to do."

The priest turned and tromped up the cellar steps. Slammed the door. Dust sprinkled from the ceiling.

After half an hour, the priest's cook brought down bread and weak tea. The group offered thanks, but the cook made no reply. She climbed the steps and returned with blankets and clothing. Charlotte selected a plain cotton dress and a sweater. Asked the men to turn their backs while she peeled off her damp blouse and trousers. The men changed, too. But their new clothes did not fit well. Both Aloïs and Philippe were taller than the priest. At least now, though, they were dry and warm.

They ate in silence. Charlotte sipped the hot tea. She put down her cup and lay down on the floor. Drifted into sleep immediately.

Hours later, noises came from upstairs. The noise woke Charlotte. Men entered the house, spoke in low tones. The cellar door swung open. Harsh light flooded the room.

Four rifle barrels aimed into the cellar. At first, Charlotte discerned nothing but four muzzles, all seemingly pointed at her. Then she realized the weapons were not Mausers or machine pistols. They were BREN guns, and the men holding them wore civilian clothes. Philippe, Charlotte, and Aloïs raised their hands.

"We are all friends here," Charlotte said.

"By amazing grace," one of the gunmen said.

"Peter and Paul," Charlotte replied.

"All right," the man said. "I just needed to hear it for myself. Come upstairs. We have much to discuss."

Charlotte climbed out first, followed by Aloïs, then Philippe. She sized up the gunmen. All wore workmen's clothing. Three were very young, perhaps not even twenty. Their leader, the man who did the talking, was older. Forties, at least. Close-cropped gray hair. Clean shaven. Fit, no sagging paunch or drooping jowls.

"I am Jean-Michel," the man said. "At least, that is my name to you. I must tell you that you've come at a bad time. And you will not be going anywhere anytime soon. Please, sit."

The group sat around the kitchen table as the priest looked on. What concerned Charlotte most was the statement about not being able to leave soon.

Jean-Michel reached into his overcoat pocket, produced a bottle.

"I bring you my apologies that you are stuck with me for a while," he said. "And cognac."

"I have information that has to get to Britain," Charlotte said. She told him about her rail maps and work for Plan *Vert*. She also briefed him on Philippe's status with the RAF, and the failed evacuation flight.

"I am sorry," Jean-Michel said. "But you will have to wait."

But why? Charlotte wondered.

The priest placed glasses around the table. Jean-Michel poured. Charlotte didn't particularly want to drink on a fairly empty stomach at this time of day, but she went along.

Jean-Michel raised his glass. Charlotte hesitated for a moment, then took her own glass. The rest of the group did the same.

"To the Resistance and to France," Jean-Michel said.

Charlotte took a sip. The cognac was good, and it warmed her insides all the way down. She waited before sipping again. With her body tired, her nerves shot, and with only a little food inside her, the liquor would go straight to her head.

"I am with the *Bureau Central de Renseignments et d'Action*," Jean-Michel explained. The Central Bureau for Intelligence and Operations. "Some call us simply the Free French Secret Service," he added. He pointed to Philippe. "Our friends across the Channel, some of your colleagues in the RAF, are working with us. In a few weeks they will fly Mosquito bombers to blow open the walls of the Amiens prison. That is why our security is so tight now. We cannot have another Lysander flying into here. And our radio calls must be kept to a minimum."

Aloïs sat straight up in his chair. Stared, open-mouthed, at Jean-Michel.

"My brother is in that prison," Aloïs said.

"What is his name?" Jean-Michel asked.

"Thomas."

"God willing, in the coming weeks, Thomas will be free."

Jean-Michel went on the describe the most daring and outlandish operation Charlotte had ever heard of. The planes would fly in at extreme low level; the mission required precision bombing like nothing attempted before. With luck, the light bomb loads would breach the walls with minimum casualties. Most of the prisoners had been condemned to death, and very soon. Desperate measures for desperate times.

"We will stand by with trucks to transport those who escape," Jean-Michel continued. "This is where I can use you. Since I cannot get you out, you might as well help me. We do not have enough volunteers for this operation."

Charlotte did not hesitate. "Of course, we will help," she said. "What do you need?"

"You and your maps are too important to lose," Jean-Michel said. "You will not get anywhere near the prison. You can stand by at a safe house and be prepared to treat the wounded. Your two friends, though, can drive trucks."

"*Certainement*," Aloïs said.

"*Moi, aussi*," Philippe said.

"*Bon*," Jean-Michel said.

"When will this happen?" Charlotte asked.

"Just a few weeks, I hope," Jean-Michel said. "As soon as the flyboys say they are ready."

"Can they do this?" Aloïs asked. "Can they bomb the prison without killing everyone?"

"They say they can," Jean-Michel said. "Some of our friends will get hurt. That is inevitable. And when the Germans realize what is happening, they will lose their minds. They will probably start firing at everything and everyone. But if we do not act, they will execute all of them anyway."

"This is so crazy it just might work," Charlotte said.

"I believe they can do it," Philippe said. "I have never flown a bomber, so I cannot speak from experience. But I know what I have heard in the RAF."

Philippe described another bombing mission—one just as audacious, that had taken place back in May. In Operation Chastise, nineteen Lancaster bombers attacked German dams in the Ruhr Valley. Torpedo nets and antiaircraft guns protected the dams. But the RAF used a bouncing bomb, invented specifically for the mission, that skipped across the water and over the nets. The crews had to invent new tactics, too, bombing with great precision from treetop height.

It worked. The bombers breached two dams and caused major flooding that inundated factories and mines downstream. But the achievement came at great cost. Hundreds of civilians died in the flood, including slave laborers, and the RAF lost eight aircraft and their crews.

"If they can do *that*," Philippe said, "they can do this."

"I know you need to get to London," Jean-Michel told Charlotte. "We cannot risk any flights now, before the bombing mission. But afterwards, we will do whatever we can for you."

"I understand," Charlotte said.

"So, what do we do next?" Aloïs asked.

"We reconnoiter the area," Jean-Michel said. "Get you and the other drivers familiar with the roads. And we wait."

"What is the mission date?" Philippe asked.

"Unknown," Jean-Michel said. "But soon."

Two days later, Jean-Michel took his guests on a tour of the region. Disguised as farmers, the group rode in a horse cart loaded with hay. The horse clopped along a road lined with linden trees. The prison loomed in the distance like a fortress. Charlotte shuddered to think what horrors might be happening inside those walls. And she tried to picture what it might look like when the bombers streaked in over the trees. But her imagination failed her. She could not visualize a bomb hitting exactly where it would blow open the outer wall and do little other damage.

Jean-Michel pointed out a safe house along the way. He told Philippe and Aloïs to remember the location. It looked like a typical rural home, too nondescript to notice. By design, no doubt. No signs of activity within.

"This will become a dynamic event, to say the least," Jean-Michel said. "I might not be there to answer all your questions once it starts."

Charlotte knew what that meant. Jean-Michel seemed so nonchalant about it. Clearly, he was an experienced operative.

On the way from Amiens, the group passed an airfield. Just a grass strip with three single-engine airplanes parked near a wind sock that drooped in the light breeze. Philippe rose up in his seat for a better look. Jean-Michel pulled him back down.

"Do not show too much interest," Jean-Michel warned.

"Who uses this field?" Philippe asked.

"The Vichy government," Jean-Michel said. "It is too small for bombers and fighters, I think. But the traitors use it to fly mail between here and Vichy."

"What planes are those?" Charlotte asked.

"They are Caudron Simouns," Philippe said.

"Have you ever flown one?"

Philippe shook his head, but his eyes lingered on the airfield. Charlotte noticed the field was lightly guarded; just two young Milice goons strutting about with their carbines. Perhaps that was because the grass field and its light aircraft had little military importance.

Aloïs paid the airfield no attention. Instead he scanned the skies, as if he expected the bombers at any moment.

"What is wrong?" Jean-Michel asked. "Do you have further questions?"

"I am excited that this may free my brother Thomas," Aloïs said. "But I worry this might kill him, too."

Jean-Michel offered no answer.

Aloïs had a point, Charlotte supposed. The leadership at BCRA, SOE, and the RAF had weighed the odds. Risk versus reward. The cost of doing nothing. The Resistance and all the agencies that supported it inclined toward action—and so did Charlotte. Churchill had said to set Europe ablaze. You didn't do that by wringing your hands about the worst that could happen.

Finally, Jean-Michel spoke.

"What if we lose half the prisoners?" he said. "That is better than losing all of them to the executioners. We get no ideal choices here."

Aloïs still stared at the horizon, as if to guide the aircraft and direct their bombs by sheer force of will.

TOM YOUNG

MEMORANDUM
REGARDING: Operation Donar
Gestapo Counterintelligence Corps,
Federal Intelligence Service, Lyon
Lyon, France 15 December 1943
TO: Reich Security Main Office, Berlin
FROM: Klaus Barbie, Hauptstürmfuhrer

Vigorous interrogation of captured subversives continues to provide useful intelligence. However, their growing number in our jail facilities has presented its own set of problems. Once a terrorist's intelligence value has been exploited, that terrorist becomes purely a liability, a drain on the Reich's food resources. That individual cannot be released, of course, and has no more usefulness to this office.

Since my last memorandum, I have transferred twelve subversives to the prison in Amiens. Two died en route. Prison officials in Amiens report crowded conditions there, as well.

It is the recommendation of this office that subversives whose interrogations are complete should be eliminated with all deliberate speed.

Heil Hitler,
Klaus Barbie, Hauptstürmfuhrer

CHAPTER 18

Lisette Gerard

The Royal Navy MGB, a motor gunboat, cut a foaming wake across the English Channel. Her engines howled at full throttle. The vessel ran dark, all lights off, at forty knots through a moonless night. The wind whipped Lisette's hair and numbed her cheeks. She pulled a borrowed Navy peacoat tighter around her against the chill and the spray. The cold and the choppy water made her wounds ache.

Lisette could have sought shelter below, but she had never taken a journey quite like this. She knew she probably never would again, as well, so she wanted to feel the wind, smell the sea. And view the French coast when it materialized in the gloom.

At the gunboat's bow, she considered how the war had set her life on a course not just unforeseen, but unimagined. As a working-class girl in Toulon, she saw her future as that of a wife and mother. She had not felt deprived by that, either. She'd looked forward to a house full of children. Lisette worshipped her brother, Philippe, and was thrilled when he became a pilot. But, for her, a life of action never seemed possible.

Good thing Philippe can't see me now, she thought. The war had strained relations between them. He had turned into an overprotective uncle. Thought she should sit out the fighting in some safe billet.

Lisette's traveling companion huddled with crewmen in the forward cabin. Virginia Hall appeared to be a frail old woman. However, Virginia was anything but that. Disguise aged the American beyond her 38 years. Dye grayed her hair. Multiple skirts added girth and hid her pistol. A dentist had even ground down her teeth to better resemble a French peasant. But her limp was real; she'd lost part of her left leg to a hunting accident years ago, and she got around on a wooden prosthesis she nicknamed Cuthbert.

Virginia's code name—her *new* code name—was Saint. To the Gestapo, she was one of the most wanted women on Earth. Lisette revered her. Virginia's skill at organizing *résistants* and evading capture had become legend in the SOE and its American counterpart, the OSS, or Office of Strategic Services. Now, Lisette would work with her in a new mission: to set up safe houses, rebuild shattered networks, and activate Plan *Tortue*. To help them, the Resistance had hundreds of fighters staged in the French Alps.

Virginia came up from below and joined Lisette on deck.

"Skipper says ten minutes," Virginia called over the roar of motors and wind.

Lisette nodded. Eyed what little of the eastern horizon she could discern. After several minutes, an edge took form, darker than sea and sky. Breakers crashed onto distant rocks, defined the Brittany coast. The MGB's engines hushed to idle. The vessel slowed down and rode the swells.

"Are we ready for this?" Lisette asked.

"We'd better be," Virginia said.

That sounds like her, Lisette thought. At least it sounded like what Lisette had heard of her. No nonsense. No patience for the timid. No sympathy for fools. No excuses, just results. And, by appearance, no fear.

Lisette, on the other hand, was scared to death. She knew well the dangers. She knew firsthand how much bullets hurt. And that wasn't the worst the Gestapo could do to you. But she feared even more the prospect of a permanent Nazi Europe. She feared letting down her country. So she pressed on.

She unbuttoned the peacoat, passed it back to the seaman who'd loaned it to her. The man spoke impenetrable Cockney but behaved like a gentleman. He joined other sailors who unlashed an inflatable dinghy and lowered it to the sea. Two men descended lines down to the little boat and unstowed its oars.

"Ladies," the Cockney gentleman said, "Your launch is ready." Lisette deciphered the words only by listening closely.

Sailors helped Lisette and Virginia climb down to the dinghy. One of the two men on board yanked a cord to start its engine. The dinghy motored away from the gunboat for a distance. Then the sailors cut the outboard and rowed in silence.

When they reached the shore, Lisette and Virginia stepped onto the rocks without a word. Lisette waved to the sailors as they began rowing back toward their gunboat. She and Virginia stepped with care through the wet stones. They made their way to the weeds and brush above the high tide line.

For security reasons, they had brought no baggage. If a German patrol found people on the beach with suitcases or duffel bags, it would be obvious they had landed from the sea. Lisette and Virginia now depended on the Resistance. They hid among the gorse and underbrush, and waited.

A car approached, headlights dim with blackout lenses. Lisette hoped it was their ride. But the vehicle passed by. An hour later, another car passed. Finally, after they had waited two hours, a car approached, slowed and stopped. The passenger door opened and a man got out. He stepped toward the beach. Lit a cigarette. Took three long puffs, then dropped the butt and crushed it with his heel.

Lisette looked at Virginia, who nodded. So far, the signals were correct. Then the man said, "Saints alive, it is cold out here."

Virginia rose from the weeds. "Saint is very much alive," she said.

"Please," the man said. "Get in."

Lisette and Virginia sat in the back seat of the car. The warm interior felt good after their cold and windy boat crossing. Their contact took his place in the passenger seat, and the driver shifted into gear and sped away from the beach.

"Anthelme," Virginia said, "it is good to see you again."

Lisette didn't know if that was a real name or a code, but it didn't matter.

"It is good to see you, as well," Anthelme said, "though I hardly recognize you."

Virginia chuckled. "As it should be," she said. "I went to a lot of trouble to look this old."

"I imagine you two would like to rest up from your Channel crossing," Anthelme said. "We have a room for you in a safe place."

"Thank you for your help," Lisette said.

"We have much to do," Virginia said. "Has Lieutenant Morel arrived?"

Lisette knew that name from her SOE briefings. Lieutenant Tom Morel was a French officer organizing a Resistance force in the French Alps. The group comprised hundreds of *Maquisards* and even some Spaniards. The RAF had airdropped weapons and supplies to them, including STEN guns and Mills bombs, which were much like American hand grenades. The SOE and De Gaulle hoped the unit would show that the Resistance could carry out large-scale operations. Maybe even large enough to tie up a Panzer division.

Anthelme sighed. "No," he said. "Tom has not arrived. We have not heard from him in two days, and I fear the worst."

"Oh, dear God," Virginia said. "I hope we haven't lost him."

"We have lost many," Anthelme said.

Lisette knew the truth of that. For a year, it seemed, the Resistance had suffered loss after loss. Fighters killed, agents betrayed, whole networks rolled up. Survivors fought on in hopes of an impending Allied invasion, but when would that ever come? Many had expected it by last summer, only to be disappointed.

Anthelme took Lisette and Virginia to a house in the fishing village of Le Guilvinec. The homeowner, an elderly waterman, showed them to cots in the cellar. Lisette pulled a quilt over herself and fell asleep immediately.

She and Virginia slept until mid-morning. When they awoke, the waterman gave them hot tea and a soup made with cod. Anthelme returned with news—none of it good.

"Tom Morel is dead," he said.

Half a minute passed in silence. Anthelme's words hung over the room like a shroud. Resistance operatives were used to bad news; doom lurked in every shadow. But lately the defeats and setbacks seemed to accumulate beyond the tolerance of even the most jaded fighters.

Virginia stared into her tea cup. "How?" she said finally.

"He was killed in an operation against Vichy police," Anthelme said.

Anthelme explained how Morel's last mission came as he led the Resistance forces based in the Alps on the Glières Plateau. The Germans caught on that an insurgency was heating up in the area, and they ordered the Vichy government to crack down. The Milice and other Vichy forces attacked. The nearly five hundred *résistants* held their own for a while, fighting in the snow with little food and no heavy weapons—just the small arms dropped by the RAF.

The German army and police battalions moved in with a force of more than four thousand, supported by *Luftwaffe* ground attack aircraft. The enemy bombed and shelled the Resistance unit and sealed off the main escape route from the plateau.

The *résistants* fought on against an overwhelming force as long as they were able. Eventually the survivors retreated and scattered. More than a hundred and fifty fighters were found dead on the battlefield. Many others had been captured. Some were tortured and executed.

"We lost the battle," Anthelme said, "but we showed them how real Frenchmen fight." He added that the BBC was calling Glières Plateau a moral victory for the Resistance.

"Moral victories do not win wars," Virginia said.

"Indeed not," Anthelme said. "And now we are shorthanded."

"How does this affect our plans?" Lisette asked.

Virginia thought for a moment. Looked at Anthelme, who nodded.

"I wanted to send you down to Montauban with five of Tom Morel's men," Virginia said. "Now, I have to send you by yourself, if you're willing. We have a small network there, the ALPHONSE circuit. They are still operational."

"Of course I will go," Lisette said.

"Then we will take you to the train station this afternoon," Virginia said.

On the outskirts of Montauban, Lisette waited by the dark waters of the River Tarn. She should have been tired from her long train ride, but adrenaline kept her on full alert. She had expected to help ratchet up Plan *Tortue* to hinder movement by the *Das Reich* Panzer division; that had been her mission all along. But she hadn't expected to take direct action this quickly.

She shivered. The night was cold. Lisette hoped her contacts would arrive on time. She stood on a concrete boat ramp that sloped downward into the Tarn. Checked her watch: one minute before eleven at night. She heard a vehicle approaching along the river road. A truck pulled up to the boat ramp, lights off. The driver shut off the engine and rolled down his window. A cigarette dangled from his mouth. When he took a drag, the fire in the cigarette brightened enough to show the stubble on his face.

The man held the smoke in his lungs for a moment. Then he exhaled and said, "The tortoise—"

"Does not win the race," Lisette answered.

"*Bon soir*," the man said.

He sat in silence while they waited some more. The man introduced himself as Olivier, though Lisette doubted that was his real name. After a few minutes, a rowboat glided up to the boat ramp. Olivier offered the same verbal sign to the two men in the rowboat. They answered with the correct countersign.

The men tied the boat to a tree branch that overhung the river. Then they began unloading tools. Not weapons—the men brought no firearms other than pistols hidden in their waistbands. Instead, they unloaded grease guns, the type one would use to lubricate a vehicle. Lisette helped them transfer the grease guns to the back of the truck.

"Tonight, we service Hitler's trains," Olivier said.

The others laughed. One of them said, "You know, I was never a very good mechanic."

Lisette understood their humor. The grease guns contained lubricant spiked with carborundum shavings—an abrasive. Applied to a train car's wheels and axles, the bearings would wear down until they seized. The train would come—quite literally—to a screeching halt. Perhaps even derail if it was going fast enough.

The team departed the boat ramp and drove to the Montauban-Ville-Bourbon station. Montauban served as a railway hub. Perhaps that was why the Germans had stationed *Das Reich* there. From Montauban, they could load Panzers onto trains and reach anyplace in France within a day or two. But not with axles ground down to scrap metal.

Lisette rode in the back of the truck with the two men who'd arrived in the boat. They were dressed as railway workers. Their dirty clothes and fake IDs identified them as such. Lisette wore ragged trousers and carried the same false document. Railway workers were essential personnel, so it wasn't suspicious that the young men with her were not in some mandatory labor battalion.

At the rail station, they made no effort to hide. They parked in the employee lot and walked right in with the third-shift workers. Carried their tools like any good employee. Some of the workers gave them second looks, perhaps because they did not recognize them. But no one said anything. Lisette supposed either they were afraid to speak up—or they suspected Resistance activity and welcomed it. Two Milice guards at the front gate looked bored and did not bother to check credentials.

On a rail siding, Lisette spotted a beautiful target. From her SOE training she recognized a DRB Class 52 *Kriegslokomotive*: a German-built steam train so new that the piston rods and crankpins still gleamed with red gloss paint. Cab windows reflected light from railyard floodlamps. A swastika adorned the smokebox. A machine like this was the pride of the *Deutsche Reichsbahn*.

She got right to work. Applied abrasive-laced grease to the locomotive's roller bearings. Emptied her grease gun and picked up a fresh one. Olivier and her other teammates found two more locomotives and treated those, as well.

Then they went to work on rail cars. They began with the ones that carried cargo. Lisette greased a car loaded with artillery ammunition. They found other cars laden with crates of small arms, barrels of oil, pallets of field rations. They took their time and worked all night. They left in the most inconspicuous way possible—with the regular workers at shift change.

The carborundum would work slowly. The locomotives and rail cars might be anywhere by the time they broke down.

CHAPTER 19

Philippe Gerard

The nights grew colder. Philippe, Charlotte, and Aloïs remained with Father Fontaine and his cook. They slept in the cellar, waiting for an update on the prison-break mission.

Philippe chafed at the inaction. For the most part, he'd been on the move since 1940, usually at the controls of an airplane. Now, as Christmas of 1943 approached, he found himself sitting in a hole, doing nothing. Father Fontaine brought his guests a radio—illegal under occupation—and they followed war news from the BBC's French language service. The broadcasts opened with the words "*Ici Londres!*"—"This is London."

On Christmas Eve came news that an American general named Dwight D. Eisenhower had become the Supreme Allied Commander in Europe. To Philippe, this meant three things: One—plans must be coming together for the long awaited cross-Channel invasion. Two—the need for Charlotte and her maps to get to England just became more urgent. Three—it was time to get back in the fight. Now.

That night, Father Fontaine led a midnight mass for his parishioners. Though Philippe had never been particularly religious, he wished he could have attended. But he knew that was unwise. A stranger of military age suddenly appearing in the church would have raised questions.

He contented himself with listening to the music. The church was only steps from the house, and the strains of piano, organ, and voice floated through the walls. He recognized one of his favorite *cantiques* from childhood, "*Les Anges dans nos campagnes*": "Angels We Have Heard on High." Charlotte and Aloïs joined Philippe in the home's front room to listen. In the fireplace, a Yule log burned. The sap popped and shot sparks against the fire grate. The warmth and woodsmoke scent reminded him of younger, safer days.

When Philippe had attended mass as a boy growing up in Provence, life had seemed so secure. His father's job as a shipyard worker in Toulon provided enough income for a comfortable existence, if not a luxurious one. His mother worked as a homemaker and part-time seamstress. He was not old enough to remember the Great War; he remembered only the stories the grownups told. To a ten-year-old Philippe, war was something awful that happened in the past.

When the Nazis rose to power during the 1930s, an older Philippe followed the news with concern. But even then, he never thought they would invade France. Hadn't they learned their lesson in 1918? After his schooling, he joined the *Armée de l'Air* and trained as a mechanic. However, from the beginning, he knew he wanted to become a pilot. The first time he applied he was rejected. The second time, his application was lost. Philippe began to suspect his superiors looked down on his working-class background. But on his third try, he was accepted.

Philippe took to flight as if born for it. In the Romano R-82 biplane, the stick and rudder became extensions of his body and mind. During solo flights in the little trainer, he played with the clouds. Early on, he punched straight through a towering cumulus. The updrafts rocked him with turbulence; he learned not to do that again. But he enjoyed soaring around the buildups, even slicing the edges with his wingtip. When he gazed down on forests and hedgerows spreading beneath him, the roads and towns and villages, the rivers in their courses to the sea, all the earth seemed at peace.

Now, all that seemed so naïve.

Father Fontaine returned from the church. The priest opened the front door, and a cold blast of wind came in with him. Snowflakes swirled, fell to the floor, and melted. Fontaine bolted the door, hung his overcoat on a peg.

"How was the service?" Philippe asked.

"Uplifting, I hope," Fontaine said. "But sparsely attended. All our young men are away. Or with their heavenly father."

"I am sorry," Charlotte said.

Aloïs crossed himself, nodded.

"Forgive me, sir," Philippe said, "but I have a hard time feeling uplifted these days."

"That is understandable," Fontaine said.

"What is not understandable," Philippe said, "is how a benevolent God could let these things happen."

The priest regarded Philippe for a moment.

"I, too, have struggled with that," Fontaine said. "The war has tested my faith like nothing before. At times I have nearly abandoned my faith. But I always come back to this: Some things are not for us to understand. We can only deal with the circumstances we are given. We must do so with all the virtue we can muster. That is the one thing we can control."

Philippe let those words sink in. He was a pilot; he knew how to control powerful machines. By nature, he wanted to control everything that affected him. He wanted to control what happened to Lisette. After his dive that cost the lives of his crewmates so long ago, he'd wanted to control what people thought of him. Impossible, of course. But the priest had reminded him of what he *could* control.

"Fine words, Father," Aloïs said. "And I mean no disrespect. But my brother in prison and my parents in the ground did not deserve what happened to them. I have been angry with God for three years."

"At times, I have as well, my son," Fontaine said. "If you have read your Bible, you know how some of the saints suffered. God does not cause our suffering. But he is always present in our suffering."

With that, the priest disappeared into the kitchen. Cabinets creaked open. Glasses rattled. Philippe wondered what Fontaine was doing now at such a late hour. Fontaine returned with a tray filled with drinks.

"*Joyeux Noël*, my friends," Fontaine said.

Philippe didn't feel very joyous, but he offered his thanks. When Fontaine put down the tray on a table in the front room, Philippe counted five wine glasses containing a reddish liquid. The priest's cook was gone for the evening.

"Expecting a guest?" Philippe asked.

"I am," Fontaine said.

He gave no further explanation. He lifted a glass and handed it to Charlotte. Then he offered drinks to Philippe and Aloïs.

"Merry Christmas," Charlotte said.

Philippe took a sip. A sweet taste with a hint of fruit. "Very good," he said. "What is this?"

"White wine with blackcurrant liqueur," Fontaine said. "The Germans seem to prefer our red wine, as they have taken nearly all of it. We make the best of our white."

"Then let us also toast to a better New Year," Philippe said.

The *résistants* clinked their glasses together, drank. Philippe wondered how many of them would live through the New Year, but he kept those dark thoughts to himself.

A few minutes later, a knock sounded at the door. Four raps—three in quick succession, followed a moment later by a fourth. Perhaps some sort of code. Father Fontaine nodded, stepped to the door. Slid open the peephole and peered through. Unbolted the door.

Jean-Michel entered. Tonight he traveled alone. He removed his scarf and leather trench coat. Underneath he wore a shoulder holster. He carried a large-frame automatic; Philippe couldn't determine the make.

"Christmas greetings, comrades," Jean-Michel said.

Father Fontaine handed him a glass, offered him a seat.

"You look as if you are very much on duty," Charlotte said.

"Always," Jean-Michel said. "But especially tonight."

"How so?"

"I just came from the radio. We have a date for our prison break."

Aloïs sat straight up in his chair. "When?" he asked.

"Just a few weeks. The RAF needs to select crews and conduct specific training. Then we go."

"Does this mission have a name?" Charlotte asked.

"Not officially," Jean-Michel said. "But I like to call it Operation Jericho."

CHAPTER 20

Philippe Gerard

A leaden sky hung over Amiens. Snow carpeted the ground. The cold numbed Philippe's fingers as he sat at the driver's seat of a Citroën U23 parked among a copse of trees. Inside his gloves, he curled his fingers into fists. That did little to warm them. He couldn't use the heater now, because the trucks needed to keep their engines off until the drivers heard the airplanes. No need for the Germans to spot the rising exhaust of trucks at idle. If all went according to plan, something else would soon draw their attention. Aloïs sat beside him, shivering. They eyed the prison from across an open field.

Another truck, with Jean-Michel at the wheel, sat in front of Philippe's vehicle. Five other trucks were hidden in the area. Philippe checked his watch. Noon. It was time.

Despite the cold, he rolled down his window to listen. No sound came but the chirp of a lark. In the distance, a dog barked.

Were the planes not coming? Had the mission been canceled?

Worse, had the planes been intercepted by the Luftwaffe? Had the Germans known the Mosquitos were coming? It would not have been the first time a Resistance mission had been betrayed.

"Where are they?" Aloïs asked.

Philippe shook his head.

THE MAPMAKER

For a moment, he let his worst imaginings run wild. He pictured the bombers spinning in flames down to the English Channel. Disappearing in a splash of fire and brine. Then he reminded himself that anything could cause a brief delay: An unforecast headwind. A minor mechanical repair. Mist causing difficulty in forming up.

Two minutes ticked by with no sign of the Mosquitos. In the truck up front, Jean-Michel glanced back at him. Shrugged.

At 12:03, Philippe heard Merlin engines.

He looked up. Scanned the sky. Saw nothing.

Aloïs stuck his head out of the passenger side window. Peered upward.

"I don't see anything," Aloïs said.

But the engines grew louder. Philippe scanned again, across all points of the compass. Still, he saw nothing.

Then his eye caught movement. Low. Very low. Even though he knew this would be a low-level bombing mission, he'd been looking way too high.

There. Just above the tree line. *Just barely* above the tree line, he spotted three aircraft. Coming in from the east. With each second they grew larger and louder. Now he could make out the twin engines and the bulbous canopies.

"There they are," Philippe said. Pointed low.

A moment later he could discern the two men in each aircraft: pilot and navigator/bombardier. The bomb bay doors were already open. The planes flew so close to the ground that their propellers kicked up dry snow. The sight put Philippe in mind of a speedboat cutting a white wake.

"Yes!" Aloïs shouted.

The three aircraft sliced over the prison, barely above the roofs. Oval shapes tumbled from their bellies. For a moment, Philippe saw no result, no explosions. The bombers pulled up, arced into a climbing turn.

Then, in rapid succession, the blasts began. Booms split the early afternoon. Fire and smoke erupted from within the prison.

Of course, Philippe thought. *Delayed-action bombs.* To give the low-flying aircraft a chance to get away.

"Hah-hah!" Aloïs cried.

Philippe peered at the prison's outer walls. From what he could see, the walls remained intact. Either the crews had missed, or the first bombs were intended for guard quarters.

A minute later, two more Mosquitos appeared. This time they came in from the north. They flew just as low as the first flight of bombers. Plumes of snow rose behind them. For a moment, one of them dropped out of sight—so low the prison walls hid it. Then the aircraft pulled up and turned. Behind it, an explosion erupted.

The second bomber streaked across the compound, barely cleared the rooftops. Fire and smoke billowed from its bomb blasts.

"*Mon Dieu*, I think they've done it," Aloïs shouted. "I see a gap in the wall."

Smoke obscured the prison now. Philippe squinted, scanned the structures. When a breeze swept away some of the smoke, he saw that Aloïs was correct: A bomb had opened a hole in the northern wall.

From within the prison, a klaxon sounded. Philippe and Aloïs laughed.

"They're a bit late with their alarm, aren't they?" Aloïs said.

The bombers were not finished. Three more appeared, just feet above a road lined with poplars. Philippe shook his head in amazement. How many aircraft were coming? What brilliant coordination had set up this attack from multiple directions?

As he watched the third wave approach, something else caught his eye. Movement, up high. He glanced above.

A single-engine aircraft rolled into a dive. Black cross on the fuselage. Swastika on the tail.

A Focke-Wulf 190.

The enemy fighter banked hard. Descended into the attacking bombers like a falcon swooping toward prey. Fire speared from its wings. Rounds from twin twenty-millimeter cannons knifed toward a Mosquito.

The bomber turned, dodged. The cannon rounds slammed into the ground just behind it. The 190 pulled up and climbed.

But the Mosquito had not yet escaped. Another 190 plummeted into the melee. Curved over the prison compound. Lined up behind the Mosquito and began firing.

The bomber rolled into a steep turn. Practically stood on its left wingtip. Tracers streaked over it. Philippe's right hand tightened into a fist as if gripping a control stick. Mentally, he flew evasive action with the Mosquito pilot. Imagined the g-forces pressing him into his seat.

"Come on, come on," he whispered.

But this was a losing battle. The German aircraft pressed its attack. Dived low. Turned. Fired again.

This time the geometry worked for the enemy. Rounds arced into the Mosquito. Slammed into the left wing. Punched along the fuselage. A burst of cannon fire blew off the tail.

The Mosquito cartwheeled into the ground and vanished in a ball of fire. The flames splashed like liquid across the snow and into the trees.

"Swine," Philippe hissed.

Black smoke rose above the crash site. The 190s circled, maneuvered for firing positions.

The bombing continued. The delayed-action bombs kept exploding inside the compound. Philippe noticed another breach in the wall. Behind it, figures scurried about the prison grounds. Men began to exit through the breach and sprint into the snow.

Another single-engine fighter plane roared across the compound. Philippe feared it was another enemy searching for another victim. But then he discerned two white stripes under each wing.

"A Typhoon!" Philippe called out. He pointed as the friendly fighter banked and climbed, daring the Focke-Wulfs to a fair fight.

None engaged, at least that Philippe could see. But another pair of Mosquitos took aim at the prison. Their bombs tumbled loose. The aircraft pulled up. There came that excruciating pause of the delay fuses. Then more explosions erupted. The bombs blew open two more breaches in the walls.

The growl of engines faded. Was it over that quickly?

Philippe glanced at his watch. He'd spotted the first bomber at 12:03 p.m. Now it was 12:08. Five minutes.

Though the skies grew quiet, pandemonium rose within the compound. The klaxon still wailed. Beneath it, shouts and screams. Gunshots registered.

Jean-Michel waved from his truck. "*Allez*," he shouted. Time to go.

Philippe started his engine. Shifted into gear. Pulled out of his hiding place and accelerated along the road. Followed Jean-Michel's vehicle. The tires kicked up the dry snow like white dust.

Philippe glanced over at the prison. Flames and smoke rose and spread. From this angle he could not see all the openings in the wall.

The drivers headed for the large breach at the corner. Already, prisoners scurried through it. As he got closer, Philippe could better see damage inside the walls. Some of the buildings had been blown open and set afire. One wing of the compound appeared to have slumped, as if built of wet straw.

At the large breach, the trucks skidded to a stop. Philippe set his parking brake. Left the engine running. He noticed other trucks, even a couple of cars, speeding up to other breaches. They had come from other hiding places near the prison. Philippe opened his door, leaped from the driver's seat. Opened the tailgate.

"Get aboard," he shouted. Two escapees clambered into the truck. More ran through the openings. Some stopped and looked about. When they spotted the trucks and cars, they took off running toward them.

"Let's get inside," Jean-Michel ordered. "See if we can help more get out."

"*Oui*," Aloïs said.

Jean-Michel had briefed them about this moment. No doubt some of the inmates would be in shock, trying to understand what was happening. Perhaps conditioned to obey and cower, they might not recognize this brief chance to escape. They might need some help. Aloïs needed no encouragement. He ran inside.

Philippe followed Jean-Michel and Aloïs through the breach and into the prison yard. There, he saw more inmates fleeing the prison.

Two bodies lay in the snow. One wore a German uniform. The other appeared to be an inmate. Flames licked through the main building's roof. Smoke poured through broken windows. Jean-Michel and Philippe entered through the nearest door. Inside, smoke hung thick. Philippe took a breath, and the smoke went down his chest like sand. He began to cough.

The power had gone out; he could see little in the darkness. Then he recognized figures running through corridors, stumbling over rubble. He nearly tripped over a body. Philippe could not tell whether it was a guard or a *résistant*. He drew his Webley, ready to shoot any guard he might see.

"Get outside," he shouted to anyone who could hear. "We have trucks waiting for you."

In the darkness and smoke, Philippe lost sight of Jean-Michel and Aloïs. He found a young man leaning against a wall. Blood streamed down his face. Philippe grabbed him by the arm and pulled him to the door. Shoved him through. Pointed.

"Run that way," Philippe ordered. "Get in the truck." The man nodded, staggered across the prison yard.

Back inside the building, Philippe began searching the hallways. To his surprise, he encountered only prisoners—no guards. Most seemed to understand what was happening. They streamed down the corridors and fled. Outside a cell door, he spotted a figure kneeling beside a downed man.

"Leave him," Philippe said. "Escape while you can."

Jean-Michel had issued instructions: Save as many as possible as quickly as possible. That meant an awful triage—sacrificing those too badly hurt to move.

"No," the man said. "I am a doctor."

A Resistance doctor, evidently. The man wore civilian clothes, not a uniform.

"Sir," Philippe said, "if you don't leave now, you probably never will."

"I know that," the man said. "I will help the wounded."

Two more prisoners joined the doctor. They lifted the prostrate man and carried him inside the cell. The placed him on a bench, which the doctor had set up as a makeshift operating table.

Philippe marveled at their self-sacrifice. For all they knew, the Germans would machine-gun everyone left at the prison in reprisal for the raid and escapes. But this doctor and his aides did not seem to care.

"*Vive le France, monsieur,*" Philippe said. He left the doctor to his work.

Back in the corridor, he found Aloïs.

"I cannot find my brother," Aloïs said. "I cannot find Thomas."

"Maybe he's already outside," Philippe said.

Aloïs had promised not to spend all his time looking for Thomas. Jean-Michel had told him the mission did not include saving particular individuals. With tears in his eyes, Aloïs ran off to help more *résistants*.

A prisoner sprinted past Philippe. The man carried a set of keys that jangled as he ran. Keys to cells, presumably. Philippe followed him through the smoke and dust.

They stopped at a cellblock where men shouted and screamed. Three men occupied the first cell: an older man with gray hair and two younger men. Fire raged just meters down the corridor, and they were still locked in their cells. The inmate with the keyring fumbled with the keys. Selected one. Shoved it into the lock.

"*Dépêchez-vous,*" a man in the cell said. "Please hurry."

The key didn't work. The inmate tried another one.

"We're going to burn!" another prisoner shouted. "Please help!"

The second key didn't work, either.

"*Rapidement,*" the third man called.

The third key turned in the lock. The inmate with the key ring yanked open the cell door. The three *résistants* scurried through the door. One of the younger men disappeared through the smoke, ran down the corridor. The other two inmates stayed.

"We will help you get more out," the older man said.

At the next cell, the first key worked. Four more men escaped. Philippe and the other rescuers worked their way down the cellblock, freeing the men inside. At the last cell, with two men inside, the lock turned but the door jammed. The ceiling sagged, bound up the iron door. The paint on the ceiling began to flake and bubble. Fire on the second floor, too, Philippe realized.

Flames flickered so close now Philippe could feel the heat. He sweated and coughed.

The door opened only three inches. Just enough for Philippe and the other men to get their fingers around its edge. He holstered his pistol. Placed both hands on the door.

"Let's pull together," Philippe said. His fellow rescuers took hold of the door. "You men shove from the inside," Philippe added. Then he shouted, "Pull!"

The door scraped open another inch.

"Again," Philippe ordered. "Heave!"

The men pulled and pushed. They gained two more inches. The ceiling began to blacken and drip.

"Can you get through now?" Philippe asked.

One of the men inside pressed his shoulder through the opening. But he could not get his head through.

"Once more," Philippe said. "Everybody heave!"

Philippe pulled so hard he felt his fingers would break. The iron door grew hot. The rescuers groaned and strained.

The door yielded two more inches. The first prisoner wriggled through. His cellmate followed.

Inside the cell, the ceiling collapsed. Burning rubble, along with a foot-wide wooden beam, slammed to the floor. Smoke and dust filled the air. Nearly blinded, Philippe coughed and hacked. Dug for his handkerchief. Placed the cloth over his nose and mouth.

"Let's get out of here," he shouted through the handkerchief. "Follow me."

CHAPTER 21

Charlotte Denneau

At the safe house, Charlotte waited with two new friends, Elise and Camille. Just this morning she'd met the two Resistance nurses. She had helped them set up a makeshift medic station in the kitchen of the rural home. They'd placed a pillow and blanket across the table. Stacked bandages and tourniquet cloth along the counter. Positioned jars of sulfa powder and burn salve by the sink. Prepared syrettes of morphine.

They'd heard the explosions, the distant booms. The screams of engines and the wail of a klaxon.

Then silence.

For what felt like an eternity, no trucks came. No word came. Nothing. Just the chirps of birds and the normal sound of traffic. Charlotte began to wonder if the mission had failed altogether. Had the bombers all been shot down? Or had their bombs not breached the prison walls? Had the attack accomplished nothing but killing *résistants*?

To Charlotte, that seemed possible. Perhaps the pilots had not bombed with the precision the mission demanded. Were the Germans laughing now?

Then two trucks pulled up. The vehicles drove around the house and parked in the back. Tailgates dropped. Men jumped to the ground.

Charlotte counted thirty. Elise opened the kitchen door. Camille readied a pitcher of water.

"Come in," Elise called. "Get inside, quickly."

The men tromped up the steps, filed into the kitchen. They smelled of smoke but looked elated. Wide eyes. Broad smiles. They kept quiet, spoke in whispers.

"*Merci, merci,*" they repeated.

Most looked uninjured. Elise offered them water, then directed them to the cellar. Ordered them to remain quiet.

A man came in with a bad burn on the side of his face. His cheek oozed with fluid, looked like half-cooked meat. Charlotte took his arm, helped him lie down on the table. Camille began examining him. The next patient walked in cradling a hand crushed by falling masonry. Charlotte shuddered at multiple compound fractures, the sharp ends of exposed finger bones. The man said nothing but clenched his jaw in obvious pain. Elise gave him a shot of morphine.

Finally, Jean-Michel, Philippe, and Aloïs entered the safe house. Jean-Michel and Philippe looked jubilant. Aloïs looked heartbroken.

"You did it," Charlotte said. "You actually pulled this off."

"Well, mainly the pilots pulled it off," Jean-Michel said. "It was a wonder to behold."

"Were there casualties inside the prison?"

"Oh, yes," Jean-Michel said. "I saw several myself. But this is better than losing all of them."

"Did most of the prisoners escape?" Elise asked.

"Unknown," Jean-Michel said. "Many did, I know that. They have been taken to various safe houses."

"Some chose to stay," Philippe said. "To help the wounded too hurt to move. There was a doctor who stayed. What courage."

The burned man on the table spoke up. "I know him," the man said. "Dr. Mans. Dr. Antonin Mans. You say he could have escaped but did not?"

"*Oui,*" Philippe said.

"That does not surprise me. That man has the heart of a lion and the soul of a saint."

"Such men will win the war," Jean-Michel said.

The same could be said of you two, Charlotte thought. She admired courage, and Philippe and Jean-Michel had shown plenty of that. Charlotte especially respected how Philippe had been so determined to get her out of France. But the war kept throwing up obstacles.

The burned man held still while Camille dabbed salve on his face. Aloïs remained quiet. He had not spoken since he'd arrived. And he did not appear to savor this victory. Charlotte could guess why.

"You didn't find your brother?" she asked.

Aloïs shook his head. "No sign of him."

"Perhaps he wasn't there at all," Charlotte said. "The Germans certainly have other prisons."

"I fear the worst," Aloïs said.

The burned prisoner appeared to be listening, but he said nothing. Charlotte moved to his side, by the kitchen table.

"Friend," she said, "do you know of any transfers out of the prison? Anything?"

"This brother," the man said, "what was his name?"

"Thomas," Aloïs said. "Thomas Lefevre."

The man stared at the ceiling. Sighed.

"I have bad news," he said. "The Boche shot him. Two weeks ago."

Aloïs staggered, placed his hand against the wall. Closed his eyes and let out a wordless wail. Charlotte embraced him.

"I am so sorry," she whispered.

"I have no family left now," he said.

"They would have eventually shot all of us," the man said.

So the planned executions, Charlotte thought, the reason for this desperate mission, had already begun.

The man described how Thomas had been one of a dozen prisoners chosen for the firing squad. In a way, the man said, it was an honor to rank among those twelve. Of all the *résistants* at Amiens, these were the ones most hated by the Germans. The ones who had done the most damage to the Reich. The most dangerous. The most feared. Klaus Barbie, the Gestapo chief in Lyons, had listed them by name.

"When they marched them out to the wall," the burned man said, "none of them cried or begged."

A guard blindfolded the men while the firing squad stood by, their breath rising in the cold air.

"Thomas refused a blindfold," the man recounted. "He looked his executioners in the face. I do not know if they felt ashamed, but they should have."

The warden called the firing squad to attention. Read the execution order. The rifles barked. The men fell. Blood spattered the wall behind them.

An officer drew a Luger and walked down the line of fallen prisoners. The third man from the right was moving. The officer pointed his Luger, fired a *coup de grâce* to the man's head. At the last prisoner down the line, the officer stopped again.

"That was Thomas," the burned man said. "He did not speak, but he raised his hand. He gave the V for Victory sign. Defiant to the end."

That infuriated the German officer. He emptied his Luger into Thomas, fired round after round.

"Then they made us load the bodies into a truck," the burned man said. "We knew our time was coming. Some of the *résistants* vowed to go out like Thomas."

Charlotte placed her hand on Aloïs's shoulder. "I know you are grieving," she said. "I know you are in shock. But you should also be proud of him."

Aloïs did not speak for several seconds. His lower lip trembled. His eyes welled. Tears streamed down his cheeks.

"I am proud, yes," he said. "But I will avenge him. I will go kill Klaus Barbie myself."

"Please do not do that," Jean-Michel said.

"Why not?" Aloïs asked.

"You will only get yourself killed. You can imagine how well protected he is."

"What do I care?"

"You will care if they capture you and he tortures you to death."

"They will not capture me. I will make sure of that."

Aloïs looked determined, beyond reason. Charlotte decided to argue with him anyway. Maybe her words would sink in later, after he cooled down and became more rational.

"Believe me," she said, "the BCRA would have killed Barbie by now if they thought it was possible."

"So what?" Aloïs said. "I will try anyway. Someone should have tried already. I will die trying if I must."

"You will do precisely that," Philippe said. "Fight for the cause, absolutely. But do not waste yourself."

Aloïs regarded Philippe for a moment. Said nothing. Charlotte tried to gauge Aloïs's expression, and she didn't like what she saw. He did not seem distraught or despondent. He no longer appeared grief-stricken. He looked resolute.

The next morning, Aloïs was gone. Charlotte had slept across from him in the cellar. She woke to find his blanket, loaned by the safe house owner, folded neatly on the floor. He'd taken his backpack, his coat, and his .45.

She chided herself for not hearing him get up, for not stopping him. But Jean-Michel advised her not to think that way.

"You could not have stopped him," Jean-Michel said. "I believe he has decided to die for France. Sooner rather than later."

"Jean-Michel is right," Philippe said. "If Aloïs has determined he wants to die in battle, you cannot stop him. Believe me, I know."

Outside, a fresh dusting of snow settled on the tire tracks, the boot-prints, and the bloodstains. Jean-Michel and Philippe drove several of the freed prisoners to other safe houses farther from Amiens. The Resistance wanted to disburse them as widely and as quickly as possible, to prevent recapture.

That evening, when the two men returned for dinner, Jean-Michel flashed a smile—the first Charlotte had seen from him. Somehow he had gotten his hands on a bottle of Pinot Noir. He twisted the corkscrew with a practiced hand, popped out the cork. Poured just a bit into several mismatched glasses for Charlotte, Philippe, Elise, Camille, and the half-dozen prisoners who remained with them. He raised a glass.

"To Operation Jericho," Jean-Michel said. "To the RAF, to the people of France, and most of all, to you, my friends. May God bless you."

His eyes watered as he downed his wine. Then he shared the intelligence he'd gathered.

"My numbers are not precise," he said, "but we believe the prison held more than 800 inmates. More than 250 escaped. The Boche are conducting a manhunt, as you might imagine, and some, no doubt, will be recaptured. We must remain cautious."

Charlotte folded her arms, nodded. If even half of those who escaped remain free, she considered, that's more than a hundred lives saved. More than a hundred to rejoin the fight.

"What about casualties?" she asked.

"Again, my numbers are estimates," Jean-Michel said, "but we think more than ninety of our compatriots died in the bombing. There are almost as many wounded."

Sad but inevitable news. Charlotte had actually expected worse. In war's awful calculus, she chalked this up as a win. The Germans might have murdered every *résistant* in the prison in an immediate reprisal. Jean-Michel explained why that hadn't happened.

"One of the bombs scored a direct hit on the guard quarters," he said. "We do not know if that was simply luck, or if the pilots were just that good. But in any case, many of the guards died instantly."

And for some reason, he explained, the enemy was slow to react. The Germans did not send forces for more than two hours. Apparently, they had never planned for anything this audacious.

As Jean-Michel spoke, an airplane buzzed overhead. The noise faded into the distance.

"That's one of theirs," Philippe said. "They are scouring the countryside for escapees."

Jean-Michel chuckled. "They will not find the ones we drove out today."

"Why is that?" Charlotte asked.

"They are underground," Jean-Michel said. "Literally."

He described their hiding place: a series of caves out in the countryside, once used for growing mushrooms.

"The locals took the escapees to the entrance," Jean-Michel said. "I have no idea where that is."

Charlotte smiled. The Resistance enjoyed at least one advantage: The enemy could never know the territory like the natives.

"What is our next move?" she asked.

Before Jean-Michel could answer, Philippe spoke up.

"I know what mine is," Philippe said. "I want to go look at an airplane."

"What?" Jean-Michel said.

"Remember that airfield we drove by when you first brought us here? I would like another look."

"Whatever for?"

Philippe placed his forefinger against his lips as if in deep thought. After a moment, he said, "I am a pilot. I need an airplane to do my job. There are airplanes at the field, are there not?"

"Are you mad?"

"No madder than the Brits who thought up this prison raid."

"It is insane," Jean-Michel said.

"But consider," Philippe said, "the Nazis will no doubt set up a dragnet to find escaped prisoners. They will be looking for *résistants* everywhere—on the roads. But not in the air. And the airfield is so close we do not need to cross intersections and meet checkpoints along the way."

Jean-Michel placed his hands on his hips. Stared at Philippe with his mouth partly open. Shook his head. And smiled. That was only the second smile Charlotte had seen from him.

MEMORANDUM
REGARDING: Operation Donar
Gestapo Counterintelligence Corps,
Federal Intelligence Service, Lyon
Lyon, France 20 February 1944
TO: Reich Security Main Office, Berlin
FROM: Klaus Barbie, Hauptstürmfuhrer

Though several subversives who escaped from the Amiens prison have been recaptured, a number remain at large. This office—along with Gestapo departments in Paris, Marseille, and elsewhere—is redoubling efforts to find the escapees. Those efforts include aggressive interrogation of those in our custody, along with monetary rewards for those who provide information.

An air strike by British forces in cooperation with terrorist elements in France was frankly an unforeseen event. This suggests a greater level of coordination between London and subversive forces than previously realized. Radio counterintelligence, coupled with thorough interrogations and swift punishment for saboteurs and spies, should discourage the communications necessary for such operations.

Terrorist elements may feel emboldened by the recent prison break. I shall emphasize to my officers that as a possible Allied invasion becomes more imminent, we must act without mercy toward enemies of the Reich.

Heil Hitler,
Klaus Barbie, Hauptstürmfuhrer

CHAPTER 22

Philippe Gerard

O ver five days and nights, Philippe and Jean-Michel drove by the airfield at different times. They wanted to learn the patterns of its Milice guards.

There wasn't much of a pattern to learn. Sometimes there were as many as three guards. Sometimes there was just one. Sometimes they seemed to patrol with purpose, walking along the fence line. Sometimes they just stood around and smoked. Sometimes they drank. One night, two of them got into a fistfight. On the last night, a woman came by when there were three guards on duty. She entered a hangar, and one of the guards went in with her. When he came out twenty minutes later, the second guard went in for half an hour. Then he came out and the third guard took his turn. The woman left around two in the morning.

"This would have been a good time to act," Philippe said. "They have their minds on other things."

"These low-lives probably always have their minds on other things," Jean-Michel said.

The three single-engine Caudron Simouns did not fly every day. During the time Philippe and Jean-Michel watched the airfield, there were always at least two of them on the ramp. On the last night, while the guards spent time with the woman in the hangar, one of the Simouns came in and landed. From their truck, Philippe and Jean-Michel watched long enough to see a mechanic refuel the airplane.

"That is the main thing I needed to know," Philippe said. "They service the airplanes as soon as they return. It would do no good to steal an aircraft with little fuel in it."

"I still think this is insane," Jean-Michel said. "If you get off the ground, the Germans will probably shoot you down. And in the unlikely event you make it to Britain, the Brits will shoot you down."

"A Simoun is not much of a threat," Philippe said. "Rudolf Hess managed to fly to Britain in a Messerschmitt Bf-110."

Philippe reminded Jean-Michel of the bizarre story: Hess, Deputy Führer of Nazi Germany, stole a fighter plane and flew it to Scotland in 1941. Supposedly, he wanted to negotiate peace terms with the United Kingdom. Hess ran out of fuel and bailed out over Scotland. He found the British were not in a talking mood. They took him prisoner.

"He's still there," Philippe said. "I imagine he will be there for a long time."

"Serves him right," Jean-Michel said. "But I still think you're crazy."

"Perhaps I am. So, why are you helping me?"

"Because I'm as crazy as you are. That's why I'm in the BCRA. But also because you will need more help."

"I will?"

"Indeed. You are a flier, not an infantryman, and I can see how little you know of small unit tactics. What you want is a raid to seize and steal equipment. Very well. Such a mission requires more people than you and me and Charlotte."

"How many more?" Philippe asked.

"To keep this from becoming a suicide mission, at least six. These Milice guards appear incompetent and complacent, yes. But they can always call for help. We do not know how far away that help might be."

Jean-Michel explained the basics of a raiding team. Riflemen would need to seal off the area. There were two roads leading to the airfield. That required two pairs of Resistance fighters. Then the assault force would go in. That required fighters to take down the guards as quickly as possible. Jean-Michel also wanted a man whose sole job would be to find and cut the air field's telephone wires.

"This is more complex than I realized," Philippe said.

"Nothing in this business is simple."

"How soon can you get these men?"

"Two days, I believe," Jean-Michel said. "How quickly can you get the airplane off the ground?"

"That depends. If the first plane we try has fuel, oil, and a good battery, five minutes. If I have to go to another of the three Simouns, then more time."

"What if you cannot get any of them to start?"

"I doubt that will happen," Philippe said, "but it is a possibility."

"If it does happen," Jean-Michel said, "we will destroy the airplanes and retreat."

That made sense to Philippe. If the raid at least robbed the Vichy government of some airplanes, it would not have been for nothing.

Two days later, six men arrived. They spoke little. They did not smile. They did not offer their names.

And they looked hard. They dressed in black sweaters and trench coats. They were thin and unshaven. One wore a patch over his left eye. Another sported a scar that ran from his right ear down to his chest.

Their weapons were British and American, presumably airdropped by SOE. Two carried the ubiquitous STEN gun. One hefted a BREN light machine gun on a tripod. The rest carried Lee Enfield carbines. All wore web belts with grenades and .45 handguns.

Philippe listened as Jean-Michel briefed them in the safe house. They asked few questions; they seemed to regard the raid as entirely routine. Only one thing seemed to surprise them: They glanced at Philippe when Jean-Michel explained that the primary goal was to steal an airplane. Once he got airborne, they would destroy the rest. If he could not get airborne, they would destroy them all.

The group decided to go ahead right away. Charlotte gathered up her maps. Philippe strapped on his gunbelt with the Webley in its holster. Jean-Michel gave them a loaf of bread and two canteens filled with

174

THE MAPMAKER

water. In the deep pockets of his overcoat, Jean-Michel placed a revolver and a dagger. At midnight, he drove them to the airfield. The assault team drove in a separate truck.

When they came within sight of the airfield, Jean-Michel turned off the vehicle's headlamps. He slowed down, crept in the darkness to a copse of poplars by the airfield's perimeter road.

The assault team stopped their own truck and dropped off two gunmen, who climbed into the back of Jean-Michel's truck. The rest of the team continued around the airfield to an entrance on the other side. Charlotte and Philippe rode in the cab with Jean-Michel as he drove up the road to the airfield's main entrance. They stopped several hundred yards from the airfield's gate.

The two assault team members jumped down from the truck bed. One of the fighters eyed the wires that stretched from poles along the road. Philippe supposed he was noting the telephone connections. The man pulled on black gloves and checked the wire cutters in his pocket. His partner appeared with a blanket folded over his arm.

"What is that for?" Philippe whispered.

"There is barbed wire at the top of the fence," Jean-Michel said.

For several minutes they watched the guards patrol the airfield. There seemed to be only two. They strolled in opposite directions along the fence. They smoked, carried their rifles slung over their shoulders.

"When the guards get well away from the gate," Jean-Michel said, "Henri and Claude will go over the fence."

A few minutes later, the two men sprinted through the darkness. Philippe lost sight of them for a moment. Then he saw two shadowy figures at the fence. They threw the blanket across the barbed wire. Both clambered over the fence. One remained close to the fence, crouched low, clutched his STEN gun, and waited. The other, with the wire cutters, disappeared into the darkness. A few minutes later he reappeared next to his comrade. Waved the wire cutters.

Jean-Michel drove toward the airfield. At the sound of an approaching vehicle, one of the Milice guards began running toward the gate. He kept his weapon slung across his shoulder. Perhaps he expected the

175

normal routine; he would check the identification of a Vichy pilot about to fly some errand for the regime.

A burst from the STEN put him on the ground. Jean-Michel stomped the accelerator. Crashed through the wooden barrier lowered across the gate. The *résistants* inside the fence rushed toward the truck, ready to defend its occupants. One stopped and fired toward the hangar at a target Philippe could not see.

Jean-Michel raced across the ramp. Skidded to a stop beside the three Simouns parked in a row. Philippe leaped from the cab. Headed for the nearest aircraft. Jean-Michel held a flashlight for him as he opened a fuel filler cap on top of the left wing. Good—that tank was full. He checked the right tank. Full as well. He kicked the chocks away from the tires.

At the darkened hangar, lights flickered on.

"Damn it," Jean-Michel said. "Somebody's waking up." He thrust the flashlight into Charlotte's hands. "Hold this for him. You two fire up this airplane and get out of here."

Philippe climbed atop the left wing. Yanked open the door. Slid into the pilot's seat. Charlotte entered on the right side. Flung her map bag, the canteens, and bread into the back of the plane. Played the flashlight across the instrument panel.

Philippe had never flown this model. He thought of how Saint-Ex had flown a Farman from France to Algiers back in 1940 when the *Armée de l'Air* was evacuating. Saint-Ex had never flown that model, either. But he wasn't in this big a hurry. And the airbase wasn't under fire. Philippe scanned the panel, searched for the fuel primer knob. There.

He twisted the knob. Pulled it toward him. Felt the fuel coursing into the lines. Pressed in the knob. Pulled it back out again. Repeated the process four times. Now, where was the battery switch? Philippe swept his fingers across the panel. Found the switch next to the starter button. He flipped the switch. He waited for the hum of current and a bounce on the voltmeter.

Nothing. Dead battery.

"*Merde*," Philippe hissed. He pointed to the next aircraft. "We'll try that one," he said.

176

Charlotte grabbed her things and climbed out the right door. Philippe exited and slid down the left wing. Gunfire chattered around him. Jean-Michel squeezed off shots with his pistol. Philippe forced himself to ignore the firefight.

At the second Simoun, he repeated the process: Checked the fuel. Kicked away the chocks. Climbed in and primed the carburetor. Flipped the battery switch. The panel lit up with backlighting.

"There are more men outside," Charlotte warned.

Philippe glanced through the windscreen. Dark figures darted across the tarmac. A stitch of gunfire felled one of them. Another of them swung a weapon and returned fire. Philippe brought his attention back inside. Shoved the fuel mixture to full rich. Cracked open the throttle. Flipped the magneto switch to BOTH.

"Come on, my dear," he whispered. "Start for me."

He pressed the starter button. The starter rattled. For a moment, Philippe thought its shaft had sheared. Then the propeller swung around, once, twice. Three times.

The engine fired. Belched smoke. Exhaust filled Philippe's nostrils. The whole aircraft shook and vibrated.

Jean-Michel turned and grinned. Then a bullet took off the top of his head. He dropped from sight.

More gunfire echoed from across the ramp. Apparently, a number of guards had been asleep in the hangar. The Resistance fighters positioned outside the airfield had rushed in to engage. Men crouched, ran, fired, took cover.

Charlotte pulled her .45 from her bag. Gripped it with both hands.

Philippe watched the oil pressure rise. Released the parking brake.

Two bullets punched through the windscreen. Splinters, either of lead or Plexiglas, stung Philippe's face. He glanced at Charlotte. She appeared unhurt. The rounds had passed right between them.

With a shove of the throttle, the Simoun began to roll. Philippe taxied across the tarmac, toward the runway. Pushed up the power to taxi faster.

On the right side of the aircraft, a man raced up to the Simoun. Aimed a rifle.

Charlotte fired through her window. Two quick shots. Beyond the two white holes, Philippe saw the gunman fall.

Philippe rolled down the taxiway, steering the nosewheel with the rudder pedals. Didn't bother to look for a wind sock. Wind direction didn't matter tonight—he just needed to get to the nearest end of the runway.

At the runway threshold, he lined up on the center. Pressed the throttle all the way to the stop. The propeller blurred into invisibility. The Renault engine screamed. Philippe released the toe brakes.

The Simoun began to roll. The centerline stripes grew shorter and shorter as the aircraft accelerated. Philippe guessed 80 knots was more than fast enough for the Simoun to get airborne. As the airspeed indicator swung through 80, he eased back on the stick.

The Simoun lifted into the night. Muzzle flashes sparkled from the ground. Something slammed into the tail, then into the cowling. But the aircraft continued to fly. Philippe pulled the stick back farther, pitched the nose up. He wanted the Simoun's best angle of climb, to get out of range of small arms.

"Are they still firing?" he asked.

Charlotte turned in her seat. "I can't see them anymore," she said. "Maybe not."

Philippe banked left, watched the compass swing toward the west. He had no chart, no flight plan. Nothing to guide him but memory and the earth's magnetism. But he'd flown between France and England often enough to have some idea of his position.

The weather had cleared since the recent snows. Stars danced across the skies. With little light pollution during the blackout, the Milky Way appeared as a swath of stardust. Philippe could even make out its pink glow. Moonbeams set the ground aglow, highlighted the angles of rooftops.

"*Mon Dieu*, I cannot believe we did it," Charlotte said. "You're brilliant."

"We have not done it yet," he said. "Not all the way. Please keep scanning. We're looking for ground fire, fighter planes, anything."

178

"Yes, I will." Charlotte's seat was aft and to the right of the pilot's seat. She leaned forward to see better through the windscreen.

"Jean-Michel gave his life so we could get away," Philippe said.

For a moment he remembered his dead crewmates in the Bloch years ago. Then he pushed away the memory, deep down into some mental *oubliette*. A dungeon for thoughts he could not handle now. He would deal with that later. Tonight, he had work to do.

"Yes, I saw," Charlotte said. "Others, too, perhaps."

She sounded so matter-of-fact. Philippe suspected she had built her own *oubliette*.

When he judged they were safely away from the guns at the airfield, he changed tactics. In these clear skies, a night fighter could find him on radar, then pick him up visually with ease. He pulled back the throttle to begin a descent.

"Now we get low," he explained. "Harder to see us on radar."

The Simoun skimmed the ground. Pastures and forests flowed under its wings. Philippe prayed his low flight would avoid enemy detection. The Simoun was hardly a high-performance aircraft; its landing gear wasn't even retractable. She was designed for peacetime airmail and light cargo, not high-G evasive maneuvers. An easy target for a Focke-Wulf or a Messerschmitt.

Philippe scanned his panel. The oil temperature needle crept higher and higher. Oil pressure was low. Why? What was wrong? He checked his fuel mixture. It was still set to full rich, so he knew he wasn't running the engine too lean. What about oil quantity? He looked around the panel. No oil quantity gauge.

"Is something wrong?" Charlotte asked.

He tapped the oil temp gauge. "We're running hot," he said. "I don't know why."

Then he remembered the thumps against the tail and cowling right after takeoff. Had a bullet hit the engine? Nicked an oil line or a sump?

Philippe leaned forward, tried to get a better look at the cowling. He could see only part of it, but he spotted no damage. He checked the fuel gauge. No problem there, at least. Plenty of gas.

Ahead, breakers crashed white against the French shoreline. Philippe flew over the beach, headed out over the Channel.

He adjusted his course, turned farther west. Aimed for the Strait of Dover, which would give him the shortest route over the water. Philippe had hoped to land at his home base of Tangmere. But with the engine running hot, he decided he'd settle for anywhere in Britain. Any base. Even a highway or a farmer's field. He counted the minutes, tracked his progress over the sea.

After several miles, Philippe scanned the cowling again. He still saw no obvious damage, though it was hard to tell in the darkness. He brought his eyes back inside, checked the altimeter. Then he glanced back up at the windscreen.

"Son of a bitch," he whispered in English.

Flecks spattered the glass. Oil, spraying from the engine.

He checked the oil temperature. The needle was pegged. And the oil pressure needle read nearly zero. The Simoun shook as the engine began to run rough.

Philippe recalled flying advice he'd heard from Saint-Ex: Fly the wings, not the engine. That meant don't drag in low on approach. Fly the landing pattern so that if the engine quits, you can still make the runway.

There would be no making a runway tonight. Philippe would need to fly the engine until there was no more engine. Then he'd have to fly the wings to a controlled ditching.

He pitched up to gain altitude while he still could. That would buy more time to set up for ditching. Ideally, he'd splash down into the wind and parallel to the swells.

The coastline passed under the wheels. The altimeter registered a climb.

"Are we going to make it?" Charlotte asked.

Philippe shook his head.

"I hope you can swim," he said.

CHAPTER 23

Charlotte Denneau

Charlotte could swim, but she knew it hardly mattered. In the cold waters of the winter English Channel, she and Philippe wouldn't last long. Hypothermia could claim them long before a U-boat surfaced to take them prisoner. Rescue by the Allies seemed only remotely possible. No one knew they were coming. At least not yet.

"Can you reach someone on the radio?" she asked.

"I'll try," Philippe said. He reached over to the radio set and tuned a frequency. Fiddled with knobs on the radio for a moment, then lifted a hand microphone.

"Handy," he transmitted. "This is a French civilian aircraft over the English Channel. How do you read?"

No answer but static.

"Handy, Handy," Philippe called. "This is a French civilian aircraft. How do you read?"

More hiss.

"Who is Handy?" Charlotte asked.

"That is the call sign for the RAF's Blackgang radar station."

For a moment, Charlotte pondered the wisdom of making a radio call in the clear. What if the Germans were listening, too? But she realized the alternative was dying of exposure. There was no choice.

Philippe called a third time. The response, if it was a response at all, was unreadable. Just a warbling amid the squelch. Charlotte couldn't make out words, or even the language.

"I'll just transmit in the blind," Philippe said. Then he keyed the microphone again: "Any station, any station. This is a French civilian aircraft with Allied personnel. Repeat, we are Allied personnel. We are east of the Isle of Wight. Our engine is damaged. We are going down in the water."

More warbling and hiss.

Philippe repeated his position report. Then he said to Charlotte, "Look around the airplane. See if you can find anything we can use. Especially life jackets."

Charlotte unbuckled her seat belt and crawled aft. Her search revealed no life jackets. No provisions, other than the canteens and bread from Jean-Michel. Just a maintenance logbook in a plastic pouch and a Very pistol with flare cartridges. She returned to her seat and showed Philippe the flare gun.

"*Bon*," he said. He shoved the Very pistol into his coat pocket. Then he prepared Charlotte for ditching. "*Écoutez-moi*," he said. "I cannot bring up the landing gear. That means the aircraft will probably flip when it hits the water. That will be disorienting. Tighten your harness. But keep your hand on the buckle so you can release it when you need to. And unlatch your door now. You'll never get it open in the dark and underwater."

Charlotte followed his instructions. She watched him pop open the door on his side. The slipstream kept the doors closed, but they remained unlatched.

The engine ran rougher, made a grinding noise. The Simoun vibrated as if it would shake apart.

"My maps!" Charlotte said. In their map case inside her canvas bag, they would get soaked. All the work, all the risk, all the *lives*, would be for nothing. The bag had protected the maps and charts from light rain well enough, but it would provide little help in the open sea.

Charlotte remembered the maintenance log in its plastic pouch. She reached behind her, grabbed the log. Tore it from the pouch and dropped it. Then she selected the most important maps—the ones with the most detail on rail lines. Stuffed them into the pouch and snapped it closed. She placed the pouch into her canvas bag and looped the strap over her head and across her chest. About half her charts and drawings remained outside the pouch, unprotected from the water. She hoped they'd at least remain intact. Perhaps they could be dried out and salvaged later.

A bang sounded from the engine. The vibration stopped.

The engine went silent, dead. The only sound came from the wind whispering across the wings. The Simoun began a slow descent.

"I don't know the best glide speed for this thing," Philippe said. "I guess around ninety."

He showed no emotion. Charlotte realized he was too busy to get scared. For that, she envied him, because she was terrified.

Moonlight lent a copper hue to the sea below. The waves grew larger as the aircraft descended. Charlotte scanned the water. She saw no ships in any direction. She didn't know what would be worse: getting picked up by a German vessel and turned over to the Gestapo, or dying a slow death of exposure. Or drowning.

She eyed the compass. Philippe was still heading west, trying to get as close to the British coastline as possible. The shore did not appear in the windscreen; Charlotte saw only the waves heaving as they stretched to a dim horizon.

The air, untroubled by turbulence, offered a smooth ride as the Simoun glided toward the sea. The quiet descent felt almost tranquil— and entirely dissonant with the danger that lurked below. The plane seemed suspended in the sky. For a moment Charlotte felt transported to an alternate reality above and away from the war.

But the war and its dangers became immediate again when Philippe turned to line up with the swells. The altimeter read one thousand feet and descending.

"Brace," Philippe said.

Charlotte clutched her bag with one hand and held on to her harness buckle with the other. The dark water rose to meet the aircraft. The wheels touched the waves.

The world upended. Or so it seemed to Charlotte when the Simoun pitched nose down into the Channel. The tail swung up and over. The sea rushed in. In that moment, Charlotte sensed little but vertigo and cold. Saltwater silenced her involuntary scream. She coughed and gagged. But she retained enough presence of mind to open the release on her harness. With her elbow, she shoved open her door. Tried to escape the airplane. But something trapped her.

In the black water, she could not see what held her by her shoulder. She struggled. Felt the panic of drowning. Choked as seawater fill her nostrils.

Then whatever murderous force tried to drown her—perhaps the harness's shoulder strap—released her. She pulled herself through the open door.

The cold water numbed her. Charlotte felt she was fighting through frigid mud. But somehow she popped to the surface. Gagged again. Vomited seawater. Found herself floating next to the Simoun, which lay awash and upside down.

She tried to call out, but managed only a wordless rasp. She coughed again, spat out water. Struggled to keep her head above water.

"Philippe," she said. Tried to shout, but hardly whispered. Coughed again. Took in a deep breath and shouted, "Philippe!"

"Here," Philippe yelled. The noise came from the other side of the aircraft. "I'm here," Philippe said. He climbed, dripping, onto the Simoun's underbelly. "Give me your hand," he said. Stretched out his arm.

Charlotte reached for his hand. Missed. A swell lifted the aircraft and pulled it away from her.

"Philippe!" she screamed. She kicked, tried to swim. Found her efforts useless against the current.

Another swell caught her. This time it pushed her back to the Simoun. Her head hit the fuselage. Dazed, she lost consciousness and slipped beneath the surface.

When Charlotte came to, she was lying between the Simoun's landing gear struts. Somehow, Philippe had pulled her from the sea. She vomited water again. Then a coughing jag racked her lungs. She sucked in a ragged breath. Began to shiver.

Philippe held onto her, kept her from sliding back into the Channel. She wanted to thank him, to say *something*, but she lacked the strength. She could only breathe and shiver. She did notice that the strap for her bag was still looped over her chest, so she still had the maps.

With each minute, she grew colder. She supposed that if she were still in the water, she'd be dead by now. Philippe had lain down on top of her, helped keep her from sliding off. His embrace implied no intimacy; it was simply a matter of survival. His body heat warmed her—but only to a more survivable level of misery. She almost wished she'd drowned. Then, at least, this would all be over.

Charlotte had no idea how long they drifted in the frigid water. She felt Philippe shivering just as uncontrollably as herself. When the sunrise revealed his face, she saw his lips were blue.

She knew they couldn't last much longer. More than likely, they would die in each other's arms. And soon. Charlotte wondered what future she might have had with Philippe in better circumstances. When she finally found the strength to speak, she whispered, "You did your best. I thank you."

He did not respond. With the heel of his hand on the bottom of the aircraft, he pushed himself off her. Raised himself to a sitting position. His hands trembled.

"Do you hear that?" he said.

Charlotte heard nothing but the slap of waves against the Simoun. She shook her head.

"Do you hear that?" Philippe repeated.

Still nothing.

But a moment later she noticed a faint buzz.

"Aha!" Philippe shouted. He pointed into the sky. "There. It's a Defiant."

Charlotte peered upward. She discerned a single-engine aircraft circling overhead. She did not recognize it, but Philippe clearly knew what it was.

"That's the RAF's Marine Branch," he said. "They patrol for downed aircrews. Maybe someone heard our radio calls."

Philippe fumbled for the Very pistol in his coat pocket. With shaking hands, he opened the breech. Dug into the pocket for a flare cartridge. Dropped it. The cartridge rolled into the water. He shoved his hand back into the wet pocket and found another cartridge. His fingers trembled so violently Charlotte doubted he could load the flare pistol. But finally, he inserted the cartridge and closed the breech. Aimed straight up. Pressed the trigger.

The flare launch blinded Charlotte for a second. But then she watched the flare arc into the sky like a miniature comet. The Defiant rolled into a descending turn. Whooshed over Charlotte and Philippe. Rocked its wings.

"They see us!" Philippe cried. "They see us!"

"What will they do?" Charlotte asked.

"They will send a boat or a seaplane."

"*Dieu merci*," Charlotte said. "If it gets here in time."

They waited for what felt like hours. Charlotte was sure she would have died from hypothermia if Philippe had not lain over her. Perhaps her own body heat saved him as well. There was nothing romantic in the embrace; it was purely a matter of survival.

But the sea brought another torment. The swells rose higher with the sunrise. Lying on the underbelly of the aircraft, Charlotte could not see the horizon. Nausea overtook her. She began vomiting again, this time from seasickness. But she hadn't eaten anything in so long she brought up only bile. Vomiting brought no relief. Philippe threw up, too. He retched and coughed.

Despite the cold, Charlotte grew thirsty. She drank from the one canteen Philippe had managed to save. But she could not keep even water in her stomach. Philippe suffered in the same way. He drank deeply, then vomited.

Eventually, the sound of aircraft engines rose in the distance. Charlotte forced herself to sit up. Shaded her eyes with her hand. Scanned the western sky. For long seconds she saw nothing.

And when she spotted the planes, her heart sank. The noise came not from a rescue aircraft, but from a formation of bombers way up, droning toward the Reich.

She watched them inch across the heavens. Wished she was aboard one of them. Anywhere but on this ditched Simoun, with cold water washing across it. Salt spray stung her eyes, added to the discomfort of cold and nausea.

As she eyed the bombers, she did not notice the other aircraft. Philippe rose up on his knees. Turned and pointed.

"There!" he cried.

Charlotte turned around and looked. A strange machine approached, just a few hundred feet above the water. A large biplane with a tub-like fuselage. The thing looked to Charlotte like it could barely fly. A single propeller mounted amidships, above the fuselage, pushed the aircraft over the Channel. Pontoons hung from the lower wings. The plane bore the red, white, and blue roundel of the RAF.

"What is that?" she asked.

"A Walrus," Philippe said. "I think it's a Supermarine Walrus. It can land in the water and pick us up."

"Thank heaven," Charlotte said.

The Walrus descended as it approached. When it touched down a hundred yards away, spray enveloped the aircraft. For an instant, Charlotte wondered if the plane had crashed. But it emerged atop a swell, cut a white wake across the sea. Rocked with the waves as it slowed. Turned toward the Simoun.

A crewman opened a hatch in the bow of the Walrus. Waved to Charlotte and Philippe. He lifted a floating throw ring attached to a line. When the Walrus came within thirty yards, the crewman called out.

"Good morning, sirs," the man said. Scottish accent. Then he added, "Ah, good morning, sir and ma'am."

TOM YOUNG

The seaplane's engine hushed to idle power. The prop turned so slowly one could almost count the revolutions. The Walrus drifted closer. Philippe pointed to Charlotte.

"Take the lady first," he shouted. "She's terribly cold."

"Yes, sir," the crewman said. "I suspect you're both right chilled. Can you catch a line?"

"Yes."

The crewman heaved the throw ring with a practiced hand. The ring sailed across the water and splashed next to the Simoun. Philippe reached for it, picked it up. But he shivered so hard he could not hold onto it. The ring dropped into the sea and floated away from the Simoun.

"Let me help you," the crewman said. "We'll get you inside and sipping hot tea in a jiff." He took hold of the line and pulled it hand over hand back into the Walrus. Held onto the throw ring. Turned toward the cockpit and made a hand signal toward the pilot.

The pilot revved the engine slightly. The Walrus nosed into the Simoun with a gentle thump. The crewman in the bow pitched the throw ring into the water.

"Ma'am, I'm going to take hold of you and pull you in," he said. "If you fall or I drop you, just grab ahold of the line."

Charlotte stretched out her arm. The man took her by the hand.

"Can you stand up?" he asked.

Charlotte tried to rise, but her cold-numbed joints would not obey. She felt the man's grip slipping from her hand. With her other hand, she reached for the Simoun's landing gear strut to steady herself. Started to get up.

A swell knocked her off balance. The crewman lost his grip altogether. Charlotte tumbled into the water.

She felt herself sinking. She tried to kick, to swim. But she could not move. Now she was so cold she could not even form thoughts. Charlotte knew she was about to drown. And she didn't care.

Something tightened around her chest. A force hauled her upward. She saw daylight again, but could not comprehend. Then she saw the line wrapped around her, and the drenched crewman pulling her aboard the Walrus.

The crewman placed her on a fold-down cot in the belly of the aircraft. Another man wrapped blankets around her. A moment later, the men pulled Philippe inside. They strapped him down on another cot, and they covered him with blankets as well. One of the men closed the bow hatch. The engine howled. Charlotte felt the aircraft plow through the waves and accelerate.

The Walrus lifted off the water. Bounced across the top of a swell. The plane shuddered with the impact. Then its wings took full purchase of the air.

The pilot rolled into a climbing turn and set a course for England.

CHAPTER 24

Lisette Gerard

Two Daimler-Benz trucks and a Mercedes staff car sat parked outside a boarding house in Montauban. Lisette and Olivier watched the vehicles and the building from a block away. It was two in the morning; they hoped they would see no activity and no passersby.

A brief encrypted radio contact from Virginia Hall had given them the go-ahead for this mission. Resistance intel had confirmed officers from *Das Reich*, the 2nd SS Panzer Division, used the boarding house for billeting. One part of Plan *Tortue* called for destroying or disabling as many German vehicles as possible. *Das Reich*'s main motor pool, dozens of tanks and trucks, would have made a good target—except it was too heavily guarded. Virginia deemed it more practical to hit the three vehicles that were usually parked at the boarding house.

"Do you have your tools ready?" Lisette asked.

"Of course," Olivier said. He didn't need much in the way of tools. Just a chisel and a ball peen hammer. He showed them to Lisette, then slid them back into his overcoat pockets. "What about you?" he asked.

"Right here," she said. Lisette didn't need much, either. Just a flint cigarette lighter. She showed him—a brass trench lighter from the previous war.

The street remained quiet. The night hung heavy with mist. The damp deepened the cold and slicked the cobblestones. Made Lisette's shoulders hurt, as well. Her wounds had healed, at least technically. But in wet weather, her body remembered the bullets. She ignored the pain as best she could. Reminded herself she was too young to feel old.

Lisette and Olivier began walking toward the German vehicles. If their plan worked, they would need to hit only one of them. The fire would take care of the other two. If flames spread to the boarding house and killed some of the enemy, so much the better.

Lisette realized the thought gave her no remorse. Sometimes she wondered if the war was hardening her in ways she could not undo. Before the Germans invaded, she wanted only to be a loving mother someday. A simple wish from a simple girl. But would a woman inured to violence still make a fit mother?

The question would have to wait. If Lisette lived to have children, she wanted them to grow up free.

When they reached the first truck, the boarding house door opened. A man in a leather coat emerged. Officer's cap on his head, cigarette between his fingers. Lisette felt a spike of dread in her chest. But she remembered her training.

"Good evening, sir," she said. She giggled. Placed her arm around Olivier's waist and weaved across the sidewalk like a pair of drunk lovers. Walked a half mile away, well out of sight in the darkness.

"That was close," Olivier whispered.

Lisette breathed a long sigh. They waited and watched for an hour. Lisette became hyperalert to every sound. She noted every distant train whistle. Heard every dog's bark. Jumped at the screech of two cats fighting.

"Do we abort?" Lisette whispered. Technically, Olivier was in charge. But he treated Lisette more like a colleague than an underling.

"I don't think so," Olivier said. "If we come back again, the weather might be better. More people out and about."

"*Bon*," Lisette said.

They watched for another fifteen minutes. Nothing moved on the street. Olivier pulled out his hammer and chisel. Strode toward the boarding house. Lisette followed him with lighter in hand.

He chose the middle vehicle, one of the trucks. Got down on his knees, crawled under the Daimler-Benz.

Lisette heard two quick bangs. Olivier scrambled out from under the truck. Fuel poured from its ruptured tank.

The pool of gasoline spread under the staff car and the other truck. Lisette waited for the fuel to spread a little wider.

She flicked her lighter. Dropped it into the fuel.

The flames lit off with a *whoosh*. For an instant, the fire's glare blinded her.

Lisette and Olivier sprinted down the street to a waiting getaway car.

CHAPTER 25

Philippe Gerard

In his hospital bed at Colchester Garrison, Philippe could not contain his rage. He glared at Squadron Leader Venable and the SOE man, Milton. Or whatever the hell his name was. Philippe sat up. His water glass trembled in his hand. He hurled the glass against the wall.

Milton ducked. Glass shards and water droplets showered him.

"YOU SENT HER BACK?" Philippe shouted. "I brought her out because the Nazis almost killed her!"

"Lieutenant Gerard, you will maintain your military bearing!" Venable yelled. "I could have you court-martialed for this."

Milton straightened his jacket. Adjusted his bow tie.

"That won't be necessary," he said. "I understand how the Lieutenant must feel. But it was Lisette's decision. Purely voluntary."

"You should not have even given her the opportunity," Philippe said.

"Well, it wasn't me personally," Milton said.

Philippe folded his arms. Looked out the window. British rain, slanted by a winter wind, lashed at the panes.

"The other news we have for you, Lieutenant," Venable said, "is that the RAF has approved your transfer back to the *Armée de l'Air*. When the doctors release you, you will rejoin your old unit in North Africa."

"Good." After a moment, Philippe added, "Sir."

Still furious, he kept his eyes on the window. He decided not to push his luck and say what he was thinking: *Good, because I have had enough of you Brits.*

Finally, he looked at Venable and said, "How is Charlotte?" He hadn't seen her since their rescue in the Channel. And he was surprised how much he missed her.

"She is well, under the circumstances. She is recovering from hypothermia, just like you. I say, that was quite sporting of you to steal an airplane and make your getaway." Venable placed his hands on his hips. "That is why I'm not sending you to the brig this instant."

At Duxford Airfield, near Cambridge, Philippe strapped himself into the pilot's seat of a P-38 Lightning. The RAF had turned the base over to the Americans, who designated it USAAF Station 357. Just as Saint-Ex had said, the P-38 was indeed a "flying torpedo." The fastest, most powerful aircraft Philippe had ever flown. And the strangest-looking. A central nacelle housed the cockpit, flanked by two engines mounted at the front of twin booms. The booms connected to a tail section with a pair of horizontal stabilizers. To Philippe, the Lightning looked like something out of the distant future. And it looked fast even when sitting still.

After getting clearance from a flight surgeon, Philippe had received an assignment for P-38 transition training at Duxford, under tutelage of American instructors. The first thing he'd learned was that he spoke English—but not American. When the Brits referred to Greenwich Mean Time, they called it "Zed." To the Yanks, GMT was "Zulu time." "Brakes off time" was "takeoff time." Many aircraft components had French names, such as "aileron" and "fuselage," but Americans murdered the pronunciation. Some of their accents were indecipherable. And who in heaven's name was "y'all?"

Philippe wondered how Saint-Ex, who spoke little English, had ever gotten through P-38 training.

His instructor, a captain from Texas named Bobby, slapped the side of the aircraft.

"Hey, Phil," Bobby said. "You saddled up and ready to ride?"

194

"Ah, yes, sir." Philippe hated the new nickname but didn't say so to the captain.

"All right. We'll fly what we briefed. You stay on my wing. We get out to the practice area and you show me the maneuvers. Then we'll do a short cross-country route. If it all goes well, I'll sign you off and you'll be a sure-enough Lightning driver."

"Yes, sir."

"You do good today and when we finish the debrief we'll have ourselves a cool, refreshing barley pop."

"Very good, sir."

Evidently, Captain Bobby was talking about having a beer. Philippe would have preferred wine, but he'd raise a glass of anything to celebrate qualifying on the P-38—and getting free of this crazy American instructor.

The captain climbed aboard his own aircraft, and Philippe pulled on his leather helmet and gloves. A crew chief rolled a fire extinguisher in front of Philippe's plane and stood fire guard for engine start. The crew chief gave him a thumbs up, and Philippe flipped on the battery switch.

The whines and hums of a high-performance airplane waking up gave Philippe a little turn of anticipation down in his gut. The artificial horizon trembled, then steadied itself as its gyroscope began spinning. He turned the fuel crossfeed switch off, checked the mixture levers in idle cutoff, switched the oil cooler flaps to AUTO. Flipped on the generator and magneto switches for the left engine.

"Clear left propeller," Philippe called out the window.

"Clear, sir," the crew chief answered.

Philippe pushed up the switch for the left engine's inertial starter, waited for the starter to wind up, then pressed ENGAGE and PRIME. The left engine sputtered, coughed, and roared to life. Philippe pushed the left mixture control forward, and he checked to see the engine's oil pressure rising.

He repeated the start procedure for the right engine, then let both engines idle until their temperatures reached 40 degrees Centigrade. While he waited, he closed and locked the side windows. Captain Bobby had put the fear of God into him about not forgetting to close those windows. Open canopy windows would disturb airflow over the twin tail of the P-38 and cause all kinds of problems.

"That ain't a design flaw," Bobby had told him. "You can't build an idiot-proof airplane, 'cause idiots shouldn't be flying."

Philippe looked to his left, at his instructor's aircraft. Bobby signaled with a thumbs up, and Philippe responded with the same gesture. Bobby called the tower for taxi clearance, and his aircraft began to roll. Philippe released his parking brake and followed the instructor's P-38 to the departure end of the runway. At the tower's clearance, Bobby accelerated down the runway. A few seconds later, Philippe rolled onto the centerline and pressed his throttles forward.

As the Lightning gathered speed, the centerline stripes grew shorter and shorter. When the airspeed needle crept past ninety miles an hour, Philippe pulled back on the yoke, and the aircraft leaped into the sky.

Fields, pastures, and fence lines of East Anglia flowed beneath him. A farmer waved from a horse cart. The P-38 shuddered in light turbulence caused by thermals rising from the ground during the early-spring sunrise. Philippe joined up on Bobby's wing, switched to a discrete frequency they could use for their own conversations.

"Wow, look at all those bases," Bobby said.

Philippe scanned the ground. From this altitude—climbing through 5,000 feet—he could see air base after air base dotting the countryside. He'd heard Britain described as an "unsinkable aircraft carrier." And from this perspective, he saw why. Every few seconds, it seemed, he overflew a base marked with a triangle of intersecting runways.

The bases were busy, too. At one, B-17 Flying Fortresses lined up on a taxiway. At another, P-51 Mustangs lifted off. At yet another, B-24 Liberators climbed to join formation.

Perhaps France has a future, Philippe thought. All this power, all these men and machines massing just across the Channel from Hitler's Fortress Europe. The sight made him think of physics classes on potential energy: a coiled spring, a drawn bow, a ticking bomb. He wondered what the *résistants* back home would say if they could see all this.

Bobby turned toward the northwest, away from the busy airspace. Philippe followed. After a few minutes, Bobby radioed: "All right, partner. I've cleared the area for you. Show me a recovery from a full stall."

Philippe checked his fuel mixture levers at full rich, shoved the propeller pitch levers to max RPM. Pulled the throttles back to idle and let the aircraft slow down.

As the plane decelerated, he held more and more back pressure on the yoke to maintain altitude. The nose crept higher. Near stall speed, the wings began to buffet. Then the Lightning broke into a full stall, no longer flying. The nose dropped through the horizon. Philippe found himself looking through the windscreen at trees and fields.

He advanced the throttles, held the nose down until the aircraft picked up speed. Flying again now, Philippe eased the nose back up to the horizon.

"Very good," Bobby radioed. "Now gimme a steep turn."

This was pretty basic stuff. Philippe had done this in every plane he'd flown. But the USAAF wanted to check boxes before it turned over a hundred-thousand-dollar aircraft to a foreign pilot. He'd flown his first few flights with Bobby in a two-seat training version of the P-38. But the two-seaters were few and in high demand. Once he'd received his solo endorsement, he never saw the training model again.

Philippe rolled into a sixty-degree turn. The horizon twisted across his windscreen. He added a little power. The airspeed indicator held steady at 200 miles per hour, and the altimeter locked onto 5,000 feet as if the machine were on rails.

He followed with a loop and an Immelmann turn. The Immelmann—a half loop with a roll back to level flight—put him on his instructor's six o'clock, in perfect firing position. However, Philippe didn't expect to do any firing when he rejoined the 2/33 in North Africa. There, he would fly a photorecon version of the P-38, known as the F-5. The F-5 carried cameras instead of guns. If he got jumped by a German fighter, he'd have to outrun it or outmaneuver it. Not exactly a dogfight if he couldn't shoot back. Still, the tactics might save his life. The instructor put him through a series of turns and dives to make himself a difficult target.

"All right, enough of that," Bobby said. "Let's see if you can find Stonehenge."

Philippe rolled his eyes. He'd been finding tiny pastures at night in the Lysander, and now the Yanks wanted to know if he could find an obvious landmark in broad daylight. Yet he didn't complain. He'd served in the *Armée de l'Air* and the RAF long enough to understand military bureaucracy. Why should the USAAF be any different?

"Roger that," Philippe said. "I'll take the lead."

He pulled a chart from a lower leg pocket of his flight suit. Unfolded it across his kneeboard. Noted his position, took a bearing on his radio compass. Bobby banked to the right, then joined up on Philippe's wing.

In cruise flight, Philippe took a moment simply to enjoy flying the P-38. Though he'd logged no more than twenty hours in the Lightning, he already felt part of the machine. The aircraft was so maneuverable its flight controls seemed an extension of his mind. He could transmit his will through fingertips on the yoke. And at high altitude, the aircraft actually became part of his body, in a manner of speaking. Up there, where he'd do his photo work, he could not live without supplemental oxygen. The mask and hose became as vital as his heart and lungs.

When the rolling hills of Wiltshire passed under his wings, Philippe looked for the runways of RAF Lyneham, near the town of Swindon. Then he turned south.

And there it was—on the Salisbury Plain, the famed stone circle. For a moment, Philippe mused about flying over the prehistoric monument in some of the twentieth century's highest technology. A thing beyond the imagining of Stonehenge's builders. But how far had we really come? Philippe had heard rumors of concentration camps turned to death factories; this modern war had brought depravity on an industrial scale.

A radio call interrupted his dark thoughts.

"Very good," Bobby said. "Next waypoint."

That one was even easier. Philippe rolled onto a southeasterly heading. He changed frequencies, checked in with Blackgang to tell the radar operators he was leading a flight of two friendly aircraft. Then he looked for a town at the confluence of the River Test and the River Itchen.

Barrage balloons floated over Southampton. Philippe and Bobby soared high above them; they were meant to impede low-flying German dive bombers. For years now, the *Luftwaffe* had made repeated raids against the port city. But the British kept repairing the docks and rebuilding the factories.

The docks bristled with cranes for loading cargo and ammunition. Ships lined the docks. In fact, as Philippe scanned through the barrage balloons, he realized he'd never seen so many ships. The docks were full—and scores of vessels waiting their turn lay at anchor in Southampton Water: freighters, landing ships, all manner of warships. Philippe was not a Navy man; he wouldn't have known a battleship from a destroyer. But he knew that even for wartime, this was a tremendous massing of force.

Farther down the channel at Portsmouth he saw the same thing: rows of ships under a skyline guarded by barrage balloons. The scene made him wish he was flying a photorecon bird right now; he would take a picture for Lisette.

That was fantasy, of course. He had no idea where Lisette was. And any photos Philippe took from the air would be classified. One could not see them without proper clearance and a need to know. But he burned the images into his mind as if exposing a roll of film. Perhaps the long-awaited Allied invasion wasn't just a dream. The aircraft at East Anglia and the ships in southern England evidenced an industrial might he could hardly imagine, now ready to launch at its target.

Over Portsmouth, at the controls of one of the hottest aircraft in the skies, Philippe felt something in himself he had almost forgotten. An emotion so long dormant he needed a moment simply to recognize it. What was the word in English?

He set a course back to Duxford. Bobby stayed tight on his wing. Philippe scanned his gauges, saw his Allison engines were humming perfectly. The sun climbed high now; visibility at altitude exceeded a hundred miles. When he checked in with Duxford's tower, the controller gave him a new barometric altimeter setting: three-zero-four-six. He twisted a knob to roll in the new number. Such a high barometer reading promised continued clear weather.

Philippe remembered the word he sought. Yes, that was it. Glimmer. He was feeling a glimmer of hope.

CHAPTER 26

Charlotte Denneau

For years, Charlotte had lived in the shadows. Dodged the Gestapo and the Milice. Subsisted on meager rations. Slept in attics, cellars, and in the woods. Just recently, she'd almost drowned.

Now, in the luxury of Danesfield House, she wondered sometimes if she *had* drowned—and gone to heaven. The British Air Ministry had requisitioned the country estate near Medmenham, in Buckinghamshire. They'd renamed it RAF Medmenham. The mansion dated back to 1899, and it now housed the Allied Central Interpretation Unit. Here, photographic analysts examined practically every image taken by British, American, and Free French reconnaissance aircraft.

Charlotte's maps had arrived at Danesfield House ahead of her. While she recovered in the hospital, analysts dried out her papers and salvaged nearly all of them. The maps augmented recent aerial photographs and filled in details not visible from high altitude. This morning, the staff served her tea and an English breakfast of fried eggs, back bacon, and black pudding in Danesfield's library. While she ate alone, she admired the mahogany wainscoting, the fire crackling in a marble hearth, the shelves lined with volumes of Geoffrey Chaucer, William Blake, Jane Austen, and William Wordsworth. When she asked why she was getting such special treatment today, rather than eating in the dining hall, she was told only to expect a visitor. When the man arrived, he introduced himself by the name of another English author.

"You may call me Mr. Milton," he said.

Charlotte doubted that was his real name, not that it mattered. In his gray tweed jacket, he looked like a professor of the literature that filled the room. Red tie and a red pocket handkerchief. She guessed his age at fifty. His accent suggested a British education as impeccable as his dress.

"Pleased to meet you, sir," Charlotte said. She rose to shake his hand.

"And you are the famed 'Tigresse'," Milton said. "You have done capital work."

The man paused the conversation when a waitress brought him tea. The waitress refilled Charlotte's cup, as well. After she left, Milton continued.

"We have already forwarded your targeting information to the RAF's Bomber Command and to the American Eighth Air Force. Most helpful, I must say. Rather fortunate you saved everything when you went for a swim."

"Not an experience I would care to repeat," Charlotte said.

"Indeed not. You have earned a rest. I trust you like it here at Danesfield."

"I do, sir. This place is beautiful. But what comes next?"

Milton leaned back in his chair. Sipped from his cup of Earl Grey. "That, my dear, is up to you."

He explained that she had a choice. She could find work supporting the war effort here in Britain. She could go home to the United States. Or she could take a new assignment in the field.

"What sort of assignment, sir?"

"You know our, ah, points of interest as well as anyone else. If you like, we could transfer you to the chaps here at the Central Interpretation Unit. Train you up in photographic analysis. That wouldn't take long; the work uses some of the skills you already have."

Charlotte raised her eyebrows. She hadn't seen that coming.

"That does sound interesting," she said.

202

"A bit tedious compared to the swashbuckling life you've been leading," Milton said. "But I can make it more interesting."

Milton told her the Allies had photorecon units in North Africa. During the war's "next phase," as he put it, the units would move forward to bases around the Mediterranean. The dynamic situation would call for a great deal of intelligence, analyzed as quickly as possible.

"Your friend Lieutenant Gerard will be rejoining his old French unit, alongside some Yanks," Milton said. "How would you like to go with him? Look at the photos he takes. Tell us what you see."

Milton smiled for the first time during the meeting. Clinked his cup onto his saucer.

Charlotte didn't need long to think. An opportunity to work with Philippe again? So many of her old colleagues were dead. Philippe represented a living link to a cause—*her cause*—not yet fulfilled. She felt a connection to him perhaps deeper than romantic love. With him, she had a chance to keep fighting alongside the French for France.

"I'll do it," she said.

"I thought so. You're a ruddy fire-eater. You could take a well-deserved rest, but I rather doubted you would."

Charlotte supposed that was why this mysterious Mr. Milton worked for SOE. He was certainly a good judge of people. He'd guessed correctly that a woman who could have stayed at home would not quit now. Her father's connections could have gotten her into any women's service she wanted: the WACs, the WASPs, the WAVEs. All relatively safe. But to her parents' horror, she'd chosen the most dangerous work imaginable.

A debriefing followed. Milton asked Charlotte for as much detail as she could remember about all she'd done and seen in the past few months. He took no notes, just listened and nodded. She described the Milice attack on the farmhouse, her flight through the countryside to shelter with the *Maquis*. The roadblock shootout with the Gestapo, the deaths of Pierre and Christophe. Her partnership with Aloïs, and the refuge provided by the Blanchets. Joining up with *El Espectro*, and the ambush on the Nazi officer. The crash of the Lysander, evading capture with Philippe. The bombing raid on the Amiens prison, and the flight to freedom in a stolen Simoun. Ditching in the Channel and nearly dying from hypothermia and drowning.

Her memories tumbled one after another. Charlotte had been trained to notice things, so she recounted each time she'd observed German forces. She also described all the Resistance assets she'd encountered. How they were equipped, what weapons and communications gear they used. What they lacked, what they needed.

Milton did not seem surprised by any of it. Perhaps he'd heard more harrowing stories in other debriefings. When Charlotte finished, he said, "Very good, my dear. You have provided actionable intelligence."

"Thank you, sir," Charlotte said. "Perhaps I should not ask, but can you tell me anything about the people I left behind?" She wanted to know about the Blanchets, Pablo and his *El Espectro* guerrillas, the BCRA fighters who helped steal the Simoun, Aloïs and his insane hunt for Klaus Barbie.

"I will see what I can find out," Milton said.

That afternoon, Charlotte began her training as a photographic interpreter, or PI. She found most of her colleagues were women. They showed her how to place a stereoscope over paired stereo photos to view the image in three dimensions. Numbers on the bottom of the photos included the date the picture was taken, focal length of the camera, and the altitude of the reconnaissance plane. The photos depicted German troop positions, V1 and V2 launch sites, factories, docks, and submarine pens in occupied France.

Charlotte studied the enemy's tactics for concealment, which ranged from smoke screens to nets and false roofs to alter the outline of a hangar or rail station. She learned to tell the difference between a dummy airfield and the real thing. The stereoscope could help identify a flat cutout shaped to look like a Dornier or a Focke-Wulf. She learned to recognize the lines of dots that on closer inspection became "dragon's teeth" or concrete tank obstacles. Widely dispersed buildings surrounded by berms suggested an ammunition dump. Shadows could give away tall structures such as water towers and oil derricks

The analysis of shadow and light reminded her of her art training. She found the work fascinating, and a perfect extension of talents she had already developed.

Two weeks after his first visit, Mr. Milton returned. As before, he met with Charlotte in the library. This time, they shared afternoon tea before a blazing hearth.

"How is your training going?" Milton asked.

"Very well, sir. I appreciate this opportunity."

"We appreciate you taking it. Now then, you wanted news of your fellow *résistants*."

"Yes, sir."

Milton put down his tea cup. Crossed his legs. "I wish I had better news," he said. "Your friend Pablo, the Spaniard who led the *El Espectro* guerrilla force."

"Yes?"

"His full name was Pablo Hernandez."

"You speak in the past tense," Charlotte said.

"I am sorry. He, along with most of his fighters, died in the battle at Glières Plateau."

Charlotte stared out a window. Mist rolled through the gardens of Danesfield House. The hedges and water fountain vanished in the fog. The dangers of war seemed to approach right up to the panes.

"I thought he was invincible."

"Alas, no one is," Milton said. "But he and his people certainly gave a good accounting of themselves."

Charlotte nodded. "Yes, I have seen them in action. And Aloïs? Do you have news of him?"

"I'm afraid so. He died in a gun battle in Lyon, just outside the Hotel Terminus."

So he got as far as Klaus Barbie's headquarters, Charlotte realized. A suicide mission. And maybe that was his intent. Aloïs had lost so much, perhaps he wanted to rejoin family and friends on the other side.

"What about the Blanchets?" Charlotte asked. "Lyam and Marie."

"The Gestapo came for them. They used their potassium cyanide pills. The Gestapo got nothing."

"And the men who helped us steal the airplane?"

"Unknown," Milton said. "Sometimes the BCRA's ways are impenetrable even to us."

Charlotte gazed into the fireplace. Despite its warmth, she felt as if the cold mist outside clutched at her heart. So many people in the Resistance had given their lives, sometimes in awful ways. And several had died specifically so Charlotte could get out with her maps.

She felt the weight of duty like a great stone across her shoulders. Her mission demanded that she give meaning to those deaths. Somehow, she needed to *earn* those deaths.

THE MAPMAKER

MEMORANDUM
REGARDING: Operation Donar
Gestapo Counterintelligence Corps,
Federal Intelligence Service, Lyon
Lyon, France 13 April 1944
TO: Reich Security Main Office, Berlin
FROM: Klaus Barbie, Hauptstürmfuhrer

Terrorist elements have begun harassing German military units with greater aggression. In this office's jurisdiction, we have observed attacks against the 2nd SS Panzer Division, "Das Reich," currently posted to Montauban. Most notably, three of its staff vehicles were destroyed by fire. In addition, some of the rail cars used for the division's logistics have been sabotaged.

Gestapo officers, assisted by French Milice forces, are pursuing leads with all deliberate speed. Further, this office has held discussions with Das Reich's leadership. The division commander reports that, if necessary, he will authorize his own retribution strikes against communities that harbor subversives.

On a related matter, we continue to extract useful information from captured terrorists. They confirm that transport assets, especially locomotives and railroads, are priority targets for the subversives. We intend to use this information to our advantage.

Heil Hitler,
Klaus Barbie, Hauptstürmfuhrer

CHAPTER 27

Lisette Gerard

The airdrop began like all the others Lisette had witnessed. At 0200 local time, Lisette, Olivier, and two other *résistants* gathered in a forest at the edge of a pasture outside Montauban. Right on time, she heard the radial engines overhead. When the aircraft flew over the pasture, Olivier flashed a code with an Aldis lamp. The plane circled, lined up for the drop run. It flew with lights out, but starshine revealed its silhouette. Lisette guessed the plane a Halifax bomber from the RAF.

Five white parachutes blossomed from its belly. A light breeze slanted them away from the drop zone. The parachutes, along with the cylinders they carried, landed along a fence line at the pasture's border. The chutes spilled their air and collapsed. The silk transformed into mere tarps draped over the stone fence.

The team gathered up the cylinders and took them to Olivier's shop, which amounted to little more than a tool shed behind a rural safe house. By the light of an oil lantern, Olivier opened the cylinders.

The first two contained nothing unusual: STEN guns, ammunition, and medical supplies. The third contained something Lisette had never seen before. The cylinder appeared to be filled with black rocks. Olivier upended the cylinder and spilled the stones onto his workbench. Strangely, he did not seem at all surprised.

"Is this some kind of joke?" Lisette asked. What madness would risk a plane and its crew, along with a clandestine drop zone and a Resistance team—for this?

Olivier laughed.

"No, love," he said. "This is no joke. In fact, this is pure genius."

Olivier explained that the "rocks" were fake coal, specially molded with cavities for plastic explosives and detonators. He opened the rest of the cylinders. They all contained fake coal, along with detonators, explosive, and paint bottles with varied shades of black.

"We paint the coal to match what the enemy uses locally, so the explosive coal does not stand out," Olivier said.

"And you place it in the coal tender of a train…" Lisette speculated.

"Exactly. And when the fireman shovels it into the firebox—boom!" Lisette folded her arms, shook her head in wonder.

"Yes," she said, "It's ingenious, as you say. But why wasn't I briefed on this?"

"These kits are fairly new," Olivier said. "We used to do this the hard way, by drilling holes in real coal. But half the time, the coal would just break apart. Very frustrating."

"I am impressed. You are quite the engineer."

"Oh, I cannot take credit. Exploding coal goes back to the American Civil War, I believe. And those crazy Brits at SOE came up with these kits."

"Very good. But how do we get it where it needs to go?"

"We have patriotic friends who work for the railways," Olivier said. "They can take one or two of these and carry them in their lunch boxes. That is the best way. But occasionally, we place them ourselves."

"Why do you need detonators when the explosive will be exposed to fire?"

"Sometimes we ignite the coal in the coal tender. Then the whole load of coal catches fire, and that's very hard to put out."

A raging blaze impossible to extinguish? Lisette found that fitting. The Nazis had brought hell to most of Europe. So the Resistance would bring a little bit of hell to their trains.

Two nights later, Lisette hoisted a STEN across her shoulder. The weapon's long sling extended across her chest, and she positioned the gun so it hung low by her right hand. When she donned an overcoat, the STEN disappeared. She practiced opening the coat and bringing the weapon to bear. She found it took about a second. Her wounds did not hurt so much this evening; perhaps the barometric pressure was high.

The mission, in theory, was simple. Resistance scouts had spotted a locomotive halted along a lonely stretch of track outside Montauban. A forest lined both sides of the track, and the train had stopped just short of a trestle across a narrow stream. No one knew why the train had stopped. Perhaps carborundum-laced grease had locked up its axles.

The locomotive pulled no freight. Its three flatbed cars sat empty. Maybe that's why it was lightly guarded; the scouts said they noticed no sentries—just a frustrated engineer standing by his train with a cigarette dangling from his lips. But the coal tender was full. The tender carried a heaping mound of coal. For Olivier, that presented a fat, tempting target. He assembled a team that consisted of himself, Lisette, and two other fighters.

Through a clear night sky, a gibbous moon threw tree shadows onto a frozen ground. In the previous few days, a springtime thaw had begun, turning the forest floor to mud. But a late cold front had iced the carpet of dead leaves all over again. The leaves crunched underfoot despite efforts by Lisette, Olivier, and two other teammates to step quietly.

They halted twenty yards from the railroad track, still hidden in the forest. Olivier patted his knapsack. He had brought two lumps of explosive coal, a redundancy just in case a detonator failed.

"Let's just watch for a few minutes," Olivier whispered.

At first, the train looked abandoned. Lisette saw no guards or crew. Then flashlight beams dotted the ground on the other side of the locomotive. Two men walked the length of the train. They appeared to carry no weapons as they inspected the flatbeds and the caboose, though Lisette knew they might have concealed handguns. After the men satisfied themselves there was nothing amiss, they climbed aboard the caboose.

210

"That's right," Olivier muttered. "Go back to sleep."

From her training, Lisette knew that in a sabotage mission like this, one hoped not to fire a shot. Real operations seldom went so easily, but she began to think this one might become the exception.

Unless...

A vague suspicion entered her mind. Was this too easy a target?

No, she decided. Trains all over France had halted because of the carborundum grease and other sabotage. Here was the latest one. So we burn it.

She checked her watch: one in the morning. Olivier waited half an hour for the men in the caboose to fall asleep. Then he motioned for the team to move forward.

Lisette and the others crept to the edge of the woods. Olivier paused and watched. Then he looked at Lisette and nodded. Signaled her two teammates with a thumbs up. They readied their weapons.

At the rail bed, Olivier moved forward alone. He planned to toss the two coal bombs into the tender unseen, then slip back into the woods. Lisette and the others would provide overwatch and covering fire if things went awry.

The operation went according to plan for about twenty seconds.

Olivier reached the railroad bed and climbed the embankment. Reached into his knapsack. Fumbled with the first coal bomb—Lisette supposed he was having trouble arming the detonator. Finally, he tossed the bomb into the coal tender.

He hefted the second coal bomb. Took a moment to arm it.

Before Olivier could throw it, a man hopped down from the locomotive.

"*Tu arrêtes!*" the man called.

Olivier looked up. Heaved the second bomb into the tender. The man drew a handgun.

Lisette swung the STEN, just as she'd practiced. Pressed the trigger and fired a burst. Cut down the man at the locomotive. She felt nothing as she watched him fall. Burned gunpowder stung her nostrils.

Armed men poured from the caboose. At least five of them. Armed with rifles, they came out firing. Olivier sprinted for the woods. A round sent him sprawling.

Where did all these guards come from, Lisette wondered. They must have remained hidden for days if Resistance surveillance had missed them.

So the locomotive *was* bait.

Lisette's two teammates opened up. Two of the men from the caboose went down. The others kept shooting. Their muzzle flashes flickered against the side of the flatbeds.

Two thumps sounded from within the coal tender. An orange glow, at first more like sunrise than fire, rose among the heaps of coal.

Down on one knee, Lisette raised her weapon again. Aimed at the remaining guards. Squeezed the trigger to put down covering fire for Olivier.

Flames licked above the edges of the coal tender. The firelight revealed Olivier at the edge of the forest. He was trying to get up.

"Help him," Lisette shouted.

Now the flames towered. They ignited branches that overspread the railroad track. Fire danced in the treetops and raged through the coal tender.

Lisette's teammates ran forward. Lifted Olivier by the arms. Lisette kept firing to make the guards keep their heads down. The *résistants* dragged Olivier back into the forest, and the team retreated farther into the trees.

The guards did not pursue them, to Lisette's relief. Instead, they busied themselves with fire extinguishers, trying to save the locomotive. Perhaps when they laid their trap, they expected a gunfight but not a firebombing.

Deep in the cover of the woods, Olivier gritted his teeth and let out a groan. A bullet had slashed across his calf. The round ripped a deep graze wound, but it could have been worse. No bones appeared broken.

With her palm, Lisette shielded a flashlight and examined the wound. Blood pumped through with every beat of Olivier's heart.

Treatment would have to wait. Lisette knew they needed to get away as quickly as possible. The coal fire would be visible for miles. Just a matter of time—probably only minutes—before additional German forces rushed to investigate.

"Let's get him out of here," Lisette said. "Take him back to the truck."

She scanned the forest to get her bearings, then led the way through the woods.

CHAPTER 28

Philippe Gerard

As soon as the C-47 Skytrain touched down at Maison Blanche airfield in Algiers, Philippe saw the change since he'd last been there in 1940. Warplanes, mainly American, staged in neat rows. Fighters on one ramp: Thunderbolts, Lightnings, and Mustangs. Bombers on another: Liberators and Flying Fortresses. Transports on another: Skytrains and Commandos.

Fuel trucks serviced the planes in orderly procession. Mechanics atop work stands tended engines. The scene stood in contrast with the disorganization and near panic Philippe had witnessed four years ago. Maison Blanche was no longer a redoubt for a defeated *Armée de l'Air*. Now it served as a base for an Allied force with the upper hand. Philippe had read how the war had gone badly for the Americans in North Africa until that profane and colorful general, George Patton, had taken command. Since then, the Yanks had poured shiploads of money and materiel into this place.

Charlotte sat across from Philippe in one of the canvas seats that lined both sides of the aircraft. He'd been overjoyed that she would accompany him to Algiers. At the very least, they would continue their professional friendship. And he wondered if that would lead to something deeper.

"Look familiar?" she shouted over the engines.

Philippe shook his head. "*Non*," he said. "This looks like a real base. When I landed here before, it was just chaos."

He didn't add that he'd been demobilized the very next day. Neither did he add that his sister should have been here from the beginning. Lisette would have been relatively safe working in Algiers as a nurse. But she'd joined the Resistance, escaped France, and then *gone back in.* Philippe was still furious about that. He had received no more word of her whereabouts or activities. Security reasons, of course. When he thought of her, he worried himself sick. So he tried to keep his mind on his flying.

A cab took Philippe and Charlotte to the Hôtel Aletti. Like the airfield, the Aletti was transformed by the Allied victory in North Africa. To Philippe, hope and anticipation hung in the same lobby where capitulation had once reigned. Officers in clean uniforms sat around tables and smoked or played cards. They wore the insignia of the United States, Britain, Canada, and the Free French forces. Other men wore gabardine suits with neckties and pressed shirts. Philippe guessed they represented foreign ministries or the OSS and SOE. A few women in elegant dresses accompanied the men. Agents themselves, perhaps, or wives and local lovers.

A phonograph played a tune Philippe had heard in Britain: "Comin' In on a Wing and a Prayer," by the Song Spinners. He supposed half the men in the room had lived those lyrics. Aromas of cigars, perfume, and the cumin and paprika of Algerian cooking filled the air. To Philippe, that marked another contrast. His nostrils were more accustomed to sweat, fuel, and exhaust.

Philippe chose a table with a view of the main entrance. He wanted to watch for his old friend Saint-Exupéry. Saint-Ex had promised to brief him on life in the revived 2/33 Recon. A tuxedoed waiter came by the table. Philippe ordered two Sidecars. When the drinks came, Charlotte took a sip, then closed her eyes and tilted her head back. Her expression suggested she'd just tasted the nectar of the gods.

"I can hardly remember the last time I had a cocktail," she said.

"Neither can I," Philippe said. He sipped his own drink, savored the mixture. For a moment he let himself imagine himself out of the war, in some brilliant future peace. A world of good friends, elegant cocktails, and gourmet food. But he reminded himself that hard fighting and flying remained. And Lisette was back in harm's way. More than likely, things would get worse before they would get better.

Heads turned when Saint-Ex walked in. Acquaintances greeted him, shook his hand, patted his back. When he scanned the room, Philippe waved. Saint-Ex spread his arms wide and called out, "*Mon ami!* You are here."

The two men embraced, then Saint-Ex asked, "Who is this ravishing creature?"

Philippe introduced Charlotte. "She is as French as she is American," Philippe said. He left out details on her background; he knew the lobby could harbor spies as well as friends. He said only, "She will interpret the photos we take."

"*Bien*," Saint-Ex said. "Most of the time I never even see them."

"By the way," Philippe said, "congratulations on your promotion." Saint-Ex now held the rank of major.

"*Merci.*"

The author wore an American-style A-2 leather flight jacket over his uniform. Lines creased the skin around his eyes. He looked heavier. Older. And despite his joy at seeing Philippe, tired. When he shifted in his chair to cross his legs, Philippe saw him wince in pain. Old crash injuries, perhaps.

"So, how are you?" Philippe asked. "Really."

The waiter came back, and that gave Saint-Ex an excuse to delay his answer. He ordered bourbon. Like the A-2 jacket, perhaps that was something he'd picked up from the Yanks.

"I have to fight doctors and politicians just for the privilege of fighting the Germans," Saint-Ex said.

He described the flight surgeons who thought him too old to fly the P-38, too wracked with cholecystitis. He suspected supporters of de Gaulle wanted him sidelined. Plus, he had run a P-38 off the end of a runway earlier in the year. Destroyed a hundred-thousand-dollar airplane.

"To err is human, to forgive, divine," Saint-Ex said. "But neither is American policy. For a time, they grounded me."

"*Non!*" Philippe said.

"Imagine that," Saint-Ex said. "I have piloted cloth-winged airplanes through storms in the Andes. But the Yanks do not think I can fly."

"They are a strange lot," Philippe said. "You should have seen the Texan who checked me out in the Lightning."

Saint-Ex shifted in his chair. Winced again.

"The doctors are not entirely wrong," he admitted. He took a long pull of his bourbon and added, "I do have pain. Were it not for aspirin I could barely climb into the cockpit."

"I am sorry," Charlotte said. "I admire your courage to fight on."

"*Merci,*" the author said. "I believe eventually we will win. But I worry about what comes after that. I fear that perhaps next year, many in France will be shot."

"Some will deserve it," Charlotte said.

Saint-Ex shrugged.

Philippe pondered his friend's attitude. He had never seen the man so depressed. He decided to change the subject.

"So, tell me about the 2/33," Philippe said. "Who remains with us?"

"Gavoille is still the commander, bless his soul." Saint-Ex listed a few more familiar names.

"I cannot wait to fly with them again," Philippe said.

Saint-Ex leaned in to whisper, so that only Philippe and Charlotte could hear: "You won't be flying out of North Africa for long. We are about to deploy to Italy. And after that, the rumor is Corsica."

Philippe looked at Charlotte, who raised her eyebrows. She nodded with a hint of a smile. Philippe could guess what she was thinking: Bases closer to France.

The Italian campaign had become a bloody slog, but it was making progress. The Allies held Sicily, and were now fighting their way northward toward Rome. With bases in Italy or Corsica, photorecon aircraft could range farther into France. Spend more time over German positions. Get more and better images.

From his briefings, Philippe knew the 2/33 would provide intelligence for an invasion of southern France, in conjunction with the cross-Channel landing from England. The southern assault, dubbed Operation Anvil, would help crush the Germans from two directions.

"I remember when our flying seemed so pointless," Philippe said. "Now, perhaps, we will do some damage."

"I hope so," Saint-Ex said. "But if our photos become more important, the *Luftwaffe* will try hard to keep them from ever being developed."

The old aviator had a point. A Lightning carrying rolls of high-value film would become a high-value target.

Two days later, Philippe found himself at Pomigliano Airfield outside Naples. The field bore all the traits of a forward air base in the European Theater: Tents and Quonset huts—prefab steel buildings that resembled a giant coffee can cut in half—sprang up overnight. They housed all the functions needed by a flying unit: Operations, Mess Hall, Engineering, Briefing, Armory, Photo Section, Weather, Billeting, Hospital.

Philippe's old unit put him back to work at once—on a mission he'd never expected. Vesuvius, the volcano that incinerated and buried Pompeii in 79 A.D., spewed ash and lava again. Pompeii Airfield had already suffered the fate of its namesake city. Hot ash and cinders settled on scores of B-25 Mitchells and other aircraft. The eruption melted Plexiglas, burned control surfaces, and dumped enough vomitus from the earth to weigh down planes and tip them onto their tails. The damage rendered squadrons of aircraft beyond repair.

Commanders needed to know if they should evacuate other bases. They ordered 2/33 aloft to photograph Vesuvius's crater, the ash column rising from it, and the pyrocastic flows oozing down its slopes. Charlotte and other analysts stood by to review the photos.

Philippe climbed aboard his Lightning while the American crew chief stood by to pull the chocks.

"Try to stay out of the ash, sir," the crew chief said. "It'll play hell with your engines."

"We have a saying in France," Philippe said. "*Il ne faut rien laisser au hasard.*"

"What's that mean, sir?"

"Leave nothing to chance."

"I like it," the crew chief said. "Makes my job easier."

Saint-Ex manned the aircraft next to Philippe's. Farther down the flight line, squadron commander René Gavoille mounted up. Philippe settled into his seat and strapped in. Unlike many of the fliers, he had not given his aircraft a name. He had no wife or sweetheart for whom to name it. He felt great fondness for Charlotte. But as a Resistance agent, she'd been under orders not to get involved. Part of him hoped that might change in her new role.

His Lightning—technically not a P-38 but an F-5 photorecon model—was so new it still smelled like a new car. The Yanks, ever fond of nicknames, called the F-5 "Photo Joe." It carried five state-of-the-art cameras, which could capture images straight down or from an angle. Not weighed down by guns and ammunition, the F-5 could fly higher and faster than other P-38s, or most other fighters, for that matter. One flier had painted a motto on his ship's fuselage: "Unarmed and Unafraid."

Philippe admired the bravado, but he judged it more aspirational than factual.

A black tower of ash and tephra loomed on the horizon like God's own wrath. Philippe tried to imagine what the Pompeiians must have thought when hell began to fall from the sky. Then he put that out of his mind and concentrated on his checklists. The Nazis had brought their own brand of hell into the modern world, and Philippe had work to do.

As the crew chief stood by with a fire extinguisher, Philippe started his engines. Watched the oil temperatures and pressures come up and stabilize. Set his elevator tab at three degrees aft and his rudder tabs at zero. Double-checked the prop controls at full increase, and clicked his oxygen mask into place.

He looked across the ramp at Saint-Ex's Lightning and Gavoille's aircraft. Their propellers blurred with speed, and exhaust blasted behind the engines. In turn, each pilot called the control tower for taxi clearance.

Philippe released his parking brake and followed Saint-Ex to the departure end of the runway.

The wind gusted to thirty knots. Philippe felt his wings rocking with the gusts even before he took off. He watched his squadron mates climb into the sky, then he rolled onto the runway and pushed up the throttles. With so much wind on the nose, the Lightning reached flying speed more quickly than usual. Philippe climbed into rough air. The needles on his panel bounced and jiggled with the turbulence. The atmosphere itself seemed angry, as if all the elements conspired against him. Philippe brought up the landing gear and pitched for best rate of climb, hoping for smoother air aloft.

The three Lightnings did not fly in formation; each was assigned to photograph a different sector. But Philippe switched to an interplane frequency so he could communicate with them, just in case anyone ran into trouble. The first transmission he heard brought an expression of awe.

"Mother of God," Saint-Ex said.

Vesuvius boiled like a portal from the underworld. From its crater, ash spewed so dark and thick it looked more like oil. A lava dome bulged on the southern slope. Philippe watched the dome split open and spill liquid fire downhill. The ash cloud bent with the breeze and rained destruction ten miles downwind.

The scene put Philippe in mind of the beginning of the earth—a planet's birth in storm and flame. Would the end look like this, too? For a moment he felt puny, his powerful airplane an insect flung against all the might of the natural world.

"We'd better stay upwind and use the oblique cameras," Gavoille said.

"Yes, sir," Philippe said. "We do not want to find out what this stuff does to pistons and valves."

"Once again we face the great problems of nature," Saint-Ex radioed.

Philippe's old friend must have been thinking of a line he'd written: *The machine does not isolate man from the great problems of nature but plunges him more deeply into them.*

Here was proof in dramatic form.

Philippe climbed to stay out of the ash. He glanced at his outside temperature gauge and noted the air growing colder with altitude. His K-17 cameras needed to stay warm for reliable operation, so he flipped the camera heat switch. That activated a heater with an electric fan. Time to go to work.

He dug into a leg pocket of his flying clothes and pulled out a U.S. World Aeronautical Chart. He opened the WAC chart only partially, having pre-folded it for easy handling in flight and to display only the sectors he needed. He clipped the chart to his kneeboard. Turned onto a heading to photograph the towns of San Sebastiano and Massa di Somma.

For a few moments, the Gulf of Naples glittered in clear air below him. Whitecaps highlighted a sapphire sea. The sun shone so brightly that Philippe donned his aviator's glasses. Even through the darkened lenses, the rays caused him to squint.

In short order, he found he could not get images from directly over either of the towns. Both lay at the foot of Vesuvius, and the wind pushed the ash in their direction. Philippe activated his cameras to photograph the obscuration, then descended for shots at an oblique angle. Even that perspective showed little but Vesuvius's ejecta settling on San Sebastiano and Massa di Somma.

"I hope they have evacuated," he whispered to himself in his oxygen mask. Philippe had little sympathy for Italy and its Fascists. But he realized the farmers and shopkeepers below may not have cared much for Mussolini, either.

After their mission, the Photo Joe pilots convened at Pomigliano Airfield's makeshift officers' club. Pinup girls and a dart board lined the walls of the Quonset hut. Planks laid across two oil drums formed a field expedient bar. Most of the Americans drank beer. The French preferred wine, some of which had arrived in the auxiliary tank of an aircraft.

Philippe raised his glass and examined the Bordeaux. Skeptical, he took a sip. Somehow the wine remained drinkable. He detected no notes of 100-octane gasoline.

He waved to Charlotte when she entered the club. Introduced her to Gavoille. Saint-Ex poured her a glass of wine. No one told her how the wine got there.

"How did the eruption look?" she asked as she took her glass.

"Awful," Philippe said. "Have they developed the photos?"

"Not yet."

"I do not believe we will ever use Pompeii Airfield again," Saint-Ex said.

"Are we safe here at Pomigliano?" Charlotte asked.

"For now, I think," Gavoille said. "Of course, we will make that call based on what you see in the photos."

An American pilot interrupted the conversation with a shout from across the room: "Hey, it's Major X. Thanks for the vino, buddy."

Saint-Ex smiled and waved. Then he rolled his eyes.

"They cannot pronounce my name," he said, "so that is what they call me."

"You seem in a better mood," Philippe said. "How are you feeling?"

"Ah, a bit bemused, I would say," Saint-Ex said.

"Why is that?"

"Before we took off on this mission, I consulted a fortune-teller. I do not know what possessed me to do such a thing."

"What did she tell you?" Philippe asked.

"Evidently, she did not recognize my uniform. She must have thought I was a sailor. She told me I would die in the waves of the sea."

Then Saint-Ex shrugged. Downed what remained of his wine in one gulp.

CHAPTER 29

Charlotte Denneau

Thanks in part to the rages of Vesuvius, the 2/33 kept on the move, and Charlotte moved with it. Philippe's and Saint-Ex's old squadron had become part of the American Third Reconnaissance Group, under the command of Colonel Elliott Roosevelt, son of President Franklin Roosevelt. She found herself in Sardinia, at Alghero Airfield, hard at work with her stereoscope. As the Americans put it, her primary weapon became her "Mark 1 eyeballs."

Mediterranean breezes ruffled the tent flaps as she analyzed photos developed in a dark room on the base. Walls dating to the 16th century enclosed the coastal town of Alghero. During Charlotte's rare hours off, she walked cobblestoned streets and visited historic sites such as the Alghero Cathedral, which dated to the 1500s.

But for most of her waking hours, she concentrated on the problems of the 20th century. Operation Anvil would follow the main cross-Channel landing, Operation Overlord, and trap the Germans with a great pincer movement. French, American, and British forces would land by sea and air. One of her first tasks involved figuring out where the airborne troops would land.

She attended a pilot's briefing one morning when the 2/33 commander, René Gavoille, sent his men out to fly. At the front of a Quonset hut, backdropped by a map of the southern French coastline, Gavoille outlined the mission.

"We intend to put ashore French Army B and the American Seventh Army," the commander said. "Naturally, they will have naval and air cover. Some of the soldiers will arrive by parachute and glider."

Parachutists couldn't touch down just anywhere. Trees, large rocks, and powerlines could break ankles, legs, even necks and spines. And the gliders, towed to release points by C-47 Skytrains and other powered aircraft, needed smooth landing grounds. Earlier glider operations had brought disaster. During Operation Husky, the invasion of Sicily, scores of Waco and Horsa gliders got released too early because of anti-aircraft fire. Soldiers drowned when their gliders ditched in the sea.

Also, rough ground could cause a glider to cartwheel. Worse, the enemy could drive stakes into the soil to tear up a landing glider and the men inside.

"We need to locate open fields away from gun emplacements and free of obstacles," Gavoille explained.

An hour later, four F-5s took off from Alghero. Charlotte watched them climb into a cerulean sky. They crossed the tiled roofs of Alghero village, and the roars of their engines grew faint. She kept eyes on them until they diminished into dots among scattered clouds that threw shadows onto the Med below. The pilots were Philippe, Saint-Ex, Gavoille, and Lavigne. Lavigne was the only one Charlotte hadn't met.

She passed the time by listening to war news on the radio. Nowadays, every time she switched on the set, she hoped to hear of the Allied invasion beginning. Still no word of that today. But the news was good. The BBC told of Allied forces starting to break out of the Anzio beachhead in Italy with the help of a big artillery bombardment. Soviet forces had retaken Crimea. German U-boats, once the terror of the seas, seemed to sink every day. They fell to depth charges dropped by British and American planes using airborne radar.

After lunch, she visited the airfield's control tower to watch the Photo Joes return. She leaned on the railing atop the concrete building, outside the main control room. Sea breeze ruffled her hair and spun the anemometer mounted on the roof. An American serviceman joined her by the railing. He said he was a weather observer for the USAAF.

"Sweating them in, huh?" the weatherman said.

"What's that?" Charlotte asked.

"Sweating them in. That's what we call it. You counted the planes going out. You pray you get the same number back."

"Yes, yes. That's exactly what I'm doing."

Several minutes of silence passed. Then the weatherman pointed into the sky.

"There's one," he said.

Charlotte shaded her eyes, looked up.

A dot, barely visible, descended from the scattered cumulus. The dot grew larger. Gradually it took the twin-boom shape of a Lightning. Descended lower. Louder now, the aircraft overflew the field and turned into the landing pattern. She watched the landing gear extend. The plane lined up on final approach, and it scattered a flock of sea birds as it crossed the airfield fence. Touched down safely. Turned off the runway and taxied to the ramp.

Near the base of the tower, the Lightning rolled to a stop, and its pilot shut down the engines. When the propellers stopped turning, a man chocked the wheels. The pilot opened the canopy and climbed down. From his mannerisms, she knew immediately it was Philippe. He went straight to the tower.

After several minutes inside, Philippe appeared on the roof with Charlotte and the weatherman. He still wore his leather flying helmet and life vest. His oxygen mask dangled from a strap on the helmet. Sweat streaked his face, and he looked worried.

"Glad to see you on the ground," she said.

"Lavigne's in trouble," Philippe said.

"What?"

"He got bounced by a Focke-Wulf. The Kraut bastard shot out one of his engines. I think he's wounded, too."

"*Mon Dieu.*"

Charlotte turned to watch the clouds and the runway. Another aircraft descended for landing.

"That's Saint-Ex," Philippe said. "He is okay. Gavoille joined up on Lavigne's wing. He ordered Saint-Ex and me to get back to base ahead of them."

Saint-Ex landed safely. Like Philippe, he taxied to the ramp and shut down his aircraft. Climbed the tower to watch for his friends.

"Lavigne and Gavoille were right behind me," Saint-Ex said.

From inside the control room, the sounds of indistinct radio traffic grew louder. Across the airfield, a siren sounded, and two trucks rolled from the fire department. An ambulance followed behind them.

Their sirens drowned out the noise of approaching aircraft. Charlotte saw them before she heard them. She pointed at two Lightnings in close formation. One trailed smoke from its right nacelle.

"There they are," she said.

Philippe and Saint-Ex looked up. With Charlotte, they watched the two planes descend into the traffic pattern. For a moment, Charlotte considered how this job was more similar to her old work with the Resistance than she'd expected. The photos, like the drawings, maps, and other intelligence, always came at a cost.

The undamaged Lightning broke away from the other aircraft. Entered a descending turn to set up for final approach. Touched down normally and taxied off the runway.

"Gavoille's back, at least," Philippe said.

"Why did he land first?" Charlotte asked.

"If Lavigne prangs it in, he could foul the runway. No point losing two airplanes. And they are both low on fuel."

The damaged Lightning entered the pattern, flew parallel to the runway. Began a slow descent. Smoke still wafted from the right nacelle, but thinner now.

The plane did not turn. Kept straight as if to fly away.

"Come on, Lavigne," Saint-Ex said. "Turn base."

Finally, the Lightning turned crosswind to the field.

"Looks like his landing gear are down," Philippe said.

"One more turn, *mon ami*," Saint-Ex said. "Turn final now."

"He is really dragging it in," Philippe said. "Very low."

"Gavoille said he sounded like he's losing blood," Saint-Ex said. "Maybe in and out of consciousness."

"Oh, no," Charlotte said.

Down at the ramp, Gavoille raised his canopy. Stood up in the cockpit to watch Lavigne come in.

Lavigne turned onto final approach. Even Charlotte could tell he was too low. The Lightning skimmed the ground. Then the aircraft banked left.

"Center line, *mon ami*," Saint-Ex said. "You are almost home."

Lavigne did not turn back onto final. The aircraft continued its left turn until it struck the ground. The left wing separated. The twin tail rose into the air.

And then the entire aircraft disappeared in a boiling explosion. Black smoke rose above the rocky field outside the base. The fire trucks and ambulance sped through the gate and raced toward the crash, but Charlotte knew the effort was hopeless.

"*Dieu du ciel,*" Saint-Ex hissed. *God in heaven.*

Philippe closed his eyes. Shook his head. Charlotte placed her hand on his arm and did not speak.

For a long time, no one spoke. Eventually, Saint-Ex walked to the far corner of the tower roof. Sat down, fished a cigarette from his flight suit, and lit it. Took a drag and stared off into space.

"Is Saint-Ex all right?" Charlotte whispered. "I mean—"

"I know what you mean," Philippe said. "The answer is no. This morning he gave me his chess set. He loved that thing. He said someday we will play chess in a better place."

Charlotte let the statement sink in. For a moment she wanted to believe Saint-Ex had meant playing chess in a free France. But she realized he meant something farther away. She let tears slide down her cheeks while she gazed across the airbase at Lavigne's plane, still burning.

CHAPTER 30

Lisette Gerard

The radio confirmed what Lisette had sensed in the air, felt in her bones. The Allies were wading, firing, blasting ashore at Normandy.

Lisette had known because her coded messages had become more and more specific on how to stop, or at least slow down, *Das Reich*, the 2nd SS Panzer Division. Now, the BBC's French service was broadcasting instructions in the clear to the wider population. The announcer said, "Every minute lost to the Germans is a minute gained by the Allies. A car stuck on the road can delay traffic for ten minutes—and blocking an enemy transport for ten minutes may ensure the success of an Allied operation."

The broadcast urged people to help friendly forces, to guide parachutists, to warn Americans and Brits of traps and minefields.

Lisette and her colleagues had done their work well. *Das Reich*'s rail cars screeched to a stop with ground-up bearings. Their coal tenders burned. Their locomotives exploded. The trains that did move hit sabotaged tracks and derailed.

With no other option, the 2nd SS Panzer Division took to the highways. Resistance lookouts watched the tanks and troop-carriers head north from Montauban on the N20. When the column turned left onto the D704 toward Groléjac, the *résistants* were waiting.

Lisette and Olivier hunkered down along a disused rail bed that overlooked the road. Olivier's leg wound had mostly healed, but he still limped when he got tired.

A driver traversing the highway would not have seen the two of them hidden behind trees and brush. But they and a dozen other fighters had a good view of the highway below, which led to a bridge across the River Dordogne.

She could hardly believe this thing was finally happening. Four years of occupation had turned all of France into a prison. Neighbors became turncoats. Radio stations became propaganda sewers. Rations ran short and tempers shorter. But now, Lisette imagined the Allies just over the horizon: their artillery pounding Nazi bunkers, their aircraft obliterating German bases. Their soldiers advancing, the Boche retreating. The beginning of the end, God willing.

Lisette wondered what Philippe was doing now. Was he flying? And where? What would he say about her return to the fight? He'd probably be angry, she knew. So protective. She wished he could be proud of her—the way she'd grown up fast in France's time of need. Maybe he would be someday.

The river flowed to Lisette's left. To her right, a country lane bisected the D704. She gripped a STEN gun and looked down the lane as far as the evergreens permitted. Checked her watch.

"The car is late," she whispered.

"But so is *Das Reich*," Olivier said. "Ticklish business."

Lisette took his meaning: A car driven by *résistants* needed to block the D704 just before the German column arrived. Too early, and other traffic might back up, alerting the enemy. Too late, and the Panzers would roll by unimpeded.

Birds chirped. Leaves rustled with the breeze. Lisette listened closely, even shut her eyes to concentrate. The sound she waited for came faintly at first, almost imperceptibly. She heard a low rumble. Metallic clanks joined the thrum of engines.

"Here they come," Olivier said.

"And still no car," Lisette said.

She caught glimpses of movement between the trees. Vehicle after vehicle rattled along the D704. On many, she recognized the profile of the main gun on a Panzer IV. Three-digit numbers marked the turrets. Their mottled camouflage paint blended with the vegetation. Crewmen wearing headphones and goggles peered from the hatches.

Lisette began to count them. She stopped at twenty. Dear God, there were so many. The *résistants* could inflict pinprick damage at best.

Finally, a car sped down the intersecting lane. Slid to a stop just as the first Panzer arrived.

"Suicide," Olivier muttered.

The plan had called for the car to block the road in time for the driver to get away. Too late for that now. The lead Panzer opened up with one of its secondary weapons, an MG 34 machine gun. Raked the car with gunfire.

The driver never had a chance. The car shook as rounds slammed into it. The driver slumped over, disappeared from view.

The tank crewmen in the first two Panzers ducked below their hatches. Clearly, they recognized an ambush.

"Hold your fire," Olivier ordered.

Lisette waited. The *résistants* had anticipated this. No point wasting ammunition against the side of a tank. Eventually the column would pass through the intersection. The fighters could wait for something with thinner skin, such as a truck or troop-carrier.

The lead Panzer shoved the car forward a few feet. Backed up. Steered around the riddled vehicle. Other tanks followed, rumbling across a shallow ditch. Their tracks clattered through the soil as easily as over pavement. The Panzers swayed back onto the highway and continued toward the bridge over the Dordogne.

Finally, a half-track troop carrier appeared. Helmeted soldiers aboard the vehicle hunkered low. But not out of sight.

Lisette took aim across the berm of the railroad bed. Settled her sights on one of the soldiers. Pressed the trigger.

230

The STEN shook in her hands as it spewed nine-millimeter slugs. Two of the troops fell to her rounds. Then the STEN jammed.

Lisette released the magazine. Smacked it against the ground. Slammed the mag back into the gun and racked the bolt. Beside her, Olivier kept firing. Lisette heard the chatter of gunfire from other Resistance positions.

With her weapon cleared, she opened up on another troop carrier. German soldiers ducked for cover. She thought she hit at least one of them.

The enemy returned fire. The Panzers flayed the trees with their machine guns. Some of the troops leaped off the carriers, found cover, and blasted away with small arms. Bark and wood chips rained down on Lisette and Olivier. Dirt flew when rounds slammed into the railroad berm in front of them.

Lisette emptied her magazine. Ejected it, inserted another. Fired until that mag emptied. Olivier cleared a jam—the damned STENs jammed all the time—and ran through the rest of his own magazines.

After what felt like forever, the firing died down to individual shots from the soldiers' Mausers. The column inched forward. Lisette guessed the *résistants* had stopped it for twenty minutes. She and Olivier remained motionless until the last Panzer sputtered across the Dordogne.

When the enemy went out of sight, the fighters tallied their losses. Ten of their number had died. In the car that had blocked the road, the driver had been practically torn apart. Close-range automatic fire left the man unrecognizable. Shattered windshield glass glinted in pools of blood. Other fighters had died in their ambush positions above the road.

"Was slowing them down a bit worth all this?" Olivier asked.

"We will probably never know," Lisette said.

That night, they listened to the radio for more coded messages. Their instructions were clear: Flank *Das Reich*, get ahead of them. Ambush them again. Harass them all the way to Normandy. Link up with the "Jedburgh" teams parachuted in by the American OSS and the British SOE.

In a barn outside the village of Tulle, Lisette and Olivier met a three-man team that went by the code name SULFA. They never gave individual names. The team consisted of a French lieutenant, an American captain, and a British sergeant who served as a radio operator. They wore green neckerchiefs cut from the parachutes that had dropped them into France. Lisette liked that bit of dash.

"This ain't the first rodeo for these *Das Reich* boys," the Yank said. "They were in some of the worst fighting on the Eastern Front before they got transferred here."

"So, they are hardened troops," Olivier said.

"*Oui,*" the French officer said. "*Très dangereux.*"

"We have seen them in action," Lisette said, "but only briefly."

"Yeah, well, you're gonna see them in action again soon," the Yank said. "The commies are planning to hit them hard right here in Tulle."

"He means the FTP," the French officer said. "The *Francs-Tireurs et Partisans.*"

"Where do we come in?" Lisette asked.

"The enemy uses a little teacher college in town for a barracks," the French officer explained. "The FTP will attack the barracks. Set the Germans on their back foot, perhaps."

"*Das Reich* plans to link up with their mates in Tulle," the British radio man said. "God willing, they won't find many of them left."

The Jedburgh men explained how they and Lisette's team would observe from the hills above Tulle. Cut off any Germans who managed to escape. Report the results to London.

The next morning, Lisette peered down at the village nestled in the Corrèze valley. Tulle Cathedral's spire anchored the village, and a warren of centuries-old streets spread from the cathedral. The college lay just beyond the cathedral, at the foot of a hillside dotted by trees.

She watched from the cover of a sparse forest. Olivier kneeled in brush next to her. Farther to her left, the Jedburgh men took cover. Lisette and Olivier carried their STENs. The Yank gripped a Garand rifle, while his French counterpart held a Thompson submachine gun. The British radio operator wielded a rifle Lisette had never seen before:

a De Lisle carbine. The Brit had explained how it included an integrated noise suppressor. To make it even quieter, he'd loaded it with subsonic .45-caliber ammunition. No loud crack from a bullet breaking the sound barrier.

They did not have to wait long for action. At the edge of town, trucks disgorged FTP guerrillas. Dozens of them. Lisette had little experience around the communist *résistants*. She hadn't realized they could muster this many men in such an organized manner.

The guerrillas flowed through the streets in silence. Surrounded the school building in a maneuver that might have been choreographed by a master director. Other fighters took overwatch positions to cut off exits—or to block German reinforcements. Lisette saw a man with what appeared to be a pair of metal tanks strapped to his back. He carried some sort of nozzle attached to the tanks by a hose.

"Is that a…flamethrower?" Lisette asked.

Olivier raised his binoculars.

"That's exactly what it is," he said.

Gunfire chattered from around the school. Perhaps the FTP men were shooting down sentries, or maybe the *Wehrmacht* soldiers were firing from inside the building. In any case, the shooting rose and fell in spurts. Lisette couldn't determine exactly how it started.

A guerrilla shattered a window with the butt of his rifle. Threw a grenade inside. With the thump of detonation, dust flew from the window.

The man with the flamethrower swept his nozzle across the base of the front wall as if watering petunias. But he was spraying fire. Flames crept up the wall until they licked at the eaves. The flamethrower operator walked around the building, spreading fire as he went.

A side door flew open. Soldiers fled the school, some firing automatic weapons from the hip. Most of the men fell to the *résistants'* bullets. A few disappeared into the streets. Pops of rifle fire followed them. Lisette could not tell how many of them escaped.

"Watch out," Olivier said. "Some of them may get up here."

Lisette gripped her STEN. Scanned the hillside and trees below. At the school building, a man on fire ran out the front door. He sprinted thirty yards, a human torch, until a volley of mercy fire put him down.

Movement, much closer, caught her eye. Glimpse of a German helmet coming up toward the hillcrest. Then another. Then the two German soldiers appeared, running, stumbling away from the town.

Lisette raised her weapon. But before she could bring it to bear, the two soldiers fell. She'd heard no shot. Then she remembered the Brit with his silenced carbine.

Another stray enemy soldier appeared. He, too, fell. This time she heard a sound, just barely. More like a whisper than the report of a gun. Similar to the *pffft* when one opened a soda bottle.

Lisette and Olivier exchanged a glance. Olivier raised his eyebrows. Then he turned and pointed to three more of the enemy running up the hill. One fell to the soundless carbine. Lisette and Olivier opened up on the other two. The one shot by Lisette spun with the impact of the rounds, then collapsed.

Shots registered from the other side of town. More of the enemy falling to Resistance guns on overwatch, Lisette presumed.

When the firing died down and the battle ended, Lisette, Olivier, and the Jedburgh team retreated to the barn that served as their temporary headquarters. She wondered what would happen with any prisoners taken during the operation, but that decision was left to the FTP. Her job was to keep moving, get ahead of *Das Reich* again, hit them once more.

She slept little that night. Images of the battle, of the man on fire, replayed in her mind. In the late morning, she and Olivier joined the Jedburgh team as they brewed coffee over a fire outside the barn.

Lisette took a steaming mug from the French officer. Closed her eyes and savored a sip. It had been so long since she'd tasted real coffee. A shout from the Yank startled her. She opened her eyes to see him pointing to a figure running toward them.

She dropped the mug. Brought up her STEN. But then she saw the figure was a girl, unarmed. Perhaps fourteen or fifteen. As the girl

THE MAPMAKER

drew nearer, Lisette saw she was distraught. Tears streaked her face. Her cheeks flushed red.

"*Messieurs*," she cried, "*Mademoiselle*, are you *résistants?*"

"We are," the Yank said. "How did you find us?"

"The FTP told me," the girl said. "They sent me to tell you.... "

She stopped to catch her breath. Leaned forward and placed her hands on her thighs. Mud spattered her skirt. She appeared to have run a good distance, probably all the way from Tulle. The girl drew in ragged gasps that degenerated into sobs. Lisette embraced her.

"What is wrong?" Lisette asked.

"More Germans," the girl said. Stopped for more wracking sobs. "More Germans came."

"*Das Reich*," the Yank said.

"No doubt," the French Jedburgh man said.

"They drove out the FTP," the girl said. "Now they are killing.... "

"What?" Lisette said.

"They arrested all the men in town," the girl said. "They are hanging them."

Her sobs turned to a long wail. *No doubt the poor child knows most of the men being murdered*, Lisette thought.

"Let's see if we can confirm," the Yank said. "Let London know."

An hour later, Lisette, Olivier, and the Jedburgh team crept to a tree line on a hill overlooking Tulle. When Lisette first saw what was happening in the streets, she did not comprehend it despite the girl's warning. She needed a moment to process the scene. Then she needed another moment to believe her own eyes—to understand it was real and not a nightmare about a small town in hell.

SS troops milled about. Panzers blocked intersections. And corpses hung everywhere.

Bodies dangled from trees. From balconies. From lampposts.

Lisette began to sweat. Her heart raced. She took deep breaths, felt she might suffocate.

Control yourself, she thought. *Observe. Think. Report.*

"Bastards," Olivier hissed. "Dear God, what bastards."

235

"Reprisal killings," the British radio man said.

"What can we do?" Lisette asked. A rhetorical question. She wanted to charge down the hill, firing her STEN. But that would be suicide.

"We radio what we saw," the French officer said.

"Then we make a plan and ambush them again," the Yank offered.

Olivier raised his binoculars. When he lowered them, his eyes welled. Passed the binoculars to Lisette.

When she looked through the lenses, she wished she had not. Corpses stared with dead, open eyes. Purple faces. Blue tongues lolled from open mouths. She tried to count them. Stopped at forty when she could not stand to count anymore.

At one corner, three SS men tied a young man's hands together. Then they forced him up a ladder. When he stopped, one of them slammed him in the back with a rifle stock. He shrieked. They hit him again and he climbed. At the top of the ladder, he screamed once more. Next to him, a noose dangled from a telephone pole.

A soldier followed him up the ladder. Yanked the noose around his neck and jerked it tight. Jumped down and kicked the ladder.

The man swung from the telephone pole. The short drop did not break his neck. He kicked, struggled, and swayed for five minutes.

The SS men laughed while he died by strangulation.

THE MAPMAKER

MEMORANDUM
REGARDING: Operation Donar
Gestapo Counterintelligence Corps,
Federal Intelligence Service, Lyon
Lyon, France 9 June 1944
TO: Reich Security Main Office, Berlin
FROM: Klaus Barbie, Hauptstürmfuhrer

Criminal actions by terrorist elements have increased exponentially following the Allied landing against Fortress Europe. Clearly, these miscreants feel emboldened, and that the Fatherland's armies will not hurl the Allies back into the sea. Some seem to believe they can attack our forces with impunity. Operations have begun to correct their misapprehensions.

This office, in concert with Waffen SS and other forces, will seek to identify and eliminate the leaders of these terrorist activities. In situations where we cannot identify specific leaders, we will employ group punishment.

We shall demonstrate the futility of opposing our Thousand-Year Reich.

Heil Hitler,
Klaus Barbie, Hauptstürmfuhrer

237

CHAPTER 31

Philippe Gerard

Ever since the D-Day invasion at Normandy, four days ago, Philippe's spirits had flown as high as his Lightning. The 2/33 celebrated with more aux tank wine, along with Kentucky bourbon supplied by the Americans. They cheered the reports of landings on beaches code-named Omaha, Juno, Gold, and Sword. They prayed for the men and officers. They huddled around the radio for news, and applauded General Eisenhower's message to the Allied Expeditionary Force. Philippe especially noted the words of what was to come:

"In company with our brave Allies and brothers-in-arms on other fronts, you will bring about the destruction of the German war machine, the elimination of Nazi tyranny over the oppressed peoples of Europe, and security for ourselves in a free world."

The "other fronts" became the 2/33's raison d'être. Any day now, they expected, Operation Anvil would launch another front in southern France. To that end, Philippe launched on his first mission since D-Day.

He climbed away from Sardinia over a sparkling Mediterranean. Pushed up his throttles and pitched for best angle-of-climb speed. Today his target was close. Not even on the French mainland, but the Hyères Islands, just off the coast of France. Philippe wanted to get up to photo altitude as quickly as possible.

On the Hyères Islands, especially Port-Cros and Levant, the Germans had placed heavy guns that could enfilade the Anvil landing area and the sea approaches. The plan called for commandos to land on the islands and take out the enemy artillery. For such a high-risk operation, the commandos needed all the intelligence they could get.

As Philippe neared the islands, he set up his cameras for automatic operation. He flipped through a checklist binder to find a chart for the correct exposure interval for his speed and altitude. For 30,000 feet at an indicated airspeed of 205 knots, the chart called for six seconds between shots. According to the book, that provided a 60-percent photographic overlap.

All right, Philippe thought, *let's get this right for Charlotte.*

He entered the six-second setting on the intervalometer knob. Placed the camera control switch to AUTO. Flipped on the camera master switch. An amber light began to flash at six-second intervals.

Philippe smiled as he remembered a saying from the Yank pilots who flew Photo Joe missions: *Smile and say cheese, you sons of bitches.*

He completed his pass over Port-Cross, then turned and flew a photo run over Levant. All the while, he scanned for German fighters. Today, no enemy came up to greet him. Philippe imagined the Germans on the ground, huddled around radios, perhaps horrified by the news from Normandy. The thought gave him a smile under his oxygen mask.

But the smile faded as he thought of Lisette. What was she doing now? Nothing, he hoped. He wanted to believe that with the Allied invasion under way, *résistants* like Lisette could just stand down and let soldiers take it from here. But as a military officer, he knew better. She was an asset in the field. Her commanders might very well respect her, but they would not love her like a brother. They would see her and her colleagues as valued—but expendable.

And more than likely, SOE would want them to trip up the enemy in any way possible. What would that entail? And how would the Germans react to that? The Nazis in France were probably losing their minds right now. Philippe forced himself not to think about it.

When he completed his flight across Levant, he switched off his cameras and set a course back to Sardinia. Far below him, a convoy traversed the Med. The sight put Philippe in a better mood. The vessels plowed straight wakes that reminded him of staff lines on a sheet of music. A symphony in this case: He counted twenty ships.

From this altitude he could not tell the types of ships. But since his flight over Southampton and Portsmouth so many weeks ago, he'd learned more about them. He suspected LSTs, LCIs, and LCGs were getting into place for the invasion of southern France. To him, the acronyms themselves sounded like music. They stood for Landing Ship, Tank; Landing Craft, Infantry; Landing Craft, Gun. A song of liberation.

After a long, curving descent, Philippe lined up on final approach for Alghero Airfield. Clear skies and calm winds made for a smooth ride. Seabirds wheeled over the runway. They passed over Philippe's canopy as he flared for a smooth touchdown. He slowed, taxied onto the ramp, and set his parking brake. Pulled back the fuel mixture levers to shut down his engines. As soon as the propellers stopped turning, a pair of technicians came to the aircraft. They began opening panels to remove the film from the cameras. Philippe considered for a moment how his photos represented something relatively new in warfare. Aerial photography had begun during the previous war, but now it was greatly refined—enough to create nearly a God's-eye view of the battlespace. A poet might muse on man overstepping his bounds, but as a combat pilot, Philippe had a war to fight. He just hoped these photos would do more good than the ones he'd taken from his Bloch MB.174 in 1940. If victory came, then he, his country, and his countrymen would have redeemed themselves.

Philippe unplugged his oxygen mask and headset cord, stuffed his charts into a lower leg pocket of his flight suit. Climbed down from the Lightning and headed for Operations.

In the Ops building, nothing more than a Quonset hut by the control tower, he debriefed with an intelligence officer: photo runs complete, no enemy fighters encountered. Then he debriefed with a maintenance officer: no major writeups, some static on the VHF radio.

He read a message chalked onto the schedule board: MANDATORY PILOTS BRIEFING 1500.

In the briefing room, Philippe joined Saint-Ex in the first row of folding chairs. Cigarette smoke hung in the air. Aircraft recognition charts lined the left wall. The charts displayed silhouettes of friendly and enemy fighter planes—P-51s, P-47s, Fw-190s, and Bf-109s. Pinups decorated the right wall—including Betty Grable, Rita Hayworth, Lana Turner. Philippe's favorite showed Carole Landis in a flier's A-2 jacket. In the next room, a clerk clacked away at a typewriter.

"Any idea what this is about?" Philippe asked.

Saint-Ex shrugged. "*Non*," he said. "But I suspect we are deploying forward again. Corsica, most likely."

Philippe's old friend looked tired. He, too, had flown a mission this morning. He still wore his flight suit, the back stained by sweat. The imprint of his oxygen mask still indented his cheeks. Like Philippe, Saint-Ex had papers jammed into a leg pocket, but they were not aeronautical charts. They looked like notebook pages marked with scribbles and drawings. Philippe took that as a good sign. If Saint-Ex was still creating, still thinking of stories, then perhaps he had not sunk too low into depression.

Gavoille, their commander, entered with a briefing book under his arm. An orderly called the room to attention. Philippe, Saint-Ex, and their fellow aviators stood at attention.

"At ease," Gavoille said.

The boss took his place at a rostrum. He wore a grim expression, which was out of character for Gavoille. Philippe wondered if the unit had taken another loss.

"As you may have heard," Gavoille said, "we are packing up again. In two weeks, our new home will be Poretta Airfield in Bastia, on the island of Corsica."

The men cheered and applauded. Pulling up stakes again would be a chore, to be sure. A "bag drag," as the Americans called it. But it meant moving closer to France. Closer to the fight. Closing with the enemy.

But the cheers did not draw even a hint of a smile from the usually affable Gavoille.

"There is more," he said. "We will continue our schedule of photographic missions. However, the Staff advises me that Operation Anvil is scrubbed. Canceled."

A beat of silence followed the commander's words.

Then the room erupted in curses, murmurs, questions. Philippe, for his part, sat mute. He felt as if a gut punch had knocked the breath from him. Saint-Ex tipped back his chair and stared at the ceiling.

"WHAT?" a flier called from the back of the room.

Gavoille glared.

"Sorry," the flier said. "I mean, what, sir?"

"Prime Minister Churchill believes all resources must be directed toward the front that has been opened in Normandy," Gavoille explained. "He fears a landing in southern France will become a fiasco like Anzio."

Earlier in the year, the Allies had continued the Italian Campaign with an amphibious landing at Anzio. The operation went well at first; more than 36,000 men came ashore the first day. But once ashore, the commanding general paused, waiting to strengthen his force. The Germans took advantage of the delay. They bottled up the Allies on the beachhead. "I had hoped we were hurling a wildcat into the shore," Churchill had remarked, "but all we got was a stranded whale."

"Politics," Saint-Ex whispered. "Damned politics."

Philippe's notions of serving his country sluffed off him like dead skin. For a moment he had fancied himself useful. Effective. Striking a blow. Redeeming himself completely. Now he felt like a chess piece. A pawn shunted aside as greater moves took place elsewhere on the chessboard.

Just a few hours ago, at an altitude of 30,000 feet, purpose and resolve had filled his spirit. All that drained out of him now. A decision made in London, by people he would never know, left him empty, without direction. His mind reeled like a radio compass that had lost its signal, the needle turning aimless circles. No course, no bearing. No anything.

CHAPTER 32

Lisette Gerard

In the back room of a café in the village of Limoges, Lisette, Olivier, and an American from the Jedburgh team waited for a local Resistance leader. They knew her only by the code name of Tabby. She wasn't just any volunteer; she was an officer with the BCRA. While they waited, a *résistant* watched the front of the café. If he gave the alarm, Lisette and her colleagues would slip out the rear entrance into the woods.

Tabby was late. Lisette didn't like that. No one else did, either.

"She better have nine lives," the Yank officer said.

"How much longer do we stay here?" Olivier asked.

The Yank looked at his watch.

"Just a few more minutes," he said. "Then we beat it."

He seemed to be thinking of what concerned Lisette—and neither she nor anyone else said it out loud. Had their contact been arrested? Or worse, was this a setup? Everything in this business was a calculated risk.

Two coughs sounded from the main dining room. That signal from the *résistant* on watch meant he'd spotted Tabby, and all was well. A door creaked open, and Lisette heard boot heels on a hardwood floor, murmurs in French. A moment later, the woman entered the back room.

TOM YOUNG

She pulled back the hood that cloaked her blonde hair. Dim light from the room's oil lamp revealed a young woman, no more than thirty. The folds of her shawl parted, and Lisette saw she wore a shoulder holster over a peasant dress. Despite her youth, she had the eyes of a combat sergeant. Expressionless. Piercing.

"We almost bailed on you," the Yank said.

"I wasn't late because I was window-shopping," Tabby said. "We received last-minute intelligence."

"Spill it," the Yank said.

"Some of our colleagues have bagged a major target," Tabby said. "They have captured and, I believe, killed *Sturmbannführer* Helmut Kämpfe."

"That is good news," Lisette said. "We are supposed to impede them in any way possible."

"Yes," Tabby said. "But some of our friends may have gotten carried away. The rumor is they burned him alive."

"Damn," the Yank said. "But you ain't exactly breaking my heart."

"Yes, he deserves no sympathy," Tabby said. "But these are not *Wehrmacht* soldiers. These are *Waffen-SS*. They are zealots. They will bring the fury of hell with them."

"At Tulle," Lisette said, "we saw what they are capable of."

"So, we expect reprisals," Olivier said.

"*Oui*," Tabby said.

"Where?" the Yank asked.

Tabby shrugged. "Who knows?" she said. "Anywhere."

"So, how does this change our plans?" the Yank asked.

"It does not," Tabby said. "In Poitiers, about a hundred kilometers northeast of here, some of our British friends are waiting."

"The SAS," the Yank said.

Tabby nodded. She and the Yank reviewed what they knew of a mission called Operation Bulbasket. Men from the British Army's Special Air Service had already parachuted into the Poitiers area. They, along with Jedburgh teams, planned to sabotage rail lines, blow up fuel trains, lay mines, and generally wreak havoc for *Das Reich*.

244

"Sounds like a good show," the Yank said.

"We hope so," Tabby said. She turned to Lisette and Olivier. "This is primarily an action by the SAS and OSS," she explained. "Our Jedburgh friends will link up with them. You two watch the roads, lie low for a day or two. Gather whatever intelligence you can."

"And then?" Olivier said.

"We will find you."

Lisette and Olivier spent the night at the Avril Hotel in the village Oradour-sur-Glane. Oradour was a quiet community on the River Glane between Limoges and Poitiers. The town had never sheltered Resistance fighters because there had hardly been any enemy to fight in the area. Even the Germans passed it by. For that reason, Lisette believed Oradour made a good spot to watch for *Das Reich* as the Panzer division continued toward Normandy. She and Olivier would hold their fire, count vehicles and men, and make a report.

In the morning they ate a light breakfast of tartine with ersatz coffee. From the hotel's small dining room they watched the main street. For hours, they saw nothing but civilian cars and the occasional horse cart. Heard nothing but children's laughter, quiet conversation, and birdsong. The waiter, a boy of about sixteen, gathered up their dishes.

At two in the afternoon, the rumble of engines and tank tracks sounded in the distance. Lisette stepped outside to look. Down the street, she spotted a light plume of dust. Went back inside and told Olivier what she'd seen.

As she spoke, a woman burst into the hotel. She panted from running hard, and her hair spilled uncombed across her shoulders. She ran through the foyer and told the man at the front desk, "They are here. They are blocking the streets."

Lisette and Olivier looked at one another.

"Why would they do that?" Lisette asked.

Olivier shook his head.

A moment later, a town crier entered the building. The old man told the staff to pass the word that everyone had to gather at the market center.

"Why?" the waiter asked.

"An identification check, they say."

Lisette felt a rush of cold, a surge of pain through her scarred shoulders. An ID check of citizens at Oradour made no sense. Unlike Tulle, the town had not harbored a Resistance force waiting for the Germans. There had been no ambush, no sniping, no sabotage.

But the enemy wanted vengeance for their missing *Sturmbannführer*. If they couldn't find the culprits, maybe anyone would do.

"Get out of here," she whispered to Olivier. "Find a radio man and tell London."

Olivier looked puzzled.

"What do you mean?" he asked. "You're coming with me, right?"

"I'll be right behind you. But I'll have a look first. See if I can get more information."

"That's insane."

"No, it isn't. At Tulle, they killed all the men. So you have to get out. Right now. They didn't hurt the women."

"I cannot leave you here by yourself," Olivier said.

"Don't be stupid," Lisette hissed. "GO!"

Olivier sighed. Stood up, squeezed Lisette's shoulder. Turned and left the dining room without another word. Lisette heard his boots on the steps as he went to his room to get his weapon and knapsack. Then she heard him tromp down the stairs and leave out the back door.

At the market square, dozens of SS troops prowled through the crowd. They were dressed for combat, with coal-scuttle helmets and field blouses of mottled camouflage. Many carried automatic weapons. Several dripped with ammunition; links of belted cartridges hung from their necks and dangled to their waists. Nearly all kept wooden-handled "potato-masher" grenades tucked under their belts. Some checked ID cards. An officer appeared and barked orders in German. The troops began separating the men from the women and children.

Lisette blended in as best she could. Her plain dress and sweater helped her look like any country maid. After careful consideration, she had left her STEN at the hotel. If a German searched her and found it, the discovery would mean death for her and probably many other women. One gun against a Panzer division would have amounted to suicide, anyway. Her mission now was to observe, to gather intelligence. She prayed she would not witness another horror.

The officer addressed the men in French. He wore a peaked hat. SS runes gleamed on his right collar. A swastika adorned the right pocket of his tunic.

"Good afternoon, citizens," he said. "I am *Sturmbannführer* Adolf Diekmann. I shall get right to the point. We know some of you have cached weapons and ammunition here for the bandits. I need two things from you: Tell me where these caches are located. And tell me who is responsible."

No one spoke. Somewhere a child began to cry.

"We do not have all day, people," Diekmann continued. "We have things to do farther up the road, and we would like very much to get on with it. Tell us what we need to know, and you may go back to your homes."

Lisette began to sweat. Diekmann hadn't even mentioned the missing SS officer, Helmut Kämpfe. And there were no weapons caches here. What was this about?

Or was this about nothing? Maybe the Nazis didn't bother with excuses anymore.

No one answered Diekmann. That made him angry.

"I see," he said. "You want to do this the hard way. Very well. Where is your mayor? Is he here?"

An old man stepped forward.

"Good afternoon, mayor," Diekmann said. "Select thirty hostages from the men."

"I will not," the mayor said. "We have no weapons."

"If you will not give us thirty, we will take them all."

Diekmann shouted more orders in German. The troops began separating the men into groups. The soldiers shoved them, prodded them with rifle barrels. Shouted in broken French. Men who protested or hesitated got beaten to the ground.

TOM YOUNG

One soldier pointed and shouted, "Get down there to that barn."

"What is the meaning of this?" a man asked.

The soldier shouldered his Mauser. Shot the man through the chest. He collapsed as blood spurted from an exit wound in his back. The soldier racked his bolt. Empty brass flipped from the breech and spun into the grass.

In six separate groups, the men were led away from the market square. Some of the women began screaming and yelling: "Where are you taking them?" "My husband did nothing!" "My son is just thirteen!"

"SILENCE!" Diekmann shouted. "I gave you your chance."

Lisette tried to take in all her surroundings, to think of a plan. She considered trying to run for it. That's when three men broke from their group. They sprinted toward the river. A burst of automatic fire cut them down. The women's screams grew louder. Lisette stood still. Took deep breaths to calm herself.

"Get into the church," Diekmann ordered the women. "Move. Now!"

He drew his Luger. Fired a shot into the air.

Troops herded the women and children across the square toward the Church of Saint Martin. Lisette now knew the Nazis intended to kill all the men, just like in Tulle. Perhaps they might spare the women and children. For her report, Lisette tried to estimate the number of men marched away. About two hundred, she guessed.

In the distance, a long rip of automatic fire split the afternoon. Then another and another.

"NO, NO, NO!" an old woman screamed.

An SS sergeant ripped her apart with a machine pistol. For a moment, red mist hung in the air above her body.

The troops kicked and punched. Shoved some of the women and children toward the steps at the base of the steeple. Forced others through the door to the sacristy.

No one could move fast enough for the soldiers. They shouted curses and shoved. Slammed women through the doors with rifle stocks.

Bodies crunched together so tightly Lisette could hardly breathe. She found herself carried with the crowd through the main entrance

248

THE MAPMAKER

below the steeple. Inside the nave, she found a little more room to move. She ran toward the altar. Took cover behind its thick hardwood.

In seconds, the nave filled with distraught women and crying children. More automatic fire sounded from outside.

From the narthex, a soldier hurled an object over the crowd. For a moment Lisette thought it strange he would throw a stick toward the ceiling. The stick flipped end over end. Then she realized it was a wooden-handled grenade.

The grenade bounced off a rafter. Dropped into the crowd. The detonation slammed through the room. Lisette felt the blast wave against her cheeks. Shrapnel sprayed the front side of the altar.

At the center of the nave, several women fell. Others, with bloodied faces and hands, tried to claw up the walls toward the windows.

Another grenade flipped across the pews. This time, Lisette felt the blast and heat but heard nothing. The first explosion had deafened her. More women and children dropped to the floor. Some rammed their shoulders against the door, tried to escape.

The door held fast, apparently chained from the outside.

Smoke rose through the church. Where was that coming from? Lisette realized troops had set the church on fire from the outside. At one of the windows, flames flickered through broken stained glass.

Panic seared Lisette's mind. She had to escape. Anything would be better than dying like this. At the chancel, she saw a window that extended down to floor level.

From the altar, Lisette grabbed a heavy brass crucifix. Ran to the chancel window. Smashed through the window with the crucifix. Glass shards stung her hands. She smashed again and again until she tore an opening large enough to jump through.

Lisette dropped the crucifix. Climbed through the opening. Cut her hands but hardly felt it. Let herself drop to the ground. She fell hard, landed on her side. Felt ribs crack. Scrambled to her feet and ran.

She got about ten meters from the church. Then a force tore through her. Bullets spun her around. More rounds shattered her legs, put her on the ground. She lay on her back. Stared up at the sky. Tried to move. Found it impossible.

A deep breath brought searing pain. Then the pain eased some. Lisette knew she was dying. She watched smoke envelop the steeple. Saw a raven glide through the smoke.

More smoke and fire rose from the sacristy. She felt no pain now, just a growing numbness. Panic left her, supplanted by an odd tranquility. Then her eyes saw no more.

THE MAPMAKER

MEMORANDUM
REGARDING: Operation Donar
Gestapo Counterintelligence Corps,
Federal Intelligence Service, Lyon
Lyon, France 12 June 1944
TO: Reich Security Main Office, Berlin
FROM: Klaus Barbie, Hauptstürmfuhrer

Our SS colleagues have completed a punitive operation in the French village of Oradour-sur-Glane. Perhaps due to the high number of deaths—by some accounts more than 600—the Vichy government has formally protested.

Sturmbannführer Diekmann has ordered his soldiers not to speak of the event. His division is proceeding to meet the enemy at Normandy.

Due to the grumblings even from the French who are loyal to the Reich, their claims must be answered by counterclaims. This office suggests the following:

1) We state that the men of the village first attacked our forces.
2) Those men died in firefights with our forces.
3) Women and children in the church died due to the explosion of a terrorist arms cache hidden within the church.

Heil Hitler,
Klaus Barbie, Hauptstürmfuhrer

CHAPTER 33

Charlotte Denneau

On the island of Corsica, Charlotte could walk the ancient town of Bastia and transport herself to another, more peaceful time. Its cobblestoned streets and azure waters contrasted with the dust, noise, and sweltering tents of Poretta Airfield. To Charlotte, the air base represented the war and all its ugliness. Violence and death. But the town and its Old Port reminded her of the small things she loved about living. Aromas of pastries made with chestnut flour wafted from bakeries. The pure polyphonic lilt of choirs chanting traditional music rose from the churches. And the landmarks told of the centuries: The Citadel overlooked the harbor and its stone jetties. Within the Citadel, bombings had scarred the Palace of Governors, but the place still retained its old-world charm. Green hills rose above the ramparts into morning mist that burned away into gin-clear afternoon skies.

One hot morning, while she waited for the latest photos to be developed, she strolled down to a jetty that extended out into the harbor. A lighthouse stood at the end of the jetty. Sea breeze lifted her hair as she took the stone walkway down to the lighthouse. Charlotte thought she might enjoy a few moments of solitude, gazing out over the water, before returning to her duties.

But then she saw a figure seated at the base of the lighthouse. The man slumped against the lighthouse wall, held a bottle in his left hand. Charlotte took him for a town drunkard. She turned to leave, to avoid any contact with the derelict. But something made her look again. The man was wearing...flight clothing. She stepped closer, and recognized Philippe.

Charlotte ran to him, kneeled beside him. He was unshaven, smelled of wine and sweat. Dried blood caked the knuckles of his right hand. He turned to look at her with bloodshot eyes. Squinted against the rising sun.

"*Bonjour,*" he slurred.

"Philippe, what happened to you?" Charlotte asked. "Did you get into a fight?"

He shut his eyes tight. Opened them again.

"No," he said. "I don't think so."

"You're drunk. Dear God, have you been here all night?"

"Ahh," Philippe said. Made a show of looking at his watch. "*Oui*, if it's daytime, then I guess I have been here all night."

"What happened to your hand?"

Philippe stretched out his right fingers and winced. He lifted the bottle to his lips with his left hand. When he found the bottle empty, he hurled it away. The bottle shattered against jetty stones. Glass shards flecked the water.

"I punched a wall," Philippe said. "Seemed like a good idea at the time."

"Why did you do that? What happened?"

Philippe stared out over the harbor for a moment. Then he dug his wounded hand into a zippered pocket of his flight suit. Found a small wad of paper. Passed it to Charlotte.

"This is what happened," he said.

Charlotte opened the paper. Through the wrinkles and wine stains, she saw it was a telegram, transmitted in English:

3.44 PM LONDON TELEX

MINISTRY OF DEFENCE REGRETS TO INFORM
YOU OPERATIVE LISETTE GERARD DIED IN THE
LINE OF DUTY ON OR ABOUT 10 JUNE 1944 STOP
NO FURTHER DETAILS AVAILABLE AT THIS TIME
STOP SPECIAL OPERATIONS EXECUTIVE EXPRESS
THEIR PROFOUND SYMPATHY STOP +++

"Philippe, I'm so sorry," Charlotte said. She pulled him to her, held him in an embrace. He began to weep. Deep sobs shook his shoulders. After a few moments he pulled away from her. Wiped his nose and eyes with a handkerchief.

"Those bastards sent her back," Philippe said. "She had done her part, and they sent her back."

Charlotte looked again at the date mentioned in the telegram.

"Ten June," she said. "That was a month ago."

"And why did it take them so long to tell me?"

Charlotte placed the telegram into one of Philippe's pockets. Took his hand.

"I do not know," she said. "There is no telling what the circumstances were, and when SOE learned of it."

Philippe pushed himself against the lighthouse wall to sit up straighter. Stared out across the water.

"I can imagine the circumstances," he said.

"Don't," Charlotte said.

Gavoille took Philippe off the schedule for a week of bereavement. Charlotte spent as much time with him as she could. They took long walks through Bastia and along the waterfront. Most of the time they did not speak, and she did not force conversation. She believed she could help best just by being there. His depression never seemed to ease.

One afternoon, Philippe said, "There was a time when I wanted to die to prove a point. But now if I die, it proves nothing. Accomplishes nothing. And if I live it accomplishes nothing."

Charlotte took his arm and said, "You mustn't think that way. You are still serving your country. We just can't see the big picture."

Philippe laughed, but the laughter came with bitterness.

"I thought the big picture was our whole mission," he said.

Charlotte wasn't sure how to answer, so she said nothing.

After a week, Philippe resumed flying missions. He lamented to Charlotte that they were entirely pointless. He and the rest of 2/33 continued photographing German positions on the Hyères Islands, Draguignan, Toulon, Marseilles, and elsewhere in southern France.

Charlotte spent hours with her stereoscope, poring over the photographs. She recorded enemy movements and activity in ports and along rail lines. She did not know what London would do with that information, if anything. But she sent it anyway.

Though little was happening along the southern coast of France, action came heavy in Normandy. Allied forces pushed out of their beachhead, and Charlotte followed news about the capture of Saint-Lô and Coutances. The victories thrilled her, but the broadcasts and intelligence reports made it clear the Allies paid in blood for every kilometer.

One of the biggest problems was supply. Eisenhower and other leaders had counted on using French ports to keep fuel, food, and ammunition flowing to their soldiers. But the Germans had wrecked the port in Cherbourg and laid mines in the harbor. The enemy was also fighting hard, with large garrisons of troops, to hold onto ports in Brest and Saint Malo.

To Charlotte, the clear solution was to take France's southern ports, which Operation Anvil might have accomplished. But she accepted that she did not make decisions—she only supplied information to the people who did.

Still, she felt the frustration that corroded morale across the entire Mediterranean Allied Photo Reconnaissance Wing. Charlotte could see that Philippe, Saint-Ex, and the other French aviators in MAPRW took it especially hard. No doubt Philippe wanted to redeem his nation and avenge his sister.

"But now," Philippe told her, "I just bore holes in the sky and convert 100-octane fuel into noise."

"Sounds like you've been talking to the Americans," Charlotte said.

"I have. They don't like it any more than I do."

On the morning of July 31, Charlotte joined the fliers for breakfast in the mess hall. She chose an American-style breakfast that day: greasy bacon and powdered eggs. Philippe chuckled at her when she put down her tray beside him. He had chosen his usual *pain et beurre*, rolls and butter, with what the Yanks called their "trash can coffee." It was the first time she'd seen him smile since he'd learned of Lisette's death.

"Are you flying today?" Charlotte asked.

"No," Philippe said, "but he is."

Philippe pointed to the door, where Saint-Ex had just entered. He cut a burly figure in his flying suit and A-2 jacket. The skin sagged under his eyes. The author walked as if his old injuries hurt more than usual. He took his bread and coffee and sat across from Philippe and Charlotte.

"Big party last night, Major?" Philippe asked.

"Not really," Saint-Ex said. "Dinner with some people in Miomo. Nice little restaurant there."

Saint-Ex said little else while he ate. Charlotte could not tell if he was unhappy about something or just focused on his mission.

"At least you have good visibility today," she said.

"*Oui*," Saint-Ex replied. "The Yank meteorologist said the weather was 'clear and a million.'"

Charlotte smiled. Saint-Ex's English had never been good, but perhaps it was improving if he'd understood the weatherman's slang.

After breakfast, Charlotte and Philippe walked out to the flight line to watch Saint-Ex take off. As he started his engines, Charlotte realized she'd never come this close to a Lightning while it was running. Dear God, that thing was loud. Even at idle, the propellers kicked up a frightful gale. The blast swept away wisps of exhaust smoke that belched on startup.

A mechanic stood fire guard with a large extinguisher while Saint-Ex ran his engine checks. Then a marshaller guided him with hand signals out of the Lightning's hardstand. The aircraft rolled down the taxiway, turned onto the runway, and accelerated for liftoff.

THE MAPMAKER

Charlotte watched the Lightning climb into a cobalt sky over an amethyst sea. Saint-Ex turned to an on-course heading. His aircraft grew smaller with distance until it vanished.

After lunchtime, Charlotte was working at her desk, bright lamp over the stereoscope, when Philippe entered the tent. He stood in the glare of the open tent flap. For long seconds, he did not speak. He just stood with his hands on his hips, looking down at the floor. Took a long breath.

"Philippe," Charlotte said. "What is wrong?"

"He's overdue."

"Who? Saint-Ex?"

"Yes. He should have been back half an hour ago."

Charlotte needed a moment to process the implication. A cold ingot formed down in her chest. *No, not this*, she thought. *Please, not this.* The unit did not need another loss. Heaven knew Philippe did not need another loss.

She rose from her desk and embraced Philippe. He held her so tight it squeezed her ribs.

"What do we do?" she asked.

Philippe released his hold on her. "We go to Ops," he said. "Listen to the radios. Pray."

In Operations, they found the 2/33 commander, Gavoille, along with an American lieutenant.

"What can we do, sir?" Philippe asked Gavoille.

The commander opened his mouth to speak. Then, overcome with emotion, he swallowed his words. Shook his head silently and turned away.

At the radio, the American lieutenant keyed a microphone, transmitted in the blind for Saint-Ex. No response came except static hiss.

Philippe went to the window. Stared into the blue abyss as if he might will his old friend out of it somehow. Keep him among the living through sheer concentration. Charlotte joined him. Placed her hand on his back.

"Could he have bailed out?" she asked. "Crash landed?" She had seen how the fliers went to the flight line practically dripping in survival

257

gear: parachute, life vest, first-aid kit, sea-dye marker, signal light, and inflatable raft. Surely they didn't carry these things for nothing.

Philippe lifted his upturned palms in a gesture of…resignation. Yes, Charlotte realized, it was remotely possible Saint-Ex was still alive somewhere. But not likely.

The American officer called again on the radio. Still no answer.

The static seemed to pierce Philippe's heart like a stiletto. He took a deep breath, as if about to try to talk without choking up. When he did speak, the words came out barely above a whisper.

"One night back in 1940," he said, "before the fall of France, Saint-Ex and I went to the mess for dinner." Philippe paused, closed his eyes, then continued. "We noticed some of our comrades were missing. Do you know what he said to me?"

"What?" Charlotte said.

"He said, 'Those who are late never get back. The night has swung them into eternity.'"

"It's not night yet," Charlotte said.

But the night did come, and it came in silence. No radio call. No thrum of a Lightning's engines. Just an empty Mediterranean sky that dimmed slowly to black.

At dark, Gavoille transmitted a radiogram:

TO: MAPRW HQ
FROM: 2/33

PILOT FAILED TO RETURN. PRESUMED LOST

CHAPTER 34

Philippe Gerard

Philippe sat in his Lightning at Poretta Airfield. He had strapped in and closed the canopy. Connected his oxygen mask and comm cord. A crew chief stood by as fire guard. Everything was ready for startup.

The crew chief must have wondered what was wrong. Philippe ignored the man's hand signals. Instead of flipping the battery switch and beginning the engine start checklist, Philippe watched the sunrise. Scarlet veils stretched over the sea. The dawn's rays turned the water to claret, the low, scattered clouds to vermillion. Even the wings of white seabirds flushed pink in the early light.

He would never see the sunrise again.

Philippe had determined to join Saint-Ex in the next world. With Lisette gone, he had no family left. With Operation Anvil canceled, he had no real mission left. No purpose, no home, no future that he could see from the depths of depression. *Rien*. Nothing.

For a moment he considered whether it was selfish to take his own life in an expensive aircraft. A pistol round would suffice. But with Anvil scrubbed, entire squadrons were being wasted. Besides, Philippe did not want anyone to find him with his head blown open. Better just to take off and disappear.

Such dark thoughts had come to him often back when he flew the Lysanders for the RAF. He'd hoped death in combat would clear his name. Now he hoped only that death would bring relief. He would join Lisette and Saint-Ex in whatever lay beyond this world of violence.

The question was how to make it happen. Surely somewhere to the north, a German pilot was firing up his 109, eager for a kill. If an enemy fighter rolled in on his six o'clock, he could just hold his wings level. Make himself an easy target. Go out in a blaze of glory. But if the Germans would not oblige, he could plunge the Lightning into the sea. Terminal dive. What would happen when you exceeded a Lightning's Never Exceed speed? Would the wings rip off?

One way to find out.

Philippe placed his finger on the battery switch to start his one-way journey. Glanced up at the crew chief. But the man was no longer looking at the airplane. He was pointing to something across the ramp. Philippe twisted in his seat to see.

A woman was running toward the flight line. She stopped to consult with a guard. He checked her ID, then waved her on.

It was Charlotte. She headed straight for Philippe's plane. Carried a sheaf of papers in her hand. What could she possibly want?

Philippe considered ignoring her. The interruption irritated him. There was dying to be done. Had he forgot to sign some silly paperwork in Ops? He was long past caring about such trivia. He could fire up his engines and keep her away from the aircraft.

But curiosity got the better of him. He raised his canopy just as she reached the Lightning. The crew chief moved a stepladder into place so she could talk to him. She climbed the ladder. Dropped the papers into his lap.

"Thank God I caught you," she said. "I thought you'd be gone." Breeze scattered her hair across her face, and she brushed the locks away to reveal a smile. On any other day, that rare smile would have warmed Philippe's heart.

"What is it?" he asked.

"We just got intel from London. Eisenhower wants the ports down here. Operation Overlord has advanced so quickly that supply lines are getting long, and the Normandy ports can't handle it all."

"You mean Anvil is back on?"

"I don't know. But Eisenhower is talking to Churchill, and Roosevelt's backing him up."

"What's all this?" Philippe asked.

With a gloved hand, he thumbed through the papers. Most were hand-drawn diagrams with a few scribbled notes.

"Railroads, as best I can remember them." Charlotte pointed to the top page. "You see the lines coming north from Marseille and Toulon. The Germans have sabotaged the ports pretty bad. But the railroads might be in decent shape. The Resistance hit the rail lines hard elsewhere in France, but not so much down here."

Charlotte explained that once Allied engineers repaired the ports and rails, supplies could flow north from the Riviera pretty easily.

"And they want to know the condition of the railroads?"

"Exactly," Charlotte said. "Get me some pictures."

Philippe leaned his head back against his headrest. Closed his eyes. Considered the meaning of all Charlotte had just told him.

"So, the mapmaker has made more maps," he said.

"Yeah, I did. Sorry they're so sloppy. I had to work fast to catch you."

Philippe leaned as far toward Charlotte as his straps would allow. Kissed the top of her head. For an instant, her perfume swept away the reek of oil and fuel.

"Thank you for this," he said.

"I thought it might give you something better to do on this flight."

Philippe considered how to answer. Finally, he said, "You have no idea."

Charlotte frowned as if puzzled, but she didn't ask questions. She squeezed his hand so hard he felt it through leather gloves.

"You better get back here, flyboy," Charlotte said. "I want those photos."

Fifteen minutes later, Philippe lifted into the Mediterranean sky with an agenda entirely rewritten. His mind raced with motivation. His thoughts spun with the altimeter as the Lightning leapt for altitude. His ship climbed so fast he nearly missed going on oxygen as he crossed 10,000 feet. He clicked his mask into place and checked the oxygen quantity light. As he inhaled and exhaled, the blinker on the oxygen regulator flashed white, black, white, black. The oxygen felt cool going down. He took a deep, life-sustaining breath. He now cared about maintaining his body; he wanted to live at least long enough to complete this mission.

The cockpit felt comfortable for now, but Philippe knew he needed to stay ahead of the temperature drop as altitude increased. He moved the heat knob to full hot. Warm air began flowing, filtered by an intensifier tube from the right engine's exhaust.

Now he could turn his attention to navigation. From a leg pocket he pulled a WAC chart, then clipped it to his kneeboard. He fumbled through Charlotte's hand-drawn maps until he found one that depicted Marseille. At the top, she had scribbled in English: RAILWAY REHABILITATION???

An odd phrase, Philippe mused, for a woman who had dedicated much of her efforts to railway *destruction*. With a black pen, Charlotte had traced rail lines leading north from the port city. These must be the rails that might be easily repaired. Philippe oriented Charlotte's diagram with the more detailed WAC chart. Took a felt pen from a sleeve pocket and plotted a flight path. The flight path—and the photographic path—would begin with Marseille's rail station and continue up toward Aix-en-Provence and farther toward Lyon.

At 30,000 feet he leveled off. Set his prop controls, fuel mixtures, and throttles for cruise flight. Heated up his cameras and went to work.

As methodically as he could, he photographed the areas Charlotte had marked. Watched the camera light flash its regular intervals. Kept a steady scan that covered the camera controls, the aircraft instruments, and the outside. So far, at least, he saw no enemy fighters.

When he covered the area marked by Charlotte's first map, he crumpled the paper and let it drop to the cockpit floor. Banked into a turn and went to work on the next sheet. Her plan was ambitious. Quick mental math told him he'd barely have enough film for everything she

262

wanted. He resolved to fly steady and true, not to waste a frame. Without the ability to look straight down and see precisely what the cameras saw, he relied on landmarks and dead reckoning.

On his fifth pass, just as he crumpled Charlotte's last diagram, he scanned outside again. Saw nothing but dots of frost forming low on his canopy. He brought his eyes back inside and checked oil temps, ammeters, and fuel pressures. Everything looked good. Then he felt a twinge of...animal fear.

Wait a minute, Philippe thought. *Dots of frost should be white. Not black.*

He looked down and to his left again.

Bloody hell. Those are airplanes.

As they climbed, they took the form of Bf-109s. Eight of them. Rising on his nine o'clock. Right over the coastline.

Muscle memory took Philippe's hands through the drill he'd learned from his crazy American P-38 instructor: *Prop levers forward, mixtures to AUTO RICH. Jettison the drop tanks.*

Philippe felt the aircraft shudder as the drop tanks fell away. He'd already emptied them, and now he burned out of his mains. With the elimination of the drop tanks' drag, his airspeed began creeping up. He pushed his throttles to the WEP setting: War Emergency Power, maximum manifold pressure.

"Come on, my dear," he whispered into his oxygen mask. "I need everything you have."

The 109s rose higher and gained on him. He was over the Med now, between the mainland and Corsica. And the 109s were between him and home base.

What to do next became a judgment call. With no guns on this photorecon bird, Philippe couldn't fight; he could only run. But how? Stay headed for home and hope the enemy planes couldn't outclimb him? Turn tail and fly directly away from them? Given the Lightning's speed advantage, they'd never overtake him if he did that. But then he'd be flying away from Corsica and getting low on gas. He'd have to ditch or bail out. His critical photos would wind up at the bottom of the sea.

Philippe decided to stay on his heading. Didn't look like the 109s could reach his altitude in time to get within firing range.

He did some quick math in his head. How fast was he going? Not a simple question in an airplane at high altitude. The thin air induced instrument error. For a rough estimate of true airspeed, he took his altitude in thousands, multiplied by five, and added his indicated airspeed.

Think, he told himself. *Thirty times five is 150. Airspeed indicator shows 250 miles an hour. They won't get high enough fast enough to get a shot at me.*

Or will they?

The damned enemy fighters looked bigger every second. Now he could see the *Balkenkreuz* markings—the black crosses on the fuselages and wings—and the swastikas on the tails. And they were still hanging on his left side. They had not passed below him.

Maybe he had misjudged. Maybe the winds gave the German pilots some kind of advantage. No doubt they'd set their engines to max continuous power, just as he had. They were almost certainly pitching for best rate of climb speed, hoping to get close enough to send him spinning, burning, and exploding into the sea.

Before Charlotte had come to his plane, the 109s would have been welcome guests. He would have held his wings level and let them do their worst. It would have been over by now. His Lighting would have fallen to earth in pieces.

But no more. Now if they splashed him, he would make them work for it. They kept getting higher and bigger, and they seemed locked on his left wingtip. In a few more seconds they'd get into position for a deflection shot. Tricky marksmanship, but if all eight of them opened up, somebody would get lucky. Already Philippe had pushed his Allison engines to the max. If he asked them for more, he might lose both of them. Along with the film and his life.

There was only one way to go faster without blowing up the Allisons: Dive.

Philippe glanced at the dive chart taped to his kneeboard. He noted that the lower he got, the faster he could go, based on indicated airspeed. Beyond the graph's envelope, his controls might lock up as he approached the speed of sound. Engineers didn't understand it all, but air did weird things when pilots flew that fast. Fliers in powerful aircraft had entered dives and found themselves unable to pull out. A shock wave or something blanked out the flight controls.

Very well, then, Philippe thought. *I will go that fast and no faster.*

He eased back the throttles and dropped the nose. Airspeed rose quickly, so he cut the power a little more. The altimeter needle began unwinding, and the Lighting zipped downward through the altitude of the enemy fighters.

Now they were directly on his beam, right at nine o'clock. The 109s opened up. Tracers cut paths toward Philippe, but the bullets passed behind him.

His eyes moved in a constant circuit between the dive chart, the airspeed indicator, and the enemy. He passed through 20,000 feet and let his speed come up by 30 miles an hour. The German fighters turned to chase him, to try to get on his six o'clock. Ideal firing position.

Now Philippe had no choice but to outrun them.

Tracers passed beneath him. The 109s were firing from too far behind.

If they gain on me now, Philippe thought, *they'll have me dead to rights.*

Come on, my dear, he urged the Lightning. *I promise I will never hurt you like this again. Just give me a little more speed.*

At 10,000 feet the airspeed needle approached 400. No time for mental math now. More tracers flashed below, and Philippe let the Lightning accelerate.

The yoke began to vibrate.

Philippe hadn't checked the dive chart for a few seconds. It was hard to do math homework while running for his life. He tried to pitch up to shave off a little speed.

The controls wouldn't move.

So, this is how it happens, Philippe thought.

The Med rushed at him. Tracers no longer zipped around him but that didn't matter. The Germans had killed him just the same.

Eight thousand feet.

Philippe pulled back on the yoke with all his strength. He could not budge the controls.

Oh, God, he thought. *Charlotte, I'm so sorry. We came so close.*

Something in the universe did not want man flying so near the speed of sound. The compressibility of the air made it impossible. At these velocities, air no longer flowed like a liquid. It behaved in inexplicable ways. To pilots who ventured into this realm, the offended air inflicted the death penalty.

Six thousand feet.

I'm so sorry, Charlotte.

Five thousand feet.

Philippe just wanted to slow down. He wanted to pull back on the elevator just a little. But it was so heavy. So, so heavy. He needed help, some kind of mechanical advantage.

Like the bellcranks in the elevator trim control.

A tip from that crazy Yank instructor, Bobby, came to him now. Philippe reached below the throttles and nudged the elevator trim wheel with his thumb. The yoke came back just slightly. Philippe pulled harder. Strained and gritted his teeth.

This has to work, he thought, *or I have about a minute to live.*

The Lightning shot downward toward the sea, but at a gentler angle.

Philippe moved the trim wheel again, and that helped him pull back a bit more.

G-forces began to press on him. The altimeter wound through 3,000 feet. Invisible weights bore down on his torso.

I am not going to make it, he thought, as his vision began to dim. *So very sorry, Charlotte.*

He thumbed the trim wheel again, pulled harder.

That made the g-forces even worse. The world changed from color to black-and-white. The sea below lay flat gray. And rushed at him.

The yoke danced as if demons yanked the elevator and ailerons. Philippe pulled harder. The invisible weights crushing him doubled in size. His very blood turned to lead. Breathing became a struggle.

It's over. Please let it happen quickly.

Fifteen hundred feet.

The windscreen cracked. The glass popped loud as a rifle shot.

Philippe's vision tunneled, broke into particles.

One thousand feet.

Now Philippe was blind. He hoped unconsciousness would make his death painless.

With his last flicker of consciousness, he pulled harder on the yoke. Felt it give just a bit.

At twenty-six feet above the Mediterranean, the Lighting pulled out of the dive. Salt foam flecked the broken windscreen. The aircraft shot across the sea at a speed few men had survived.

Philippe's vision returned. He took a deep breath of oxygen.

Am I still alive?

I'm still alive!

Philippe drew in another long breath of oxygen. Then another, and another.

Thank you, my dear. We did it.

Let's go home.

He bumped the throttles and started a gentle climb. Far behind him, eight Bf-109s, low on fuel, turned back for their base.

CHAPTER 35

Charlotte Denneau

Through Charlotte's stereoscope, Philippe's photographs revealed a trove of intelligence. She worked late into the night, moving the stereoscope with her left hand and scribbling shorthand notes with her right. From the first images over Marseille, she found a rail system the Allies could use with minimal repairs.

Marseille's main rail station, *Gare de Marseille-Canet*, had suffered little damage. The roundhouses remained intact. Coal stores had not been burned. Best of all, Charlotte identified dozens of locomotives and scores of rail cars.

The railroads themselves might need work, but nothing the engineers couldn't handle. The Germans had blown a trestle at Aix-en-Provence. They had also blown spans over the Durance and Buëch Rivers. But with prefabricated Bailey bridges, the Allies could throw a span across a river without needing a crane.

Railroads often ran alongside rivers, and Charlotte also noted where barge traffic could move. The enemy had destroyed bridges in several places. But she found stretches of the Rhône where tugboats could operate.

The ports themselves were a mess. The enemy had scuttled ships, sown mines, and destroyed piers. However, Charlotte realized the

American and British navies knew how to clear a harbor; they'd had plenty of recent experience at Normandy.

In the dark hours of the morning, Charlotte sent a report to London. Then she burned her notes.

At breakfast, she found Philippe in the chow line. "You look tired," he said.

"I *am* tired," Charlotte said. "But it's a happy tired."

"Meaning?"

Charlotte considered what to tell him. She wasn't supposed to discuss her reports with anyone outside the Allied Central Interpretation Unit. And certainly not in an open mess hall. She put down her coffee and placed her hand on his wrist.

"You did good," she whispered. "Very good."

"I am glad it was worth it." When they took their seats, Philippe described his escape from enemy fighters that nearly ended in disaster. Then he raised his coffee mug and said, "Here's to still being here."

Charlotte clinked her own mug against his.

"Absolutely," she said. "Dear God, what a close call. And you're flying again today?" Philippe was dressed in his flight clothing.

"*Oui*, but not in that aircraft. I took it past its limits, and engineering says the ship needs a thorough inspection before it can fly again."

"Be careful, please."

Charlotte touched the front of his leather A-2 jacket as she spoke. Philippe was becoming more than a colleague. Life could end at any moment; he had proved that again yesterday. She realized she could not stand the thought of losing him.

Philippe and his squadron mates flew hard for three more days. Each morning, Charlotte met Philippe for breakfast. Bade him goodbye and Godspeed with a furtive kiss. Then, from the control tower catwalk, watched him and his friends lift off into the cobalt infinity of the Mediterranean sky.

During the days, she noticed other planes, larger planes, descending to the south. Bombers were deploying to the airfields that dotted the Corsican coastline. Her own base, Poretta, was hardly alone. The Allies had established so many air bases on the island that the Americans called it the USS Corsica, an island that amounted to a giant aircraft carrier.

One afternoon she received a rare invitation—to attend a pilots' briefing. She thought she knew the briefing's purpose, but she dared not speak it aloud. The pilots suspected, too. When she joined Philippe in the briefing room, the place buzzed with anticipation. Cigarette smoke hung in the air. Among the men, she saw more smiles in ten minutes than she'd seen in two weeks. Gavoille entered the Quonset hut, and an orderly called everyone to attention. Gavoille was smiling, too.

"As you were," he said.

Everyone took their seats.

Gavoille hesitated. Scanned the room. He let the suspense build for a moment, like an entertainer with perfect timing.

"Gentlemen," he said, "and lady…" He gestured toward Charlotte. "We are back in business."

The room erupted in cheers and applause. The men stood as they clapped, and Charlotte stood with them. The celebration went on for half a minute. Then the commander motioned for silence. Charlotte and the fliers—*her* fliers, she considered them—returned to their seats.

"The Allied invasion of southern France"—Gavoille paused for a few more hoots and claps—"now has a new name. Welcome to Operation Dragoon."

More cheers. Someone called out, "Sir, what the hell is a dragoon?"

Gavoille chuckled.

"Horse-mounted infantry, in the old days," the commander said. "But I can assure you the Germans will face much more than horses."

Laughter rippled across the room.

Then Gavoille took a more serious tone. "As you might imagine," he said, "we are about to get very busy. Flight orders might change at the last minute. An invasion is a dynamic situation, and decision-makers far above my pay grade will want information. I am told Roosevelt and Churchill themselves have reviewed our photos."

"And so they should," Philippe whispered.

When Charlotte returned to work, she found new orders sent by secure radiogram from the Central Interpretation Unit. As a secondary mission, they wanted her to look for evidence of atrocities by German forces. The order gave no details, no suggestion of what she should look for. She supposed the CIU bosses themselves weren't sure what to look for. But an order like this wouldn't come from nowhere. They must suspect something...awful.

That night, the pilots threw a party in the officers' club. Someone brought in another drop tank of wine, along with cases of beer. They hired a local bartender, who served cocktails spiced with Cap Corse aperitif. Charlotte wore a red dress she bought in Bastia. When the phonograph spun out "Der Fuehrer's Face," by Spike Jones and His City Slickers, the crowd laughed at the mocking lyrics. Charlotte raised her cocktail glass when the song began its *Heil!* refrain, followed by the Bronx cheer.

She noticed Philippe's smiles faded quickly. She pulled him to a table, and they sat together.

"I imagine you're thinking of Saint-Ex," Charlotte said. "He would have loved this day—and this evening."

"Right on both counts," Philippe said. "I do miss him. He would have been right here at this table, showing us card tricks."

Philippe looked like he was about to add another thought. He opened his mouth to speak, but said nothing.

"What?" Charlotte asked. "Is there something else?"

"*Oui.* I received another telegram from SOE today. More information about Lisette. They said she died in what appears to have been a massacre at Oradour-sur-Glane."

"I'm so sorry, Philippe." Charlotte took his hand in both of hers. "What did they say?"

"Only that the 2nd SS Panzer Division appears to have done the murders."

Charlotte thought of her latest message from CIU. Was this what they meant? Maybe—along with heaven knew what else. There were rumors of horrors in concentration camps far beyond what she'd already heard about Buchenwald. She wanted to tell Philippe about the CIU order. But for now, he had no need to know. And her orders were classified.

"Lisette was a fighter," she said, "just like you and me. I know you thought of her as your baby sister. But she was a warrior like all of us." As Charlotte spoke, she swept her hand to show she meant everyone in the room.

"Maybe there is comfort in that for me later," Philippe said, "but not...." He did not finish his sentence.

"I can only imagine what you're going through," Charlotte said. "But, as our British friends might say, it's sporting of you to show up tonight and celebrate."

"I cannot say I am happy," Philippe said. "But I am happy to be here. I cannot bring Lisette back. But now I can do something about it. And I am happy to be here with you."

"You're sweet," Charlotte said.

Movement at the front of the room caught her eye. At the bar, Gavoille was chugging from a mug of beer. Placed his arm around an American flier. Listened to something the Yank said, laughed loudly. The commander then climbed atop the bar, his beer still in hand. Ignored the beer that sloshed out. He waited for the latest song on the phonograph to end.

"May I have your attention, please?" Gavoille shouted. Conversation hushed. The commander placed his free hand on his hip and began belting out *La Marseillaise*, the French National Anthem.

> *Allons enfant de la patrie,*
> *Le jour de gloire est arrivé!*

Everyone stood. All the French and the French-speaking Americans sang along. Charlotte's eyes filled with tears. Gavoille directed his drunken choir by pumping his fist into the air.

At the end of the evening, Charlotte invited Philippe to her room. She did not make the decision on the spur of the moment, or under the influence of drop tank wine and Cap Corse. Like everything else she did, she had given it thought. He was one of very few men who understood her life, who knew what she'd done. Most men, she supposed, wouldn't even *believe* what she'd done, let alone understand it. She and Philippe had shared risk and mourned deaths, yet due to fortune or God's grace remained among the living. Perhaps they would never find anyone who could fully relate—except one another.

In her Quonset hut, Charlotte enjoyed more privacy than most of the men on base because so few women served at Poretta. The time she spent with Philippe in her bed felt natural and effortless. She held him close until the sun shot rays through the cracks at the door.

They ate a leisurely breakfast in the chow hall. No missions were scheduled that morning, so the fliers could sleep off their hangovers. Gavoille greeted them as they sipped their coffee. The night of celebration had left his eyes bloodshot, but other than that the 2/33 commander looked happy.

"Lieutenant Gerard," he said. "Engineering tells me they have completed the inspection on the F-5 you overstressed. Despite your best efforts, she remains airworthy. She is yours again."

"Very good, sir," Philippe said. "I believe that aircraft brings me luck."

"Indeed. She needs a name."

"Ah," Philippe said, "yes she does. And I have an idea."

Philippe flew the next morning. From the tower, Charlotte watched him taxi from a hardstand darkened with oil from dripping cylinders. She waved when the aircraft rolled past her. When she saw the freshly painted nose art, she laughed.

At the departure end of the runway, Philippe began to accelerate. He reached flying speed, and he lifted into the Mediterranean morning in an airplane named *Mademoiselle Charlotte*.

CHAPTER 36

Philippe Gerard

For days, the pilots of 2/33 flew routine missions in the hot Mediterranean summer. But that ended in mid-August, when the invasion of southern France began.

By the predawn hours of August 17, 1944, Corsica fairly trembled with the thunder of departing aircraft. Philippe preflighted his Lightning by flashlight as bombers lifted off from Poretta, Solenzara, and a half dozen other bases. Today was the third day of Operation Dragoon, and Philippe had just received orders for a high-priority mission.

The first gleam of sunrise revealed scores of B-24 Liberators and B-25 Mitchells rising in formation. The sight thrilled Philippe. Made him sense victory was possible, perhaps even close at hand. He so wished Lisette and Saint-Ex could see this. He mourned them, and he knew he would forever. But his feelings for Charlotte took the edge off his pain. And today's mission in her namesake aircraft made him feel…effective. A small but important cog in the machine to liberate France.

As long as he could pull it off.

He launched behind the first wave of bombers. "Deconfliction," the Yanks called it. The last thing he needed was to collide with another plane or to get clipped by a stray falling bomb.

In the climb, he set his propellers to 3,000 RPM with oil and coolant shutters on AUTO. And how *Mademoiselle Charlotte* wanted to fly. The vertical speed indicator showed nearly 4,000 feet per minute as she reached for the heavens. If he had asked too much of her before, she had forgiven all.

By now the sun rose high enough that Philippe wore his aviator's shades against the glare. Through broken clouds below, the light dappled the Mediterranean. The glare eased when he turned to the northwest, into haze shot through with pastel layers: blue over pink over amber.

The radio buzzed with peril:

"Fighters three o'clock low."

"Got heavy triple-A."

"One, no, two falling out of formation."

"Taking fire over Camel Red sector."

Already, enemy antiaircraft guns had begun exacting their price. Philippe's intel briefing had told him he'd encounter a threat he'd not seen in a while: flak from heavy guns. Flak could send shrapnel ripping through wings, engines, flesh, and bone. The largest calibers hurled shells higher than *Mademoiselle Charlotte* could fly.

During his time with the RAF, fighters had posed the primary threat. That held true, as well, with most of his missions in Lightnings. The 2/33 pilots suspected it was a German fighter that had killed Saint-Ex.

But today, he'd need to photograph a target shielded by a hornet's nest of flak cannons. Back in 1940, during the Battle of France, he'd taken fire from relatively light mobile guns. They'd thrown enough sharp steel to tear up his Bloch and kill his crew.

Today, the briefers warned, would be worse. The Nazis had had years to construct emplacements for their heaviest weapons.

When the altimeter needles swept through 20,000 feet, he broke out of the haze. Entered a sky clear as a mountain stream. Above him and to the west, a formation of Liberators found air cold enough to form condensation trails from the heat of their engines. The bombers inscribed a score of white lines toward their target.

Philippe leveled at 30,000. Set his throttles and prop levers for cruise. Trimmed his control surfaces so he could hold course and altitude with only his fingertips.

Through a break in the clouds, he spotted the Riviera coastline. Blue-green surf slid over brown-sugar beaches. Then the clouds opened further to reveal...an armada. Ships of the invasion fleet—bullet-like shapes on the water—stretched to the horizon. Smoke and fire boiled from the muzzles of a battleship. In another sector, a flotilla of landing craft marked their progress with white wakes that, to Philippe, mimicked the contrails of bombers.

God have mercy on the Germans, Philippe thought, *because we will not.*

He checked his heading, continued toward his own target. The American Twelfth Air Force wanted photos of the harbor at Toulon. Vessels from the old French navy, now operated by the Germans or the Vichy government, might pose a threat to the landing force. The French had scuttled much of their fleet rather than let the vessels fall into the hands of the enemy. But even an immobilized wreck with its keel in the mud could be dangerous if its guns still worked. French ships in the wrong hands had plagued the Allies before: Back during the invasion of North Africa in 1942, the French battleship *Jean Bart* had blazed away at American vessels and ground troops.

What warships still lurked at Toulon? And once the Allies took over the port, what repairs would it need to support the invasion? Philippe's job was to find out—if he survived. Intelligence had revealed scores of flak guns guarding the harbor. The gunners' job was to kill Philippe, or any Allied pilot who ventured overhead.

Philippe checked his charts, checked his course, checked his panel. Good, the cameras were warmed up and ready. Engine manifold pressures and oil temps normal. Oxygen quantity sufficient. Fuel level fine.

Ahead, over the nose, he spotted Toulon and its harbor, with the distinctive hill rising above the port. Quays, piers, and wharfs jutted at irregular angles. Ships lay at anchor and at dockside. From this altitude, he could not identify any of them with the unaided eye. That would become Charlotte's job, in consultation with naval advisers. Philippe needed only to take the pictures. And survive long enough to bring them back.

He started his cameras. Pressed the chronometer button on his panel to time a 60-second photo run.

And the gunners started their fire.

Black puffs stained the sky in front of him. The first three rounds exploded beneath him, ten o'clock low. Maybe half a mile out.

Philippe's palms began to sweat. He took a deep breath of oxygen, concentrated on holding heading and altitude. To get useable photos, he had to fly his course straight and true—no matter what came up at him.

He knew moments like this haunted the dreams of bomber pilots. During their bomb runs, they could take no evasive action. They could only fly right over the target and hold speed, course, and altitude to give the bombardier a stable aiming platform.

Another trio of flak bursts blossomed ahead of him. Closer this time.

The bastards are ranging me, Philippe thought.

Flak gunners, he knew, could choose from different tactics. They could set up a curtain of fire over a target and simply wait for the aircraft to fly through it. Or worse, they could aim. With continuously pointed fire, they could dial in a plane's speed and altitude. Fine-tune with each salvo. Set fuses to explode at the correct altitude. Track the azimuth and blow the aircraft out of the sky.

Philippe kept his compass, altimeter, and airspeed indicator locked as if on rails. If Lisette could face death for the mission, so could he. The amber photo light winked as his cameras whirred.

Steady, steady, he told himself.

In the next instant, black ink vomited from a clear sky. A flak shell burst right in front of him. Shrapnel raked *Mademoiselle Charlotte*. Sounded like hailstones pounding a car.

Pain stabbed through Philippe's left leg, arm, and hand. The aircraft yawed off course when his torn muscles spasmed. He corrected, leveled his wings. Glanced downward. Blood spattered his flight suit, his gloves, and the throttle quadrant.

The gunners had him dead to rights.

No doubt they were making their final adjustment. The next salvo would send him to earth trailing smoke, fire, and pieces.

But Philippe wasn't dropping bombs. He had no bombardier requiring precise speed. His cameras mainly needed precise heading and altitude.

Philippe gripped his throttles. Felt blood squish between his fingers inside his glove. Yanked the power to idle.

The airspeed needle plummeted. Philippe pitched up to hold altitude as the aircraft slowed.

The gunners fired again. Leading him too much now, the rounds burst ahead of him. Metal shards flecked his canopy. But the engine instruments indicated no serious damage. No apparent flight control damage, either; *Mademoiselle Charlotte* handled normally. And once more, he was about to ask all she could give.

The chronometer's second hand ticked through fifty seconds. Fifty-five. Sixty. Philippe held course for another moment to make up for his slower speed. The photos might show more overlap now. Charlotte would figure it out. But finally, he had the pictures. Mission accomplished, as long as he made it back.

At one minute and five seconds, and just above stall speed, Philippe pushed the yoke forward. Punched the throttles. Rolled into an accelerating, diving turn.

He glanced over his right shoulder. Shells exploded above him. His nose sliced through the horizon. The airspeed needle came alive. Swung past 150, then 200 miles an hour and kept going. Land and sea rushed up at him.

Now, nothing devised by man could calculate a firing solution quickly enough to hit him. With mathematics and gravity on his side, Philippe blasted across the coastline. His compass, altimeter and airspeed indicator danced a ballet of constant motion. The Riviera rotated beneath him. The ships, buildings, hills, and trees grew larger.

Finally, beyond the guns' range and below their elevation, he rolled out of the turn. Pulled out of the dive. Shot across the waves like a bolt from a crossbow.

By the time he descended for Corsica, the adrenaline was wearing off. His wounds were beginning to stiffen. And they hurt like hell. On the downwind at Poretta, he asked the tower to roll the ambulance.

Philippe turned onto final approach. The pain distracted him so that he nearly forgot to lower his landing gear. The wheels locked into place just in time to avoid a go-around.

He touched down, turned off the runway, and rolled down the taxiway. The ambulance followed him to the hardstand. A truck with the film technicians followed close behind. He set the brakes, shut down the engines. As soon as he opened his canopy, a crew chief mounted a ladder and helped him out of his harness.

"How bad are you hurt, sir?" the man asked. He glanced at the blood that smeared Philippe's flight suit, the seat, and the controls.

"They got my leg. Maybe it's not as bad as it looks."

Two medics jumped out of the ambulance to help the crew chief. As the crew chief tried to pull him from his seat, Philippe groaned. Pain seared from a wound above his knee. When he tried to stand, he saw shrapnel embedded in the side of his leg. His arm and hand hurt, too.

Particles swam before his eyes. His vision blurred.

Philippe came to on the tarmac beside his aircraft. The medics kneeled beside him.

"Just lay still, sir," one of them said. "You passed out, but we caught you."

"We're gonna roll you onto a stretcher now," the other said.

Philippe tried to relax, to let the medics move him as needed. During the short ride to the base hospital, the ambulance seemed to find every bump and mudhole. Each one hurt. At the hospital, a nurse scissored open the leg of his flight suit. Pulled off his jacket and gloves. Blood dripped from the left glove. An American flight surgeon examined him.

"You're lucky, Lieutenant," the flight surgeon said. "I don't see anything life-threatening. But I'll have to cut some of that metal out of you."

Philippe closed his eyes and nodded. The medics wheeled him into an operating room. The nurse placed a mask over his face. His pain began to fade, and he surrendered to unconsciousness.

He awoke to see Charlotte sitting beside his bed. She held his right hand, the uninjured one. He smiled at her. Felt a warm numbness. She stroked his hair.

"You really gave me a scare," she said.

"Sorry," he whispered. "How long have I been asleep?"

Charlotte looked at her watch. "They brought you to the hospital around noon. It's eight in the evening now."

Philippe tried to move his left arm. He saw bandages around the arm and over three of his left fingers. A gown covered his legs.

"How bad?" he asked.

Before Charlotte could answer, the flight surgeon spoke up. The doctor strode across the room in his white coat, clipboard in hand.

"You needed a seamstress more than a doc," the flight surgeon said. "I pulled a big chunk of shrapnel out of your leg. A bunch of little pieces out of your arm and hand. Lemme see." He consulted his clipboard, ran his finger along a sheet of paper. "Twenty-five stitches in that leg. Ah, six, eight, eleven, fifteen, nineteen in your arm. A few along your ribs on the left side, too."

"Can I still fly?"

"Whoa, cowboy. Not for a while. But you don't have any permanent injury, if that's what you mean."

A sigh of relief escaped Philippe's lips. As his thoughts became more organized, he turned his mind to the mission. He considered how he might ask Charlotte what he wanted to ask.

"Did you like the picture postcards I sent you?" Philippe said. By now, the photos would have been developed, and she'd have had time to analyze them.

Charlotte gazed up at the ceiling. Clearly, she took his meaning and also needed to judge what to say. When her eyes met his, she said, "Very much so. Our friends, ah, liked the pictures, too."

"They said they were useful?"

"Oh, yeah. They want to go see for themselves."

The flight surgeon ordered a week of bed rest for Philippe. And light duty at least until the stitches came out. On the third day, Philippe tried

280

walking on crutches. It hurt, but he found he could move under his own power. As his condition improved, he got bored. He wanted to get out of the damned hospital ward and go outside. He wanted to see more of Charlotte. And he wanted badly to know more about the mission.

After a week of recuperation, he asked the flight surgeon if he could go to dinner with Charlotte.

"Hmm," the doctor said. Then he offered a knowing grin. "Yeah, you can go to dinner. But that's all you can do. I don't want you busting my stitches. Understand?"

Philippe often found American humor more grating than amusing. But this time, he felt too happy to take offense. Charlotte met him at the hospital in a jeep she'd signed out of the motor pool. Philippe climbed in and stowed his crutches in the back. He wore his best uniform, with the blue service coat of the Free French Air Force. Charlotte wore her red dress. Greeted him with a kiss and a bottle of Vin de Corse.

"Thank you for bringing that," Philippe said. "But will the restaurant let us bring our own wine?"

"Probably not," Charlotte said. "We're going to drink it before we get there."

Philippe smiled, but he didn't ask questions. Decided just to let the mapmaker lead the way. On the short drive in to Bastia, Charlotte pulled off the road. She found an overlook that presented a view of the Old Port, the hillside above it, and the sea beyond. The setting sun lit the water an electric blue. Philippe guessed the visibility at a hundred miles.

From her bag, Charlotte produced two ceramic coffee mugs.

"I liberated these from the chow hall," she said. "Not exactly fine crystal, but they'll do."

She uncorked the wine. Philippe held the mugs while she poured. With her thumb and forefinger, she flicked away the cork.

"Ah, so we're going to finish the bottle," Philippe said.

"Indeed, we are."

Charlotte took her mug, clinked it against Philippe's.

"À *ta santé*," she said.

"And to yours."

Philippe took a sip of the rich red wine.

"I suppose you'd like to know what happened after we analyzed your photos," Charlotte said.

"*Oui*, but I did not wish to rush you."

"Well, your photos showed at least four French ships in enemy hands."

As Charlotte continued her story, Philippe's pain, anguish, and self-doubt fell away. Her words assured him he had not fought in vain. Reminded him Lisette and Saint-Ex had not died for nothing. They were warriors, like Charlotte had said.

She told him the photos captured the battleship *Strasbourg*, the cruiser *La Galissonnière*, a destroyer, a submarine, and other vessels in Toulon harbor. Some of the ships had been scuttled, as expected. But the damned things still had guns. Maybe they couldn't move, but they could fire.

"The day after you got the photos," Charlotte said, "the 321st Bomb Group at Solenzara sent three dozen B-25 Mitchells. They scored several direct hits."

She added that a photo run the next day, by another 2/33 pilot, showed good BDA—Bomb Damage Assessment.

"They took out those naval guns," Charlotte said. "There are Free French and American troops ashore right now who are still alive because of you and those B-25s."

Philippe took another sip from his mug. Charlotte's words sank in like the wine warming the back of his throat.

"What about the bomber crews?" Philippe asked. "Did they all survive?"

Charlotte nodded. "They all made it back," she said. "They had some wounded, though. The flak was pretty heavy."

"I'm sure it was."

The next several minutes passed in silence. Philippe closed his eyes and let the last of the day's sunlight warm his face. Sea breeze brushed his cheeks. He wanted to photograph this moment in his mind, to capture this scene with this woman for as long as his memory might last.

He opened his eyes. Took another sip.

"The flight surgeon says he'll put me back on flying status soon," he said.

"I know."

Philippe looked out across the Mediterranean. A "Photo Joe" Lightning flew over the beach, on approach to Poretta. Farther out, Philippe discerned Allied warships on the horizon. Their shapes shimmered in the heat waves. Above them, a bomber formation descended toward Corsica.

There was much work left to do.

MEMORANDUM
REGARDING: Evacuation
Gestapo Counterintelligence Corps,
Federal Intelligence Service, Lyon
Lyon, France 25 August 1944
TO: Reich Security Main Office, Berlin
FROM: Klaus Barbie, Hauptstürmfuhrer

This office shall close as of this date. Sensitive files have been destroyed as directed.

Heil Hitler,
Klaus Barbie, Hauptstürmfuhrer

EPILOGUE

Operation Dragoon's forces, including French, American, British, Canadian, and Greek troops, overwhelmed Germany's Army Group G. Many of the enemy troops were demoralized draftees from outside Germany. Under the command of U.S. Lieutenant General Alexander Patch, the Dragoon task force liberated Toulon on August 27, 1944. The task force liberated Marseille on August 29. Both ports went into operation quickly.

Meanwhile, forces that had advanced from Normandy entered Paris on August 24 and 25. Charles de Gaulle gave a victory speech on the 25th. Philippe and Charlotte listened on the radio, held each other, and wept at de Gaulle's words:

> *Since the enemy which held Paris has capitulated into our hands, France returns to Paris, her home. She returns bloody, but quite resolute. She returns there enlightened by the immense lesson, but more certain than ever of her duties and her rights.*

During the first week of September, Philippe received a request—not an order—for a special assignment.

"You do not have to fly this mission," Gavoille told him. "If you do not want to, I understand. In that case, I will fly it. But I could not let 2/33 take this sortie without telling you about it."

The flight plan called for a Lightning to fly to Marseille, refuel, and take off again for a photo run. The target: Oradour-sur-Glane, where Lisette and hundreds of others had died at the hands of the 2nd SS Panzer Division, *Das Reich*.

Already the Allies looked ahead to the war's aftermath. They expected war crime tribunals. Prosecutors would need evidence.

"*Bien sûr*," Philippe said. "Of course I will fly it. I thank you for the opportunity, sir." He spoke dry-eyed, in a firm and even voice.

"Are you certain?" Gavoille asked.

"As certain as I have ever been of anything."

In a newly repaired *Mademoiselle Charlotte*, Philippe descended for Oradour. The Allies had pushed the Germans out of the region. In fact, Lyon had just been liberated. Without the threat of antiaircraft fire, Philippe took his time. He felt more like a crime scene photographer than a surveillance pilot.

Below, he found the cocoa-colored channel of the River Glane. Checked the landmarks against his chart. The Glane did not stretch wide like the Loire or the Seine; overhanging trees concealed much of its course. With his finger on the chart and eyes on the stream, he followed the water until he spotted Oradour.

Philippe eased back his throttles for descent. Rolled into a bank to line up for his first photo run at 5,000 feet. Activated the cameras. From this relatively low altitude, he did not have to wait for analysis to know what his cameras captured. He saw well enough with his own eyes.

He found not a village, but the skeleton of a village.

The Nazis had torched every building. Every home, every shop, even the church. What kind of people would set fire to a church? The ceilings and rafters had burned away to leave only fire-stained stone walls.

No doubt, people had been inside some of these buildings during the fires. Philippe still hadn't learned how Lisette had died. Was it in that house? In that church? He prayed her death had come quickly, but he'd probably never know.

A lump rose in his throat. But Philippe did not weep into his oxygen mask. He gripped his throttles and the yoke, summoned all his skill and professionalism. He could not bring back his sister, but he could document for the world what these monsters had done. Send some to the gallows.

Yet he felt no sense of vengeance, no burning anger. The anger had come before, and he knew it would come again. But now Philippe acted purely as a functionary, helping bring matters to account.

He sensed the Lightning's vibration through the controls, felt himself part of the aircraft. Held altitude and heading with the precision of a test pilot. He completed his first run, reversed course, and set up for another pass. Lower this time, down to 3,000.

The lower altitude magnified details. Burned cars sat on their rims, the tires melted away. Scorched trees clawed the air with black limbs. Rubble spilled into streets where walls had collapsed.

Nothing stirred in the town. Not a person, not a cat. Not even a bird. Oradour lay utterly deceased. To Philippe, it appeared the earth had ruptured to reveal some part of the underworld, a village in Hades, ghostly and silent.

His camera light blinked its progress. Film rolled and exposed, for commanders, for courts, for history. The Lightning named *Mademoiselle Charlotte* flew over a mourning but free France, giving voice to the dead.

HISTORICAL NOTES

This book is a work of fiction, backdropped by real events. My character Philippe Gerard initially appears while flying a Westland Lysander for the British Royal Air Force's Special Duties Service. When I first envisioned a French pilot flying for RAF special ops after the fall of France, I wondered if that was a flight of fancy. But during my research, I learned there were at least two Frenchmen who did exactly that. Group Captain Hugh Verity's memoir, *We Landed by Moonlight*, became my primary source for that part of the novel. In fact, Verity served as the model for my character Squadron Leader Hugh Venable.

Charlotte Denneau and Lisette Gerard are also fictional characters, but they are inspired by real women of the Resistance such as Virginia Hall, Violette Szabo, and Charlotte Delbo. In fact, the "real" Virginia Hall makes an appearance in Chapter 18, though her conversation with Lisette is, of course, imaginary. The sabotage techniques used by Lisette and her teammates, such as "exploding coal" and grease guns spiked with carborundum, are real.

The author Antoine de Saint-Exupéry is the novel's most prominent real-life figure, though all scenes and conversations with him are fictional. He's best known for his children's story, *The Little Prince*, but he also wrote of darker matters. Saint-Ex flew with the *Armée de l'Air* during the Battle of France and chronicled the experience in his searing memoir *Flight to Arras*. Later in the war, he rejoined his old unit and continued the fight. On the morning of July 31, 1944, he took off from Corsica and never returned.

In 1998, a fisherman off Marseille netted a bracelet inscribed "Saint-Ex." Two years later, a French professional diver in the same area discovered wreckage of a photorecon variant of the P-38 Lighting. Subsequently, a salvage team recovered parts with a serial number that corresponded to the aircraft the author took on his final flight.

In 2008, a book titled *Saint-Exupéry: The Final Secret* quoted former Luftwaffe pilot Horst Rippert as saying he believed he shot down Saint-Ex. Rippert added that he could not be sure—and he hoped he was wrong because he enjoyed Saint-Ex's writing.

Some of the novel's details about Saint-Ex, such as the story of his visit to a fortune-teller, come from an excellent nonfiction book about him. *Saint-Exupéry: A Biography*, by Stacy Schiff, was a valuable resource. Schiff's book also mentions that Saint-Ex's unit photographed the erupting Vesuvius in 1944, but my depiction of his flight over the volcano is fictional. I first discovered Saint-Ex's writing as a kid growing up in rural North Carolina. Our one-horse town, Oxford, had a two-horse library, and I found Saint-Ex while thumbing through the card catalog. I was looking for anything to do with flying. His work transported me from the tobacco fields of Granville County to the Saharan sands, the Andes peaks, and wartime European skies filled with smoke and shrapnel. I took his stories as an invitation to his world—to write and to fly.

Aerial photorecon missions like the ones flown by Saint-Ex and Philippe began during World War I with handheld cameras carried in biplanes. The equipment and procedures became much more sophisticated during World War II, as depicted in this novel. Aerial surveillance evolved further during the Cold War. You might say Saint-Ex's P-38 variant was the forerunner of aircraft such as the U-2 Dragon Lady and the SR-71 Blackbird.

Memoranda from Gestapo officer Klaus Barbie intersperse the novel. The memos are made up, but Barbie was all too real. Known as the "Butcher of Lyon," he tortured Resistance fighters and Jews as Gestapo chief in that city. After the war, he escaped arrest and made his way to

South America, where he lived under the alias "Klaus Altmann." During the 1970s, Nazi hunters Serge and Beate Klarsfeld tracked him down. In 1983, the Bolivian government arrested him and extradited him to France. Barbie's trial on multiple counts of crimes against humanity began in 1987. The court sentenced him to life in prison. He died in prison in Lyon in 1991 at the age of 77.

Charlotte's encounter with Pablo, the Spanish leader of the fictional *El Espectro* guerrillas, has historical grounding. Former Spanish Republicans fought against the Nazis in France. When Pablo takes his leave of Charlotte, he refers to heading for the French Alps to continue his fight. In March of 1944, thousands of German troops and French Milice attacked a smaller Resistance force in the Alps during what became known as the Battle of Glières Plateau. Under siege in bitter winter conditions, most of the *résistants* were killed. A monument now overlooks the site of their courageous last stand.

While sheltering with the Resistance, Philippe and Charlotte take part in the attempted liberation of the Amiens prison. That, too, is a real event. RAF Mosquito bombers blew holes in the prison walls and allowed many Resistance prisoners to escape. I tried to depict that attack accurately, based on historical accounts. The raid's commander, Group Captain Percy Charles "Pick" Pickard, and his navigator, Flight Lieutenant John Allen "Bill" Broadley, died during the mission. Popularly known as Operation Jericho, the mission did not initially carry that code name. According to historian Robert Lyman, a 1946 French film came out under that title. The raid has since become known by that name.

The massacres at Tulle and Oradour-sur-Glane are also real events. After the D-Day invasion on June 6, 1944, the 2nd SS Panzer Division, known as *Das Reich*, headed for Normandy. Resistance fighters made every effort to impede them. Following an attack on German forces already in Tulle by the *Francs-Tireurs et Partisans*, the Panzer division arrived there on the evening of June 8. The next morning, Germans rounded up all the men between the ages of 16 and 60. Ninety-nine died by hanging.

The next day, *Das Reich* arrived in Oradour. Under the command of *Sturmbannführer* Adolf Diekmann, they torched the village and tried to kill everyone there. More than 600 died. According to some accounts, the massacre came as a reprisal for the killing of *Sturmbannführer* Helmut Kämpfe, reportedly a friend of Diekmann's.

To this day, Oradour remains as the Nazis left it. In 1946, French President Charles de Gaulle ordered the preservation of Oradour's ruins as a permanent memorial. You can still see the rubble, the rusted cars, and the silent stone walls where hundreds were locked into the burning church. Much of what we know about what happened in the church comes from the testimony of the only survivor, Marguerite Roffanche. She leapt from a window, took five bullets, and hid in a garden. She was rescued the following day.

Diekmann did not live long enough to face trial. He was killed in Normandy on June 29, 1944.

Philippe feels at a loss when the invasion of southern France is canceled, and then he finds purpose again when the operation gets revived. That reflects real events. British military leaders worried that Operation Anvil might draw too many resources away from the Italian campaign. But later, as the need for more port facilities became apparent, the mission was resurrected under the name Operation Dragoon.

After Dragoon launches, Philippe plays a pivotal role by photographing French warships in enemy hands at Toulon harbor. That, too, comes straight from the pages of history. In a 1982 article for *Air Force Magazine*, World War II veteran Dino Brugioni describes bombing the vessels from his B-25 Mitchell. Brugioni's article notes that the bombing mission took place after aerial reconnaissance confirmed the warships' presence.

Brugioni joined the Central Intelligence Agency in 1948. He was considered one of the world's top experts on imagery analysis, and he became a strong advocate for using aerial photos as a historical source. He died in 2015 in Stafford, Virginia.

As of this writing, the generation that won the Second World War is rapidly leaving us. Before long, all of them will have reported to a higher command. We owe it to them to remember their sacrifices, to honor their victory over Nazism and Fascism, and to preserve the freedom they passed on to us.

Tom Young
Alexandria, VA
June, 2024

ACKNOWLEDGMENTS

Without strong support, I could not have brought this novel to print. My wife, Kristen, always my primary editor, helped me shape the storyline. Her mother, Laurel Files, and mine, Harriett Young, also offered input that helped polish the manuscript.

My old friend Jodie Tighe, in a literary correspondence that goes back decades, offered input on French language and culture. My newer friend Fiona Shrimpton provided valuable help on French habits and conversation.

My American Legion comrade Ken Dalecki worked for *Kiplinger Washington Editors* and *Congressional Quarterly*. He retains a razor-sharp editor's eye, which benefited this book immensely. Ken served in the Vietnam War, and is a past commander of American Legion Post 20, which is affiliated with the National Press Club in Washington, DC.

Nothing happens in this business without tireless literary agents—and my association with agent Michael Carlisle of InkWell Management now goes back fifteen years. Thank you again, Michael, for all you do.

I write these acknowledgments with a note of sadness. Two friends and mentors who have critiqued all my previous books have completed their earthly missions.

I dedicated this novel to one of them, Lieutenant Colonel Joe Myers. Joe and I flew many thousands of miles together with the 167th Airlift Wing, West Virginia Air National Guard. Joe was an aviator and warrior with the heart of a poet and philosopher. All who knew him became the better for it. At his memorial, I watched his ashes drift cloud-like from an aircraft over our home base. The ashes spread and dissipated, and they seemed to vanish before touching the ground. I found that fitting. Joe's spirit yet flies.

And the spirit of Dick Elam yet sails. Beginning when I first set foot on the campus of the University of North Carolina at Chapel Hill, he encouraged me to write, and he set the bar high. A teacher in the truest sense of the word, this Navy veteran and avid sailor helped bring out my best work, as he did for hundreds of others. You might say my first class with him never ended. To this day I remain his student.